Created with Vellum

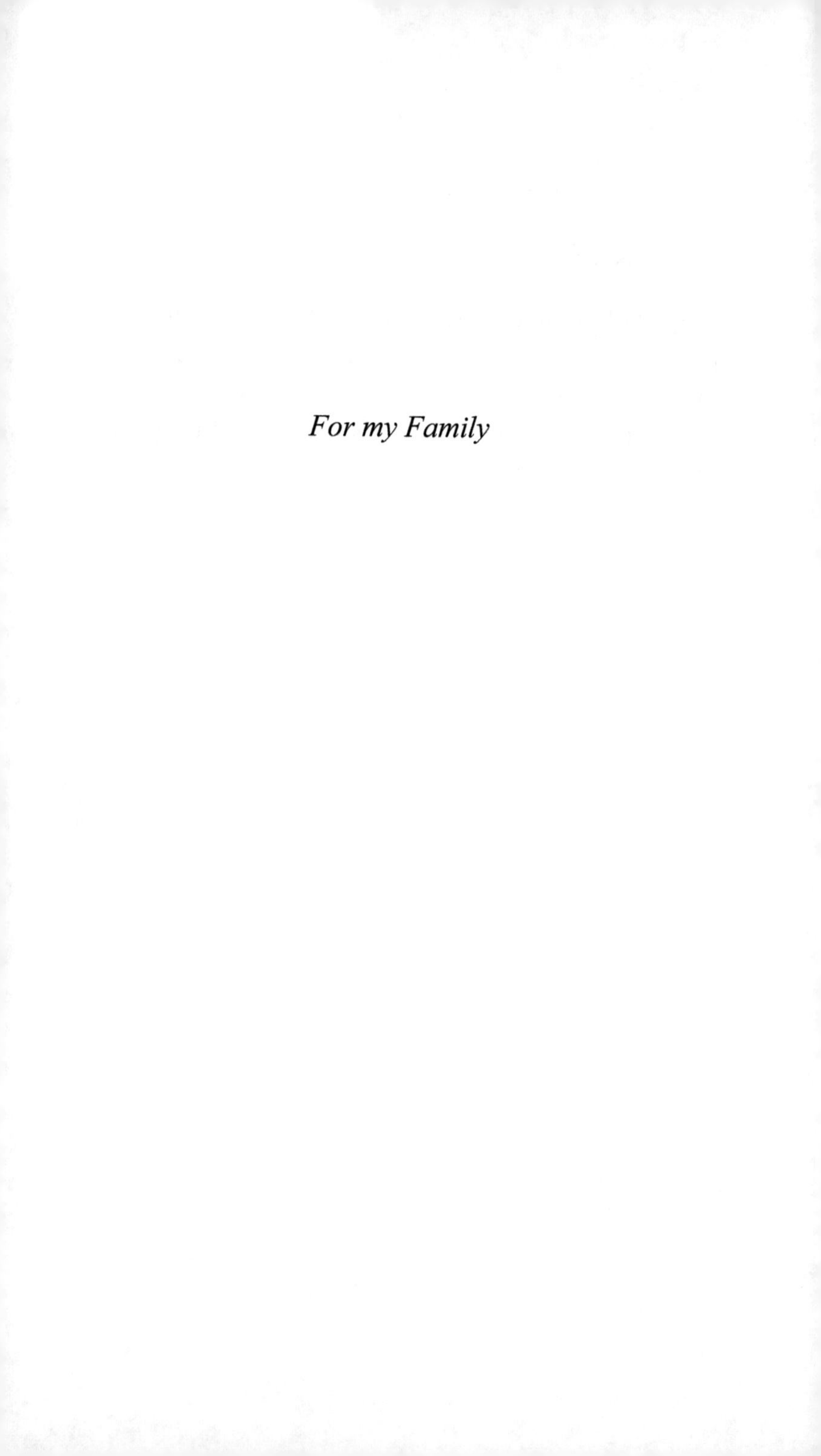

For my Family

DEADLY CONFLICT

DEADLY CONFLICT

E L RUSSELL

CONTENTS

1.
2.
3.
4.
5.

6.
7.
8.
9.
10.
11.
12.
13.
14.
15.
16.
17.
18.
19.
20.
21.
22.
23.
24.
25.
26.
27.
28.
29.
30.
31.
32.
33.
34.
35.

36.

37.

38.

39.

40.

41.

42.

43.

44.

45.

46.

PROLOGUE

For centuries, several small communities of Homo Evolutis, a new species of human being, had sought refuge from corporate greed, rogue government agencies, and brutal exploitation of their powers from secret paramilitary factions seeking their powers.

The largest Evolutis Cohort, led by Elizabeth Stosak, consisted of renowned medical researchers, brilliant physicists, forward thinking engineers, and savvy social scientists. Under her leadership they began a discussion that would soon lead to construction of an additional sanctuary in Antarctica buried beneath 5000 meters of rock, ice, and snow.

With the house lights ablaze in the huge auditorium, a replica of her favorite lecture hall on the UC Berkeley's campus, she met with her Cohort in the SPA, located in an underground facility on Thirasia, in the Greek Cyclades.

Wearing her white desert robe adorned with a satin blue sash, side arm, and curved Kanjhar knife, Elizabeth summarized the trials her Cohort faced during their emerging years including the kidnappings of Shannon and her three children. Those acts set in motion a war with a secret fundamental sect of ancient people known as the Followers.

She spoke to their minds. <We control inter-dimensional space and time by folding it. We also view remotely, reposition objects and ourselves to far away places. We can disrupt matter at will, yet the true nature of our skills remain unsolved mysteries to our most competent scientists. We seem to control everything, yet understand nothing.>

Her eyes fell on Oliver, sitting at the end of the first row. Partner and confidant, he'd always lift a shaggy brow and slow smile letting her know her presentation moved smoothly. His position as a renown economist did not diminish his ability to discus these topics of her lecture. He understood more than most the international and intragalatic importance of their abilities and often chided her for her inability to give their new abilities a scientific basis.

She addressed these concerns to the audience even though he hadn't raised the question today. <Our brains have morphed neural networks into a new region of the brain behind Broca's area. It's from that growth that the astonishing skills from our first awakening come.>

Her eyes jumped to his and then back to the assembled.

<I have tried to understand why that development is not yet understood.>

He grinned at her attack of her own argument.

She continued. <We assumed our genome was responsible for our augmentation, but so far, labs have not located any significant changes to the basic structure of our DNA. Your understanding of the human genome of our immortality through self-healing and self-immunity can only be explained by understanding the changes to the epigenetic settings of each gene.>

She smiled inwardly. She was the top bio-geneticist, and for all that, he was a brilliant economist, it had taken some time to educate him to the concepts that he now challenged her to explain scientifically.

<Computing the optimal settings for each epigene have been frustrating because the huge number of combinations of epigenetic settings needed to express a significant genetic change was astronomical and beyond current computer capacity.>

She grinned back at him. When had he become the science advocate? Then she voiced the hope on the horizon. <I believe as more of us have our

second awakening, the answers to these questions and the scientific explanations of our development is attainable, especially the untapped power of our biological guests; the 100 trillion cells that constitute our microbiome.>

Low chatter rippled through the audience.

She raised her voice. <I must warn everyone that having new powers also increases the list of enemies and species who up the threat of conflict for want of the knowledge of the biogenetic information that separates us.>

A shouted question from the audience stopped her presentation. However, instead of a reply, she waved her arms for attention and then held up one hand like a traffic cop at a busy intersection, while pointing to her temple with the other.

The audience fell silent and waited in anticipation. Her eyes danced across the front row scanning everyone close to her while she focused on the news entering her mind. Disbelief covered her face and she walked slowly to the edge of the stage to share what she had learned. She opened her mind and again spoke mentally to the entire assembled audience.

<Security reports the discovery of a huge interstellar sphere parked at L2. It is identical to the space ship we gave to Cato and his group of

Followers to search the galaxy for their origins.> She shook her head slowly. <It appears to have been abandoned.>

THE SPACE SPHERE

The SPA at Thirasia

Elizabeth repositioned to the SPA's rampart high atop a renovated monastery on Thirasia, across from the extinct volcano and the tourist destination Santorini.

Oliver followed. "What the hell happened to them, Liz?"

"To Cato? We haven't established that it's the same sphere we made for him." She paced, nervously biting her lower lip. "Tobin said he'd meet us here."

She folded her arms and shook her heads. "Imagine, that boy in a mysterious sphere. He's hidden at L2, a place referenced only by its relative physical description close behind the moon, forever out of earth's sight, might be the one they'd created for Cato and several hundred Followers, or not. Other than a copy, though, she couldn't imagine what else it might be. Months ago, they had made two spheres for Cato's journey across the galaxy. As one of the five Lagrangian points, where the gravity of the earth, the moon, and the sun conspire to produce five stable places, L2 was a safe place to hide something as large as the space-sphere. The odd thing was Cato never discussed returning or making any additional contact.

Much to her relief, Tobin, her college-aged nephew, the inventor, and creator of the spheres, appeared at her side. Eager to investigate, she went to the point of their meeting. “I have to see it now.”

He tipped his head in greeting to Oliver then turned to her. “Then, let’s go, we need to check that thing out.” With everyone standing in a tight circle, he carefully removed a small semi-transparent sphere about the size of a golf ball from a pocket deep inside his robe and held it in his hand for all to see.

Elizabeth bent close. The bright, almost invisible orb, which nestled around an inscribed twelve-sided dodecahedron, never ceased to amaze her. Possessing a tiny floating ring, it looked like a crystal model of Saturn. The beauty of the thing was mesmerizing, but what it could become was a marvel beyond belief.

Tobin placed the sphere on the flat stone ground, and then touched both sides to make a copy before returning the original to his robe. “This is the miniature from which I built the two for Cato and his Followers.”

“Tell me, Tobin,” she said, holding Oliver’s hand and backing away, “could Cato or one of his Seekers have made an exact copy?”

Tobin shrugged.

“I gave them a small one and showed them how to copy it and change its size to the two-mile radius space-sphere as you’ve seen me do. So yes. Any Seeker can figure out how to do it. Watch."

Tobin stood like a faux magician pointing toward the small sphere with his index fingers. He smiled at her and then touched them together like a schoolboy making a finger gun. He slowly backed away spreading his arms wide over his head. The sphere, containing an almost invisible network of twelve pentagons fused together by thin green edges grew above them until it filled half the rampart.

“READY TO GO?” He grinned with eyes like twin lighthouse beacons.

Oliver placed a few affectionate pats on his back.

“It’s beautiful, my boy. You’re quite the craftsman. Your pride is well warranted.”

The three repositioned inside, and in return for his praise, Tobin offered his uncle the helm. “Care to drive?”

Oliver raised an eyebrow. “Uh . . . umm . . . can you tell me how?”

A hoot of laughter escaped Elizabeth’s lips before she could catch it. “I thought you were paying attention every time you were in one of these things.

“Not so much, it seems.”

Tobin took pity on him. “You remember the spheres we built Cato? The one we’re in is the same as them only one-hundredth the size. Concentrate on this sphere and imagine you see it behind the moon.”

OLIVER SAID WITH SOME ANNOYANCE, “That’s it? That’s all you’re going to tell me? You must be kidding. You sound like George saying, ‘All you have to do is imagine it, and if it is in your repertoire, your mind will do the rest.’ “He put his hand on his forehead and drew it slowly over the top of his head. When he removed his hand his hair stuck out over his ears.

Elizabeth smoothed his spiky hair and cupped his chin in her hand, "That’s no explanation at all.”

"You know we can't explain all the science behind our powers. Even George, who knows more physics than anyone, can only speculate on most of it."

OLIVER LOOKED like he'd swallowed something sour. "So, I just pretend I can fly this thing?" For seconds he folded his arms across his chest and then shook his head. "Nope, that won't work."

ELIZABETH POINTED HER FINGER. "You're better than you think."

Following her direction, he saw a tiny crystal-like orb reflecting sparkles of bright sunlight. His eye grew wide, and he muttered something in Norwegian. "I did it? Is that all there is to it?"

"GREAT PILOTING, Uncle Oliver, take us closer for a complete fly-by."

"HOW DO WE ACCOMPLISH THAT? WITH ANOTHER REPOSITION?"

"SEE, even the largest of the space spheres has the thin ring around it. That ring is your mind's link to moving the sphere. The ring causes the space around the sphere to bend, thereby creating an artificial gravity within, which determines the sphere's perpetual bottom." They drew near, and the mysterious sphere filled their view. In fact, it was an independent world with land and lakes and buildings. It was fully sustainable for life, which was the purpose when they designed the originals for Cato and his Followers for their galaxy exodus.

Oliver's brow furrowed. "Perpetual?"

Elizabeth bobbed her head. "No matter how the sphere moves through space, gravity inside the sphere is always the same." She pointed at her feet. "And it's always down there."

"Ah, I remember the time we trekked across the ice fields on a dog sled you put inside your first sphere. We had gravity, and you used the ring to steer it."

The memory of them huddled like spoons in a utensil drawer, wrapped in fur-lined clothes, suddenly warmed by repositioning inside a small sphere caused her to smile. "I should've let you drive some."

"Nonsense, I had barely awakened."

"It's easy, my dear. You use your mind to disrupt that bending, and the sphere's effort to return it to equilibrium makes it move."

"Ah."

"Use your mind to make a tiny rotational lift of any part of the ring, and you'll go slowly in that direction. Depress any part of the ring down to back away from that direction. The more you move the ring down, the faster you go."

"So you intend me to drive?"

"Go easy until you get the hang of it. Then, there's no sub-light speed you can't attain immediately. Move us closer, and then we'll want a viz before we go inside."

ELIZABETH HUFFED IN EXASPERATION. "I don't see a damn thing that gives us any indication of what's going on. It certainly seems identical to one of Cato's spheres. It looks like the sphere he took off with except there's no sign of Followers inside. I don't sense them underground either."

"We still need to reposition inside for a closer look."

Elizabeth put a hand on Tobin's arm. "I am the one who will be going inside. You two will watch my back. Ollie, I need you to scan the space around the sphere. If you see anything odd, pull me out. Don't wait to see if it's a threat. I can always return later. Got it?"

He nodded and squeezed her hand. "Careful, love."

She gave an inelegant snort. "Just another rabbit-hole."

BECAUSE SHE'D HELPED Tobin design the sphere, Elizabeth knew every square inch of it. She suppressed her first impulse to go to Cato's control center, and instead, repositioned inside the medical facility. Everything was in its original place and never used. How could that be? A cold chill ran up her spine. She hoped she'd placed Ollie with Tobin out of harm's in harm's way because she needed him. But Tobin's been a bit impulsive lately, and she wondered if Tobin was a good choice for Ollie

She scanned the area again looking for abnormalities. The portable console screen in the corner was different. One of the newer models looked like a rectangular nine-foot by four-foot of clear glass on wheels. When activated, however, she knew it became an interactive computer screen.

She touched the start icon, hoping for a message. Within seconds, a realistic image of

George appeared. George? Although the image's facial expressions gave her the feeling he really recognized her, she knew her longtime friend and collaborator was a cleverly disguised realistic recording. Nevertheless, he might have a clue as to what was happening.

"George, What the—"

"Elizabeth, good to see you were able to find us."

"Us? Who is—"

Before she could finish, the image of George raised a hand and continued, "No doubt you figured out this is a non-interactive recording. So, for once," the image chuckled, "I'll be doing all the talking without one of your insightful questions. I know you have many, so I'll get on with the answers."

Oh, great, she wanted a conversation with one of the top physicists on earth and a fellow Nobel Prize winner to boot, and instead, she gets his questionable sense of humor and answers to questions she might or might not have.

"First answer, you asked me to make this recording." He grinned. "Yes, Elizabeth, that was an answer. You are the one who demanded this recording be made. You always were a bit on the dictatorial side, but I like that about you."

<OLLIE, Tobin, are you hearing and seeing this?>

Their affirmative <yes> came in unison.

"But I digress. The answer begs another question, doesn't it?" He paused as if giving her time to ask and wore that gleeful expression he got when he had an arcane physics tidbit of knowledge to impart. "Ready? Here it is, the answer to your question is only if you believe time travel is possible."

As though knowing she needed time to think, the image of George wavered in silence before her. Time travel? What were the implications of that in this context?

"Elizabeth? Are you with me? I know your mind is churning with what I said, but we need to move on."

It was hard to remember her friend was not actually there. His timing was so attuned to her reaction. Her mind was stuck on the concept, just as he'd guessed.

He waited a moment more, giving her time to marshal her thoughts. "The next answer is, yes. Time travel is possible, but only if you do not interfere with the mind's control of it." He laughed, "I should have taught my classes this way when I was a teaching assistant at Rice." His recording didn't pause this time. "All right, the last answer. Because only the mind is capable of avoiding a time-travel paradox."

<Again the mind,> Oliver's voice sputtering into her head. <George puts time-travel on the same level as piloting a sphere.>

She couldn't refute that. <Wait. There's more.>

"So to be fair, I'll stop frustrating you with answers. It'd be best if you sat down and talked this through with someone live and I have just the person." He paused like he expected her to ask the question.

His image stilled, and she worked at digesting what she'd heard. It was all too bizarre. If she'd told him to do this video, she'd surely have told him to make more sense?

George counted on his fingers. "When you entered this room, two things occurred. One, the system confirmed you were here, and two, it sent a Q-bit, a small piece of quantum code, to someone alerting her of your presence. My time is up. Be sure to visit me in Chicago when you can."

He raised a hand in what she thought was to say goodbye, but instead, he pointed his finger down and wove it in a circle. "You should turn around now." The screen went blank.

Her breathing hitched and the hair on the back of her neck stood up. She was no longer alone on the sphere's medical center. Why hadn't Ollie pulled her out? She turned, preparing for the worst.

Instead, she found herself staring face-to-face with herself.

REFLECTION

Lagrangian point L2

Dumbfounded, Elizabeth barely sensed Oliver's question.

<Liz, what's the matter? You haven't moved for several minutes. Are you okay?>

<Uh. so far.>

<What the hell does that mean?>

<It's difficult to say. Can you see or detect anyone in this room other than me?>

Oliver reacted by repositioning her back to the safety of their sphere. "What the hell, Liz? You're making no sense."

She observed his behavior for clues about how much more of this he understood than he let on. "Thanks, Ollie. I think I needed that break. I'm going back now. Keep an eye on me, but I don't believe I'm in any danger."

He protested, but Tobin intervened. <She'll be safe, Uncle Oliver. Don't hold her back.>

Elizabeth returned to the large sphere and backed up slowly to a small conference table, falling more than sitting into her chair. She locked eyes on a slightly older Elizabeth. Time travel. That's what George had said. Why hadn't the George image told her she'd meet a version of herself from the future? Clasping her hands together so they wouldn't shake, she leaned forward on her forearms. "Explain."

The figure walked toward her and Elizabeth studied her, Not bad. Her laugh lines were possibly more pronounced, perhaps not used for laughing. This encounter must be something serious. The spring in her step was for haste, not one for joy. The future version of herself had a bearing of resolve and when she walked to the table and sat, Elizabeth dubbed her Liz II. It was all too freaky. From the facial structure to her mannerisms, Liz II was the same, but older.

Liz II spoke.

"I am not a clone."

"Then what are you? Can you read my mind?"

Liz ii shook her head.

"I believe I remember it. Oliver and Tobin cannot detect me because I don't wish to be seen or recorded. Neither they nor you will remember anything about this visit."

Elizabeth frowned, "Then, why go through all of this, . . . this show if it means nothing?"

Liz II spoke calmly. "I am adjusting all of you to a new timeline. One where none of you remember exploring this site and finding me. In fact, you will only remember that you found nothing here."

“Timeline? When we finished here, do you intend to reset the clock? How? By sending us back in time?" She pushed her chair back and remained sitting saying, "All this is rather silly." Elizabeth raised her voice. "What do you want?”

Liz II showed no reaction. “As you guessed, I am a future version of you.”

“That’s not an acceptable answer. It doesn't explain anything."

Liz II began to pace. She balanced her left elbow on the back of her right hand resting on her chest and punctuated her speech with a finger.

Elizabeth found this lecture mode irritating, and her eyes narrowed.

Liz II continued. “As you see, I am you. Yes, you heard me correctly. My DNA, my microbiology, my memory are all the same as yours. I am, in fact, you.”

The younger Elizabeth stared deep into her eyes, looking for an explanation.

Liz II continued pacing in lecture mode. “To understand, you must accept the premise that within limitations, controlled by the mind, time travel does, in fact, exist."

Time travel. It was a concept she and Tobin discussed often. The folklore of MeMa's recent behavior suggested its existence. "I accept your premise. Then why are you here?"

Liz II shook her head. "I can't tell you that."

"Why is the sphere here?"

"I can tell you nothing."

"What the hell is the point of all this?" Elizabeth sank back in her chair and folded her arms. "What do you expect me, us, to do?"

Liz II extended a hand. "I am here only to show you something important."

Elizabeth knew by making contact with the woman she gave her access into the deep state of her mind and hesitated. Ridiculous as it was, she didn't want Liz II altering her mind. She didn't like the idea of herself in her mind? This is ludicrous.

The older Elizabeth said, "Trust me."

The younger Elizabeth accepted the offered hand.

RETURNING to the smaller sphere to face Oliver and Tobin, she shook her head at the uneasiness itching its way up her spinal cord. “The sphere’s empty, no one is there.”

That wasn’t right.

“There’s only a deserted island. No fish, no flowers, no Followers, nothing.” She hesitated as a fleeting flash of uncertainty held her motionless. She had vague feelings about what might happen next. She didn’t like it. She hated not knowing. “Take me home. There’s nothing here. The sphere has been abandoned. There's work to be done at home.”

“Oh, crap,” Tobin, said. “This may well be one of those practice space-spheres I made for Cato that got lost. I launched it at the moon a short time ago while attempting to pilot it remotely and I lost it.”

“You lost it?” Oliver was generally very low-keyed, but his voice rose an octave. “A thing that size? You just left it to bounce around in space?”

Tobin nodded. “Not so big by cosmos size. It’s possible I left it at L2 and forgot about it.”

Elizabeth lowered her brows and gave him a stern look. “You and I know that is not possible. You have the mind of a steel trap. You’d never forget something like that.”

Tobin shrugged as if it were of small importance to him. “Do you want me to collapse the sphere?”

She shook her head. A squeezing on her heart and the headache escalating within her temples had become an annoying distraction. "No, leave it in L2 for now. We have other concerns." Damn. It would be nice to know what the hell they were. Tobin should go to Sally. That was a completely bizarre and random thought. Things were not making sense in her normally logical mind. Nonetheless, she patted him on the arm and made the suggestion. "Maybe this is a good time for you to take some time off and go visit that girl you met in Egypt."

Tobin's brows shot up. "You mean Sally? That's a great idea, can you help me convince Mom?"

TOBIN AND TINA AT ULURU

Ayres Rocxk

Tobin hadn’t been with Sally in Cuddly Creek for some time and he was impatient to see her, but Tina asked him to stop. Old habits were hard to break. From birth, he had been there for his sister and she for him. Their bond as twins had grown while still in the womb and their closeness was powerful. He repositioned to her vestibule and announced his presence. Few Evolutis homes or apartments had the need for doors.

<What’s up, Tina? I have places to go.>

<Hey, Tobin. Come in, I’m ready>

“Ready? Ready for what? You called me.”

“We’re going to see Sally, right?”

“Not exactly. Anyway, I only stopped by because I thought you needed something.”

“Well, yeah, I do. I don’t know how to get to Cuddly Creek without you.”

“Have you never heard of alone, Tina? I want to go alone. I want to get away from everything for a while. That means you, too.”

"Oh, come on, Tobin. I won't get in the way. I like Sally. I'll just say hi."

"But I am not going to see her. Okay? I need a break from all the family drama. I can't think of a better place than Cuddly Creek."

"Great! You'll take me?"

"No."

"You're worried about something, aren't you?" Tina chewed her bottom lip. "Does she know you're the same guy who took her to Ayres Rock and are you sure it was two years from now?"

"I'm not sure we got around to that. I may have mentioned it."

"Does she know how important the drawings and notes on the yellow slips of paper are to us?"

"No, she couldn't know and I didn't tell her." He looked at his twin. Except for her softer and rounded edges, seeing her was almost like looking in the mirror. She exasperated the hell out of him when he was searching for privacy . . . or trying to keep a secret. "Where are you going with this,

Tina?"

"There seems to be little doubt that some version of you met her two years ago. I'm thinking now, there's no reason to assume it was two years ago from now. It could be four years or eight, or . . .

well you get my drift. We don't really know the timing of that visit to Ayres Rock with Sally."

"A serious thought, considering our time travel plans." He abruptly shook his head. "Wait, this can't be. You and I know I built the spheres for Followers space travel over a year ago. So why would I visit with her and give her the notes for building the sphere now? Crap. You think I changed the timeline? MeMa's gonna slaughter me."

Tina hooted. "Tobin, you crack me up. Think about it. MeMa would have killed you lo-o-o-ng ago"

He rubbed his head. "Contrary to logic that's reassuring. Let's look at this carefully." Now he and Tina were back to the familiar ground of problem solving. Together, they could figure out most anything.

Tina offered, "Is it possible Sally was still mad at you when she give me all the notes you had written back then? Although she gave them to me willingly to pass on to you after I met her in Egypt, maybe you were not completely forgiven."

He glared at her. "We parted on the best of terms."

"Okay. Maybe there was information you missed in the note or maybe it was torn off somehow."

“Hmm.” Rather than dismiss the suggestion out of hand, he thought back and went over every fact he knew. “Sally did say she tore one of the notes to pieces.” He rubbed his chin. “When I asked her what was on that sheet, she said it was something about ‘my family being in trouble.’ By then, I knew we were in trouble and I didn’t ask for details.”

“As far as trouble goes, one or the other of us has been stalked, shot at, or kidnapped for at least the last several years.”

Tobin slapped his forehead “Holy shit, Tina, I need to see that paper.”

“You remembered something.”

“Something’s vague, but it’s definitely a memory. It could have something to do with the sudden appearance of Cato’s sphere. I remember I left my notes to her sticking out from under the rock next to her sleeping bag so she’d find when she woke up the next day. I need to go back to that time. I can remotely viz our campsite on Ayres and read the note before she tears it up. I’ll do it from a distance and the paper will still be under the rock in the morning. That’ll work.” He threw his hands in the air. “See, no change to the timeline.”

Tina folded her arms and spoke with as much authority as she could muster. “If time travel’s the problem, MeMa says we are capable of remotely viewing through both time and distance, so you don't have to leave this rook to check on your papers."

Tobin returned her challenge. "Sure, no worries. You solved that problem. By the way when did you have hat lesson with her? I don't remember mine."

She frowned. "Okay, good point. I've never done time travel either so take me with you."

"Okay. You made your point as well."

He always gave into her and it was easier to do it sooner rather than later. What the hell, she'd had her second awakening the same time he did, so he knew the skills were in her brain's repertoire. It was a skill she needed, knowing how to time-travel safely and it wasn't like he was on some secret spy mission or even a tete a tete. He snorted. Much as he'd like to be. He realized she knew enough about his skills to teach her without MeMa's help.

"Throw some warm things in your back pack. It's a bit wet and cold down there this time of the year. Keep in mind, we will not be talking to Sally."

"I'm packed."

He could see sparks of anger flash in her eyes every time he mentioned Sally. "Okay. Out with it. You're not still angry with me for being with Sally?"

"Tobin, I realize that the first time . . . I mean the actual first time . . . you were with her, you didn't know that Mom and Aunt Elizabeth were speculating about the possible negative impact of an Evolutis microbiome's impact on Sapiens. You didn't know you could initiate awakening by close physical contact. So on that count, I say you are innocent."

"Jeez, thanks. I didn't know I needed your pardon."

"But now that you do know, you need to be more careful. How much does Sally know, Tobin? I mean about us?"

"You and me?"

"No, dimwit, pay attention. Us as in Evolutis?"

"Lord. Do we have to go through that again? After you and mom met us on that riverboat in Egypt, I repositioned Sally to the SPA and told her about becoming a new species."

"You need to take things slow. You know how difficult the transition to Evolutis is for some people. Look at your own family, for god's sake. Sarah was a mess."

"You're a little late for that. I think Sally's started the change and when she makes it, I'll be there for her. She knows what to expect and I'm monitoring her. Christ, listen to me. I've been watching over her and I'll be there whenever she needs me." He wasn't about to admit to his sister he was concerned on that score as well because more and more of his time seemed to be tied up with family affairs off planet. It was one of the reasons he needed time to be alone with Sally.

"I heard that."

"Heard what?" He should have known she'd hear his thoughts. Although the Cohort members couldn't read minds, the twins had an extra sense of each other from MeMa's interventions while they were still in the womb.

"You said you weren't going to see her. Just now I heard you say you were. What's the deal? Are you or aren't you?"

"Believe me, if I were seeing her this trip, you would not be along."

TINA STOOD about a kilometer from Ayres Rock and vized the sleeping figures of Sally and Tobin from another time. It was eerie, to say the least. She wanted to wake him to see himself gazing down. They would ask each other so many questions their tongues would probably wear out. She chuckled. Too bad it was against time travel rules.

Her twin stood next to her and then sent a virtual projection of himself to stealthy search for the note he'd left by the sleeping bag next to Sally two years ago.

She shivered, not sure if it was from the chilling evening desert air, the effects of time travel, or maybe the fact that she could see triple Tobins.

She monitored his rapid search of the note, worrying all the time that one of them, or one of their friends sleeping nearby, with would wake up.

A bright moon facilitated her vizing. When he lifted the rock near the backpack, Tina could see the relief in his face. His mind said all she needed to hear. <Got it.>

<Me too. Let's return to your place. This part of the world is getting too crowded.> She marveled at the number of campers on the rock. <This place seems rather busy tonight, perhaps the local tribe should charge extra for nighttime tickets.>

He stood next to Tina and in spite of the ample distance from Ayres, whispered "I only needed to see the half top of the missing papers. That's where the sketches are. The last time I saw them, I couldn't make out anything wrong with them."

Tobin ran his finger's back and forth across his chin. Except for the sketches he'd given Sally, he and Tina had solved the problems in building the spheres together. She knew all of the ins and outs as well as he did. He had hoped she would see something in notes they gathered that he had missed. “Now that we know we’re looking for something important in the design, check your viz again. Do you notice something we didn’t catch before?”

She ran her finger’s back and forth across her chin in a manner identical to her brother. “We need to go over this step by step. We’ll figure it out. We always do. Start at the beginning.”

“I didn’t see anything in the sketches about a problem with the sphere. What I think I saw is an enhancement. The problem is I’m not clear about what kind of enhancement I drew.” Tina’s presence, whether angry, teasing, or collaborative, always centered him. That’s what he needed now. Focus. “After I built one of the first spheres . . . and after you and I finally figured out how to get in . . . and out of it,” he snorted at the memory of that particular problem, “I thought about the sphere they called Spaceship Earth at Epcot. It led me to think of my first idea, the thought that putting something inside a plain sphere would make it make it stronger. You know, like the rods of steel to make concrete stronger.”

"Right. You put a dodecahedron inside and blew it up like a balloon until its corners blended with the sphere just like rebar in a construction site."

"Exactly, George told me I could still achieve the strength I wanted by simply expanding the inside object until only the corners merged with the sphere. I wanted some space between the flat sides of the dodecahedron and the sphere."

"How come? What did you want the space for?"

"A small apartment, storage, plant pods, you know, anything."

"Why bother? Put 100 people inside a sphere and two-seconds later let them out at Alpha Centauri. With repositioning, time's not a factor." She laughed. "Besides, I can't imagine one hundred Evolutis ever wanting to go to the same place at the same time. We can't expect each sphere to behave like a bus. You'd need 100 spheres positioned about the galaxy. Besides, once you've been somewhere, your mind remembers its location and you can always reposition there again. You don't need an entire space portal."

"I remember now. What you said reminded me." That was how it always worked. They bounced ideas and questions off each other until their thoughts crystalized.

"I did? Did you remember more?"

"Much more. That's why the original sphere we saw at Disneyland kept sticking in my mind. Think about it, all those people in the park from all from different places. I imagined the line of them marching into Disney's sphere, selecting one of the, say 11,000 triangular spaces, as their unique portal to take them home."

Tina's eyes grew huge. "Wow. And this could work in outer space. So to make the first leg of a journey, I would reposition to a portal sphere. That's what you'd call it, right?" She didn't wait for a response. "It could be in parking orbit, say, around L2. Once there, I pick the portal within the sphere that would take me instantly to where I want to go, like planet z for example. The next time I want to travel planet z from home, I could just viz it and reposition there because now that I've been there, I know the way."

Tina grinned like someone in the loony bin. "That's brilliant. How will a first-timer know which portal goes where?"

Tobin felt his mind on fire. They had played this discovery game often. "Our yet-to-be-created app will give each portal the ability to offer a perpetual preview viz, you know, like a travel poster. No, maybe more like a movie trailer of the target location. Yeah, more like that. So the first time traveler can see and record the place in his or her mind."

"Clarification, Brother, do you mean 'first-time traveler or a 'first time-traveler?"

His face beamed with the new vision. "Ah hah, That's a great question. If the initial setting was to a specific place and to a specific time at that place, there is no reason to assume the portal will be different for a different time. The portal would work with something like a dial-up and the traveler could choose a given time in history. Imagine a portal-sphere, or even two, hidden behind L2 or L3 for people on earth to use. They could have a thousand or more windows to the best most interesting places in the galaxy." Tobin grinned at his sister. "Can you see it?"

Her grin matched his. "It has real promise. I'm impressed."

"You'll help me build a prototype?"

"Are you kidding? Best summer camp ever."

THE ELEVATOR

The Rampart at the SPA

Sticking her hand in the closing door's gap, Sarah caught the elevator door. God, she couldn't wait to get out in the sun. Underground was fine for work, but she needed some outside time in her day. Doing something active, anything outside always calmed her down.

Taking a deep breath, she readied herself for the slow ascent. Sure, it was great that the new security system stopped anything dangerous from coming into their fortress, and it was a fortress, but in order to pass through the protective sphere, the elevator had to travel so slowly it would challenge the patience of a snail. She gritted her teeth to stomp down the anger that always followed her impatience.

Another hand held the door and Benjamin stepped in with a broad smile for her.

"You," she frowned, "can wait for the next one."

"Well, yes it's me," he said looking down to check. He raised an eyebrow and flashed his beautiful white teeth again. "At the rate this thing moves, I would be waiting until next week for the next one."

What he said was hard to refute. She gave a token nod then she turned her back on him the way people generally do in an elevator. She heard him stifle a chuckle or at least make a poor attempt at it and it made her steam. She crossed her arms and ignored him. "Jerk."

<I heard that.>

<Damn.>

<That, too.>

"Like hell you did. I blocked you off." She whirled around and glared at him. She wanted to throttle him. "First, you blew me up . . . then you practically killed me . . . and then you kidnapped me." He made her so mad she had trouble putting a coherent phrase together.

"Not precisely true on all counts. Your thoughts, by the way, are written all over your posture." His grin returned.

Buttoning her mind up good and tight so nothing got out, she turned away from him once more to stare at the elevator door. It wasn't fair that he was so good-looking… and tall. And why the hell was he so damn charming? Not that she noticed. His damn precise beard, on the other hand, was too fascinating to ignore. How did he keep it just-so on his square jaw?

She sensed a change and turned. "What happened? I don't think we're moving."

"Although we were going so slow it was hard to tell we actually were moving, you are correct. The elevator has stopped." He hit the emergency button one more time and got no response.

"God, if we could just reposition out of here." Sarah heaved a big sigh. "This security thing is a pain in the neck." Ugh. She looked at her cellmate. The waste of time was killing her, especially with him.

"Anger is also a waste of time," he said. "I don't suppose we could use this time to bury the hatchet?"

"What?" Sarah glared at him. Her mouth gaped open and her brows knit so close together they looked like a single line. "We should make peace? Are you out of your mind? There is no we."

He stood leaning against the side of the elevator with his arms crossed and totally at ease. He raised a brow as in anticipation of what she'd do next, no doubt.

She didn't hesitate. "You have the nerve to say you're willing to forgive me for being kidnapped by you? Well, doesn't that make total sense?" She swiveled around to glare back at the elevator door, willing it to open and let her out. This was unbearable. She stood ramrod straight and within minutes, got a crick in her neck all because he was a freaking pain in the neck. Oh, damn. Rotating her head in a circle to relieve the pain, she took a deep breath, trying to relax her shoulders.

"You might as well get comfortable. It looks like we're going to be in here for a while."

She avoided his eyes b y checking him out. Benjamin wore a pair of upscale slacks and a long sleeved white dress shirt. The contrast to his smooth dark skin emphasized his breathtaking good looks and Sarah hated him all over again. He rolled up his shirtsleeves and unbuttoned another button at his neck before settling on the floor, his long legs stretched out casually in front of him. With his ankles crossed, he looked like owned their small square of real estate and was there to collect rent.

Bastard. Giving in to the reality of the situation, Sarah decided to sit. However, she drew her legs up to stay as far away from him as possible and he had the nerve to laugh at her effort.

He didn't even have the good manner to put a hand over his mouth to subdue his outburst.

He's definitely a Jerk, Jeez, she had no imagination. She needed another personal pejorative for him. Wishing she weren't drawn to him by some perverse twist of fate, she did her best to ignore him.

They sat in silence until she couldn't stand it any more. She lowered her chin and without looking at him asked the question that had been eating away at her, "Why'd you do it?"

"Do what?"

"What the hell? Are you kidding me? Everything . . . bomb me . . . kidnap me . . . give me to your sister Adrianne. And she hurt me, Benjamin. She hurt me really bad." Sarah crossed her arms and tried to escape his eyes by putting her head down on her knees. God, yes, the woman had hurt her. The punishment for not buckling down to Adrianne's brainwashing was excruciating. She still woke in the middle of the night sweating and shaking in fear of the pain starting again. She ran her fingers through her dark hair and said, "Your sister is the devil, Benjamin. She's rotten to the core."

"Yes."

"Yes?" She thrust her chin forward. "You agree with me and still you gave me to her?"

“Yes.”

“You’re in league with her. You’re partners. You… you…” she sputtered in an effort to find the right words and hit her thigh with her fist when the only thing that came out was, “Jerk.” God, again.

“You said that already.”

“It’s worth repeating.”

“Let me explain,” Benjamin said, his face impassive.”

Sarah lifted her chin high and turned her head to the side, wanting to hear but not wanting to admit it. There was no way she would ever . . .ever forgive him.

Benjamin re-crossed his arms and began. “The Followers charged Adrianne with finding an awakened young person. The assignment came with the expectation that they, the Followers, would convert her find, in this case you, to their group.” Benjamin dropped his hands to his lap.

His voice was resigned and Sarah thought maybe she detected shame. He should feel ashamed.

“It is a practice I do not approve of, but Adrianne goes after it with a vengeance and her methods are . . . uh, rough. I did everything in my power to talk her out of taking you. I got nowhere.”

He had her full attention now. She knew from first hand experience that to say Adrianne was rough was a euphemism beyond any she'd ever heard. She turned toward him. "She's a sadist, Benjamin, and you know it. She's a monster."

He grimaced. "Yes, her techniques are cruel and calculated, but I'm not sure I could defeat her without killing her and I could never do that, Sarah. So I went with her, theoretically as an accomplice, but in reality, to protect you."

"Not so good at the job were you? In fact, you sucked." She raised an eyebrow, daring him to refute her statement. That she could even talk about it was a testament to hours spent in therapy.

"You've got to admit you weren't helping."

"Helping to kidnap myself? What am I missing here?" Dammit. She'd let him make her angry . . . again. She took a deep breath. He would not rile her. She wouldn't let him.

"You kept me drugged." She shot at him. "You wanted me to wait around for you to come up with something when I didn't even know whose side you were on?"

Benjamin had the good sense to lower his eyes.

"And then, your solution was to whoop me away to some God-forsaken cabin in the snow-bound woods and make me your prisoner instead of Adriane's? What's wrong with that picture? Was I supposed to guess that you were doing a good thing? You're kidding, right?"

"I can see how it must have looked to you," he admitted. "I wanted to make sure you would be safe from my sister. If you were loose, she would have honed in on you like a boa constrictor on a rat."

"It didn't much work, did it?" It sure as hell hadn't. Adrianne had found them almost immediately.

"That's because you announced to the world where you were." He ducked his chin to hide a grin and then totally lost it. He threw his head back and laughed. "Girl, for someone who didn't know what the hell you were doing, you let loose with some powerful brain muscle. It's a good thing you finally lassoed those incredible powers under control now." He wiped his knuckles across thick curly lashes to catch his tears of mirth.

"You may think that's funny, but when Adrianne took me, she did unspeakable things to me." Anger consumed her again. "I was like an experimental mouse in a cage to her. She stabbed me with needles . . . with mind altering drugs… and beat me with invisible . . ." She stopped, a look of such horror on her face Benjamin half rose to come toward her.

Sarah held out her palms. “You stay away from me. It was your fault she had me.” She took a couple of long steadying breaths, reminding herself she was no longer imprisoned and glared at the man responsible.

Benjamin sobered and sat back down, instantly. “Sarah, I tried everything I could to prevent it. He lowered his head. She overpowered me.” It was a confession on a whispered mumble.

“Excuse me? What did you say?”

He glowered at her. “I said, damn you, she overpowered me.” He locked gazes with her and his lips stretched in a thin straight line. “I could not keep you safe. I could not keep my damn sister from taking you.” He dropped his graze and rubbed his forehead. “After knocking us unconscious, she imprisoned me . . . locked me up. When I finally got loose, I couldn’t find you anywhere . . . and believe me . . . I tried. Finally, I discovered Adrianne held you in a chalet high in the Switzerland Alps . . . for all the good that did me. I couldn’t penetrate her security. Furthermore, every time I tried, you were diabolically punished.”

“I remember,” she said through lips drawn thin. God, did she remember. The pain was so bad she couldn’t stay conscious half the time.

He studied her face for a moment before he went on. "When the Followers said you had been ruined for them, my sister made a deal with a paramilitary security company called Darkwood. They also wanted the powers you had to offer, but for a different reason than the ancient people. Adrianne is a loner, Sarah. She never agrees to work with anyone unless there is a great deal in it for her. Did you learn anything about this Darkwood group while you were with her?"

"What? Are you stupid? Did you forget the part where they kept me drugged the entire time trying to brainwash me? I was surviving, Benjamin, from minute to minute. That was all I was doing. I closed my brain and feelings to anything from the outside. I breathed . . . one breath after another. If Tobin's dream training hadn't been so powerful, it would never have gotten through to me. I did everything in my power to shut out everything incoming."

Sarah detested pity. She jerked her head away from his compassionate look and cursed herself for showing weakness. She thumped the wall of the elevator with her fist. "When will they get this freaking slow-ass elevator working again? It's getting damn hot in here." She ran a hand up and down a long brown arm, which was only a shade lighter than Benjamin's. Her mother kept telling her they made a handsome couple and Sarah kept telling her there was no couple in the equation.

Apparently, Benjamin still thought they could at least be friends. “As you know, Tobin was furious with me. He’s a damn big guy and he packs a wallop.” He rubbed his chin in memory. “I was sure he broke my jaw, but if it hadn’t been for him, and his dream training, we would not have been able to get you out. You are so strong, Sarah . . . both inside and out. What happened to you would have broken a lesser mortal. I can’t tell you how much I admire you for that.”

Whenever his gaze penetrated hers, Sarah felt all mushy inside and she didn’t want him to have power over her that way. Jerk, she reminded herself. “How do you explain your actions in Svalbard? You delivered Elizabeth and Oliver to the Followers. They went in a peace mission, yet you gave them up. They were drugged and powerless.”

“I was monitoring your aunt and uncle with Tobin. You saw that he and I were working together when you finally escaped Adrianne and dropped in the sphere.” He slid around the elevator to sit next to her. “We’re on the same team, Sarah. We have battles coming up that will require that we work together. As a team, we all will be stronger without the animosity.”

She pursed her lips and crossed her arms, leaning away from him. She didn't want to give up her anger. It helped her keep her distance. He was dangerous to her. He distracted her. She needed him to stay away. She stood and paced in the small area. Two strides and then a turn, two more strides and another turn, and so on.

Benjamin unfolded his long legs and came gracefully to his feet in front of her. He lightly held her upper arms. "Peace.? Cut me some slack. Let's start over without the distrust." A small smile started on his lips and it filled his lovely brown eyes.

Damn. I'm losing it. She stood totally still . . . giving no resistance. She started falling . . . toward him.

The elevator lurched and Benjamin pulled her to him just as the door jerked open.

A technician stuck his head inside. "Sorry to interrupt. You folks okay?"

THEY ARGUE WITH MEMA

The Rampart at the SPA

Awakened abruptly by a voice in the middle of her deep sleep, Elizabeth, gasped as her heart flipped into double-time pounding. She drew in long slow breaths and hoped MeMa had something important to report. <Daughter, I need to speak with you on the rampart.>

Ducking her head from beneath Oliver's strong protective arm, she slipped free and slid to the far side of the bed trying not to wake him and put on her terry cloth robe.

She re-positioned to the rampart where the cool breeze made her glad she'd worn her robe. Wrapping it tighter around her slim waist, she let her eyes roam in search of MeMa. In her black Victorian gown, the ancient woman all but disappeared into the shadows and Elizabeth almost missed her. She walked toward the matriarch, who stood gazing over the rampart wall at the Aegean Sea below. Shannon arrived and surprised her, but

MeMa apparently expected to meet with both of them and motioned them closer.

Skipping the social niceties, Shannon launched straight into attack mode. “You’ve been absent from this Cohort for a long time, Mother. What could be so important it could not wait until morning?”

Ignoring Shannon’s anger, MeMa said, “Good evening, Daughters. We must talk.” She gestured to three wooden Adirondack chairs in the corner. They sat and waited for her to speak.

Shannon sat in the chair, stood, sat again and crossed her arms, radiating anger. Elizabeth understood why. Too often in recent history, the old woman, with her vast years of knowledge, experience and power, was missing when the Cohort needed her.

Elizabeth shuddered at the memory of the volcano’s heat closing in, at the kidnapping of the twins, at the excruciating pain Sarah had undergone in the hands of . . . she shook herself. The woman was here now, that was what mattered.

Shannon’s annoyance was understandable and great enough for both of them. Elizabeth stifled her own resentment in favor of gaining information. She greeted the matriarch in the formal ancient way. “Good evening, Mother, we have been without your council for too long. We have questions.”

MeMa nodded, her sage old eyes danced at Elizabeth's courteous greeting. "I am here to share what I learned speaking with my closest and most trusted Seeker friends across the globe. I know you both want to hear what news I have of our future."

She leaned forward slightly and opened both hands. "I am afraid, however, simple knowledge of the future is not as important as realizing how important patience is at the core of our problem."

Shannon snorted then regained control and sat stone-faced. Elizabeth wasn't sure she could sit through another of MeMa's dissertations on patience either and was hopeful the words 'our problem' meant that in this go around, MeMa was not advocating waiting.

MeMa tapped Elizabeth's forearm. "Knowing what might happen is important, but only if the reaction to the problem recognizes the need for patience. Too often solutions turn out to be short-lived because long-term consequences were ignored."

MeMa tilted her head toward Shannon. "As someone with extensive research on the human brain will attest, the decision capabilities of the pubescent sapiens teenager are flawed, I believe, due to rapid development in the brain requiring vastly increased connections between neurons. As a result, teenagers often make impulsive and risky decisions."

Shannon couldn't hold back any longer. "I'm sorry my need to ensure that we have seen our last kidnapping is my priority, but we are only young by your standards and I cannot help being impatient about the safety of my children."

MeMa's eyes narrowed. "The acquisition of Snyder's area initially produces the same results in adults as the rapid development brain does in teenagers. I, along with my associates, loath kidnapping and agree these issues must be addressed to stop the pain and suffering your family has endured. Our strategic solutions must be implemented only after the long-term consequences of our action is understood."

Shannon said, leaned forward. "While we absolutely need a permanent, strategic solution, I need an immediate tactical response to the kidnapping threat. Now. Not latter."

MeMa gave a slight bob of her head. "Yes, I understand, however, we must respond tactically within the context of a greater strategy."

Elizabeth gnashed her teeth, squeezed her palms in tight fists. What a merry-go-round of double-talk, obfuscation, and delay of truths, all these were familiar characteristics of MeMa's communication.

No wonder impatience gnawed at her best friend. "Of course, Mother. I wonder, could you give us your recommendations for what we call the bottom line, that which allows us to address our concerns . . . ah, sooner."

Shannon sat back in her chair, folded her arms and waited, a mulish expression covering a steaming facade. MeMa's ability to detect their thoughts made it was fruitless to block their frustration.

The ancient woman raised her brows. "We have concluded it is time for the Cohort to become an invisible people."

Elizabeth's jaw dropped and she quickly snapped it shut. "Meaning what, exactly?" She glanced at Shannon, who remained silent and unreceptive. "Are you suggesting we adopt the same methodology of the Followers and find some place to hide? To simply disappear?"

MeMa shook her head, "No, the world needs the Cohorts. You must remain in sight, but as Worlders."

Elizabeth, a brilliant biogenetic scientist and Shannon a superb brain scientist were unable to string together a sentence. Neither spoke. Where was MeMa going with her conversation? None of it made sense. How could MeMa see the large picture while focusing on minor tactical considerations such as putting us in the world to proselytize?

"Have either of you wondered why the Followers made the decision to sequester their families in Svalbard under a mountain of ice?"

"Of course we gave it thought," Elizabeth said, "It's clear to us their fundamentalism and paranoia drove them there."

"That is hardly an accurate conclusion." The old women's tone was sharp, even angry.

"Have either of you experienced first-hand persecution? Have either of you watched a family member burned alive at the stake?" Bitterness crept into her voice. "Have you ever been denied food and shelter?" Her quivering voice rose, "Have either of you had to watch a family member or friend die of a mysterious illnesses, helpless to prevent it?"

Elizabeth softened her anger. "We know of your terrible suffering, Mother. We know the history of persecution and disease in Europe."

MeMa continued as if she hadn't heard, or perhaps because she needed to repeat the story to keep it alive. "I lived through it." She raised her chin as if in defiance. "Were you aware that when we finally met as a group and gathered on the shore of northern Norway for the last leg of our exodus from Europe on our journey to Svalbard, we were met not with more ships, but by forty-nine Seekers?"

Elizabeth's eyes popped wide. "The trek across the Svalbard ice is a myth?"

MeMa shook her finger, "Oh, the trek occurred across ice, Daughter, but the ice we crossed was not in Svalbard, we walked across Norway. Once we got to the its northern coast we met Seekers who repositioned us across the ocean to the underground community on Svalbard."

"I don't understand," For the first time, Shannon showed interest. "If you had powers, why didn't you use them in Europe? Why did you even have to flee? Why didn't you confront your enemies?" She threw her arms out. "You could have ruled Europe. Hell, you could've taken over the world."

"No, you need more context, Daughter. We learned to detest those who subjugated people in the name of nobility and warred in the name of religion. We did not want to become like them or live among them. They were driven by greed and prejudice and we wished only for separation from them. At that time, we only wanted to create a safe society in which we would live in peace. Most of the Follower leadership believed their stay on earth was only for a short while. They spoke of an interstellar people called the Children of the Light who they believed to be their ancestors, the ones who would one day return for them."

Elizabeth had trouble looking as though she cared. How many times had MeMa told them this story? True, it was an amazing story, but she wanted to get on with the current problems, like why was she talking to herself in her dreams and what was George doing on L2? She believed in the concept of time travel, but there was something more going on and she was damned if she could figure out what.

MeMa droned. "But there is more, Daughters. You must appreciate how opposed the Followers are to killing. Fighting, combat, and war, they are all based on the premise that in order to win, the enemy must die. Is that not so?"

"Assuming both we and the Followers are both Evolutis, then those of us who recently awakened have not finished evolving, correct?" Elizabeth commented dryly.

"And you say this is relevant to kidnapping?" Shannon asked. "How? I want those bastards who kidnapped my children. To me, that's war. I'm not a Follower. I don't think like them. I want these people to die. You think that's blood-thirsty?" She spit the words through clenched teeth, "I want them to die in my hands."

"I understand, Daughter. Many of us standing on the northern shore escaping persecution felt as you do." MeMa had barely moved during her entire recitation. It was as though the memories, dredged up from so very long ago, exhausted her. "But we knew our first job was to guarantee the survival of our families for centuries to come."

"Mere survival?" Elizabeth asked, "Is that the crux of what you are about to propose to us today?"

With what appeared to be great effort, MeMa draw her ancient body taller in her chair. She repeated what she had said earlier. "This Cohort must develop the patience to become invisible to the world."

"What?" Elizabeth and Shannon chorused.

Shannon spoke first. "You believe we are foolish to assume we can work successfully with governments, corporations, and the military?"

MeMa nodded. "You cannot work with them as Evolutis without destroying any future chance for a successful transition of Sapiens into Evolutis. It took some 25,000 years for Sapiens to absorb the Neanderthals." She gazed deeply into her eyes. "We have neither the numbers nor the time to repeat that coup."

Shannon jumped to her feet and began to pace, shaking her arms next to her head. "With all our work in medicine and all the people we helped transition to Evolutis, you expect us to hide under a glacier?" She turned and pointed a finger at MeMa, "How can you expect me to simply continue working at Johns Hopkins pretending nothing has happened? If we were to deny our ongoing conflict, then how's that different from denying we are a new species? This is going to take more than a few disclaiming Internet videos and tee-shirts saying, 'Sorry, science prank!'" She sat and with her elbows on her knees, supporting her head while she glared at MeMa.

Elizabeth eyed Shannon and knew what she would soon say would permanently strain their relationship with the matriarch. "Mother, could you tell us more about the wisdom of patience?"

"I can tell you both that having recently had their second awakening you are vulnerable to impulse and the need for immediate satisfaction."

Shannon raised her head. "Do you refer to the millions of additional neural connections our brains develop to support a second awakening?"

"Yes, precisely. In your case, you went after rogue government agents to gain information almost killing several in the effort."

She looked at Elizabeth. "In your case, daughter, you actually killed two men."

Elizabeth felt anger welling up. “Vald deserved to die.”

MeMa stamped her foot. “No child, I do not speak of Vald. In fact, he has been rescued by his people and is actively working on his revenge. Because you were impatient and impulsive, his now raging need for revenge could have been avoided by a well thought through strategy and a patient response.”

Elizabeth stood in anger. “What? He lives? Vald is alive? How can that be? I shot him out of the solar system.”

“His minions intercepted his flight.”

“He lives. He lives. He lives.” Elizabeth couldn’t catch her breath. Her breathing grew rapid and shallow. Her head buzzed and she was burning up from the volcanic heat.

“Elizabeth. Elizabeth.” Shannon took Elizabeth’s arm and shook it firmly. “Look at me. You are okay. You hear me? We are both okay. Focus on my face. We survived the volcano and at least for now, Vald is not here. Breathe. That’s it. Are you good? Are you back with us?”

Elizabeth wasn’t sure. She still had nightmares and knew that Shannon did too. “Yes. I’m okay.” That bastard. How could someone that rotten have anyone who cared enough about him to save him?

She saw MeMa watching her. What was she doing there? She rubbed her palms across her forehead. She needed to get a grip. Shannon's eyes narrowed at MeMa. "He still deserves to die. How many did he kill before he left Elizabeth and me to die with my children? I repeat. He is a monster and the world, hell, the galaxy, would be better off without him."

MeMa placed a hand on Shannon's knee. "I agree, the Time Overlords and I think you are on the right path in preparing the world for an Evolutis majority. We should network with politicians and DARPA." Elizabeth hoped for a more relaxed discussion after MeMa's departure, "Meanwhile, we must become invisible as an Evolutis nation yet we can still remain among the general population. Don't you think that's possible? All we need to do is hide our facilities and protect our young. We're smart enough to create the rest of the plan."

"I don't know," Shannon said in frustration. She stood abruptly. "Why must we live always looking over our shoulder? With all our children constantly at risk, it's difficult to think beyond the moment. If it's not about protecting my children, then I'm not interested." She spoke through clenched teeth and balled her fists. "I can't work with you on this. Not now, anyway." She turned away and vanished.

Understanding Shannon's distress over MeMa's her apparent casual attitude for the safety of her children, Elizabeth could hardly fault her anger.

SHANNON'S MISSION

Berkeley Campus

MeMa tried to explain. <Grandfather, they fail to understand.>

<We knew this might be the most difficult part of the mission. However, you must continue to reveal your true nature and intentions for them without telling them about their future as we know it.>

Elizabeth almost whispered. <They would listen if they knew. I must share the message with the right people.>

Seth shook his head. <No, I have explored that part of the timeline and it leads to chaos, confusion and disaster. It generates too much divergence. There is a correct time for that action and we must endure until it arrives.>

<I defer to your wisdom, Grandfather.>

<Please, do not call me that.> He stroked his beard. <You must reveal yourself soon.>

ELIZABETH SIPPED her tea and worried about Shannon and the meeting. Her friend's anger was well founded, as far as she was concerned, but it had deflected MeMa's purpose. At least she thought it had. She was fairly certain MeMa had come with something to tell them. Shannon's impulsive behavior seemed beyond what she had witnessed since her friend's freshman year at Rice. She had hoped it had to do with the damn sphere at L2. Dammit, there was an immediacy about it telling her something else must be at play. What the hell was it? Damn MeMa and her muddy smokescreens.

She gazed over her cup past her small flower garden to the Berkeley campus and waved at Ollie, who was casually climbing the grassy hill toward the back patio. Warmth spread though her as he returned the greeting and drew near.

She stood and waited until they were within comfortable speaking distance to tease him about walking. "Too tired to reposition?" He frequently balked at the action saying he was afraid he'd end up on Timbuktu.

He laughed. "Funny. My office window was open and I could smell fresh cut grass. Something dearly lacking in Tobin's space balls."

"Ah," she replied. "Nothing like it. Come sit. I have tea."

After a long warm hug and a quick kiss, he settled next to her and gazed at her vista. “It is lovely here on your patio. The view is spectacular and private and the weather couldn’t be more perfect.” After a few quiet moments he asked in a soft voice, “How are you doing?”

She made a wry twist of her lips. She had shared most all her thoughts with Oliver and in this case, about her concerns about Shannon.

He patted the back of her hand. “Any word about her?”

“No.” She looked away. Shannon wasn’t the only thing on her mind. She wasn’t sleeping well and could make no sense of what her dreams were about. Nightmares, really. She woke afraid and breathing hard. Garbled voices in her head terrified her and she couldn’t understand the words. Although she tried to keep her fears to herself, she could tell from Ollie’s look of concern he knew something was going on. Asking no questions, he would gather her close and just hold her. Lord, she needed him.

“Interesting what MeMa said about making rational decisions soon after the second awakening. It reminds me of the impulsive behavior we associate with puberty. Remember when she buzzed the Rice campus with that damn plane of hers? We all thought it was a great joke, but the administration wasn't so pleased. Go to her. Let her vent. Find out if she is capable of making rational decisions. She needs you. See if she has any plans . . . bone headed or otherwise."

"She doesn't, that I know of, and right now I'm the bad guy in her mind because I supported some of MeMa's idea."

"Try again. That's what best friends do for each other."

"I can't seem to defend my concerns to her where her children are involved."

"Then don't." He lifted her hand and gently shook it between them. "Go. She needs you."

She squeezed his hand. "Thanks, Ollie." Elizabeth had no idea where Shannon might be so she followed George's advice and opened her mind. Ah, of course. The gazebo. She saw her sitting alone in black scrubs, blending into the shadows of the white structure adjacent to her family estate in Baltimore. Before repositioning, she grabbed two glasses and a good bottle of wine.

"HI." Elizabeth raised the bottle above her head. "Got a minute for an old friend?"

Shannon dimpled her cheeks and cleared the small circular table beside her wicker chair. "Sit," she said, pointing to another chair.

“James still in China?” Elizabeth asked by way of conversation. Her friend’s husband was the head of the multi-million-dollar Trident International conglomerate and was often away.

“Yeah.” Shannon wiped her hands on her scrubs and reached for the wine bottle. “I’ve given up keeping tabs on my Gulliver’s travels. James could make his treks about the world so much easier if he would just reposition, but prefers good old train travel. I don’t know how he views a train that runs at 120 miles per hour as ‘good’ but it makes him happy.” She poured two glasses and handed one to Elizabeth, making eye contact for the first time. “MeMa says you are correct about Vald.”

Elizabeth pulled her chin in. “Really? I find it strange that both MeMa and Vald have spent the last several centuries doing their own thing in their own way trying to influence events in this world for their own purposes.”

Shannon sipped wine as her brows jerked high. “That doesn’t sound like you. Where did that come from?”

“First, it’s from MeMa telling me her life story from 1206 on.”

“Humph,” Shannon snorted. “I suspect it goes back farther than that.”

"That may well be. The second thing is, it seems MeMa spent a good deal of time with us and our parents when we were kids."

"And later when we were at Rice as well. Funny, how she never stood out, but she was there. I remember her now. Didn't she dress like a nun? Why didn't we notice her earlier?"

Elizabeth put her glass down and leaned forward, resting her elbows on her knees. "You can bet it has something to do with MeMa hocus-pocus. She told me she was on the verge of quitting her Rice project because she couldn't find a suitable seventh."

"MeMa and her damn sevens. Okay, so in combinations of seven, Evolutis is stronger, but they were so powerful anyway, why is it always such a big deal to the woman?

Elizabeth pointed at Shannon. "For whatever reason, when a brilliant high school senior won a national science research prize and transferred to Rice in the second semester of her senior year in high school, her problem was solved"

Shannon responded with a dry voice. "So I guess all this is all my fault."

"Good one. But seriously, you aren't even in the running with Vald around. His danger to us began in the 1300s when he passed himself off as a persecuted European during the Black Plague exodus and ingratiated himself into the Follower leadership." She threw up her hands in disgust and anger. "That bastard."

Shannon grimaced. "Everyone has a plan for us. Screw them all."

If that wasn't the lead Elizabeth was looking for, nothing was. Even if she started an argument, it was time to ask. "What's your plan, Shannon?"

"We need to know more about the bastard. I want to research him to death. I want to discover every single aspect of his being and then science the shit out of him until he dies. I'm starting with his well-documented hubris to get close to him. I can't say more than that and I tell you this in confidence only because of our friendship. I trust you not to share this."

Elizabeth held her breath hoping to hear more. When none came, she couldn't hold it back. "What are you saying? Are you going to find him? He tried to kill us. Are you trying to give the bastard another chance? The man terrifies me. He gives us both wake-up-in-the-middle-of-the-night-screaming-nightmares. And you are going to him? Are you out of your mind?" She was screaming. She couldn't help it. Just talk of the bastard made it hard to breathe. She shut her mouth and drew deep breathes through her nose. God, she felt lightheaded. She'd had some harrowing experiences in her live, but near-death by volcano ranked right up there.

"I'm not going to wait alone on some street corner to be taken." Shannon shouted back. "I've had enough." She vanished.

Well, dammit to hell, so much for being a friend. All she'd managed was to screech at Shannon and make her leave . . . again. For all that she'd said don't tell, there wasn't really anything to say. Who did she know who could be more diplomatic?

A CALL

MeMa's Victorian Home

A summons from MeMa was a command. <Daughter, I need to speak with you in private. Come to my home.>

WITHOUT HESITATION, Elizabeth repositioned to the ancient woman's Victorian residence. An image of a small, dark vestibule guided her to the location and she smiled to herself at the realization someone as traditional as MeMa would adopt the new Evolutis social practice of having guests arrive in a vestibule before barging into the house.

The only light in the small windowless room came from a short blue and white porcelain French jar lamp, which struggled to illuminate the small room's dark wood paneling. A portion of the wall to her left opened, offering brighter light and the scent of fresh pine needles.

Out of darkness, into the light. She entered her matriarch's sitting room, marveling at the decor. MeMa sat on a low Victorian occasional chair. The green cushions on the seat and back were supported by the dark wooden curlicues of the décor's time. The deep luster of the wood was proof of years of love and care. The ancient woman opened her arms in welcome. "My sanctuary."

Slightly longer than wide, the room was almost too busy absorb all the small details. The maroon walls were barely viable behind large portraits of family members in gilded frames, polished ornate mirrors, and wall sconces. Bold crown molding with acanthus leaves edged the ceiling and a wooden chair rail ringed the walls.

"What a wonderful chamber." Elizabeth couldn't take her eyes from the spectacular mirror above the fireplace. "Your Pier mirror is exquisite. She smiled at her hostess. I also love the smell of your Christmas tree. Is it a permanent fixture?"

MeMa returned the smile with warmth not always apparent. "I enjoyed watching your mind examine every piece of furniture and every knickknack while your brain asked a million questions. Where did it come from? How old must it be? How did I get it? Of what value do I hold each piece? You have long fascinated me with your leaps in deduction. I saw you had answers to most of the questions you asked."

Heat rose in Elizabeth's cheeks. She felt like a voyeur. "I would love to talk with you about every item in this room. They are lovely. However, I suspect you brought me here for more pressing matters."

"While I also look forward to a time we might talk about my acquired pieces, you are correct, we have other problems to discuss. Tea?"

She accepted the cup and waited expectantly.

"Know that we can speak freely in my home. I have taken steps to ensure our speech and thoughts are secure." She offered her guest scones from a dish sitting on a small table with three curved legs. "The marble on this table is from Greece. It is known as Imathia green marble. I found it right after he acquired this comfortable green chair. They go well together." As she spoke she slowly ran the tips of her fingers in circles over the smooth stone.

Mesmerized, Elizabeth said nothing. She noticed objects in the room that had nothing to do with the conversation. A toy train set sitting under the improbable Christmas tree was in disarray, as if left by a child called away for lunch. A man's slipper sat carelessly under a nearby chair. A pair of reading glasses rested on the arm of a chair. The room looked like people other than MeMa lived there and she heard the male pronoun again in her mind. For all that she wanted to ask who 'he' was, she felt it would be intruding.

For moments MeMa paused as though remembering and then finally spoke. “In our last meeting, Shannon was angry. I am afraid I have some bad news in relation to that.”

Still wondering about the ‘he,’ the old woman mentioned, Elizabeth reined in her attention at the mention of Shannon. What was she into now?

“I should have said, *potentially* bad news, Daughter. Shannon has taken it upon herself to find Vald and learn his true intentions.”

Elizabeth hung on to a calm exterior like a drowning man holds on to a raft, but by god she was furious. She dared not speak for fear of giving herself away. How many times had she gone after Shannon at risk to her own life . . . not to mention the life of Shannon’s children? Hell, at the risk to other Cohorts as well. Damn the woman. She wanted to kick somebody. She took a deep breath. “Exactly *how* is that bad?”

“She is attempting to probe into her future as a gleaner in her own mind.

“What the hell? That can’t work. Please explain.”

“She knows as a gleaner she can only *observe* . . . with no control or over the body she occupies, even if it is hers. That is so she cannot alter the timeline. Those of us who have done extensive time travel know physical travel into the future is a fantasy. Even if we were to ignore those facts as Shannon has, her vain attempts trigger alarms bring her to the attention of the Time Overlords who monitor *all* time travel with assiduous deliberation.

"So she has had no success."

"Not unless she had figure out something no one else can. Time travel has thus far been limited to the past."

She crossed her arms and stared so hard at Elizabeth she felt MeMa held her responsible for Shannon's actions. Her own experience with time travel was limited. She made a mental note to talk to Tobin and George. Maybe together would be good.

MeMa continued. "Time travel is not only limited to the past, it is limited *only* as far *into* the past as the time traveler has lived. Time travel in groups, are enhanced by the oldest person in the group. This piggy-backing effect currently allows us to travel back to 200 *B.C.* The current limit exists simply because there is a Seeker alive today who was born in that year. He survives as the oldest living member of our species and has acted as a shepherd for others who want to travel to the past."

"Meaning he can guide them *anywhere* back in time, *including* as far back as 200 B.C. because he was there."

"That is what I said, daughter."

"And once having made the trip, all members of that piggy-backed group can make subsequent trips that far back in time on their own."

"Yes."

Touched a nerve. "I only wanted clarity, Mother." She wished MeMa would get to the point. "Who *is* this time traveler?" The wall opposite MeMa's green chair held the largest portrait in the room. While the other two walls contained smaller paintings with two or more people and pets in them, this larger one had only one person, a striking man in his middle years with piercing blue eyes.

Aware of MeMa's pause while her mind once more went wandering, Elizabeth responded as a student caught passing a note. "B.C. as in Before Christ? That covers a lot of years. Got it. He can't go any farther back than 200 *B.C.* No one on earth can. But then—"

"While George supports the idea that no ability exists that allows us to actually travel to the future, he has mentioned several experiments conducted at the quantum level that support a brief level of pre-cognition," MeMa continued.

"The experiments are as baffling as they are interesting." Elizabeth had read about them. Some particles reacted seconds even minutes before an experiment was initiated.

"That's hardly time travel to the future."

MeMa blinked once, slowly. "The important thing we have learned from our one-directional time travel to the past is we *must* have deep respect for controlling and preserving our timeline. This awareness led to the establishment of Watchers, who are powerful Seekers who monitor the timeline and are alerted by disruptions when the integrity of timeline is threatened."

Elizabeth felt uncomfortable by MeMa's long meaningful pauses and deep gazes. Was she supposed to know something? What?

Was as though he woman could predict Elizabeth's thoughts. She finally said, "This brings me to my friend, Seth, He is a Watcher and a powerful Seeker. After our last meeting, I grew concerned with what Shannon might do so I asked him to monitor her."

MeMa paused and offered Elizabeth the plate of scones, which she waved away and struggled over a response. One part of her mind wanted to admit her friend was impulsive and the decision to monitor her was a good one, but instead said, she blurted out the question that had been in her mind from the beginning of this bizarre conversation. "Who is the *he* you keep mentioning?"

"Do you mean Seth? All Seth could tell me was that Shannon's efforts, although fruitless, were focused on Vald. As I said, he and I believe she has been trying to find him. History tells us the man is an unpredictable psychotic killer, so if she has any chance of being successful, she will need our protection."

"History also tells us that the bastard left her miles under ground next to an active volcano that almost blew her . . . and me . . . and her children . . . to kingdom come. Will Seth continue monitoring her?"

The portrait was definitely *not* Seth, she decided. The old woman was obfuscating . . . *again.* Lord. She was a master. So who *was* the guy in the painting?

"Seth has offered his services. When you meet him, note I often address him as Grandfather." She gave a small chuckle. "It is a little joke between us. He does not appreciate that title, but after all, he has earned it."

"How is that?"

MeMa folded her hands over her lap. “He is the one. Seth is the oldest known living member of our species.”

That was a surprise. And she was going to meet this person.

“Is something wrong, Sister? Your mind seems to be drifting.”

She couldn’t refute that, but sensing her social call was about to end, she tried one more time. She pointed to the portrait of the man on the opposite wall. “Is he the ‘he’ you mentioned?”

MeMa’s face softened, but what began as a smile dissolved into a sigh. “Yes, that’s the man.”

That was it. She said no more and Elizabeth sat in silence. She had intruded enough.

The silence grew and the matriarch grew more agitated before she spoke. “I have decided to present you with a festering conundrum. What do you remember of the search you made of Cato’s space sphere up at L2?”

“I found nothing conclusive. It seemed to have been abandoned yet there were no salient clues. We can’t even be certain it was Cato’s. It *looks* identical but the damn things are so easy to copy.”

MeMa raised her chin and tilted her head back, blowing out air. It was an unladylike gesture from one so reserved.

"Have you had difficulty sleeping since then?"

"No." She rubbed the back of her neck. "Yes. Maybe. Why do you ask?"

The old women sat taller as if she had come to a decision and was addressing the troops. She took in a deep breath and re-folded her hands in her lap. "Your future you, with the assistance of several of your future friends, did what we have long thought impossible. You physically traveled back in time from your future to deliver an urgent message to an earlier version of herself, to you."

Elizabeth lifted a hand to her forehead. *What* was the woman saying? "I . . . I remember nothing of that." Wouldn't she remember? She was sure she would. Flashes of nightmares blipped in her mind. Nothing she could hold on to. "You said a message?"

MeMa skipped the question, as she so often did. "Something happened in her future time that requires your intervention."

"Yes?" No? What was the old woman not saying?

"After you were shown the event, it became a part of your mind's memory that you could share with whomever you recruited to be on your response team."

"You are talking about what I saw on this supposed visit that I don't remember? How am I supposed to share that?"

"We attempted to *remove* the memory of it from your brain, but that is always an incomplete process."

"Remove it?" Damn, she hated people who repeated things. "We, as in you and who? You mean memory fragments are what keep me awake at night?"

"That and probably voices giving you cryptic messages. We, Seth and I, argued a long time about the wisdom of letting you witness this terrible event before you could put together a trusted team come up with a solution, especially without any explanation."

"A solution to what? Your memory scrub worked well enough, it seems." It was getting harder and harder not to shout at MeMa. In truth, she wanted to shake her like a rat terrier. The damn woman doled out information like an hour-glass with a cork in it. "How long have you known of this event that you need me to witness?"

"For centuries," MeMa said. "I had to work on my own to *create* my team. You have only to *select* yours. I can say no more about that aspect of this concern."

"What? What are we talking about, a team for what? Why don't I get centuries to work on a solution for . . . for god knows what?" Elizabeth felt like Alice falling through the looking glass. She was having a conversation about a cataclysmic event that was a total mystery to her yet she was supposed to prevent it.

"Seth and I, along with several trusted Seekers have been examining the personal timelines of everyone close to the problem that created this event. Simultaneously, we are looking for a successful resolution. Now, for the first time, there appears to be a clear and safe path toward such a solution. That's where you and your original cohort come in. We have an idea for a lasting stalemate of galactic proportions." She lowered her eyes and began pleating her skirt. "We have to work through something first with you," she said to her lap.

"What?" Elizabeth said. "Something with me?"

MeMa raised her head. "There was an unexpected problem in the timeline we have to work through. It concerns you."

"Me? I thought you said I would have to be the center of the team that fixes whatever is that is about to happen."

"And you are. Here is the problem that only you can resolve for us. Would you rather see the event now or at some time in the future, closer to the time of solving it?"

"What's the problem?"

"If you see a recording of the event now, you have the extra burden of having to keep it secret until you select a team and create a solution. Thinking and worrying about the problem will have a negative impact on the selection of your team. "

"How else could this move forward?"

"Ah, so Seth has said." She sat on the edge of her chair and caught one of Elizabeth's hands. "If we let the timeline play out, certain situations will arise that will force you to assemble a team now to address various intermediate problems that will arise. Our study of the timeline says these additional, ah, conflicts will make your final selection stronger and will add to your leadership skills as well. But only if you have not seen this greater problem."

"Simply put, I need more field work, right?"

"The downside is that you will feel more pain. Your anxiety could accumulate and your reaction may cause you to be more irrational and put your team at risk. There is a high probability that one or more of the teams you put together now may not survive and will thus be unavailable for the final solution."

Christ. Now she was in charge of teams of people who could die . . .for what? She didn't resist a sharp reply. "It is hard to imagine that *knowing* could cause *more* anxiety than not knowing. What the freaking hell are we talking about?" She bit her tongue. One did not talk that way to the matriarch of the clan.

MeMa patted the air in front of her. "It displeases me to be vague about this, but remember, we are *extrapolating* what might happen, without certainty."

"Are you saying what I think you are? No matter which scenario I choose, to know now or to know later, different pieces of my memory of it will be erased from my mind."

"Yes, however inefficient that process may be."

"I understand." She just wanted to get on with it. She felt like she was on a merry-go-round with her eyes closed being quizzed on what she saw.

"Once you pick your team, you will be able to travel back in time. Do you see the advantage? You will be able to take as long as you require to develop a solution before you have to return to present time to implement it."

Elizabeth stood. "I changed my mind. I choose *not* to know.

ELIZABETH AND SETH CONFER AT HIS VILLA

Cyclades, isle of Mykonos

All though she was expecting his contact, upon hearing his voice in her mind Elizabeth still couldn't react to him as she would with any normal person. <Sister, I am Seth, we must meet about our Sister Shannon.> It was disconcerting to have him in her head. <Of course. But first I must speak with Oliver. Give me ten minutes.>

<Oliver? Of course, please extend my invitation to him. I live on Mykonos near the top of the island just past the windmills. Here's a viz of my rooftop garden for you to zero in on. By the way, from what the Watchers have learned of Vald, there is a good chance we will be monitored, so use your best blocking app, if you catch my drift.>

She furrowed her brow. What the hell did Shannon get into? <Got it. Mykonos in ten.> That settled it. She was going to kill the woman herself when she found her.

<Ollie, put on shorts and a t-shirt. We're meeting someone for lunch in the Cyclades and we need to do it on the QT, so turn on your best brain blocker.>

BASED ON MEMA'S statement that Seth was the oldest living Evolutis, the twenty-two hundred year-old man who greeted Elizabeth and Oliver on Mykonos defied all belief. He was beautiful, no two ways about it. At six-foot three, he stood as tall and well muscled as a demigod. Steely blue eyes regarded her surprise with amusement. His thick head of silver hair was pulled back into a ponytail, tied low on his neck, seeming to pull his cheeks into a permanent smile.

Standing at the edge of his horizon pool, he opened his arms to the dark blue Aegean beyond and below. <Welcome to one of the best views of the Aegean.>

I'll say. Elizabeth couldn't take her eyes off the man. Perfect white teeth between a short white mustache and beard accentuated his tan. He exuded virility.

Although they, the Cohort, all altered their genome to appear relatively young, they did not measure their life in centuries. Her experience with people of that age was restricted to MeMa, Cato and his Followers. They accepted the concept of *hundreds of years* to those dried apple dolls with their wrinkles in wrinkles.

Apparently oblivious to the contradiction of age and good looks, Oliver viewed the city below and commented on the weather. <The cool air up here is a nice relief from the heat below.>

<True,> Seth said from beside him. <And it is nice to be removed from the city, although the base line in the music from beach front discos manages to drift up in a visceral rumble.> He led them to comfortable patio chairs and waved an arm. <Please. Sit.>

Once the niceties were taken care of, Elizabeth waited no longer. <Your invitation although gracious, comes with a dark side. What's happened with Shannon?>

Seth smiled a kilowatt smile that threatened to derail Elizabeth's train of thought. <Allow me to put this in context for you. My parents were what can best be described as refugees. They arrived here from a planet from the other side of the galaxy fleeing persecution from the Silva.>

<You are not of Earth?> *That* was a surprise. <How can you be Evolutis?> She hadn't meant to blurt that out, but his statement had thrown her for a

loop. <Does everyone live that long where you are from? Who are the Silva? Where is their planet? Did they follow you here?>

<The Silva are a people who exist to dominate. They come from the planet Spes. The name is similar to your Latin word for space. It was once my parent's home. I, however, was born on Earth.>

Oliver sat on the edge of his chair. <Why were your parents persecuted?>

<Because they weren't Silva.>

He stated the facts in a flat voice, void of emotion, but Elizabeth knew there was great feeling under the surface. How could there not be? Seth was not her idea of an alien. Accept that he was better looking than anyone she knew and couldn't appear more human.

<If your parents are not of Spes and not of Earth, where are they from?> Oliver asked. <How did it come about they chose Earth? How did they even find it? How far did they have to travel? How did they get here?>

Seth snapped out of an apparent trance and looked directly at both of them. <Many current Seekers have asked the same question, but in truth I have little in the way of facts or substance to tell you. Their original metal space capsules have long since tuned into iron oxide at the bottom of oceans.

Neither my parents, nor any of the people on Spes for that matter, had any knowledge of folding space to create the beautiful spheres you make. They were left to create simple devices.

When my parents made the exodus from Spes, their civilization was a little more than one thousand years older than earth's. Although they had the power to reposition, their space ships, think steampunk without the steam, were basically metal tubes filled with air and food. They were forced to reposition blindly from one solar system to the next because they did not know what their destination held in store for them. Other than naked eye astronomy, they lacked any technical tools for navigation. If they couldn't see suitable planets once they arrived in a strange solar system, they'd return back to the last safe planet they had encountered and try again in a slightly different direction. The goal was to find our galactic antipole, our twin planet across the Maelstrom. Eventually they did and here I sit, the first Evolutis to be born on Earth.>

Oliver said, <So your parents were Evolutis. Is everyone on Spes an Evolutis or is this an evolution from your parent's previous planet?>

She also wanted to nail him down for clarity, but held up her hand knowing they had to get on with business. <You opened the door to a year's worth of questions, which I would dearly love to pursue, but this thing with Shannon is time sensitive. What can you tell us about her and Vald?>

Seth rested his elbow on the arm he had wrapped around his waist and cradled his handsome chin. He couldn't figure out what had precipitated Vald's rescue and he did not like it. Normally, a careful dissection of the facts showed him the answers. He knew Elizabeth shot the twisted Follower into deep space with an anywhere else as a destination. He shook his head and gazed out toward the Aegean. <Somehow, Vald's minions figured out it would be a good idea to hang out in order to intercept him.>

<How did they know to be there?>

Oliver hadn't said much until now, but he didn't let that pass. <That makes absolutely *no* sense. How could they possibly anticipate where Vald would be?>

Seth slapped his leg. <Good question. Yet, they were waiting for him. Maybe his hubris allowed him to believe Elizabeth couldn't kill him.>

He glanced at Elizabeth with a realization he did not know her as well as he would like to. As the leader of the Cohort here on Earth, she had her finger on the pulse of all happenings. He wanted to know what she knew . . . always. If he was to protect Earth in any meaningful way, he would have to know her better. It may have been the adoptive planet for his parents, but to him, Earth was home and he held it a dear as any Earthling. He held Elizabeth with a locked gaze and after a pause asked, <Were you going to kill him?>

Elizabeth is a strong woman and she wanted Seth to know she was his equal who expected honesty from her at all times.

She didn't hesitate. <I had *every* intention of killing Vald. Believe me, I'm *devastated* he is still alive. I will *never* forgive him for the devious plans he orchestrated and you can bet your ass Shannon willnever forgive him, either.>

Seth cleared his throat. <Nevertheless, within minutes after you dispatched him in his tight shrink-wrap sphere, his minions collected him safely aboard their spacecraft.> He extended an open hand. <Possible mental communication?> He rubbed his hand over his square chin evaluating what he knew of the man. <Although it would taken more power than any Silva I am aware of, it is possible he could have made mind contact. You should know the space craft they picked him up

with was a copy of the one Shannon *showed* him how to build.>

Elizabeth shook her head slowly. <What the hell are you talking about? Why would she *ever* show him how to do that?>

<That is part of the mystery, is it not?> Seth snorted a short laugh. <Where you aware that when Vald learned his staff had wagered on where they would find him, he killed the ones who got it wrong. The grapevine has it he called it incompetence.>

<How did you learn of this?>

Oliver's look of patent disbelief made Seth grin and he nodded once. If the man only knew what and how he got his facts, but there would be time for that later. Instead, he said, <I am only trying to be brief. MeMa is forever telling me that I Sorry, >

Oliver patted the air in front of him. <I forgot you are also a Watcher. I am amazed by the details of your . . . uh, sleuthing.>

Seth continued. <We replay events in time over and over, much like a film loop, until we reach consensus for our conclusions on our observations.> He placed his hand against his chest. <You hear one voice in your head, my voice, but that voice is a blend of many of us who have labored long on such things. As a guardian of the timeline I must first be

accurate in what I perceive and then be patient enough to trace it through time, recording consequences and possibilities.> He looked at Oliver and his mouth turned up at the corners. <It is long, tedious research that would torment a sloth into taking off at a run.>

<You're saying Shannon appeared on one or more of those projected timelines? Oh my god. You're saying she is somewhere else in time. That's what you've been telling us, isn't it?>.

<We do not follow a map of a person's total possible paths through the future. Every decision, every movement can have millions of outcomes in a very brief amount of time. We look for trends and probabilities and the probability of Shannon's efforts failing were significant in every one of them.>

Oliver raised his palms. <But you said no one can travel to the future.>

<That's one of the problems a time traveler faces. It is much like repositioning blind. You may know a certain star has a planet, but if you have never been there before, you mind's inability to calculate its position in space and time prevents you from connecting to it. And if you should connect, which future did you find?> Seth didn't wait for a response. <Our success in time travel to our past is

based on and limited to our own life span because we were there.> He laughed. <It's because our mind is till connected to that previous time that our brain can obtain and process those events.>

Elizabeth shook her finger at him. <And that's why if I travel with you, connected to you by a simple handshake, I can travel beck to, in your case, 200 B.C. Correct?>

He nodded vigorously with a grin that remained from his laugh.

Oliver winced as though he had bit into a sour apple. <Oh, does that mean she would be limited to being inside your head?>

Seth glanced at her to catch her reaction and patted her knee. <No, once there she could head hop, as we call it until she found a suitable host.>

She quickly asked, <If someone from the future were to head hop, into my mind, and I'm not sure I like the idea of that, could I accompany them back to their future?>

<That's a reasonable assumption, but their future might not be an expression of your timeline and they risk changing their time line without their knowledge or ability to fix any unwanted changes.>

Oliver held his head and rested his elbows on his knees. <Oh, my god, Seth. This all makes me happy to remain sitting on my porch.>

<I agree and often wish I had never become involved with the Watchers working with the Time Overlords. Bottom line, working in teams, the Overlords simply employ statistical studies coupled with a limited number of what? Call them probes? Then they discuss and extrapolate the probability future events in our time line.>

Elizabeth said. <Can you extrapolate Shannon's current situation?> She opened her palm and leaned forward. <Do your numbers tell you if she will die in her effort? Can you tell us if Vald be successful and earth will be destroyed?>

<It's too soon to tell. Extrapolation is never precise and the Watchers do not like to guess.>

Oliver lifted his head. <He's right, Liz. Mathematicians have long had the ability to interpolate. That is, filling the gaps in data, but learned long ago that extrapolation, finding data that hasn't happened yet is more mystical than mathematical. What can you tell us about the reasons for her mission? I don't suppose you have a theory on why she goes off on her own?>

Seth lowered his chin and stared at them like a parent tired of repeating everything. <I believe MeMa has already spoken of her impulsive behavior to go off on her own. The impulse, in part, can be shown to be a dash motherhood and a pinch

of drive of one whose brain is making millions of new connections as it reorganizes after a *second awakening.*>

Embarrassed by his manner, Elizabeth ducked her head so the rising heat in her cheek was hidden. It wasn't as if she forgotten the *second awakening* part, it was just that she thought there should be more to it. Okay, Shannon was impulsive. As far as she was concerned that was no change. *Second awakening* or not, Shannon was always like that. Impulsive. It was also acting stupid and Shannon was anything but stupid. Risking another set down, she asked Seth's opinion of her next burning question. <What, in your opinion, is Vald's next move?>

<We have been observing him for close to two thousand years. If he is true to his past, he will regroup by first taking what he needs or wants, and then fleeing to his current sanctuary. Then he will rethink his options and then irrationally lash out at those who he believes have wronged him.>

Oliver reached for Elizabeth's hand. <That means you, Liz, my love.>

She squeezed his hand. "Yes. He'll come after me."

Seth's response to her realization was almost indiscernible. <And others.>

Her voice turned cold. <Where is he, Seth? You know or have a good idea, don't you? Tell me.> She'd thought they were friends but it wasn't feeling that way now.

<We have indirect evidence that he is in Afghanistan in the area you call the *sapping grounds*>

<What is he doing there?> Oliver asked. <What could be there for him?>

<Precious and rare Earth metals. He is harvesting them for Spes.>

<Any indication that Adrianne and Darkwood are in cahoots with him?>

<We know Adrianne is aiding his effort, but we can only speculate how or why.>

Oliver balled his fists, struggling to keep his anger under control. <And Darkwood? They're the scum of the earth. What's their role in all this? We know they're as willing to kidnap or kill as Vald. What's in the game for them?>

Seth rubbed his short beard. <Short-term? My guess is Doyle's *non-Evolutis* troops will make use of their immunity to the sapping stones to provide some muscle to oversee Vald's theft of our resources. Vald himself and his Seekers would be as affected as we are by the minerals. He would need Darkwood's external help.>

Ollie asked. <Long-term?>

Seth shrugged. <Darkwood would be the army to subdue and govern earth.>

Oliver thumped his thigh with his fist <We need to *annihilate* that bunch once and for all. There're everywhere and they're in our way.>

Elizabeth reached a hand out to Seth. <I respect the Watcher's creed on non-speculation. Thank you for bending enough to offer your personal insight and candor about what might happen. I feel you've brought us up to speed. From what you've told us about Vald, he is currently in his harvest mode, gathering as much as he can, before he takes flight to his home-world, Spes, to prepare a revengeful return. Is that basically correct?>

He nodded and didn't modify her conjecture.

She held up two fingers like two pistols. <If he sees Shannon as an intelligence asset, he'll include her in his gathering and take her with him.>

<Excellent deductions, Sister, and from what I have seen of Shannon, she'll try to make the most of her presence by continuing her efforts to get him to see the wisdom of modifying his plans for power.>

Elizabeth had a bad taste in the back of her throat. What the hell was Shannon thinking that *she,* she who had almost been killed by him on at least two other occasions, had the where with all to change that maniac's mind?

As if she'd spoken out loud, Oliver voiced her thoughts. <Shannon's delusional. It will *never* happen. Vald's so full of hubris won't even begin to listen. She'll get herself killed. Considering what we know of him, none of us are safe.>

Elizabeth balled her fists and punched her thighs with an anger that had been building every time she heard Vald's or Shannon's name. Although for different reasons, the result was the same and the growing inaction was killing her. It generally did. <That settles it. We need to go after him. We need to put him and Darkwood out of business and we need to do it fast before he makes a run for it. Our goal is to pull Shannon out of where ever she is and if possible, capture and kill that Bastard.>

Oliver laid a hand on her shoulder. <Liz, you know if Shannon believes she has a chance for a diplomatic solution, she'll fight you every step of the way.>

<You're right. She's so damn pigheaded. She can go ahead and try all day, but it will do her no good.>

Seth, who had been quiet, stood suddenly and turned toward the sea. <I never tire of looking at the Aegean. The color is magnificent. It calms me.> He swiveled around to face them with anything but a calm expression. <I fear we are in for turbulent times. Finding Vald, or even unsuccessfully searching for him could destroy any temporary advantage you have in your mission. You will need to be quick and decisive.> He put his hands on Elizabeth's shoulder and looked deep into her eyes and gave her a small shake. <It is of the utmost importance that if the situation warrants, you must be able to back away and *allow* Vald to escape with Shannon.> He had not removed his hand and he gave her a second jiggle. You may *have* to make that choice, losing *her* or losing *everyone* on your team.>

He did not release her immediately and Elizabeth, mesmerized, felt compelled to answer as if it were a recitation. <Yes, I will back away if the situation warrants it in order to save my team.>

PEACE OR WAR

SPA's Rampart

Elizabeth knew from her discussions with MeMa and Seth, like a weatherman using statistical storm-like tracks, lays out possible future timelines and looks for points in time when the tracks begin to rapidly converge.

There was no question in her mind that her small band of warriors, with their brilliant minds and courage, knew that not only might this be their last chance to deal successfully with Vald, but the effort to find Shannon might end in her death. Tobin and Sarah had been in such a dangerous situation before. Tina, too, from first hand knowledge, knew what was at risk. Although Oliver had been farther from the previous deadly adventure then he wanted to be, he was close enough to experience it with a visceral reaction.

"JAMAL! I've been waiting for our arrival for days." Elizabeth ran to greet the handsome black warrior everyone else knew Benjamin with open arms. Only his 6'4" height and warrior physique kept her from raising him in the air as an expression of joy."

Instead, he hugged her close and reminded her with a soft whisper, "Call me Benjamin."

She stepped back holding both of his hands, "You look marvelous, Benjamin. Any word from your mother? Is she well?"

"Yes, and she sends her best and wishes she could be here with you. The twins are due in a week."

"Let's be sure to catch up at dinner. There is much to do for this mission, but I want to know more about your mom, Yasmin and life on the other side of the Maelstrom."

STANDING on the SPA's rampart atop the renovated monastery with her comrade warriors, Sarah inched away from Benjamin St. Phard. His presence disturbed her and she didn't want Elizabeth to notice. *Damn.* He seemed to be everywhere she went these days. She knew she and her siblings had been called together by Elizabeth for something serious, so there was no room for personal conflict, however, ignoring the man was proving more difficult than she'd thought. She focused in on Elizabeth, who was addressing the man she wanted to avoid.

"Benjamin, what have you and George put together to help us track down Shannon?"

Benjamin deposited a large black duffel bag at her feet and stepped back. "George wanted to go with us, but he is overseeing the cages you requested for our prisoners."

"Prisoners?" Sarah blurted. She felt her face grow hot and anger bubbled within. The word *prisoner* from Benjamin's mouth brought back a jumble of painful memories. She put her hands to her cheeks to cool them, yet they had abruptly turned cool and she grew dizzy with fear. Tobin grabbed her arm and steadied her as she uttered a grateful moan and then took a deep breath and rallied, glaring darts of fury at the Benjamin. Like a pot ready to boil over, one moment she was under control and the next, she wasn't. She had to keep a lid on her emotions. *The Jerk.* God, she really needed more epitaphs. Jeez, now a reference to a description on a tombstone? Did she really mean that?

Benjamin didn't help. She ignored him until she felt his gaze fixed on a point inches below and to the right of her navel. He stared at the knife she wore hanging from one hip on her belt. She felt heat rush to her face.

Abruptly, he said, "You must earn the right to wear the khanjar in battle."

She ran her thumbs under her thin leather belt, which held the sheath holding the famous curved Arab dagger on her hips. "I'll gladly show you how I earned that right, Benny." Throwing the diminutive of his name in his face as a challenge, she took a fighting stance and beckoned him forward with the fingers of her left hand, leaving her right resting on the blade's handle.

He took the bait and stepped toward her before reining in his temper. Tempering his attitude as well as his voice, he said, "Seriously, Sarah, I'm asking. How did you get the thing?"

She raised an eyebrow and plastered a big grin on her face. "None of your damn business, that's how."

He stepped menacingly closer and his big shoulders loomed over her. "I said, where?"

"She stepped back with her hand still on the hilt of the knife. "You're breathing all the air," but she folded and told. MeMa, if you must know."

“It was not MeMa’s to give,” he said.

He maintained a hypnotic eye contact and although she tried, she couldn’t look away. In fascination she noticed the knot in his jaw bunch and release with clenched teeth.

“She took it from me a long time ago.”

“What?”

“I *said*, MeMa took it from me a long time ago.”

A large strong ally moved close to her left shoulder. “I guess you lost it because it’s Sarah’s now,” Tobin said.

Tina moved in on her other side. “She earned it, perhaps you remember. She endured torture, escaped from Adrianne, fought with valor in the GrimsvÖtjn Volcano campaign, and was instrumental in finding and saving our mother, at the bottom of that freaking sapping well. In my book, that qualifies her as worthy.”

Elizabeth stepped between them. “Obviously the conversation you are having must be finished, but only *after* we find your mother.” She raised her eyes to Benjamin. “Shannon.” she said, as if he needed the clarification. “And we must also find Vald.” Then she mumbled under her breath. “And kill him. The little bastard still needs to die.” That’s what she wanted. “Then, and only then, will our business will be finished.”

Her firm reprimand subdued them instantly. They knew the seriousness of the mission took precedence over their personal quarrel. The three neutralized their expressions and stepped away from each other.

"Let's get back to the purpose of this meeting." Elizabeth looked at each of her small courageous band. As before, the twins were there, as was Sarah. In spite of Shannon's exacting protests, they were her original warriors. Benjamin, who should have been with them the first time and was not, joined them now with Oliver. "George is seeing to the construction of copper-mesh lined cells, each designed to be impenetrable by electromagnetic waves. We moved them to a deep cavern beneath the SPA that we've converted into a vault. They're locked up tighter as anything you can find in a bank." She paced in front of them. "We are not the wanton killers Vald and his crew are, so we will take prisoners. I hope they are our first residents."

Tobin, true to form, wanted the precision of the statement. "Are you sure the cells will do the job? Are you positive the prisoners will *not* be able to mentally communicate with one another or reposition?"

"Absolutely. In the copper-mesh-lined cells the prisoners will be totally cut off from anyone in community. Their crew will be unable to detect their presence anywhere.

Elizabeth swung her gaze to the individual members of her small band and looked each in the eye. "Our mission is to find Shannon. Although we are not killers, those who stand between our goal and us will only be given one chance to step aside. Let me be perfectly clear. We will eliminate, by any means possible, *anyone* in Vald's faction, including Vald, who threatens us or interferes with our efforts to locate Shannon." She saw grim understanding in each face. "We will hunt down any of Vald's rogue elements including Adrianne and Darkwood like a dogs for our basement kennels. Is that clear?"

Elizabeth stood quiet for a moment, letting the rules of engagement to soak in. She was confident her worriers knew the importance of the mission as well as the danger. She lamented the fact they were getting all too familiar with such battles.

"We hear you, Aunt Liz. No killing, unless it is necessary." Sarah, the most blood thirsty, looked at her siblings. "And if it is necessary, let them have it, right? "

After nods all around, Elizabeth added one more thing. "This is important. I want everyone to understand what finally precipitated Shannon's thinking to go off on her own after Vald."

Oliver said what Elizabeth suspected they all thought. "In my book, Shannon felt we had waited enough for MeMa and her Seekers to act. Their process was too slow for her. Once again, resolution has fallen to us, to find Shannon and take care of Vald."

Elizabeth patted the air in front of her. "That's about it, but it's incomplete. She's too smart to simply go off on her own. Furthermore, she believes to preserve our sense of honor with adherence to a higher code of conduct we owed it to ourselves to try everything . . . including this diplomacy. That is the mission she is now on. She is looking for a peaceful solution *before* we consider a more deadly conflict."

Tina folded her arms and rocked in thought. "This is so unlike her. I mean, I know those thoughts reflect her beliefs, but why would she suddenly believe *she* was the power to face Vald toe to toe? He scares me to death. Why isn't Mom afraid?"

"She probably is," Sarah said, bumped her sister's arm. "That wouldn't stop her. But you're right, what does she think gives her an edge over someone else to make mediation work?"

"Me." Tobin looked sheepish. "I'm afraid it's my fault, but I didn't think she'd go off on her own like that. I only wanted her to be stronger and be more protected . . . in case she did."

Benjamin asked, "What are you talking about?" The suspicion he generally carried of Tobin rode his furrowed brows. "What did you give her?"

"The spheres. She asked me to show her how to create one and how to use the smaller ones as a weapons." He clenched his fists and took in a deep breath.

Surprisingly, Benjamin uttered the words."Hold on. I can see you're about to tear-ass after her on your own, but you can't. We're a team."

Oliver took Tobin by the shoulders, almost as if to restrain him physically. "Your mom's a grown woman. She makes her own decisions. There is *no way* you are at fault." He gave Tobin a little shake. "You *do* see that, don't you?"

Tobin locked narrowing eyes with Oliver and gave him a non-too convincing nod.

Elizabeth added her hand to Tobin's shoulder. "She was focused on getting to Vald and learning what his plans were for us. *Protection* was also her motivation. I recently learned from MeMa that Shannon had attempted time travel into the future to learn what Vald might be up to and was frustrated when she failed at it."

"I could tell she was upset over something when she recruited me to teach her how to make the spheres."

Oliver patted his back. "Of course you did as she asked. Any one of us would have done the same. Let's have it, though. Tell us how it all played out for both of you."

Tobin shrugged. "I couldn't stand watching her worry about the family so. I had to do something to let her know we supported her. I felt the ability to copy and enlarge a sphere would give her a bargaining chip and since she didn't know how to fold space, Vald couldn't design one for his own usage. I told her how we planned to use the sphere to travel in space. She caught on to how it could be used to gain his trust immediately."

"With her intelligence, I'm sure she did," Oliver said in his dry humor.

Elizabeth laid a hand on Tobin's arm. "Think back. Was there anything else you told her?"

"Before I showed her how to copy and resize the small sphere I gave her, I asked her if she had a specific use for it in mind." He rubbed his forehead as if messaging a headache. "I *think* she believed if Vald could leave the earth with his people he'd go away and leave us alone."

Elizabeth held her chin in a moment of silence. "If she planned on seeing Vald, as you suggested, what do you think would be her plan to avoid being drugged as Oliver and I were when we paid the Followers a visit without an invitation?"

While Tobin discussed the possibilities with Tina and Sarah, Elizabeth turned to Benjamin. "When Oliver and I were in the tunnel trying to meet with the Followers and we were overcome by the drug Seekers use in kidnapping, the one that's a derivative of Rohypnol, where were you?"

Benjamin shuffled his feet and avoided eye contact. "I waited farther down the passageway for you to arrive."

"How did they dose us with the drug?"

"The rocks you handled clearing an opening to their cave had the drug poured all over them." He lifted a palm. "It has no odor. You couldn't smell it."

She raised her chin suspiciously and asked, "Why didn't the drug affect you?"

"The entrance you used wasn't a perfect seal. The warmer air inside escaped, keeping the passageway fume free.

"Son-of-a-bitch!" Oliver exclaimed. "I remember a breeze coming from inside the tunnel the moment we broke through that rock barrier. Don't you, Liz?"

"Hmm, yes. One more thing, Benjamin, am I correct in assuming the Seekers version of Rohypnol can be formulated so they can determine the timing of the onset of the drug, as in making a timed delay of unconsciousness if that is their wish? After clearing the rocks, Ollie and I must have walked five minutes before we became dizzy."

Benjamin glanced at Sarah before answering. Her glare was as cold as an arctic entry way. He dropped his head in an infinitesimal affirmative motion.

Elizabeth shook both fists close to her chest. "Ah ha. Yes. That's it. Mind that it is still speculation, but based on these facts, I think I know how they might have tricked Shannon into believing she could avoid the drug." Her smile turned diabolical. "And I know how we can use that strategy against them."

The group edged in close.

"Here's what I think happened. We told Shannon of our successful combat with Vald's Seekers and Darkwood mercenaries when we attacked them on Iceland a few months ago. If she tried to replicate those tactics she would have landed the sphere near a large pile of boulders in

Afghanistan for initial cover and protection. You know, to hide while she deliberated how she would enter the cave. If we assume Vald and Darkwood still employ their original tactic, while she waited, invisible in the sphere, a small group of Seekers would appear in a circle surrounding the underground entrance. And remembering how the drug worked from listening to Ollie and me tell our story, it only makes sense that *if* the Followers had dosed the area in front of the entrance with the drug, their own Seekers congregating there would soon show the effects. They're not immune from the effects of Rohypnol, as you know."

Tobin spoke with confidence, all shadows of the guilt he'd felt earlier, gone. "She would have waited longer than five minutes to be certain."

"At that point, it would be natural for her to assume the drug had not been used. The question is," Oliver said, "was it a clever deduction or not?"

"Right," Sarah said. "That makes sense. Then she figured she had time to reposition outside of the sphere behind the mound of rocks before making her entrance. She smacked her hand with a fist. "Something went wrong."

"They didn't dose the entrance." Elizabeth went slowly with the scenario they'd painted. "Most likely the entire area *behind* the rocks, where we hid successfully, was now covered with the Seeker drug. Anyplace she repositioned near the boulders would've dosed her. It was only a matter of waiting. Their strategy assumed she'd copy ours and had already given them control of her without her realizing it."

"Damn." Sarah kicked a pebble. "So she was probably easily subdued and taken prisoner."

Sarah's speculation raised more questions than answers and fury grew like a mushrooming angry mob. They shouted over each other offering theories and dismissing them as fast as stock market trading and it was several long moments minutes before Elizabeth reeled them back in.

"Don't be so sure she's a captive. They were clever, yes, but so are we. Our team includes some of the best chess players of the century." Looking at the twins, she gave them a knowing smile. We can come up with several variations of any plan. "We'll need to be prepared to constantly adjust our tactics accordingly and beat them at their own game. It may be a cliché, but we'll begin by assuming the best and preparing for the worst."

She rotated to face Benjamin, who studied the young team's riotous behavior with disapproval and nudged his arm. "What did George send us in the black bag?"

He knelt next to the black bag and as a father might pass out holiday treats to children, he handed each member of the team a new side arm, complete with holster and belt.

When Sarah asked for two, Benjamin said, “Sure,” without looking at her, “but you only need one. These will fire forever with no need to recharge or reload.” He jostled his in his hand. “And notice the handle’s lighter weight? It is still heavy enough to use as a good club in case something happens to the firing capability.” He smiled and handed her the second weapon, then stood and presented Elizabeth the last one. “Here you go. George had a special left-handed holster made just for you.”

Elizabeth examined the tooling on the holster. “Lovely.”

Then he handed her another gift. When she recognized it, she extended both hands held close together and as her friends watched, she slowly drew a shiny steel blade with diamond studded solid silver handle from her belt behind her, examining the ancient khanjar curved knife in silence. Rolling it over and holding it up toward the sun she experienced elation, sadness, and apprehension. The gift meant they recognized her as their leader in combat. It was time. Once again she and her small

Cohort were jumping into the Lions den. She didn't pray often, but sent off a quick message nonetheless. *Lord, let no one die on my watch.*

Oliver, already by her side put an arm around her waist. Tina, Sarah, and Tobin stood facing her while Benjamin stood behind them holding his large black bag.

Elizabeth commanded softly, "Stand close,"

Tobin said, "Shall I make one?"

Elizabeth shook her head. "We won't need a sphere for invisibility or travel. Where we're going, they will be expecting us."

Benjamin asked."Where is that, exactly?"

"Southern Afghanistan."

AFGHANISTAN

Dirt trail near stream

In an instant the blue shades of Aegean Sea changed to many shades of brown. Elizabeth and her five warrior-diplomats reappeared at the entrance of a large cave located near the top of a ridge overlooking a wide valley where a thin strip of water fed a green ribbon of land. As it snaked its way through the valley far below, a small line of tenacious trees and thorny bushes grew along its banks.

Tobin immediately assumed a position of lookout, scanning the vast valley for activity. Benjamin joined him. While Oliver investigated the cave for suitability, Tina and Sarah checked their new weapons, After several moments, Elizabeth drew them together close by Tobin so he could maintain his vigilance. "There are reasons Vald may have stopped here in Afghanistan to pillage. He is after the same things that drove nations to fight here for centuries. You will soon understand his zeal. This region is rich in rare earths and precious metals. Once known by our military as the Red Zone, the last coalition of troops, mostly American, pulled out several years ago and control of the area quickly reverted to powerful local Taliban warlords. ISIS is in the mix now and represents a large unknown growing force. Both are extremely dangerous. We must be very careful."

Oliver pointed behind them. "I assume this huge hole in the rock is our Headquarters. It's sealed it off at about 200 meters from the opening. Harris stocked-piled supplies inside that will more than adequately satisfy our needs while we search for Shannon." He glanced at Elizabeth. "I thought you said he'd be here waiting for us."

"Since the pullout of coalition troops, outsiders don't visit here," Benjamin, kicked a small stone across the mouth of the cave. "Anyone we meet will not be friendly and these guys don't take prisoners. We need to keep a low profile and constant watchfulness."

"Case in point. Look below." Tobin, standing closest to the rim of the drop-off jerked his thumb to the valley below him. "I'm vizing what looks like some locals fighting. See the ones being chased? They're down on the other side of the stream about 1000 meters away. They're headed this way and it's not looking good for them."

<Get down!> Elizabeth barked in their minds. <Minimize your profile. We stick out like road signs up here. >

Below and in the distance, eight adults in white hooded robes ran in a disorganized zigzag pattern, franticly trying to avoid a rapid succession of gunshots. Bits of dirt and sand exploded on the ground near them.

Sarah yelped. "They have no weapons! They need our help."

<Stay where you are.> Elizabeth warned. <Observe only and don't give up our *position.* We don't know who they are.>

"One man is hit!" Tina squawked. "See? He rolled behind that outcrop of rock for cover!"

"I see him." Oliver added. "He's scrambling for deeper cover and there seems to be a large bloodstain on his thigh,"

In her excitement, Tina, jabbed her elbow in Elizabeth's side. "The rest of the group has made it across the stream. Can't we help the one who was shot?" She pointed to the fallen man.

Tobin tugged on her robe. "Wait! One of the men is returning for him."

They watched in focused fascination as the pursuing party, shooting as they ran, came within 100 meters of the downed robed figure. When the rescuer swung the injured man up over his shoulder for a fireman's carry, both men's hoods slid off.

<It's John! He's carrying Harris! It's Harris who got shot!>

"Why don't they just reposition?" Sarah hung so close to the edge of the cliff in her excitement that Benjamin grabbed her robe and pulled her back. Although she glared at him, she stayed put.

"It's probability the damn rare earths," Tobin said.

Tina shook his arm. "What's that got to do with anything? What are you talking about?"

"They interfere with our powers."

"What about us, Tobin?" Sarah asked, shaking his other arm. "Does that mean we've lost our powers too?"

He shook himself loose. "We're okay. The sapping ground isn't everywhere, right, Benjamin?"

"What the hell? Talk English, Tobin," Sarah snapped,

"I got them!" Elizabeth shouted, in relief as Harris and John landed in a heap on the dirt in the mouth of the cave. <There doesn't seem to be a loss of power at this distance. I just plucked them from where they were.> Her voice became more commanding. <Hold steady, we're not done here. There are *six* more Cohorts to extract. On my

command, Sarah, take the first on the left and Benjamin, the next in line. Oliver, you get the next then Tina and Tobin, follow their line of escape. I have the last one.>

In rapid succession, the members of the chased band landed safely within the mouth of the cave.

Keeping a low profile, Elizabeth crouched down and vized the men who had been pursuing them. She grinned at Tobin. "I'll bet they didn't see that coming. I'll check on Harris, you keep an eye on the bad boys in case they make the mistake of coming this way."

She pushed back from the edge until she was far enough away to stand unseen from below, then spun toward the collection of white robed Cohorts, which included Harris and John.

"You're a welcome sight," Harris said. " What the hell happened? We trained every goddamned day, yet we got down by the river and couldn't do a damn thing." He gritted his teeth in pain.

"Hold still, man." John applied pressure with both hands to a sterile dressing he'd placed on the wound, squeezing both sides of Harris thigh like he was crushing a coconut. I think it's a through and through.

"It's great to see you, John. Let me give you a hand with his leg." Elizabeth moved to cut the pant leg off, but John held a hand out to stall her.

"Scissors won't work on the stuff these pants are made of. Harris, push your robe aside and pull your pant leg higher and hang on to it." He adjusted his grip and reapplied pressure to the small entry wound in the back and wiped the blood from the gaping exit wound in front, giving Elizabeth a quick look at it.

Working fast, Elizabeth field-dressed the wound while the others attended to the other rescued Cohorts, checking for injuries and handing out water. Looking up from her bandaging, she motioned with her hand for Benjamin to come closer. "I need to get Harris back to Thirasia's ER ASAP. Will you take him?"

As Benjamin lifted Harris, she answered the question she saw on his face. "Return with the best warrior-Seeker you can find. There are only thirteen of us with Harris out of the action. Our strategy requires at least fourteen Seekers. Hurry!"

John yelled to Benjamin, who had turned to leave with Harris, "Belay the Seeker request. I'm not in the original count of fourteen and I can handle that action now. Others back at the SPA depend on all the Seekers they have for protection."

After they left, Elizabeth leaned back against the cool interior wall of the cave. She held up her hands to examine the blood that extended up her forearms and muttered a grateful thanks to the man who handed her a wet cloth for clean up. "Harris owes his life to you, John. It was brave to go back for him. Thank god you did. Although it was a through and through, as you thought, it nicked the femoral artery and he'd have bleed out in short time. " She put the soiled cloth aside. "We didn't know what happened to you. Where did you go?"

"Benjamin told me stories of the travels he and his sister had made through this part of the world when they were young. Many of them involved crossing Afghanistan. He said he thought that Adrianne would prefer hiding in one of the hundreds of small caves here rather than going to the larger ones on Svalbard or Iceland."

He stretched out the leg he had pulled to his chin. "Do you see what I mean?" He waited for expectantly. It didn't take long.

"Ah. She's familiar with this area and would be comfortable hiding out here where it is more difficult to be found."

"Exactly. When I was in Afghanistan, I remember how difficult it was for our troops to find the Taliban in these mountains. It occurred to me my contacts, the natives we worked with, might have seen or heard something that could lead us to Shannon."

"Why didn't you tell us you were here? We were worried about you."

A mere hint of a smile tweaked his lips. "I couldn't communicate with you . . . or with anyone, and believe me, I tried. All I got was silence. I couldn't reposition, either. It was as if I'd forgotten how." He shook his head. "Have I lost my skills?"

"A logical conclusion, but no. Tobin figured it out. It's this freaking country." Elizabeth swept her hand in a big gesture toward the valley beyond. "It's packed with rare earths."

Tobin turned from his scanning duty. "Benjamin told me many years ago his people called this the *sapping grounds*, because it sapped all their strength. They learned some areas have greater concentrations than others. Depending on their quantity, they can disrupt our powers . . . sometimes more and sometimes less. Regardless of how much or how little, it's disconcerting."

John scratched his head. "Especially if you're me. I just gained my skills . . . powers . . . hell . . . I never know what to call them. I thought they'd just up and disappeared as quickly as they came. Of course. After what happened to Shannon and you and the kids in Svalbard, we should have been all over this. How could we *not* have anticipated this?" He rubbed his eyes with the heel of his hands. "You're talking large quantities of this stuff, right? Doesn't there have to be a lot for it to have that kind of affect on us?"

Elizabeth added, "I'm not sure. But r*are* is a misnomer. There are so many Giga-tons scattered about, Rare Earths are not rare at all. While, China and North Korea have huge amounts, so does Afghanistan. They just don't have the manufacturing plants to refine it that China has." She patted the ground. "Right effects of ere in Afghanistan. From what happened with you, we've learned some things today." Her brows drew together. "Are you sure you're okay?"

"Yes, once the proximity to the *rare* earths is gone."

John still looked disgruntled and Elizabeth knew the reason why. As a black-ops seal he was comfortable in any hostile environment, mostly because he always seemed to conquer it. He didn't like being caught short like he was today. She it could see it ruffled his tail feathers. John stared at her in silence for a few seconds before answering in a casual and rational tone. "You came out here on your own, earlier. Why?"

She shrugged. "I was here to satisfy my curiosity. The ability to move anywhere in seconds has given be some bad habits. How did you hook up with Harris' team?"

"I didn't. At least not on purpose." He shifted his sitting position on the hard rock floor to get more comfortable.

Elizabeth marveled at John's ability minimize his considerable contributions. "James sent you, didn't he?"

"*After* he cursed Shannon out in a *vast* array of colorful epitaphs, James told me go find his wife. As you know, on one hand he feels he chased her away and at the same time is a nervous wreck over her abrupt disappearance and suspects foul play. Once I arrived, I followed leads I got from previous war contacts about a white civilian woman working with American mercenaries in a small village somewhere near that creek bed." He jerked his thumb toward the valley where they'd found him and paused letting his word sink in.

"Americans."

"So I camped on the ridge above the trail watching for any activity that might indicate where she was."

"That trail that is nothing but rocks and snakes?"

"The very one. On the fifth day a patrol came from the south. I followed them and had just fallen in behind when they spotted Harris' men below the trail in a switchback. You saw the rest. They attacked and you know what hit the fan."

"I saw you got around them so it looked like you were dropping back to get Harris. How'd you manage that?" Elizabeth patted him firmly on the shoulder. "Thank God."

"Hold on," she said, raising a palm, "everyone needs to hear this. Tobin," she called, "the bad guys aren't crossing the stream, right?"

"Right. How'd you know?"

"This place is all about territory and that's the edge of theirs." She waved him toward her. "Bring the others."

As the Cohorts settled around Elizabeth, Benjamin returned. "Harris is getting worked on now and he'll be up and about in a day or so. He wants us to have the additional teammate so we can make the fourteen. That would still leave John as a backup. The Seeker preparing to join us is a guy named Seth. Any of you know him?"

Since her kidnappings, Sarah was *always* on guard. She made a quick scan of the entrance, both hands locked on her pistols, before answering. "I know Seth. He's old school. Tough. And when necessary, as nasty as he needs to be."

"It will be good to have his experience and power standing with to us," Oliver said.

"Right, he has skills beyond ours and has been tracking her intentions."

"Tracking? Why the hell doesn't he give us her location?" His face took on a red glow of anger.

"He may have his reasons for keeping her possible location to himself, allowing us to locate her may have a better outcome on our timeline."

He grumbled something like, "More voodoo bullshit."

She appreciated Seth's willingness as a Time Overlord to monitor them, but his expressed desire to *be with them* was in many ways a relief to concerns Elizabeth hadn't realized she had. <Thanks Harris.>

She grinned at Sarah. "We'll take all the *tough* we can get." Turning to the others, she said, "Here's a three-part pop quiz. Why did we fight in Iraq, Iran, Afghanistan, and Turkey?"

No one answered.

Oliver laughed. "Come on Liz, we know it's one of your trick questions. Don't set us up."

"Okay, Ollie, you're the next Nobel Laureate in Economics. You tell the class."

"Put me on the spot, will you?"He chuckled, "Okay. I'll play." He looked around at the small group that was sitting or leaning against the cave wall. "In spite of what many think, our government wasn't in it for the oil . . . or control over nuclear power . . . or driven by religious fundamentalism."

"So," she encouraged him, "why *did* we go to war?"

Oliver didn't give a direct answer any more than Elizabeth did. "I'll give you all a hint. John here, was running over it earlier."

Tina protested. "But Iraqi's oil, Iran's nuclear threat, and the Taliban stronghold here in southern Afghanistan . . . weren't they all good reasons to go to war?"

"My guess is that our government felt Americans wouldn't accept war for something that wasn't an obvious and immediate concern." Oliver stood and dusted off his hands. "They believed they knew the economics of oil, the dangers of nuclear power and the American fear and distrust of unknown religions, but the government was taken by surprise by the increasingly large quantities of rare earths our society demands. And of considerable importance is the monumental increase we will *need* in the future."

Tobin squatted on his heels. "So, whose in charge here?

"As an economist," Oliver said, "and more importantly, as a fan of mystery stories, I say follow the money to find the power. Whoever wants to rule here is fearful of any other power that might interfere. Find out where these guys are, and we find Shannon."

"You think they are the Taliban or ISIS, Uncle Oliver?" Tobin asked. "They're the local power . . . and they are sitting on a fortune. So you think that's who mom's working with?"

"While it is true they rule here, I don't believe they are the controlling power."

"Ollie's right." In some ways, Elizabeth wondered if that would be simpler. Anyway, the answer was Vald. There was no question in her mind about that. "Shannon's after bigger fish like Vald." She looked toward the cave entrance.

She rested her head against the wall of the cave. "When we get her back, we'll do what's necessary to find out Vald's ultimate plans. Too many bad things have happened because of his evil actions."

<GRANDFATHER, why allow them this risk? They need to prepare for his revenge. She must activate and share the message. We fear it will prematurely reveal itself to her and cause much damage.>

<This excursion to Afghanistan is critical for their teamwork to continue. Plus, their proximity under pressure accelerates the completion of their Rising.>

<This can only lead to more disappointment.>

<They will add much to their understanding of his mind. He watches them and believes he sees opportunity. He underestimates their science, but hubris is his ultimate flaw.>

NEW CONFLICT

Cohort Cave Headquarters somewhere in Afghanistan

Elizabeth stood in the mouth of their cave and stretched. If she sat there any longer she was sure she'd go nuts. She absently examined the dried blood under her fingernails, the result of her work on Harris. Although she didn't mind roughing it on occasion, a hot tub with lots of soap seemed like heaven right then. "These rare Earth's are tuning out to be our Species' kryptonite. We should have had a team of researchers study them last year's experience when Vald imprisoned Shannon in a deep well he'd stocked with rare earth stones. They rendered her too weak to escape and almost killed her."

Ollie grunted. "It's disgusting. I just hope we don't find Shannon sealed inside a brick of kryptonite. It was a close enough call the last time." He took Elizabeth's hand, "Come. Sit next to me and let the cool of the cave wall take away some of this damned heat."

He brought a canteen of cold water and she sat and wiggled into a comfortable position next to him soaking up the comfort of being close. They were near enough to the mouth of the cave to see the stark beauty of dry mountains encroaching into infinite blue skies.

It wasn't long before John joined them. When Tobin arrived minutes later, Elizabeth asked about Benjamin. "He was to be our backup protection for the survey by monitoring the immediate area so they couldn't ambush us."

Oliver passed around the canteen of water.

Tobin took a long swallow. "Benjamin went to get something so Tina and Sarah are relieving me as lookout."

She acknowledged the information with a lift of her chin, but her mind was on the landscape. "Would you all agree the effect of the rare earths varies with the concentration of the stuff?" She snorted. "Which would of course make sense. I'm thinking the stream carries dust from the local mines. The strength of rare earths on its banks may be more dense than in other places, depending how it's trapped there."

John took the canteen next and guzzled water. "This place is damn hot." Everyone laughed. It was so true the statement was absurd. "The samples we took from different locations should validate our theory. We're hoping to get the analysis back from the SPA, ASAP."

"Good, we'll need the info to have for our strategy sessions."

Benjamin arrived abruptly carrying a bulky duffle bag, which he dropped at Elizabeth's feet. "More presents from George," he beamed, taking folded garments from his black bag and tossing one to Elizabeth and one to each team member.

She looked up his tall lean frame to see a huge grin threatening to split his handsome face. His normal light brown color had darkened with the sun's exposure to a darker tawny shade that contrasted pleasingly with his white teeth. She laughed in response to his gleeful expression. "Whatever it is this time, it must be something amazing."

"These white robes may look like the simple ones worn by most Arabs, George upgraded them with a stronger anti EMP lining."

"Our new uniforms," she joked gazing around to see everyone got one, including Tina and Sarah, who had joined them. "The upgrades make them mandatory, starting now. They are lighter and in spite of the extra EMP screening they have a hood." She flipped her hood over her head and drew the cord through the toggle spring under her chin. "Hmm. Good design. It is nice and snug. No leakage."

Benjamin nodded approval. "With this robe, George says you are not only safe from an EMP burst, but preliminary tests showed a good result against sapping stones as well."

Oliver harrumphed. "How does this 'relatively safe' and 'good result' come about?"

"It has a better mesh lining," Benjamin said, adjusting his belt. "You'll like the feel of it. You'll need goggles to protect your mind."

When the enthusiasm for the robes settled, they moved the meeting out to the mouth of the cave where Sarah insisted on keeping a constant watch. Elizabeth surprised everyone with hoped for information. She spoke to no one and nodded with each word. "Shannon is alive. I saw her in one of my dreams . . . the dreams that are visions of real-time events. Men were with her, I could *not* tell if she was a prisoner or not. Fortunately, John has more intel about her possible location."

With those words, the group fell silent. Elizabeth vized a projected a map of SouthernAfghanistan to their minds that showed their cave as a white square at its geographic center. "John, you carry on with what you've learned."

"My sources tell me a Caucasian female civilian was seen near this village, depicted by the red square on the map." A line appeared connecting the two squares. "The village is eighteen kilometers following this path." He indicated another line through the mountains. "Going this way, it is sixty-seven kilometers if we stick to this path. We could possibly reposition to the spot but would need to be prepared to walk out a distance on a return trip if there are sapping stones."

"What's your plan, Elizabeth?" Harris, as always, wanted to be on top of the logistics. He had arrived unexpectedly just as John began. Although he sported a slight limp, he assured Elizabeth he was well enough to contribute.

"Oliver and I will take a sphere directly to the village. We won't be detectable and will fly high enough to be safe in the sphere from rare earths and. Initially, we'll look to see if there is evidence Shannon is there."

"What? No disrespect, Uncle Oliver," Sarah growled looking at Elizabeth, "but why are you taking him?" She placed a hand on each of her pistols. "Has he been trained in combat? Several of us are more prepared for a fight."

"Exactly, Sarah." Elizabeth reverted to her command voice. "Oliver and I will not be fighting.

We'll be observing from a safe place. We are *not* going to make contact and certainly not going into combat. I will share what I see with my mind to yours." She included everyone with her intent gaze. "Tobin, if we are threatened, pull us out and collapse the sphere where it will do the most damage. Got it?"

"Got it."

OLIVER KEPT the sphere about 800 meters above the surface while Elizabeth lay flat on her stomach against the lower curve of the sphere observing the terrain below. Puffs of smoke behind the next ridge drew their attention and when their protective bubble cleared the crest, the sad remains of a small village came into view. Mortar fire and RPG's left little of the meager buildings unscathed.

<Ollie, pull us closer.> Hovering at to 200 meters, she identified about forty Taliban or ISIS soldiers attacking a small uniformed band of five. Around them lay the dead bodies of comrades. Badly outnumbered, the five hid behind a wall that would not protect them for long.

Elizabeth alerted the team. <Are you seeing this?>

<Yes. It doesn't look good for the five still standing,> John returned.

<I thought all coalition forces had pulled out years ago. If that's the case, what's going on below?>

<The guys cornered are probably Special Forces on a secret mission. That would mean they don't expect any help from the guys who sent them and they're prepared to die without it.>

<John, do you recognize the uniforms?> She expected a positive ID after all John's years of service in Special Forces, friendly fire or foe.

<No, they're *not* wearing any specified Ground Combat Uniform of any national service that I know of. Their camouflage pattern is different and unique.>

A large explosion on the other side of the small wall knocked it down, burying the five defenders in plaster and bricks. It threw the sphere back about 100 meters before Oliver could return it close to the rubble covering the men. Elizabeth shouted short rapid commands. <The Taliban's charging! Ollie and I are leaving the sphere now. Tobin! Pull us and the five men still standing out then explode the sphere in a five-count.>

"No, Liz," Ollie shouted. "It's too dangerous!"

She grabbed his jacket. <Now.>

The pandemonium of the gunfight battered their senses as Oliver and Elizabeth deserted the safety of the sphere and slid on to the packed dirt. The din was tangible. Noise filled their heads . . . drowning out thought. Taliban bullets zinged though the air, ricocheting off bricks and exploding in clouds of sharp shards of rock and blinding sand. The Taliban bore down on them and Oliver stepped in front of Elizabeth. In a diabolical twist of irony, the gunshots gave off a sweet aroma that perfumed the chaos. The big bang of the collapsed sphere echoed around them and the last thing Elizabeth saw was the Taliban blown to oblivion.

FRENZIED CONFUSION FILLED the cave entrance. Fallen bodies, bloody limbs, choking dust, and angry shouts filled the small space. Swearing in Norwegian, Oliver stood partially shell-shocked, while the Cohorts who had yanked the seven from sure death carefully separated and examined bodies for damage. The credit for any of the soldiers surviving went to the small wall taking the brunt of the blast.

Elizabeth sat leaning against the side of the cave, breathing as heavily as she did after any marathon and watched four dazed soldiers being rushed to the back of the cave for treatment and interrogation. A fifth remained, completely covered by a blanket. She could hardly contain her nerves. “Whoever said ‘War is hell’ got that right.” Her body trembled and her head pounded. She worked to control the wobble in her voice and slid sideways to the floor.

Oliver, barely recovering himself, rushed to her, terrified by what he had seen. My God, Liz! Are you okay? He wrapped her in his strong arms and just held her.

“Ollie, I didn’t mean to make you—”

“Shhh, it’s okay. We’re safe now.” He leaned away to look at her before he pulled her close again. “These men . . . do you know why they were there? We’re questioning them.”

Elizabeth listened to what Ollie said but it made no sense of the words. “Men?” she asked and then uttered, “The noise.” Her words seemed irrelevant to nothing now that everything was quiet. She tried to hold on to Oliver but felt herself slipping away. Ollie shouted, but the words faded.

“Blood. Liz! My God! You’ve been shot, You’ve been shot.”

AN UNEXPECTED TWIST

The Cave

Tina pulled Elizabeth from Oliver's arms and gently laid her on the ground.

Oliver continued to hold her hand. "Liz, stay with me."

Elizabeth lifted her arms and looked at her white robe to see what made Oliver think she'd been shot. Except for a headache, she felt no pain. She blinked her eyes and responded in a whisper. "Not shot. Blood?"

Oliver brushed the hair back from her forehead. "See Tina? Her hair's covering it."

"Cold . . . too cold. Too much . . . cold . . . Ollie?" Elizabeth tried to make sense of what he said, but his voice grew dim. Too hard to concentrate, she grew cold and stopped caring.

Tina bent close. Very smart, well versed in many things she knew some medicine.

"She's in shock." She shouted over her shoulder, "Med kit. The bullet scratched the outer cover of her skull."

Oliver repeated Tina's command. "Med kit, now," her love repeated. He would take care of her.

ELIZABETH AWOKE in a large a dark room. Her head hurt, but her mind was totally … she searched for the word ... *quiet.* Standing on a cold floor she knew her shoes were missing. She bowed her head to look at her feet and suddenly had the strange sensation her brain was too small for her head and if she moved too fast, it would roll out through her nose and fall to the floor. She poked her right temple and a finger and felt something sticky. *Syrup? Strange.* She jerked her hand away and absently wiped it on her white hospital gown.

A vast emptiness filled the black space around her. There was no ambient light . . . yet she *remembered* seeing her toes.

"Hello?"

No response, not even an echo.

She reached out with her mind.<Hello?>

That hurt.

A distant noise, reminiscent of the switch of the stage lights she remembered from a Berkeley faculty performance, startled her. Yet no light came on. Waving her arms before her for protection, she, shuffled forward. Sensing, rather than seeing something before her, she stopped.

Darkness pushed in on her and she put her arms up to ward the stale air that filled her nostrils.

She tried again. <Hello.> Nothing but a sharp pain in her head.

She took a small steps and her hand touched something. Quickly, she jerked it back. It was soft, smooth. Then she reached again. *Velvet.*

She poked it with her finger then pushed it with her open hand. A heavy hanging velvet curtain? Ah, but if *was* a curtain, there had to be a way through. She fell to her hands and knees and slid one hand along the cold floor.

<That's it. Go under.>

"Who said that?" She whispered with the smallest sound.

<Don't you recognize your own voice?>

"Ridiculous. You can't be me."

<Go, under the curtain.>

"Can't lift it. Too heavy." She sat down and waited for help.

A noisy whirring from her far right brought another theatre memory more vivid the other one. A narrow shaft of light broke through when the curtain slowly parted and she pushed off the floor and ran through it.

Some twenty feet beyond the curtain, two overstuffed armchairs sat on a circular rug facing each other. In one, a man in a brown corduroy suit relaxed in sleep. A floor lamp stood to one side and seemed to be the only source of light.

"George? Is that really you?"

The startled figure snuffled awake and sat forward, slapping his thighs. "Liz, you found me!"

Cautious and unsure, Elizabeth stepped closer. "George? I've been shot." She tilted her head. "Why do you need to be found?"

He cocked one hairy eyebrow. "You're not dreaming, Elizabeth. Sit, we need to catch-up." Sitting on the edge of the chair, he tugged on his vest then waved his arms at the vast darkness. "Where do you think you are?"

She looked at him with suspicion. "It's an auditorium." A soft glow of light erased the darkness. "It's the Zellerbach Theater at Berkeley, correct?"

"Not to me it isn't."

"What does that mean?"

"Don't you remember? I'm at home." He pointed at the darkness behind him to the left. "Through those windows I have an excellent view of Lake Michigan from the 27th floor of my apartment. Over here, to my right—"

"I remember."

He extended is palm. "I mention it because *here*, your mind creates the reality your brain needs to stay sane. This theatre *you* see," he waved one arm toward where she had indicated, "explains the darkness you feel right now."

"You're the math-physics man, George. *Where* is here?"

"Good question, but answer this. Where is your brain and where is your mind?"

She shook her head in protest. "Ouch! No, George, don't give me the damn late night-dormitory mind-brain identity argument. Bottom line, what's going on?"

"I believe it is about your recent *second awakening*. With it, your mind acquired the power to transcend dimensionality. It's striving to understand what lies beyond the three-dimensions currently confining your brain. Your brain-mind will soon exist everywhere. To do that your brain must exist on the quantum level. You began life aware of a three-dimensional universe. This," he waved both arms wide, "is different." He smiled. "You will soon experience more powers and the consequences of a *second awakening*."

She watched in silence as he tossed two circular coasters on the carpet.

"You remember that skinny little book about an adventure in flatland? Let's say your mind first becomes aware of life in a two dimensional universe. That beer coaster there, by your foot is you. Width and length, but no height, hmm?"

She nodded.

"The other plain coaster next to you is some native life form you are visiting who is ignorant of other dimensions. See the outer black circle in the rug? That represents the walls of a room that surrounds the coasters. You're both in a room with no doors." He looked up and smiled at her. "The plain coaster guy asks you why you are in prison with him and you say you came to show him a way out." He chuckled and his stomach shook. "To get the two of you out of prison, all you do is pick him up and drop him beyond the black ring. Easy for you in your three-dimensional world, but impossible for him in a two-dimensional world."

"That's it? That's your best explanation?" She gave him her best fish-eye and picked up both coasters and tossed them on the floor beyond the rug.

George scratched his head. "I couldn't think of a good fourth-dimensional example. Perhaps with more time—"

"Let's hope so." Elizabeth fell more than sat on the other chair. "Am I stuck in here?"

"You can fold space. I've seen you move objects. You can reposition in three dimensions. Tell me, Elizabeth, how do you do that?"

"Hmm," She thought for a second. "I don't know."

"Can you tell me how it *came about* that you learned how to do those things?"

"I was taught how to do them in dream training."

"Exactly how? What did the instructions look like?"

She frowned. She didn't know. How could *that* be? Odd, now that she thought about it.

"Exactly. You don't *know*."

"And yet?"

He held up both palms and shrugged. "You still manage to do them. Is it simply a feeling?"

She thought about that and everything started to fade and disappear. *Focus on this meeting.* When she looked back at him, he hadn't moved. He gave every impression he could wait forever for her answer. She furrowed her brows deep into her forehead. "I just . . . feel the intention . . . inside. I will it . . . and . . . it happens." Her felt the heat rise to her cheeks in embarrassment. "Not exactly scientific method, is it?"

She still had no response from George.

"How do you do it?" She lashed out the challenge. "You're the Nobel Laureate in Physics. Can you say how you got here?"

Although George wriggled uncomfortably in his chair and did not speak immediately, he finally said, "That's fair turn about. I've been racking my brain thinking how one might fold space, in any dimension. All my thought experiments point to a quantum solution." He frowned. "Other than that, I really don't know."

"George! I must return to find Shannon. Did you notice the opening in the curtain I used to get in here?"

"Opening?" He shook his head, "To me, you came through my front door."

She spoke in a monotone tone, describing something she knows is nonsense. "I am in an auditorium at Berkeley and you are sitting in your high rise apartment in Chicago. Is that what you are saying?"

"It would seem so, my dear."

"And this small carpet and two comfortable chairs, is a third place, a nexus of our two worlds."

He nodded again.

"And you haven't left this nexus in some time?"

"No." He shook his head and his face remained blank. He appeared see no dilemma.

He was so frustrating she wanted to shake him. No, she wanted to throttle him. Her voice rose with her with an anger she couldn't curb. "Why am I here?"

"There may be something on your mind is working on that your brain cannot solve. Is that possible?"

That was a dilly. Of course there was something she could not figure out. Where the hell was the woman who used to be her best friend? The one who was so aggravating she didn't know what to call her.

She said with a flat voice, "I can't find Shannon."

"Umm. Do you see her here? Maybe she too has come."

Why was she wasting her time? "George, how do I get out of here?"

"Oh, you want to leave?" His face erupted in a broad grin and he seemed eager to share his thoughts on the matter. "From what you told me about your dream training, it seems appropriate that you would first assume a solution exists. Then, just imagine what it looks like. What was your favorite way of travel before your first awakening?"

"London tubes. I loved Kings Cross station, but what does that have to do with this?"

"Think, Elizabeth. How can you make that memory work for you? Make Kings Cross your meme for travel. Visualize it."

Alice must have felt like this, she thought. She grabbed his shoulder. "George, you don't have a hookah behind that chair, do you?"

He looked at her in disappointment. "Use your Kings Cross meme. You know how to do this. This is not a dream, Elizabeth. What you remember will become the reality your mind creates for your brain."

She exhaled, closed her eyes and remembered the smells and sounds of the London Tube. A faint distant sound of an approaching underground train claimed her attention. The noise echoed from the bottom of the stairway that had appeared to her left. "Oh my god, George. I have to leave." Descending the steps as fast as she could, she threw over her shoulder, "I'll see you again . . . here . . . soon."

IT WASN'T until the doors closed behind her and the train sped away that she realized they both had said the exact same words in parting and in unison. "I'll see you again . . . here . . . soon."

Her car had no other passengers. As the train continued its acceleration away from the brightly lit platform, she grabbed hold of the nearest pole in anticipation of a black hole in the wall ahead. Moving faster than any subway she remembered, it entered the darkness of the black hole with a whoosh and although she closed her eyes and held her breath. She saw something. Shannon, was outside the standing in the dark.

She waved her arms in a come-here motion. Then the window grew dark. Vald appeared and stood next to Shannon . . . smiling, too close. Stars twinkled behind them and then everything faded away.

"OUCH, THAT HURTS."

"I know. Stop moving." Oliver's voice sounded far away. "It's a nasty cut." Then his voice zoomed in on top of her. "Tina, I need the med kit. Now! The bullet scratched the outer cover of the skull."

She'd heard him say that already. Or at least Elizabeth thought she had.

"Get the compress for me and put it in my hand. She's holding onto my other arm so tight I can't move it." Oliver pulled her hand away.

She knew she was back with Ollie. Relief flooded through her and she opened her eyes. Where had she been? *A dream? Another real-time vision?* That was it. Someone pressed a wet towel to the right side of her head and she winced at the pain while welcoming the cool. She shut her eyes again and drifted into sleep.

THE NEXT TIME SHE OPENED HER eyes, Elizabeth realized she was in the SPA's hospital in Thirasia. Oliver cradled her on his lap with both arms as someone worked on her head wound. She reached up to touch Ollie's cheek and he took her hand and smiled endearingly, then hugged her hard.

"Uncle Oliver, hold her still. I don't want these stitches to leave a scar."

"Tina, it's you." Elizabeth said in recognition. Her eyes dropped and she relaxed back against Oliver, pulling his arm closer across her chest.

"I was afraid for you, Liz." He looked at her with grave concern. "We shouldn't have left the sphere. When our team transported us here, I asked how you were and you blinked once and held my arm. You never let go. You are going to be the death of me."

A head wound. George was definitely a dream. As a medical doctor, Elizabeth knew what a concussion could do to ones mental wanderings. Besides, Ollie just told her she never broke physical contact with him. She had been here all along. Yet, she had had such dreams before, ones that were of a real event. Shannon is alive. She would bet on it. "What happened?" Her question came out in a horse whisper. "Can I have some water?"

"When you brazenly, ignored my advice and *dumped* us both outside the safety of the sphere, I felt like shooting you myself." He scowled at her while holding the glass to her lips.

He trickled cold water into her mouth. Ambrosia couldn't be sweeter. "Good . . . so good." Her eyes drooped gain. "Honestly, Ollie, I'm okay and so are you." She tried to sit up.

Ollie exclaimed, "My god. You *are* aren't you? Okay?"

"No, I'm *not* okay. I'm shaken to my core."

He growled at her, "You could have gotten us both killed." His smile gone. "You were damn lucky. It was a foolish risk."

Elizabeth had the good sense to look contrite. She could see he was angry. "I'm sorry. Honest, I'll be more careful in the future, I promise."

“Yeah, right, like you never said that before. It’s damn annoying.”

She dozed and woke with a start. Lord. She couldn’t hold a thought. “Captured mercenaries. That was the reason why she was shot. What intel did we get from those captured soldiers? Did they know anything?”

“Harris and three Seekers have them. We should know something soon.” He touched her cheek and shook his head at her. “You’re hopeless and you know it.” A minuscule smile replaced his stern look.

ENCOUNTER

Interrogation at the SPA

It took Elizabeth almost an hour to convince everyone she could walk. Even then, Oliver insisted she hold his arm. The solicitous demand irritated her, but she did as requested to atone for his perceived idea of her bad behavior.

Her voice bounced to the rapid rhythm of her walk. "Every second we dawdle, Shannon may be closer to Vald's clutches. Furthermore, Vald will leave once he decides he has plundered all he can and if he does have Shannon he'll drop her into the hands of who-knows-what twisted Taliban tyrant. Hell, even that bastard may talk her in going with him."

"There you go again . . . risk taking. We haven't even scanned your head and you are *running* down this hall."

"Dammit, Ollie, Hurry." She pulled on his arm to get him to walk faster. "If only we could reposition."

"You *can't* until your head wound is cleared up and you *know* it. At least change out of that damn bloody robe. You look like you were in a barroom brawl. Use the new one Benjamin gave you."

She rolled her eyes and let go of his arm so she could walk faster. Entering the Spa's designated interrogation room ahead of him, she quickly assessed the situation. Harris sat on one side of a long oval table and faced the four captured men. Elizabeth sat next to him.

Three powerful Seekers took a position behind her. When one said, <Sister, we are ready> shewinced at the pain in her head, but gritted her teeth replied with a nod and she stood.

Standing across from the seated captives, she considered how to begin. One of the four men rose laboriously. He had a gash on his head and he steadied himself on one leg before barking out a sharp, "Ten-hut!"

The remaining three reacted immediately and stood at attention. None were steady on their feet, but that did not detract from their military presence. It filled the room.

Elizabeth bobbed her head in acknowledgement of their respect and then sat in the chair to Harris' right. "Be seated, gentleman."

Oliver came through the door and sat next to her.

“First order of business, Gunny,” She spoke directly to the man who had called the men to attention,” I want you to know we’ve brought your forty-seven fallen comrades in from the field. Is that total correct?”

“Ma’am, yes ma’am.”

She spoke to Harris without taking her eyes off the four. <Have they been told about us? Our interest here and our powers?>

<No.>

She watched as the eyes of the three of the men shifted to the fourth man who sat silently at the end of the row. The glance had been so quick she would have missed it had she not been watching for it. It identified him as their leader. On further speculation, she noticed the man’s uniform had small faded areas that, until recently, had held patches of his rank as an officer. She studied him a moment, then said, “Sir, you and your men will be returned to your base as soon as we have determined it is safe to travel.”

He almost smiled at the tall woman who so quickly gleaned the fact he was their officer. “Thank you, ma’am. How did we get here?”

She ignored his question. “We need your help, Major. A woman, a member of my family is traveling through the region we found you. She needs our assistance. Have you any intel regarding her? A Caucasian, five-foot-seven, medium length auburn hair?”

As she spoke, Harris slid a photo of Shannon across the table.

The officer took the photo and after carefully looking at it, shook his head. “I have nothing to tell you about such a woman, I’m Sorry.”

Elizabeth felt the three Seekers behind her slowly glide closer to the table when the major muttered he was sorry. She watched four sets of eyes roll upwards in surprise and apprehension.

“Who are these men?” the major demanded.

She leaned across the table and made eye contact with the enlisted men. “While your leader and I have our discussion, you three will not interfere. Understood?”

To reinforce her words, the Seekers pointed their pain sticks at the soldier’s chests. The tips of each sphere begin to glow.

The uniformed men froze, staring at the pointed weapons until distracted by the rattled gasping coming from their major.

They saw his face contorted in pain. His lips moved silently as spittle formed at the corners of his twisted mouth No words ushered forth as he struggled to breathe.

Elizabeth's mind had a tight grip on his throat. She spoke through clenched teeth, "Major, I have a splitting head ache. I'm only going to ask this one more time. Where is my friend?"

Blood flowed from the man's nose and his body convulsed repeatedly. Struggling for control of his shaking hand, he dug into his pants and laboriously pulled out a ragged piece of paper. When she reached for it, she released the pressure on his throat and he collapsed, face down, his head hitting the table with a loud thwack.

Elizabeth unfolded and read the paper before passing it on to Harris. "What do you make of this?"

He read it then gave a curt reply. "Give me a second."

After he vanished, one of the men across the table whispered, "Son-of-a-bitch. She acts just as tough as that other one."

"Yeah." the Gunny breathed, "She's like that leather-bound bitch."

Elizabeth frowned at the comment. "Tell me sergeant, what was her name and why was she with *you*?" She ended her question by pointing a finger at him.

He jerked back against this chair and his eyes bulged. "A . . . A . . . Adrianne," he stuttered.

She curled her finger and slid her hand into her lap. "And . . ."

"They met us at the location the major just gave you."

"And *they* are *who*?"

"That leather dressed woman, and a man dressed like one of them." He jerked his head at the Seekers.

"How did they arrive at your location?"

"They drove into camp in a Humvee convoy."

"How did they leave?"

"The major gave their driver the coordinates to one of the deeper mines we secured and the convoy took off immediately."

"You *saw* them *drive* away?"

He jerked his head in an affirmative.

"You and your men will be taken to your quarters and individually questioned by the hooded men standing behind me. Your answers must agree or they punish the ones who lied. Do you understand?"

"Ma'am, yes ma'am." They maintained their military bearing, but fear filled their eyes as they marched from the room, each under the heavy hand of a Seeker.

During the lull in action, Oliver said to Elizabeth. <You'd make a great prosecutor, Liz. Where did you ever get that choking technique?>

Surprise he noticed, she said, <I'm not sure, Ollie. A movie, perhaps?>

ALTHOUGH TOBIN and Benjamin remained at the cave entrance as lookouts, they followed Elizabeth's interrogation with a viz.

<What does that sound like to you?> Benjamin's brow lifted with a knowing look.

<If they were forced to drive in and out, it sounds to me like the area they chose for their base is a sapping ground.>

THE SAPPING GROUND

Afghanistan

Safe or not with her concussion, Elizabeth repositioned back to Afghanistan. Having changed into her new robe, she rested her left hand on the pistol grip of the weapon, also supplied by George, and examined her team at the entrance to the cave they called headquarters.

Pacing in front of her band, she paused in front of each to check their EMP pistols. "We are seven." The original group of Elizabeth and Oliver, with the twins and Sarah, was augmented by John and Harris. "While Seekers continue the interrogation of the soldiers we rescued from the attack, we'll move on to where we believe they are holding Shannon."

She stopped in front of Sarah. "You, Benjamin, and John may have to resort to your considerable physical skills once we actually go in. It appears that they chose to detain Shannan in an area of concentrated rare earths. I believe the concentration of those elements is the only way they could restrain her without a ton of drugs. Your robes will deflect most of the power of the sapping stone." She glanced at John and took comfort in his neutral expression. It told her he was prepared.

"I have some added protection to the robes that might come in handy." As she spoke, a Seeker passed out latex gloves to her team.

Sarah held hers at arm’s length between two fingers, rolled her eyes and raised her brows to the heavens. "Really, Aunt Elizabeth? What the heck? We’re not a forensics team."

Elizabeth laughed at her outburst. “They use a drug with their own variation of Rohypnol. We discovered the Followers painted it on rocks and on the walls in the entrance and tunnel of the cave Oliver and I attempted to enter. After touching them, we were knocked out in minutes."

"Oh, sorry." Sarah lowered her head sheepishly.

“No problem. We learn with each mistake. Let’s hope they aren’t too big. I want us properly prepared. Ah, good, here's something you'll like.” She waved to the arriving Seeker who handed out something that produced an entirely different reaction.

"Pain sticks! Aunt Elizabeth! Now you're talking." Sarah stood and spun hers, twisting around like the martial arts expert she was. "No wonder you made us train in Kendo and Shaolin stick fighting."

Elizabeth tapped her own stick on the rock floor for attention. "We were only able to simulate the stick's response in our training, otherwise, you would have spent most of your time in a hospital bed. Be careful where you point it or what you touch it to in battle." She extended her own stick slowly until it touched Sarah's chest. "If I were to do that to you during actual combat, the stick would channel energy from my mind and concentrate it as a lens focuses light. The stick becomes a lethal weapon."

Oliver examined the tip of his implement. “I don't understand how the brain generates all that power. Is there something in the stick that enhances it?"

She shook her head. "The stick reacts to the mind not the brain. The power unleashed will increase as your brain expands its interface into the greater mind." She quirked one side of her mouth. "To tell you the truth, we don't know much about this new mind and what it can do. Just be careful where you point the thing and what you touch with it when you're angry. Anger adds to the energy. Have no fear, the energy will be there when you need it." She then reached into Benjamin’s bag and removed a small box. “These special dark glasses are part of your EMP protection. Put them on and then let’s viz for Shannon.” After watching her warriors complete their dressing, she commanded, "Let's do it."

They linked arms and stood as one. Their combined energy surged until they achieved the critical mass of power known as the Seekers' Seven.

THE VIEW OF A DESOLATE, rocky valley below the small cave did not diminish Elizabeth’s confidence. Her calm whispered directions emanated from a resolve born of a desire to punish those who sought to annihilate her cohorts. "This is only the first step. We need to scout this network of tunnels and follow the one we feel has the best chance of locating evidence of Vald and the bastards she tried to work with.”

A voice in her head reminded her once more. *<Before he runs, he takes what he can.>*

She turned and led her group deeper into the small passage. Just past the first turn she indicated a section of wall. "Find a comfortable place to sit close together while we remotely viz the cave network across the way.”

Elizabeth watched Tina fidget and sat next to her. She kept hearing the same warning in her head. *After his harvest, he takes flight to prepare his revengeful return.*

"Even though we won't be able to see each other, we *will* be able to communicate with each other, right?"

She patted Tina's leg. "Absolutely, my dear. Your mom's safety remains our first goal and we will get her away from danger as fast as possible. One more thing, do *not* reposition. Got that? If you reposition into sapping stones you may not be able to reposition away. We think our robes lend some protection, but not if the concentration is high. You will have to fight and make your escape the old fashioned way, *without* your powers. Got that?"

Nods and raised thumbs signified they understood and would comply.

"Okay. Let's begin again."

AFTER THE GROUP surveyed their destination through their collective minds' eye, they decided to virtually cross the valley and enter the cave entrance. From their viz, they knew it was guarded by two otherwise hidden machine gun emplacements. Manned by two locals dressed in traditional civilian garb, their combat boots and ammunition belts were enough to mark them as combatants. They sat on their heels or rested against the wall of the cave. Elizabeth cautioned, <Don't be alarmed. They can't see or hear us. Keep an eye out for any of Vald’s people. Our virtual presence won’t stop them from sensing we are here. The tunnel splits ahead and we will as well.>

AFTER TWENTY MINUTES of exploring side passages and moving through stacks of boxes and barrels, they encountered no one.

Sarah wanted action. <This is as exciting as visiting a hardware store, Aunt Elizabeth.>

<I hear you, kiddo. We seem to be in their storeroom.>After several more minutes of silence, she added. <We need to decide on which of the seven passageways seems the most likely to—>

Tina whispered, <I have two uniformed men approaching.>

<Hold positions.>Elizabeth spoke with all the emotion of an air traffic controller. <I want everyone to stop and continue monitoring their

passageway while Sarah and I join Tina. Wait for us, Tina.>

Her command came too late. Tina had repositioned across the valley and stood close behind the militiamen. The soft pop of the displacement of air, gave her presence away and Elizabeth saw the men react.

They whirled to face her with weapons raised, but before they could fire, Tina expertly spun with one arm holding her stick close to her hip, knocking the weapons from their hands. With her free hand, she grabbed, pulled, and twisted a pinch of space that she quickly released, causing a small explosion near the men that sent them flying. They hit the floor of the cave forty meters away and slid and tumbled before slamming into the wall where the passage turned.

<Tina, take them to the cave, now. Everyone else, hold your position. Continue to viz.>

Elizabeth repositioned to join Tina at the entrance to the cave, guarding the bodies of the two men.

She made no effort to hide her anger. Tina had scared her with her reckless charge and could have been in very real anger. “You could've been killed and you compromised our power of seven.

Furthermore, you may have compromised our mission."

Tina lowered her head to avoid eye contact and mumbled, "I'm sorry, but Aunt Elizabeth they just *appeared*. They were not there more than an instant. They aren't locals, they're Vald's men dressed like locals. They've got to be like us. Not locals."

Elizabeth had a flash of insight. Tina and Tobin did not awaken as everyone else in the cohort had. They were already awakened at birth and may see Sapiens differently. She reached out and touched her shoulder. "I was afraid for you. You did well to recognize them for being Evolutis disguised as Sapiens. You reacted quickly and effectively to an unexpected threat."

Harris arrived. "We're ready to move Vald's men to Thirasia. You want anything from them before they go?"

"Thanks, Harris. I just want to know what information the Seekers can get out of them. If you'll be my direct line to the interrogation, that will work well. I'm glad you're okay and are covering our backs again. It makes me feel safer." She smiled at him and when he smiled back, it came with a world of shared experiences.

"Tina and I will continue scouting. Keep us posted."

As soon as Harris transported the men, Elizabeth and her niece returned to their positions in the cave next to their team. They continued their remote vizing of the network of caves across the valley.

FIFTEEN MINUTES later Harris spoke to Elizabeth. <The last two we sent to Thirasia are still unable to talk. They both have extensive internal injuries. However, the Seekers did get some credible intel from the four you pulled out of that skirmish in the village.>

She raised her chin. <You trust what they told you?>

<Yes, I think so. The four mercenaries we captured told us that local scuttlebutt among the troops says where we'll find Shannon, no one has seen what these guys call 'that freaking magic.' That tells me no one at their camp has seen any repositioning.>

<That raises some questions, doesn't it? Are they not repositioning because there are rare earths or because they don't want to be detected?>

<Well, it sounds to me like you're headed for hand-to-hand combat land. I understand Tina's

already given a solid accounting of her fighting skill.>

Elizabeth felt Harris had said it with pride. She knew his history as a competent combatant and how he took special interest in the group's progress. <And Shannon? What’s the word on her?>

Harris paused. <That's a bit strange, I'm wondering if we were being led into a setup or not. This wouldn’t be the first time.>

<What do you mean? What do you know?>

He hesitated. <Yes, that is, from the intel we have, she doesn't seem to be hurt.>

<The uniforms tell us she's free to walk and talk to anyone and is not under guard.>

<That could be good news. It may confirm our beliefs she is here negotiating a peaceful settlement on her own. What’s your assessment?>

<I recommend you go into Vald’s compound as you planned. Expect resistance. Be prepared for the worst, but I'll tell you, Elizabeth, from what I've been told, there is still a chance that Shannon may have gone Patty Hurst.>

<What? You mean the classic Stockholm syndrome? You think she’s accepted her captors as friends? That would be crazy? Of course, she won’t do that.> Elizabeth fumed. <You’ll have to do better than that, Harris.> She closed him out.

DEAD END

Afghanistan through Labyrinth

With the vizing of the extensive labyrinth finally complete, Elizabeth reviewed the plans for phase two of the mission. “We all see the same thing, right? There’s a smaller cavern directly ahead of this location. Let’s call it the antechamber. It’s connected to a larger chamber by a single short passageway. The larger chamber has ample space to hide weapons and men. With the semi-circle of concrete rooms built against the wall, it’s a good candidate for their command central.”

Tobin added. “I detect two men behind a low stonewall and that could play into our strategy. The center area in front of the bunker is packed full of large crates and barrels making dozens of places to hide. It is a real sniper farm.”

“The small concrete rooms have walls that shield our view.” Oliver wiggled his back against the wall to scratch it. “I wager they’re dead rooms and any one of them could hold Shannon’s quarters.

We need to be careful when we hit them. We don't want her to take any of our fire."

"Not a problem." Benjamin glanced at Sarah. "We can control our strikes, but look," he pointed ahead, "do you see the steel doors at each end of the short passageway that connects the antechamber to the great cave? It's too inviting, like they want us to reposition in there. It's got ambush written all over it."

"They must expect us to come after Shannon," Sarah said. "It would be an excellent booby trap if we repositioned into the passageway and rare earths held us captive between the steel doors."

Elizabeth could sense her team's tension and was glad for it. It would keep them alert. "We'll stage our attack to avoid any unwelcome surprises."

A grin spread split Sarah's face "We are going in."

Elizabeth had trouble containing her own excitement. "When I give the command, the inside squad, that's you, Sarah, Tobin and Benjamin, with me, will start the action by repositioning to the antechamber behind the outcrop of rocks 30 meters to the left of the door into the large cave." She projected an image of the exact spot of their arrival to their minds.

Tina eyed her brother. "What about our concern it's a trap?"

"That's why the outside squad will stay here covering their backs. We won't go in until we've checked out at least some of the trap potentials. If there's trouble, you will extract us ASAP. Tina, you monitor Tobin. John, you monitor Benjamin and me. Ollie, you have Sarah. Pull out anyone who even appears to be in trouble, but do not rush in to help. Hold your position here at headquarters and deal with them remotely."

"No offense, Sarah," Oliver said, glancing only momentarily at her, "but I'll be monitoring you, Liz." He gave Elizabeth a steely-eyed look. "We had a deal."

Her eyebrows dropped like a storm cloud. "Yes, we did. I'll promise to be extra careful and you'll back off a bit and give me some space to work."

Silence wrapped them all in an awkward blanket as the two glared at each other in a tense standoff. Finally, Elizabeth broke the tension. "Fine. You are on me. John, you'll monitor Sarah as well as Benjamin."

With Oliver and John squared away, she included Tina in her warning to the outside squad. "If *any* you sense *anything* is wrong . . . and I do mean *anything* . . . don't wait for a cry of help. Get your partner out of there. The inside team may loose their powers to sapping stones or from an EMP blast, but you, here on the outside, will remain untouched, *providing* you stay put and restrict your work to vizing from our headquarters. Got it?"

Members of both teams nodded as she made eye contact with each.

"We're ready. I'm going first to the spot I indicated. The rest of my inside squad will follow and wait in their left hand position until I indicate differently. We can do this." She repositioned.

From her location by the door, Elizabeth checked that both squads were in their designated locations, and then spoke for the last time to the outside trio. <Once we enter the passageway and then the large cave, I may not be able to make contact with you. I don't like it, but that's how it is. Fortunately, you will still be able to see us.>

Her voice sharpened as she addressed the inside team. <Listen up. I can see the short passage has limited lighting, but I will check for Rohypnol and the presence of rare earths with this special flashlight George sent. Do *not* enter until I say it's safe. If you lose a visual of me, pull me out.>

Elizabeth repositioned inside the short sealed passageway and immediately clicked on the special flashlight George had recently repositioned to the pocket of her robe. The lighted end had a small tube extension for an aerosol spray. The light emanated from several small cylinders, each emitting different wavelengths of light set to recognize different toxins. When it encountered a family of toxins with known variants of Rohypnol, the spray would glow with a specific shade of orange. All safe areas would shine a light green.

After a quick but exhaustive examination, she gave the all green signal and laughed at the pun. They went directly to the bunker’s steel door to examine it. They pushed their tinted goggles to their foreheads and took turns examining surfaces with Elizabeth’s light.

<It’s not sealed. We can just open it.> Tobin handed the light to Elizabeth and reached for the door

Sarah moved toward as well. <Great. Let’s go in.>

<Hold on, kiddos.> Elizabeth raised her arm making a bar in front of her protégés. <Stop. *Make* the time you need for caution.>

She turned to the most experienced fighter in their group. <Benjamin, push it open just enough to look in. Scan the bunker area visually before you go in. You two, go ahead and viz what you can from

here.> She stood with arm still outstretched, ready to stop Tobin or Sarah from jumping the gun.

Benjamin shook his head. <It looks clear, but until we are actually inside, we won't know.>

She gave a thumbs up. <Agreed.> And then Ollie's voice entered her mind. <We checked the roofs and the wall from here. Both are clear. Be wary of the large crates and barrels piled all over the center of the cavern. We can't see into all of them. They may still be hiding shooters.>

Tobin and Sarah cautiously pushed the door wider and Elizabeth rescanned the pile of supplies. To the outside team, she said, <Standby. Once we enter the cavern, we may lose contact.>

Elizabeth pointed with her finger. <If we reposition a few feet to the left, next to the rock wall, we'll be able to take cover behind those containers and still be close to the door. On my mark, go>

THEIR ARRIVAL FILLED THEM WITH PAIN.

Tobin and Sarah fell to their knees. Benjamin and Elizabeth remained standing . . . barely . . . and held their throbbing temples.

<Goggles! Put them on,> Benjamin shouted as he reached down and pulled Sarah's eyewear from

her forehead to her eyes. <Someone or something hit us with another EMP blast. Keep them in place, the goggles will protect the front of our brains where our powers are vulnerable. Make sure your hoods are tight around the rest of your head and face.>

Tobin had already checked that Elizabeth was properly protected while Sarah quickly examined Benjamin to see if he was all right. She said nothing but jerked a nod with her chin to say thanks and a thumbs-up letting him know his hood was good.

Crouched behind the container, Elizabeth spoke to each of them making sure the damage was not more than a painful reminder to be careful. <Stay low and still. I'm betting there's a motion detector. Stay put. I'm going to attempt to reposition to those boulders farther to the left.> She immediately vanished from the spot and twitched into view as another EMP pulse zapped her. Instead of arriving behind the rocks, she'd gone only half the distance to her destination and had landed on her bottom.

"Damn," slipped from her lips before she got a hold of herself. <Okay, everyone. This is what we've learned. It looks like the EMP is triggered by an automated system. Make sure your robes and glasses continue to cover your head and face. Otherwise, you'll get knocked on your butt every 30

seconds. I'm going to stay still and take a few seconds to recover and then I'll test a reposition behind the boulders.>

Elizabeth remained motionless except for her eyes, which continually scanned the cavern. Another RPG blast blew up a pile of rocks on the far side of the cavern. Tobin's voice entered her head and she was grateful they could still had communicate.

<We made it behind the rocks, Aunt Elizabeth. Except for headaches, we seem good to—>

A rocket propelled grenade exploded near the steel door, denting it severely and raising dust and sharp chips of rock. Four-uniformed militia appeared thirty yards in front of Elizabeth, their automatic weapons raised and ready for use. Without conscious thought, she repositioned close behind them and raked the back of their necks with her pain stick. Like puppets with cut strings, they dropped. She was lucky the timing was between the automatic EMP pulses.

<Tobin, reposition the bodies to the small passage on the other side of the door. Everyone, reposition on me.> The four men vanished, Benjamin slammed a large boulder into the partially opened steel door to close it tight, and the three arrived at her side. Mere seconds had passed before

another blast ripped through the cavern. Before the debris from the ceiling could fall, Elizabeth created a protective sphere. The concussion from a second RPG explosion propelled their protective bubble and its stunned occupants across the cavern toward a spot two-thirds up the far sidewall.

"That scared the damn crap out of me," Sarah said, breathing hard as Elizabeth stabilized the sphere's rebound. "There are obviously more men we can't see. If they aren't Followers, who are they and why didn't we detect them?"

"Good questions. For now, they can't see us. "From what they can see, we just vanished."

"Wait," Tina said. "You're saying you the *Followers* aren't here, but you think they are repositioning these soldiers into the cave to waste us?"

"That's diabolical. Definitely worthy of Vald. Clever, actually."

"Clever my ass. They're dangerous and we can't look for Mom while they are shooting at us. They're in the way."

"The fact that they can't see us isn't stopping their random firing of rocket propelled grenades." Tobin shook his head. "It's eerie how silent it is inside the sphere, yet we can see the flying bits of stone and concrete from the explosions."

“The cells. If Mom’s in one, those blasts could kill her.” Tina pressed her nose to the wall of the bubble. “What’s our next step, Aunt Liz?”

“Before we entered the bubble, I detected EMP pulses every thirty-seconds, as well.” Elizabeth pointed down at the boulders. <Sarah, someone’s still firing at our last location. Find the shooter and take him out. I’m going to get in my own sphere and shut down the EMP source. The effects may be cumulative on us and I don’t want to take a chance at testing my theory.>

Below her, one of the concrete buildings on the far side exploded from within and she heard Sarah’s excited hoot.

<Got their freaking nest, Aunt Elizabeth!>

Several men, both in uniform and in civilian dress, scrambled from the rubble created from Sarah’s hit. As they ran single file toward the large bunker at the center of the semicircle, she picked off the last man in line, then the next and the next until one after another, she rendered them unconscious and repositioned them to the small tunnel for safe keeping.

<Just a good, old-fashioned turkey shoot,> Oliver chuckled.

Elizabeth nodded. <Good job, Sarah. Harris will take them to HQ. Everyone keep your protective

robes tight. We're still not certain of the rare earths factor.>

From the safety of the bubble, Benjamin looked down at the remains of the cement room. <Uh, oh, it doesn't look like everyone made it out.>

<Sarah, go easy. Your mom could be anywhere. We don't want to hit her.>

The voice in her head spoke again. <He's completing his harvest mode gathering as much as he can.>

Elizabeth rubbed her temples. <Why rare earths?>

The mysterious voice spoke again. *<Preparation for a vengeful return.>*

<Seth? Is that you? Can you help?> Damn, snippets of dreams pushed her to her knees. We need to get a move on.

The voice declared, <Vald's doing the unspeakable.>

She saw fire in her mind . . . scorching . . . devouring . . .*horrendous* filled images filled her head and she could make no sense of them. *<He must be stopped.>*

<Liz? Are you there?>

<Ollie?> She breathed in great gulps of air. Calming air. Cool air. <It's you, Ollie?>

<Of course it's me.>

Elizabeth broadcast to both groups. <We are ready for stage two, which must be executed with precision. Keep our robes tight and goggles on.> She couldn't say that enough. She was terrified something would happen to one of them. It wasn't that she lacked confidence in them. She knew they were fighting-ready, she just didn't want any of them hurt . . . or worse and she didn't want to think about that. She called her entire team, inside and outside squads, to the roof top of the middle bunker.

<I think we're being played. Vald has cleverly set up a series of delaying tactics covering his escape plan.> The grim line of Elizabeth's mouth showed her anger. <These small cells are a complex collection of dead rooms that are shielded from all outside electromagnetic disturbances. While it's possible Shannon could be in any one of them, it's also possible that all of them could be hiding bad guys with weapons just waiting for us.>

Sarah said, <So we storm them.>

Benjamin added, <One at a time, calculated and appropriate.>

<That's an attractive possibility, but it would take too much time. I don't think we're going to see any Followers here. I think the complex has been designed to slow us down.>

Sarah said. <Well it worked. We're still here with nothing to show. All that automated fire accomplished was to play us.>

"Oh no, guys." Tina voice held momentary panic before it returned to her confident assertive self. "But we need to make certain mom isn't here, right?"

Elizabeth tapped her temple, <Mind speak only> and stood resolute. <Yes, but we have to be quick about it. <Tobin, detonate small sphere on the roof of each room. The blast has to be large enough to disorient anyone inside, but not big enough to kill them. It should rip part of the roof off and flush out anyone hiding inside.>

<Got it.> Tobin said. <Roof off. Heads on. I'll modify the size of each sphere as needed as we work around the semi-circle of bunkers.>

<When the occupants stumble out, the rest of us will disable them with short EMP bursts from our side arms. Benjamin, you're in charge of cleanup. Reposition any fallen bodies to the short passageway with the other captives. We can hold them there until we move them to the SPA. Benjamin and Sarah, cover each bunker's front door from the low wall. Tobin and I will work from the roof. Since they could have hidden snipers anywhere, Ollie, Tina, and John, cover our backs. If

something looks suspicious, spray the area with your EMP pistols. Set them at the highest level.>

<You realize that while that setting will only knock out a Follower, all we've seen so far are soldiers Are they just normal men?> Oliver took Elizabeth's shoulders to make sure she was listening. <At that level, you could kill them.>

<I don't like the idea of murdering anyone either, Ollie, but the only people you will fire on are the ones trying to kill us.>

OLD SCHOOL

Cavern deep in the Labyrinth

Tobin disrupted local space and created two small spheres. After he positioned them on the roof of the first cell, Elizabeth gave the command.

<Go.>

The din from the blasts made any normal communication briefly impossible and dust and debris shut down visibility. Elizabeth held her breath during the confusion and limited vision while Benjamin and Sarah scrambled through the rubble poking at shadows with their pain sticks. They quickly discovered and dispatched four disoriented militia to the small passage.

When the dust settled, revealing an empty, shattered room of rubble, there was no sign of Shannon. <The next one,> Elizabeth said, and they repeated the action and with the same result.

Damn. They were running out of options and still no Shannon or indication that she had been there. <Careful, everyone, this next bunker is larger.>

Elizabeth crossed her fingers as the next sphere imploded. This was taking too long. They needed to find Shannon and fast.

The sound of that detonation was wrong. <Tobin, what happened?>

<This whole thing is a dead room. The blast did *not* damage it. Repeat, no damage.>

New explosions of sand and powered stone exploded around Benjamin and Sarah, who had set up behind the low wall.

Tina and Oliver' shouts came simultaneously. <Sniper. Two o'clock above and behind the cells.>

<I'm sweeping the area,> Oliver said. <There's a tiny opening in the wall. Does anyone see—>

A small explosion erupted at the hole, thereby sealing it and throwing a shower of rocks and dust onto the roof of the main bunker below.

<Was that you, Sarah?> Tina asked while the rocks continued to fall.

<Damn right, girl.>

Tobin drew their attention exploding a larger sphere on the same cell. <Get in here. There's something you need to see.>

While Oliver and Tina covered them, Elizabeth joined Benjamin and Sarah who had dashed inside as Tobin dropped inside from the roof. Although Tobin's sphere had breached the dead room, against all odds, a smaller dead room sat within. <It's like that Russian doll thing with things inside of things.>

Benjamin, trying to viz through the copper lined wall shook his head. <I am having a hell of time vizing inside. Why would anyone build a dead room inside a dead room?>

Tobin held up a hand. <Hold your positions and take a look. The door doesn't have a lock.> He knelt and pointed to the dust on the floor. <There's only one set of footprints and they walk away from the room.>

"Small footprints." Benjamin said. "Like a women's."

Elizabeth nodded. <Just like a woman's.> She spoke softly. "That's because they belong to Shannon."

THE PRODIGAL DAUGHTER

Dead Room in the Labyrinth

Elizabeth wanted to examine the inner dead room for any clues it might hold about Shannon's association with Vald's Followers. In an effort to use their time more efficiently, She sent Tina to follow Shannon's footsteps.

<Sarah, have your EMP gun ready to spray the inside when I open the door.>

Sarah gave her a curt nod and raised her weapon.

Elizabeth pushed the point of a pain stick against the unlocked doorknob. The door slowly opened inward to reveal a single stark and dark room. Except for an army cot that took up almost half of the floor space, there was only a small square basket sitting next to a tiny table and chair. The rough stone floor added no comfort.

Following Elizabeth into the room, Sarah's eyes filled with tears "What do you think they did to her? Where is she?"

Elizabeth said, “Be tough, kiddo. You can do this.” She used the pain stick to point to a small curtain closet in one corner.”I want you to look at the clothes in there to see if they’re your mom’s.”

Hesitantly, as though the curtain were alive, Sarah pulled one side open with her index finger and stood on tiptoes to see what was on the small triangular board that served as a shelf. “How long were they planning to keep her here?” She pulled off a Jersey off the shelf and held it so the others could see.” Yes, this is mom’s. See the pin at the shoulder? That’s her good luck traveling pin.” Her voice trailed off, “I gave it to her.” She buried her face in the Jersey and sniffled. “It smells like mom, too,” she inhaled a shaky breath as she reached for something hanging in the back. “These are her favorite traveling slacks.” She pulled them down as well.

Tobin put an arm around his sister’s shoulders. “We’ll find her, Sarah. We’re close now.”

“I know. Thanks, really, I do,” she rallied. “What’s next, Aunt Elizabeth?”

Benjamin looked around. “It looks like she intended to say a while.”

Sarah held the sleeve of a tracksuit. “She always over packed so it’s hard to tell.” She dug down to the bottom of the basket and pulled out a stack of folders. Placing them on the desk, she flipped over some of the folders and said, "All of her important notes are here. All the new medicine she had teams working on." She held up one folder. "This one contains a draft of her Johns Hopkins department's budget and projects for the coming year."

Elizabeth reached for a red binder. "My god. Our most recent research on micro genomes is here." She held up the folder and waved it around. "What the hell? We've been working with Chloe on this and haven't shared it with anyone. It is Chloe's baby and she hasn't even published an article. I'll like to throttle Shannon for this, I really do. Wait until Chloe hears. She'll help me. This research was Chloe's special baby and here Shannon was sharing it with Vald? Our enemy, the monster, the goddamned fiend? What in all that was holy was going through her mind? If they didn't find her soon, it would be too late. The question was, too late for what?

Elizabeth was exhausted and deflated. Her arms hung at her sides and she bowed her head, which pounded with the sound of far-off explosions of fire and head-rattling noise. Not the explosions here in the cavern, but larger ones of cataclysmic scale. They were in her mind. As a warning. She had to do something about them. But what? *From* what? She wrapped her arms around herself as if for protection. She huffed a laugh. Some protection. She felt vulnerable, helpless. She almost missed what Sarah said.

Sarah shook her head and murmured, "What was she thinking?" Then she turned to Elizabeth. "I'm going back to help Uncle Oliver now," and vanished just as John returned from trailing Shannon's footsteps.

"I have vized her footsteps straight into the main bunker at the center of the row."

"What's your read on their strategy, John?" After all his years in black ops, Elizabeth was confident he had one. His guesses were usually close if not dead on.

"They might have pulled back to set up for another an attack," he said. "They'd have taken any prisoners with them for sure."

Elizabeth examined the closed look on his face for clues. "John, what do you really think?"

He cracked his knuckles and took a deep breath. "Vald's stalling so they can escape."

The unknown speaker in her mind reminded her, <he takes flight to prepare his revengeful return.>

Benjamin rubbed his chin. "Like to the farthest place they can find, you mean like Antarctica. Hell, hiding off the planet isn't out of the question."

John snorted. “I imagine Benjamin is right. They’ll go as far as they can. What do you think, Liz?”

“Good thought, John. I’m betting the same. Vald never struck me as the type who preferred a head-on confrontation although the bastard will do it if cornered or believes he’s unbeatable.”

She turned to Tobin.

<Tobin, how good is your mom at making these spheres? Can she make them to take care of herself?>

Surprise flashed across his face. <She’s good, very good, in fact. She can do what she needs to do to protect herself. Why?>

A voice, blasted into Elizabeth’s head bringing her response to an astonished halt. It was her voice, but different, the voice that spoke to her when she met George in his reading room only she was on the Zellerbach Auditorium stage at Berkeley. But it was *Her voice.*

NOT ENCOUNTERING RESISTANCE, Elizabeth’s team cleared the huge center bunker in seconds. It was more of a storage garage than a headquarters.

The front doors were large double doors and they discovered another identical set of doors on the opposite end that opened to a large passageway going deeper into the mountain range.

<Everyone, this part of the operation is over,> Elizabeth said. <Everyone, join me inside the huge main bunker.>

Within seconds, her band assembled. <John thinks Vald and his people are in full flight. I agree. Use remote viewing and viz this cave complex good to make sure we didn't miss anything. Look for escape tunnels and check the surface for a radius of ten miles for evidence of a departing sphere.>

With her team concentrating on details, Elizabeth ignored all side channels and other underground distractions and expanding the distance of her underground viz in broad sweeps to a five-mile radius, she discovered a huge cave that seemed to serve as the main living compound. <Found something,> she told the others. <Viz with me and tell me what you see.>

Benjamin answered for all of them. <It's packed full of Followers and Seekers.>

<My God, there's another complete ring of concrete rooms.> Sarah said. <There's space for several hundred people there.> Her eyes grew wide. <Does anyone see mom?>

Oliver craned his neck as if it would get him closer. <There're several hundred men congregating on the rooftops like something's about to happen.>

<I can't see her.> Tobin shouted.

Tina, as well as the others, kept her eyes glued to the viz. <Me neither.>

Elizabeth laid a hand on her shoulder and gave it a gentle squeeze. <I don't think we'll have to look beyond this cavern for your mom, Tina.>

John pointed over his shoulder. <I don't like this. That huge collection of boxes and barrels that was here moments ago just vanished.>

Elizabeth vized the cavern they left moments ago. All the stores, the crates, the barrels, and assorted containers, that had been piled high in the center of the cavern, had vanished as John said.

Knowing her team had her back, Elizabeth repositioned to a place in the tunnel just short of the huge vized warehouse cavern.

<We're too late! They're moving out.> Elizabeth roared. <Reposition to me, now.> Immediately, her team repositioned to her and faced the end of a passageway. Expecting to see another locked steel door, they were awl-struck by the sight of a solid wall of granite raising like a curtain before them.

Oliver spoke in a low voice. “My god, am I seeing what I think I am?”

“Believe it,” she said. “At the far end of this tunnel, we’re watching part of the surface of a gigantic sphere rise from the ground. I sense it is miles in diameter.”

The air in the passageway began to flow toward the moving mass.

To protect them from being sucked in to the vacuum created by the departing sphere, Elizabeth created a sphere around them that just fit in the narrow passageway. It held them secure while they navigated close to the ascending sphere.

Tobin’s hand went to his head “The thing is so huge I can’t make out the curvature of the sphere’s wall to calculate its size.”

Although there was no one there to fight, Sarah reached behind and gripped the handle of her curved khanjar dagger with her strong right hand. “We’re *going* to follow them, aren’t we, Aunt Elizabeth?”

“We can’t reposition inside. I did a probe and the Followers inside have applied their minds to keep us out. They’re too many, making them stronger than our seven. And when their sphere accelerates to any real speed, it will be invisible to us. We’ll have no way of tracking it. Of course, most importance, we'll have no way of knowing if Shannon is inside."

"Too bad we can't stick our sphere to it like a barnacle," Tobin said.

With those words, the huge sphere accelerated upwards, away from the surface above. Pulled along by the updraft, the team's tiny sphere was sucked out of the tunnel.

As predicted, once it began to accelerate, the large sphere quickly became invisible.

Elizabeth saw the stunned look of disappointment on everyone's face and spoke in private to Oliver. <Shannon is with them, Ollie. I have to go get her.>

<How?>

Not sure herself, she said to Tobin, "Quickly, hoover our sphere over the crater."

He returned a crisp, "On it," and placed the tiny sphere where requested.

She turned to Oliver and placed her shaking fists on his chest. "You know I *must* do this."

Oliver forewarned of yet another pending separation closed his eyes and pulled Elizabeth close, trying to push away his fear. How many times could she circle around the flame of death and survive? How close could she get before probability took her wings? After a moment, as he always had done, he kissed her cheek and whispered, “I know.”

Tobin shrank the sphere that had carried them and protected them down to pocket size and tucked it away. Elizabeth’s band of warriors silently turned to face her and waited. Oliver stood behind her, both hands on her shoulders. He was as discouraged as the others and found it hard to feel any enthusiasm for her pep talk.

“We are *not* defeated. We just need to take the next step, to figure out where they might be headed? We have some of the best minds in the universe right here. Think, dammit. Think. We know Vald. We know he likes to gather what he needs then hide. Where would he go?”

Tina’s sad voice echoed what everyone was thinking, “He’s headed for some place outside of our solar system, right? Some place *far* away.”

Elizabeth said, “That’s my best guess, Tina. Now we have to narrow down the *where*.”

Tina remained optimistic and pleaded, “Mom can’t be in that sphere. She’d have taken more clothes and she didn’t. She’d never leave her notes yet we found them in her room back in the bunker. ” Tina picked up her pain stick and turned her back to her aunt . . . her commander . . . her mentor. She and walked away. “She’s still here . . . somewhere. I’m going to find her.”

“Hold on,” Sarah said. “I’m going with you.”

Tobin held up both palms and spoke privately. <Sorry, Aunt Elizabeth, they need me.> He took several steps backward before turning and stretching out his stride to catch the girls.

Oliver hated that he had no cure for the droop in his love’s shoulders. For all that he wanted to keep her safe and happy, he worried what the future held. “They simply need to be doing something, Liz. We missed something. We just need to look again.”

John, in his succinct way added his thoughts. “A single clue could clear this mess up.”

Benjamin had his hand on his chin and studied the ground, his brows furrowed in a deep concentration. “Is it possible that Sarah and Tina are wrong about her clothes and her notes? I wonder if her records have a clue we missed.”

“Or,” Elizabeth said, “it possible that in leaving her clothes, that *is* the clue? Or her notes. Tina is right. I can’t *imagine* that she would leave them . . . unless . . . they serve some purpose.”

Relieved to see Elizabeth perk up, Oliver listened as she shot out orders.

“Benjamin, scour this complex of ruins for clues to the Followers’ destination, limitations, or anything else that closes our knowledge gap on their intentions. John, connect with Harris and see if there's any INTEL we got from the mercenaries that worked with Vald's group, then help Benjamin."

Oliver looked at her expectantly. "How about going back in time and hiding in the sphere or even taking her from her room in the cave when she sleeps?"

"That's a great idea and it might even be possible, but I'll be damned if I know how. I'll talk to George." Oliver took her shoulders. "You know, I'm the only one you haven't assigned a job. I can do more than economics, you know."

She extended her hand, "Come. Walk with me to the end of the last small passageway and check out the new edge of the cavern, the afternoon sun should allow us to view everything. First, we'll calculate the size of Vald's sphere"

ELIZABETH SCANNED the deep empty bowl-like crater left by the departing space sphere and pointed toward the far side. "The damn thing must be four miles wide. I have an idea that didn't dawn on me until I saw the sphere vanish into space. We were prevented from going inside but we could still see inside. You remember the large lake Cato's Follower's took with them? The bottom half of their sphere consisted of that lake and at least fifteen cubic miles of precious earths. I think that's the reason Vald came here to hide before he left."

"We never accused Vald of being stupid."

"Yes, but that was clever of him." She smiled for the first time since they'd started their hunt for Shannon.

"What's chasing around in your head?"

"Hear this." She grinned and sent a private message to Tobin and Tina. <Listen, you two, I need you to *use* those brilliant minds. As I see it, we have two options. One depends on you to solve a problem. I need you to approximate the volume of the lake inside the sphere. Figure how many days a lake of that size might sustain Vald's group of 400 people. Extrapolate from that number of days your best guess of what might be Vald's destination.>

<That won't work if Vald's destination is a place he's been before," Tobin said. "He can reposition the sphere point-to-point to anywhere in the galaxy and we'll never find him. But," he continued, "if he's *never been* to the destination, repositioning is off the table,"

Tina eyes widened. “That limits him to sub-light speeds which means the fastest he can travel to a place he *hasn’t been* is roughly 99.9% the speed of light. Since it takes light about 25,000 to 28,000 light years to get from earth to the center of the galaxy, Vald’s people could be in space a very long time. Since he’s not stupid enough to opt for that, we have to assume he has a nearby base between earth and the nearest star, four years away. And that’s what makes the water estimation critical and it means we have a chance of finding him.”

Elizabeth smiled. “Good thinking. You’re correct, of course and that’s why we have two options. One, get with Harris to set up six security teams to begin a search of inhabitable planets within one light year of earth. Put one expert Seeker with each team to monitor all of space within one light year for evidence of Vald’s sphere. If Vald is forced to sub light speeds they stand a good chance of picking up the sphere’s disturbance of local space. Have Harris send six spheres along the six axes in space away from Earth. Tell them to plan for a trip lasting upwards to six months unless we get new information to call them back.”

She didn’t wait for his reply. “This is important, Tobin. Make sure your Seekers know they are *not* to engage Vald. I repeat. They are *not* to engage Vald. They are to observe and report only. Got that?"

"What's the second option?" Oliver asked.

"It's bad." She avoided eye contact for a moment. "If Vald is in a position to reposition to a place he knows, one that is far, far away, we will never find him. It will give him a huge advantage, should he decide at some future time to return to Earth and wreck whatever havoc he pleases." She held her head. There was something in what she said. Her head pounded again and she saw explosions. "That option greatly increases the probability that he plans to return and settle the score with Earth."

"Of course there's always time travel if we can talk a Time Overlord into taking us down that twisted path." She kissed Ollie hard. "I have to go now." And she vanished.

HIGH ATOP THE far ridge made by Vald's departing sphere, a small figure in black leather surveyed several small waterfalls and openings in the crater below. Suddenly she pressed a speed-dial button on her cell phone. "Colonel," she cooed, showing her sharp white teeth. “*As promised,* Afghanistan is ours for the taking.”

BACK IN THE RABBIT HOLE

George's place in Chicago

Elizabeth returned to the edge of the giant crater caused by the departure of Vald's sphere. She had found too few clues from the events leading up to the exodus of the madman and his Followers and hoped her instincts would lead her to something she'd missed previously. Although she would never admit it, not even to Oliver, she was afraid. In her heart she knew that success was far from a sure thing.

Glancing around the huge crater, her gaze fell on the filling basin. Soon all that would be left of Vald's blast off would be a deep circular lake. Angered at her inability to focus on the immediate task, she directed her attention to her last visit with George. How in the hell had she created the ticket wall for the London underground at the Kings Cross junction? Or did she? Was it arrogance to think she'd created it?

Since the experience with George had begun backstage at Berkeley's Zellerbach Auditorium, she concentrated on recalling the initial trigger that generated that meeting. At one point in their discussion he'd said, "Assume a solution exists, then, imagine it." It made no sense at the time, nor did it now, yet . . . wasn't that exactly how she had told Oliver to *drive* the sphere? She shook her head. The whole *second awakening* thing was so . . . what . . . inexplicable? Baffling? George had told the process of connecting her brain to the greater mind had begun. What kind of hocus-pocus was that?

A chilly breeze rose unexpectedly from the depth of the crater and she wrapped her arms tighter around her middle. Turning her head from the updraft, she saw a gray door standing between two large rocks in the sandy soil. Faded black box letters invited her in.

ENTER. Smaller letters below said *Faculty and Staff.*

Without hesitation, she stepped through the door.

Giddy with a sense of accomplishment and control that had eluded her for days, she found herself backstage of the Berkeley auditorium.It has to be next to the entrance. She felt for the control to open the curtains and threw the switch. She turned back and found her meme had expanded to include a black box next to the gray door. Her eyes traced a thick black power cable disappearing into the dark shadows high above. The box had a yellow handle and the white letters under it read CURTAIN. She threw the switch

The curtain swayed in time to the whirr of a distant electric motor, then slowly parted. Light poured through the gap and a voice from the other side called out to her.

<Of course it does.>

“Is that you, Elizabeth? Come in. The door’s open.”

George. He was there. She’d found him. Elation filled her and she hurried through the opening, expecting to see the stage. Instead, she found herself standing in the hallway in front of George’s apartment. The sound of an elevator door softly closing behind her completed the new scene and her perception became her reality. She was in the hallway outside George’s penthouse in Chicago.

“Are you coming in or not?”

“Of course.” On entering, the same two overstuffed armchairs faced each other on the circular rug. The floor lamp still stood to one side.

George’s voice came from a distant room. “Out here . . . on the balcony. Come feel the breeze and enjoy the view.”

She rushed to his side. "There's not much time. Have you been vizing our efforts to locate Shannon?"

When he nodded, she detected a brief grin. "Where do you see humor in this, George? Do you see clues? Maybe in Shannon's clothes?"

He tilted his head, puzzled. "Meaning what? Explain."

"We think Shannon might have *allowed* herself to be captured in order to meet with Vald and establish a truce with him, but whenever she travel she over-packs. She took enough clothes and research notes to Afghanistan to take an extended trip. The odd thing is, *if* she went willingly with Vald, why didn't she didn't stop to take anything she packed when he launched the space sphere? We tracked her leaving her sleeping quarters barefooted. Vald must have decided to leave in a hurry. Perhaps we surprised him."

"No kidnapper hearing the cops are at the door is going stop an abduction to let the victim pack." He rubbed his hand back and forth across his chin. Unless—"

"Unless she wasn't kidnapped at all. I think she went on her own volition, but how can we know? Everything is still in the room they kept her in . . . or maybe she just slept there because she wanted to." Elizabeth ran both hands though her hair and wondered when she'd get a chance to wash it again. Stupid unimportant thought. She pushed it away.

"What do *you* think happened, Elizabeth?"

My best guess, you mean? I think she detected, or had short notice about Vald's sudden departure and she ran like hell to join them."

"John said none of the rooms had locks. What does that tell you?"

Frustrated, she threw out her hands. "Ma-a-aybe," she stretched out the word as she thought, "our efforts were too good. We scared Vald off before he was ready to leave. Why didn't we anticipate that? Which brings me to something else. The dead rooms are the same kind you had us build in the SPA. How could Vald's Followers know how to make them?"

George held out his palms. "Vald is arrogant, not stupid. His group embraces technology in ways that makes them a far more formidable adversary than you imagined. Did you consider the possibility that he may have had outside help?" He pointed to a chair. "Sit with me a moment. Remember time here is different." He smiled in a vague way. "It is inconsequential because we have tons of it." She sat and he leaned toward her. "We have all the time in the world."

He squinted his eyes at her as one might when examining a new discovery. "When you first *awoke*, you heard voices, but never knowingly had any visual distractions. Am I correct?"

Elizabeth held his gaze. "Define *distractions*."

"Some of the younger people you discovered who were going through their *awakening* coped with a fear of onset schizophrenia, correct? They attributed the voices they heard in their head to a mental condition. Such a distraction interfered with their acceptance of their *awakening*."

"Yes, yes, we know that's true" She shifted in her chair. In her mind, time was still of an essence in *her* reality, she was rapidly losing patience with George. "You know darn well we had trouble convincing Sarah she was *not* schizophrenic, for example."

"But *you* did not have such problems?" he persisted, holding her in her chair with the intensity of he gaze.

She said, "No-o. So-o?"

"Yet," George persevered, "Schizophrenics may have magnificent visual manifestations. They may have imaginary playmates, roommates, even lovers."

She yanked her hand away, frowning, but she maintained eye contact, aware of a possibility she didn't want to consider. Only the sudden sadness on his face made her accept the informative intent of his comment.

"Forgive me, Elizabeth." He took her hand again.

She looked at it and said, "I understand what you are saying."

He searched her eyes and waited.

"Look, I understand you are saying the mind is a powerful thing and sometimes we are confused by our perceptions. The last time I visited you, I left with the impression that my mind had expanded or connected beyond my brain. I find that hard to swallow, but I certainly can't explain a whole hell of a lot of things that the Cohort is capable of, so I am going with it because *you* said so."

Releasing her hand, George nodded and clapped his hands. "Yes, except now we can speak more of *the* mind as something separate. I sense you are aware that your brain is in communication with a greater evolving mind. The strong connection to that mind is part of your *second awakening* and your brain has had to catch up with it or cover up what it does not yet comprehend . . . uh . . . understand."

"Hmm." She was working on grasping at least some of what George said. It was never easy with him. He spoke in abstracts and hypotheticals. With a belief system that worked on concrete facts, she found things hard to believe without them.

“This is all about communication.” George held his arms wide and wiggled the fingers on his right hand. “See here? This is us in macro communication between the brain and the mind. He kept his arms open and looked at his wiggling left hand fingers. “Way over here we watch our genes in micro communication with other genes within a cell or from cell to cell or with genes within micro organisms.” He laughed looking from one hand to another. “It’s all genomic chatter!”

Elizabeth politely laughed along with him, unsure what he was getting at.

“Don’t you see? Your brain is coping by creating an interface for you to improve communication with the greater mind. It is creating visual aids like memes that allow you to communicate on a higher level so you will eventually understand, and accept this new reality’s mode of communication much like an infant has to learn to see and understand spoken words.

She sat back in her chair to stare hare at George, as if trying to read him. “Where are you on this?”

“I’m right here with you.”

She sorted. “Obtuse as always, George, but I seriously need some straight answers here. I mean what do you, the Nobel Physicist with all your brain power, make of the *science* behind all this?”

“The science underlining the universe? You mean, like The Theory of Everything?” He took a deep breath and exhaled a long weary sigh. “It’s all been too much promise and too little action in the answer department. We physicists are a long suffering lot.” He rubbed the back of his neck and stretched. “String theory, the big bang, all that dark matter, quantum theory. It’s not all accurate, and I admit, it’s been frustrating. Like Einstein said, ‘It’s an unpleasant thing to bring people into the basic laws of physics,’ but I think you know that.”

“There you go again, misquoting Einstein. I know you think it’s funny, but in fact, your friend, and fellow Nobel Prize Laureate, Steven Weinberg said that.” Elizabeth gave her head a quick shake. “Look, George, as you said, I’ve had my suspicions about those areas of physics myself, but you are sitting across from a medical researcher and genomic scientist and I think you might be flying solo on this one.”

“I once felt that way as well, Liz. He gestured beyond where they sat to the direction from which she had come. If I believed your scene, the auditorium, was only a self-delusion, I would be missing its greatest importance. This is the result of two minds connecting . . . struggling to cooperate in communication. That is the basis of our visual memes. . . yours and this," he twirled his hand overhead, "is mine. This is what is important. This, I believe is basically how you will soon communicate with Shannon." He folded his hands together and pointed at her with both index fingers. "Your mind connected to *the greater mind,* which in turn, connected to me. See? We both *needed* the *greater mind* to make that *connection*." He extended his arms to encompass their seating area. "My vision requires this setting of a chair and carpet as a base. Your vision uses an auditorium. You always did like lecturing, so it's easy for my mind to associate that with you, even if it is only the back stage of an auditorium." He chuckled. "This environment is just as real as anything you actually lived in."

"Are you implying we can have many visual memes? One for talking, one for travel, and so on."

He sat back and let his arms fall to his lap. "Yes, as long as you are able to define what you hold as real, as merely an internal perception that justifies sensory information, your meme will work."

She waved her arm at the scene before them. “Okay, but why all this? How’s it helping me locate Shannon? She could be on the other side of the galaxy by now.”

“This is better than vizing. Our brains are learning to connect us to a place where we all . . . everyone . . . everywhere . . . exists. Even with someone we love who might be across the galaxy.”

She crossed her arms. “Explain.”

“Let’s focus on Shannon. If her brain-mind connection has risen sufficiently, she would be able to see and interact within our meme immediately.”

“Risen, George? Do you mean her mind has developed like in a second awakening? Are you saying she could be here, right now, with her meme joined to ours?”

“Yes. Her mind would use something that is familiar to her to bridge the gap, possibly something that we both know well.” He shook a finger at her. “Now it’s my turn to ask about word usage. What do you mean by *if her brain-mind connection has risen sufficiently*?”

“If her mind has, as MeMa calls it, had a *second awakening*.”

Elizabeth leaned forward. “You’re saying you must first experience *more* changes and the effects of these experiences are *cumulative*? They build . . .

from one experience to the next? Is that it?" She leaned closer. George could be such an enigma. Was what he said possible? She could communicate with Shannon now? Just like that? "How do I initiate communication with her when I don't know where she is?"

He pointed to the floor with both hands. "The subatomic mind can be thought of as existing *every where*." He paused as if expecting a response, but Elizabeth said nothing and he continued. "A case could also be built for it existing *every when*, as well."

She huffed, "George, I don't have the energy to concern myself with time travel right now. Not today. *Everywhere* is more than sufficient for me right now and if this everywhere also means everyone, then if everyone *exists here*, then where in hell is Shannon?"

He pulled his chin in. "Oh. Right. That's what this is about."

She heaved a big sigh to cover the scream she was going to let lose on him. "Yes." She crossed her fingers. "You have an answer?

"You can see her and I think you can figure out where she is. I'm not sure her brain is ready to construct her part of the a meme, though." He grinned. "Does that help?"

Elizabeth's brain jumped from one idea to the next. "Incredible as it seems, yes, I believe it does." She stood abruptly, eager to get started. "Do you think all Cohorts will have this *second awakening*? Will their minds connect in this fashion?"

He bowed his head once. "I hope so, but I could be wrong on this point. This may just be the beginning. The entire process might not be completed for the entire Cohort for a long time. However, right now I firmly believe you can contact Shannon whenever you want."

She hurried toward the door. "Thanks, George. I am going to find her."

"Elizabeth." He didn't rise from his chair, but pointed to one side and shouted, "You are able to use my meme's KC button on the elevator. It will take you down to London's Kings Cross underground junction."

Instantly upon punching the KC button in the elevator, she stood in front of an automated ticket booth she recognized from London. All destinations said *Return.*

She stamped her foot. Dammit. I am not going home. I'm not finished here!

A familiar voice spoke, <Having trouble?>

It sounded like her voice, but with slight overtones of a dialect. Maybe MeMa?

<Have you considered the transfer section on the board?>

She searched the board for the word transfer. *Oh.* Way in the upper right in very small letters the categories listed under Travel consisted of domestic, intercontinental, intergalactic and intragalatic. She craned her head forward to make sure she had seen them correctly.

Intergalactic and intragalatic space travel? I'm in the deep end in way over my head! After giving Vald's knowledge of science a brief, she punched in the intergalactic number.

NEW TRAVEL

London's Kings Cross Underground

The machine popped out a ticket and Elizabeth stared at it before pulling it free. Using the ticket meant there might, in fact, be other dimensions and galaxies for her to explore. Accepting it meant she had to take the ride and it represented a commitment no less serious than stepping off a cliff.

George said the inter-dimensionality of a ubiquitous subatomic mind could be accessed using a an Evolutis brain construct of a meme. She held up the small ticket of thick paper and examined both sides, then carefully reread the small print.

Ludicrous.

For sanity, her brain must have created the ticket. She confirmed gate and track information with the sign on the platform wall and realized she and Shannon would have many long evenings and much good wine over this one. She ran a hand over her chin.

But only if this works.

Clutching her ticket with a white knuckled grip, she stomped down second thoughts. The cool air at the bottom of the long escalator smelled clean and refreshing and although this platform was quiet and had no crowds, it brought her a memory from the year she studied in London.

When the slight pressure of air heralded the arrival of a sleek cylindrical train, she craned her neck for a closer look, then drew her hands up under her chin cradling it in protection against the thunder and squeal accompanying a rush of newsprint and wind.

The train screeched to a stop in front of her and the doors slid open. Elizabeth stood, unsure, and then nimbly stepped into the empty car and sat facing forward, firmly holding on to the back of the seat in front of her.

The acceleration hurled her back against the plastic seat as though the train had shot up a steep hill. Her position near the front of the first car gave her a clear view of a tunnel ahead. As the bright light of an approaching train grew larger and larger, she braced herself for an unavoidable crash. She shut her eyes to the imminent contact and held on with a prayer.

When nothing happened, she opened her eyes and saw the sun . . . a radiant blue hue coming closer and turned her face from the escalating heat. The train suddenly veered to the side and sped by the receding star. Craning her neck, she watched its brightness fade into deep red, then cool black as she left the solar system behind.

A single bright blue dot hung in the dark region far ahead. In wonder, she watched as it grew into Vald's sphere, the one that must hold Shannon. She prayed that he had kept her alive. The train slowed and with it, came loss of gravity. Weightless, she gripped the seat in front of her and stared at the transparent bubble. Dark earth and rock filled the bottom half of the sphere with a rough terrain. Trees, water, and buildings make it habitable. Looking every bit a Christmas ornament, it appeared to need only a shake and snow.

The train veered toward the sphere and accelerated.

The voice, that was not hers yet belonged to her, prepared her for the next thing. <Only Shannon will see you, but she may not have awakened sufficiently for her mind to fully cooperate and accept your meme.>

The subway car vanished and Elizabeth covered her head, bracing for impact. It never came. She fell through dark space as though she had merely repositioned. The smell of damp dirt confirmed her arrival.

Lowering her arms, she found herself inside a huge sphere, at least several miles wide. More specifically, she was in a familiar white wooden structure that sat on a high rocky plateau. She was not alone. A figure, gazing in the opposite direction, stood not ten feet away.

<Shannon.> Elizabeth ran toward her, but as she drew close, she slowed to a walk and then stopped a few feet away. Shannon turned with a trace of a smile, yet barely reacting. Confused at the absence of response, Elizabeth said, <It's me, Elizabeth.>

<Is it really you? I mean are you real? I've tried so long to contact—>

Elizabeth grabbed her friend and hugged her hard. <You scared us all to death. I may murder you yet, but yes, I'm here.>

Her long-time friend turned slightly away and folded arms. <You *can't* be here.> She pointed behind Elizabeth. <Not with that.>

Frowning, Elizabeth twisted her head and looked at the place Shannon indicated. An involuntary squeak emerged. She hadn't realized she had arrived in a replica of the white gazebo on Shannon's Baltimore estate. It now sat on the floor of the auditorium stage at Berkeley. Immediately, she understood why it was in that precise spot. *The mind* had connected the memes that each of their minds had created.

<My God, Shannon. It's true. George believes we, as a species, have acquired Inter-dimensional time travel. It works. We did it. We're here. Together. You and I . . . we made this happen. Our minds paired at the quantum level, our minds to the greater mind. According to George, with paired minds we can be anywhere . . . entangled anywhere in the entire universe.>

<What are you talking about? I did nothing to create this. What are *you* doing?>

<It's simple.> Elizabeth laughed. <Okay, it's pretty complicated actually, but we don't have to worry about that part. Our brains have undergone a *second awakening,* which allows us to connect to a greater mind. That mind can use properties of other dimensions to communicate and travel throughout the galaxy and time itself.>

Although a brilliant researcher and physician, Shannon stood with face as blank as a stump. Only her darting eyes indicated her struggle for comprehension.

<Don't you see?> Elizabeth turned her palms up in question.

<You call what you just said an explanation?> Storm clouds gathered in Shannon's eyes. <It wouldn't hold up in any scientific study I can name.>

<Hmm.> Elizabeth tried again. <Our brains have risen beyond simple repositioning. Our perception of time . . . of where we are . . . of what we see around us . . . is exactly that, a perception only.>

Shannon's blank stare, or more like an angry glare, bore through her.

She tried again. <Shannon, nothing is real until our brain creates it. Our brains decide what our reality will be. We just have to *think* of where we want to be with our brain and this thing, *this greater mind* takes us there. I got that from George. That's what he told me. Tobin's portal sphere's are extensions of simple repositioning suited to those who have not attained a second awakening.>

Shannon curled her face up in impatience. <I hope you're not trying to get another doctorate in this business. You'll never be able to defend your dissertation.>

Elizabeth took no offence and instead grinned in delight . . . in surprise . . . in pure exhilaration. She turned in circles, arms extended, taking everything in. <*We did* do this. Not me alone, but *us*.> She pointed to stage floor. <I only did that part. See? The gazebo part, that's yours.>

Excited by what she perceived as a breakthrough in her own understanding, she grabbed her friend's hands and swung with her in a circle like little kids. <*We* did this. We met here, I mean. I didn't know where you were until you thought it and I arrived . . . here.>

Shannon nodded she was listening, but no fragment of understanding glinted in her eyes.

<I am lost for words and cannot explain this *next* thing, Shannon, but I believe we may have confirmed the theory of a bio centric universe.>

<What the *hell* are you talking about? You mean that *foolish* noise about life and consciousness being the basis for understanding the universe? You came here to sell that?>

Elizabeth remembered why she'd came and frowned. <What the devil were you doing running off with Vald? Getting on his space-sphere bound for God knows where? You don't even know where he's going, do you?> Remembering the worry and manpower that went into the search for Shannon, her anger grew <Your kids were frantic. I was frantic. Hell. Everyone was frantic.> She rolled her eyes around the vista of the sphere and the heavens above trying to calm down.

Shannon bit her upper lip and looked away. Her shoulders slumped and she walked slowly toward some small boulders nestled against the sphere's wall and sat on one, rotating back to face her friend. She jerked her thumb at the gazebo. <I'm not ready to sit in that thing. I can't believe I had anything to do with making it. This sphere, the last thing I made, took me here . . . far from home and . . .>

Her voice trailed off and she lowered her head, avoiding Elizabeth's reproachful gaze. She rubbed her temples with both hands. Shannon closed her fists and pounded her thighs. <I did *not* fail with Vald even though he's the bastard who imprisoned me a mile under the volcano then left me to die. My failure was that I thought I could reason with DARPA. I believed I could work with our intelligence community. I tried every argument I could with Vice President Galvez. My political efforts failed . . . all of them . . .miserably.>

As Shannon fought back tears, Elizabeth went to her and put her arm around her shoulders. She could feel Shannon's body tremble and pulled her closer. <How goes your negotiation with Vald and his followers?>

Shannon pushed Elizabeth away. <I left clues. My children didn't need to chase after me.>

Standing, she swiped her nose with the back of her hand.

<Your children figured that out. They read your clues. Everyone knew you weren't kidnapped and that you were looking for a solution out of the mess with Vald

<Oh, Liz,> Shannon ground out, <So with all of my political failures, it's now all about Vald. I needed Vald to trust me.> She exhaled a brief smile. <But after you put him in a sphere and jettisoned him into space, I figured he wasn't about to trust any one of us to do that again. It seemed clear to me I needed help from someone he would listen to. That's why I contacted Adrianne and asked for her support to get him to trust me using one of Tobin's huge space-spheres to help him resettle. I promised to go with him to prove it wasn't a trap. He agreed and took me along. Tobin taught me how to create an interstellar space sphere and how to capture land and water inside it for an extended voyage.>

<Yes, but surely Vald still didn't trust you. For that matter, why would he think you'd trust him?>

<Of course not. Don't you remember the Cold War? Trust is not required. It's all about crafting a stalemate. Look at it from Vald's point of view. He knows we can obliterate him and his people or at least he thinks we can. He *needed* me. He knew you

wouldn’t blow up the sphere with me on board. Arrogant? Certainly. The man could have invented the word. He *pretended* not to care if I came with them. I played along and caught up with him moments before he departed.>

<Hmm. I guess I can see that. The bastard’s so egotistical that getting him to believe he’d won you over might be easier than I’d have thought. So basically, you built him an arc and signed on.>

<Yes. I walked from my apartment in the cave, barefooted, and took my respectful place next to him.> She smiled bitterly. <He even let me drive a bit.>

Elizabeth choked and coughed on that. <He fell for your gambit, hook, line, and sinker. So you didn’t fail.> Her admiration changed in heartbeat and she spoke through clenched her teeth. <Shannon O’Quinn, there were *many,* and I do mean *many* times in your wild scheme where everything could have gone to hell and you’d be dead now.>

<But it didn’t. It worked. I’m here> Shannon heaved a weary sigh. <I’m sorry I worried everyone, but Vald *had* to go, all he needed was a vehicle.> She lifted a palm outward. <I was responsible for getting him and his people off our planet. If they’d remained, we’d be fighting forever

with little chance of a victory. Neither for them and certainly not for us. Our powers are too evenly matched.> She hung her head. <God, can you image? It'd be war forever.>

Elizabeth laid her hand on her friend's arm. What she had said was true, but there was more to it than that. Vald was still a threat to Earth. Her head pounded and visions of explosions filled her head. Somehow, Vald had fled Earth only until he could create a suitable revenge. That made him more dangerous than ever.

<You said it best when you pointed to the Earth and told Cato,'The children we seek are on already on Earth.>

They sat quietly lost in their own thoughts until Elizabeth stood and tucked her glossy brown hair behind her ears. <By the way, what was your plan for Vald's Followers before you returned home?>

<Stay with him until he found where he was going, of course, and since I know where it is, reposition home.>

It was too absurd to be serious. The tension broke and both started to laugh.

Elizabeth gasped between chortles, <So Vald can pilot this thing?>

<He can now and so can several of his Followers.> She gazed up toward the stars without

speaking for several seconds. “You know, Liz, Tobin gets this stuff. He is so damn smart, he’ll figure out the parts we don’t get and explain it to us.>

<Duh. You are right. I only thought of George.>

<Well, yeah, he’s the obvious one. I figured since I had at least *some* quantum physics in my medical prep, that I’d could learn more from George later to understand what Tobin was trying to tell me, but when I tried to answer some of Vald’s questions about folding space, I got stuck. His reaction to my ignorance seemed quite reasonable.>

<What does that mean?>

<He took my lack of knowledge as normal. I mean it was as though he didn’t expect me to know the science behind it.>

Elizabeth frowned. <Since none of the Followers seemed to have made efforts to keep up with science after their initial European exodus in the 1300s, it seems more than pompous.>

<No, Liz. I think it’s more than that. We’ve assumed that their centuries living under the ice had cut them off from science.> She nodded her like an old sage. <It’s not that they’re against science. I think they don’t need it. They don’t require science.>

Elizabeth's mental facilities went into high gear trying to make sense of her friend's statement and Shannon explained.

<If I assume the Followers don't need science and connect that concept with something else Vald said, then there is a logical conclusion.>

Elizabeth leaned forward. <Go on.>

<In all our talks together, Vald never once said the word *brain*. He always referred to the *mind.* Hear the difference?> Her voice rose as she became more animated. <If I tried to explain something, his comment of assurance always went something like, 'Ah, so your mind did such and such' or 'your mind was able to do thus and so.' That sort of thing.>

<That's how George talks. When I pushed for more detailed explanations, his comments were always about the mind, not the brain.> She began to pace. <He talked about a *second awakening*, a *rising* of the mind, or rather our brain's ability to communicate with our . . . no, no . . our *mind's* ability to communicate on higher levels. He was *particularity* clear about that point. It's *the* mind, not y*our* mind or *my* mind.>

<That must be where Vald is. Past his *second awakening*, I mean. That's why he doesn't need science. He believes he has has enough science to

create what he needs. Ugh,> Shannon said, with her hand to her head. <Sorry, that's not much clearer.>

<It'll do.> Elizabeth gazed out into the stars as if there were answers there. <I've never seen the galaxy look as brilliant before. The tilt of the galactic disk is profound. <See it?> She pointed low into the huge cluster that she no longer thought of as the Milky Way. <Just under it is Sagittarius. I use the constellation as a pointer to locate the galactic center, you know, the giant black hole. The Maelstrom.> She craned her neck forward as if to see better. <Oh, my god, we must be traveling at sub-light speed.> She could hear her heart thumping. <Quinn, tell me, does Vald know how to reposition the space sphere? Has he done it?>

<Well, of course. We couldn't spend years trying to find a planet. Earth is some twenty to twenty-five thousand light years from the center of the galaxy. He had to learn to jump. Is that important?>

She flashed a message to Shannon. <Damn right. Don't say a word. Vald's approaching. Hold my hand, Quinn.> She repositioned them to the Gazebo behind them. Close by, the floor of Elizabeth's auditorium blended into the sphere's Afghanistan terrain.

<So? Can you make whatever this is, work?> Panic had crept into Shannon's voice and it had risen in pitch. <Why the sudden need to leave? What's wrong?>

<George told me to think about a solution that *somehow* includes the meme we each created *and* we have to leave before Vald jumps the space sphere again.>

<Somehow?>

Elizabeth spoke faster. <Grab on to the rail of the gazebo and hold my hand tight.> She crossed her fingers just in case.

<You're saying I created this gazebo . . . because it means something special to me?>

<Don't you remember? How many late nights did we sat in it with some very good wine and argue the finer points of genetics? You used to laugh and say those debates would be complete if we ever taught the gazebo to fly.>

<Ye-e-e-s, but so what? That's right up there with when pigs fly, don't you think?>

<Back then, I would have. Yes, but what we know . . . what we are . . . is so different now. > <Try it with me . . . and hurry. Vald could reposition the space sphere at any time. Just imagine we can do it. Close your eyes and imagine this white wooden wonder fly.> She pointed to help

her along. <Do you see grass around it? Do you see the small table? Tell me what you see. Your mind is like a computer rendering an image. The more your let your brain work on it, the more details you'll see. Each time you think of your meme it gets sharper, more complete.>

Shannon gripped the railing so hard her knuckles turned white. <We're moving. Now faster! Things are flying by!>

<Hold on, were almost out.> She almost exploded with excitement. They had safely left Vald's space sphere behind and traveling on their shared meme, enjoyed the vision of a fanciful voyage back on Earth. She knew they were witnessing their return through their joined mind and welcomed the joy of the moment "I see Lake Liberty below! The estate is just down past the meadow." Shannon leaned to her right as the gazebo banked. "I see the pier and a small boat." Her eyes flashed upwards. "A flock of geese are flying over the lake toward the bay."

She felt a breeze hit her face and knew Shannon had accepted their expanded reality. "Go ahead, follow them. Take us faster! We're over the Atlantic. Go on until you see the rampart at Thirasia. Take us home, Shannon."

REUNION

Somewhere - Somewhen

Elizabeth hugged Shannon and cried in relief and happiness. “You did it. We made it.” Soft pops and loud squeals soon filled the rampart.

Oliver grabbed her then shook her and then wrapped his arms around her so tightly she squeaked. “That’s it. I mean it. I am never letting you out of my sight again.”

That sounded good to her. She didn’t want to go anywhere but here.

Shannon was surrounded by children when Harris and John arrived with James, who gave her the same speech Oliver had given Elizabeth. She had to admit being married to two adventure-laden women probably was hair-raising. Not as bad as the actual adventure, though. Lord, she was glad to be home. No one spoke of Shannon’s decision to leave on her own or the status of her mission to persuade Vald. There would be time for that soon. Right now, at this moment, she basked in the joy of family and friends as more of the Cohort appeared on the rampart in celebration of her reunion.

Without a word, Elizabeth and Oliver walked hand in hand toward the shadows in one corner of the SPA's rampart. Content to observe Shannon's reunion and not wanting to share the attention she deserved, Elizabeth only wanted to sit close to Ollie and regain the reality where they existed only for each other.

Oliver jutted out his chin, patted the back of her hand and said softly, "Oh dear, God. Okay. I'm ready. Let me have it. Where have you been and how does it work?"

She couldn't help grinning at him. He really did go kicking and screaming into these new concepts. "Ollie, you are the best of sports. This will blow you away." She paused, frowned, and glanced down saying softly, "MeMa. She must know of it. Of course! That's how she… hey…" She shook his shoulders and raised her voice. "Benjamin . . . By now he surely must be able to. . . . " what? She rubbed her chin, and her eyes grew wide. "Do you think the twins are there yet? Of course, they are. Tobin will . . ."

"Hey, Let me in. Tell me what's going on in that head of yours." Oliver dipped his head to frown at her under his carefully trimmed eyebrows. "Are you going to explain or just mentally brainstorm with yourself while I twiddle my thumbs?"

Elizabeth laughed and soundly socked him in the arm. "Aren't you the impatient one? Yes, yes. I can't wait to tell you."

He heaved a big sigh. "Okay, out with it. Do you think my brain can handle it?"

"Hah, your brain will do just fine, even though it is not about economics. It's your mind I wonder about. Remember the time you tried to explain the concept of cloud computing to me?"

He nodded.

"Well, it's like that. The computer is your brain, and the cloud is your mind. But this cloud connects to everyone's cloud. Our new awakening is something like that. All I . . . Or you . . . need to do is allow your brain the time to learn to connect to this cloud, which we will now call the mind."

Oliver looked at her for several seconds. That was all. No other movement. Finally, he said. "Ah . . ." Then she waited through another period of silence until he blurted out, "Sure, and just how am I supposed to figure out how to do that? It took me a month to learn to use DropBox on my computer."

She giggled. "Kiss me again."

"Liz?"

"Go on, it's not difficult." She nudged him. "Is it?"

Without another word, they kissed, for several minutes.

She held his face in her hands and spoke to his eyes. "The trigger for the rising, the second awakening, is based on our microbiology. You know, Ollie," she grinned, "all of this is pretty fascinating stuff. Our first awakening must also depend on getting a microbiologic trigger." She grabbed his shirt and pulled him close. "So kiss me, again."

He pulled her off her feet as he hugged her close.

"What are you doing?" She grinned at the smile in his eyes.

"If this microbiology is going to work, we need to do it right."

A WHILE LATER, they walked the short distance to Thirasia's extensive medical facilities, located on the floor above their apartment. Climbing the curved stairway that overlooked various open dining, socializing, and exercise, areas, Oliver shared his thoughts on what Elizabeth had told him.

“So that explains why Shannon chose to leave a trail of bare footprints for us to follow. Interesting.”

“Right, she knew any one of us that had their second awakening would be able to read the trace microbes in the prints and know it was Shannon.”

He laughed, “Yes, it’s quite amazing, really, but I’m relieved you didn’t have to kiss George to get it.”

She punched his shoulder. “Funny,”

As they approached the landing of the medical facility’s entrance, James appeared. “Elizabeth,” he extended an arm to her, “you have accomplished miracles.” Before she could respond, he pointed to the medical facility above with his shillelagh. “Shannon is indulging me by allowing her staff to do a thorough medical checkup. She’s even allowing them to scan her entire body for micro implants. I don’t trust that bastard Vald one bit. It’s a miracle she wasn’t murdered.”

His voice lowered, and he spoke in a friendly and conspiratorial tone. “Shannon doesn’t know, but I asked a personal friend of Chloe’s to do a complete psych evaluation as well. I’m sure she’ll see through that, but she’s feeling so guilty about the trouble she caused, she’ll do it to put everyone’s mind at rest.”

As they continued on their way up the gentle winding stairway, Elizabeth noticed again the architects beautiful use of the existing rock formations. Their destination was a small lounge nestled near a high, narrow waterfall that tumbled out of nowhere, only to disappear again behind an outcrop of rock. The splashing water generated a gentle breeze and a feeling of the great outdoors.

They relaxed in overstuffed chairs sitting around a low table of highly polished ancient cedar. Etched in the center was a careful carving of Earth's continents. A waiter bot, resembling a domed trashcan, silently arrived by their table and took their order. Three drinks and bowls of finger food promptly emerged from within.

Oliver toasted the departing bot with his glass, "To a good use of technology."

Elizabeth laughed and relaxed for the first time in months. She turned to James, raising her glass again. "To you. This is a lovely place. Your design is beautiful. The feeling of outside space in this solid rock fortress is nothing short of miraculous."

He looked up at the hanging plants thriving in the artificial light. "Perhaps. It is, but this great facility is already too small. If we tunnel any deeper, we'll sink Thirasia into the Aegean."

His guests chuckled and sipped their drinks as James slid forward in his seat and leaned on his shillelagh. “We need a much larger place to serve our growing needs for the future . . . for centuries, even. It must be well off the beaten track.”

“We have the whole planet,” Oliver said. “I’m guessing you have a place in mind.”

“We need more than just a hidden place. We’ll require a new way of life. I’m recommending we build a sanctuary in Antarctica beneath 5000 meters of rock, ice, and snow. While our Cohort prepares to emerge as the dominant species on Earth, many of us will need to hide in plain sight as the Follower’s Worlders once did. They will keep their powers hidden while they work within the government and research facilities to influence leaders and policies, to uncover possible persecution plots, and to detect and recruit new Evolutis.”

James glanced at Elizabeth and laughed. “Well, certainly not Afghanistan. Don’t want to go there. With all its mineral wealth, nations will be fighting and digging for decades. Besides, I’m actually getting used to our powers and the things we do. I don’t want them compromised by the presence of rare earths.”

Elizabeth rolled the ice cubes in her empty glass and grinned. “It’s about time you said that. The convenience alone should make a high-powered CEO like you love the relocating. Have you admitted your radical views to Shannon?”

“Lord no. Let her go on fretting about me.” He actually flushed. “I like it.” He turned his head and coughed.

Elizabeth helped cover his confession. “There are getting to be enough of Evolutis in the general population that people are noticing. We need to adopt a low profile.” Continuing to stare at the empty glass, she slowly positioned it on the table and said, “Now, that’s interesting.”

“What’s interesting about a low profile, love?” Oliver leaned closer and placed his empty glass next to hers.

“Spill it, Elizabeth,” James said, lifting his hand toward a near-by bot to order more drinks. “What’s got your attention?”

“There’s always space.”

RESOLUTION

Doyle's Darkwood office

Colonel Doyle had not heard from Adrianne for so many weeks he was not sure if she was still working with him. Damn, but she was a confusing piece of work. If he didn't want, or more like need her skills, he would have washed his hands of her long since. Yeah or need to ogle her body, the devil on his shoulder said. He brushed off his epaulets to rid himself of temptation and stared off into space. It had taken a long time, but when she finally contacted him, the news was good.

Afghanistan was theirs.

He savored the word, but he feared he would never see her again. Although piqued by her sudden disappearance, he hoped she would get over the last blistering guilt trip he'd laid on her. He shouldn't have told her their recent kidnapping failures were her fault. She did not receive accusations well . . . Hell. . . Or at all.

Now, suddenly, as if they were the best of pals, she'd notified him through an encrypted cell phone that she had made good on her promise to deliver Afghanistan, and all its rare earth and precious minerals, to him. He adjusted the grenades on his desk three inches to the left and drummed his fingers on the desk. At that time, he requested she remain with his team of field agents and safeguard their victory. So he was much surprised that when he entered his office, he found her perched on his desk.

"Where the hell have you—" The cold blue steel of her eyes stopped him cold. Adrianne's anger blasted from her body in copious waves and Doyle, not wanting to send her off in a huff again, tried a new tack. "Are you all right? I was concerned something . . . Did you have an accident?"

Adrianne swore in a language new to him, and he watched as his little trophies vibrated toward the edge of his desk. Diving forward, he caught the grenade just before it tipped toward the floor. Cursing softly, he once more fell into his chair and tried to control his breathing while his arm, of its own accord, adjusted the position of the small model of Mount Suribachi.

Adrianne made herself at home in the soft chair in the corner of his office. Doyle took his first good look at her and couldn't hide his shock. Her silky black hair had lost its luster and gained a strip of white just off center. The voluptuous length of black silk was gone. Now, no longer than a porcupine quill, it became a fitting description of the prickly potential for danger oozing from her visible pores.

A growl came from the chair. “That bitch. You can see what she did to me.”

Doyle could only nod with his mouth hanging open,

She unerringly grabbed at the top of her head and pulled at a fist full of white hair. “The bitch tried to kill me! For that, she’ll pay.”

The colonel sat immobile while she ranted about her near-death ordeal at the hands of Elizabeth. Her malice filled the very breath of air in the room, and it was with relief that the intercom rang to bring her tirade to an abrupt halt. A reprieve. “Bring him in,” Doyle barked before he even heard the full message. He turned back to Adrianne.

She had vanished.

WITHIN MINUTES, two Marine guards escorted Dr. Franklin Mandeep through the door and stood him in front of Doyle’s desk. The colonel opened the center desk drawer, pulled out a dog-eared folder and dismissed the marine escort without a glance.

When the last Marine quietly closed the door, Doyle instructed Mandeep to sit in the closest chair. He quickly scanned the last four pages clipped to the back of the folder, and then made a cursory examination of Dr. Mandeep's posture and body language. "It's all in here?"

"Yes . . ." He cleared his throat. "Yes, Colonel. All the preliminary research is there."

"It works?"

"Yes, sir."

Doyle used his free hand to lift up all but the last page and glanced again at it before lifting a brow and grilling the petite man with a probing gaze. "You're ready for human trials?"

Mandeep nodded and ran a nervous finger around his tight collar.

"Look," Doyle punctuated his words by thumping his finger on his desk, "the American forces have departed, and we've cleared out the Followers. Afghanistan is now a temporary vacuum that's about to suck in hordes of anyone who can carry a shovel and a duffel bag. We don't have the time to screw around with more tests. Understand?"

Mandeep glanced about like a mouse that knows there's a cat in the room. "The Taliban are still there." The statement came in a whine. The damn man always whined. “Why not take them out, kill them as well?”

Doyle slammed shut the file and spoke slowly, as an elementary school teacher might to a slow student. He shaped his hands over the desk as though they held a bowl. “Remove Afghanistan’s Taliban,” his hands moved the imaginary bowl off the table, “and welcome in the Pakistani Taliban.” He repositioned his hands over the table. “Remove the Pakistani Taliban,” his hands dumped the imaginary bowl on the floor, “and welcome ISIS or the next effing brand of Al Qaeda.”

Mandeep watched Doyle’s hands like a small animal watching a cobra.

“Manage the current Taliban,” The colonel continued, “and everyone’s happy. Get my drift?”

Understanding spread on his face. “Ah. Yes, sir. I see. I am to make a demonstration that scares the world and makes the current Taliban feel most secure, yet still afraid of us. Is that correct, sir?”

Doyle nodded. “Our special friends will get the blame for the whole operation.”

The doctor’s expression exploded into a smile. “By special friends, you mean Stosak and O’Quinn?”

When Doyle nodded, the little man laughed. “The world will despise them and force them underground like the pack of frauds they are.”

“Bet your ass.”

ELIZABETH SEES THEIR FUTURE

Berkeley Campus Home

For the first time in eighteen months, Elizabeth and Oliver spent the morning relaxing in the white wicker rocking chairs on the patio of their Berkeley campus home. They sipped ice tea, nibbled fresh scones from Edinburgh, and talked of inconsequential things.

"Liz, this scone is wonderful."

"It's almost dinner time in Edinburgh, and the fresh pastry was hard to find. Can I cook or what?"

"Actually, my Liz, my love, your repositioning skill has made you the gatherer and me the hunter. Nobody cooks much around here."

"Ah. Okay. The next time you pop over to Scotland and hunt for some breakfast."

He leaned closer and gave her a kiss. "Any time, anywhere together, love." He rubbed his hands together "Well, we have a whole semester of lecturing, department parties, and . . . uh . . ." He stopped and ran his hands over his khaki shorts. "It doesn't seem so exciting after what we've been doing. We'll have to get used to enjoying . . . Normal things again. Oliver hooked a footstool with his toe and drew it closer. "You think you'll miss the action, love?" Maybe take the METRO to the city and watch the seals on the wharf."

"Smell the seals is more like it, but if I'm not mistaken, they disappeared a few years ago."

"Spoilsport. Let's see. We haven't taken in the town for several years. We could take a tour bus through San Francisco."

"Lord, it's a good thing I know you're kidding. Where do you come up with those ideas? Anyway, I'm good for the moment watching the sun beat out the fog over the water. This view is incredible. I never get tired of the different faces of the bay.

"The action, yes, the drama, no. There was too much at stake, but this quiet interlude does leave me feeling I should be doing something.

"This is nice. No obligations, no pressure, no anxiety. I could get used to it, at least for a while."

The gravel in the front drive crunched an alert they had company. Elizabeth watched an unknown figure came around the back corner of the house and approach the patio. Although the young woman looked like a coed with her with cropped blond hair and shorts with a crisp, white, short-sleeved blouse, she had an air of confidence and purpose in her greeting to Elizabeth. Her smile was somehow reminiscent of days gone by at Rice University.

"Hello?"

Without returning the smile or salutation, Elizabeth walked down the short steps to meet the stranger. "Do I know you?" There was something familiar about her. Furthermore, the visitor had stopped several feet away, as Cohorts did in greeting. She felt a strange warmth she did not wish to acknowledge the feeling that emanated from the young woman.

"I know you're busy, Dr. Stosak, so I will deliver my message and leave."

Elizabeth momentarily slipped her gaze sideways to Oliver, who had joined her.

"Yes. What is it?"

The visitor spoke as if she'd rehearsed her pitch. "If you are comfortable with the concepts and constraints of time travel, meet me on the Acropolis at sundown, by the olive tree next to the famous Caryatids, on July 23rd in the year 1888."

The mention of the place set off a trigger in her mind, and a message flew through her head like summer lightning. "The Caryatids. Yes, I'll be there." She examined the woman with her intense gaze. What was it about her? Something. She was familiar. "Who are you?"

"I am a friend. I'll reveal my identity at the meeting place."

"Why that date? Why the Acropolis?"

The woman's cell phone made the sound of chirping baby birds. "Oh, sorry. I'm late for class. I have to run."

She vanished.

Elizabeth closed her open mouth. "That was . . . Interesting. . . I think." She climbed the steps back to the patio. "There's something about the Acropolis that I can't quite find in my brain. Seth has mentioned it several times. I need to discuss this with him before I meet that young woman in Greece. I'll ask him to join us. I like the man, and it's been a while since we last saw him. And you know how he likes as his early evening drink. He might as well have it with us, don't you think?"

"Perfect. Is Seth still advising Harris about security? I hope he isn't tied up."

"I think so. But now that things seem to have cooled down, Seth has returned to monitoring the timeline."

"Don't ask too many questions, I hear he loves to talk."

WHEN OLIVER RETURNED with three gin and tonics, the venerable Seeker had answered Elizabeth's call and had settled himself into a third rocker. He was dressed the same as they last saw him on his rooftop garden on Mykonos wearing a white mock turtle and shorts. Every hair of his long silver ponytail was tied neatly behind his head, and his short beard and mustache were trimmed as close as possible to his square chin and still be seen.

Oliver set the tray of glasses on the table and distributed them before raising his glass to Seth. "Slainte. Thanks for coming." The three sat side-by-side facing the green expanse of lawn and the lights of the campus beyond while slowly sipping their drinks and slipping into momentary silence.

"This too is beautiful, but in a different way from my patio. The fog rolling in is quite dramatic."

Yes, beautiful, Elizabeth thought and winced when Oliver stepped on her food.

"Oh, sorry, my dear, I thought you'd lost your train of thought. Time travel, right?"

She glared at him but in truth, refocused. It pleased her that Seth had accepted her invitation. He was a person of great experience and wisdom, not to mention incredible good looks. With his high cheekbones and square chin, he could grace the cover of any romance novel. She hoped she didn't blush yet put her hands on her cheeks to cool them. Damn.

She swallowed hard. “How do you maintain your level of fitness?” She flushed deeper, and Oliver nudged her foot.

Lord. “Sorry, forgive me, that was rude.”

He smiled into his glass. “I have aged sufficiently to have achieved my second awakening. Therefore, I can control my genome, if that is what you wish to know?”

“You’re on to me. Yes.” She changed the subject as fast as she could, yet apparently not enough. “When did you first meet MeMa?”

“Ah.” He sipped his drink. “As a gentleman, I must ask your forgiveness. Only MeMa should be the source of that information.”

“Of course.” She felt the heat rise again and switched to the topic that precipitated the invitation. “You’re an expert in many areas. I invited you here in hopes that you’d share some of your knowledge of time travel. I’ve been asked to meet someone in a strangely specific time in the past and at a specific place.” Elizabeth knew she could manage the trip, but she was not as confident as she’d like to be and hoped he could ease her concerns. Even though she wasn’t sure anyone had the answer on this one, as a scientist, she wanted to know how things worked.

She filled him in on the details and on the young, vaguely familiar young woman who delivered the invitation.

"How do you plan to travel in time? That is, what modality have you chosen?"

That surprised her. She wrinkled her brow and glanced at Oliver. "I'm not sure I understand your question."

Seth studied her a long moment, making her uncomfortable.

"Tell me about your plans for the trip. Will it be the first? What is your meme?"

"Yes, it will be my first time to time travel on my own. How do memes fit in?"

Elizabeth smiled and said. "Ah, you were a gleaner."

Oliver cleared his throat, but before he could ask, Elizabeth explained. "A gleaner is a time traveler who passively experiences the world through the mind of a person in another time with no control or influence over them what so ever."

"Good description. Have you tried other modalities of time travel?"

"I think I see where you're going with this." Elizabeth glanced at Oliver to see if he thought so, too. His frown said no. "When I first traveled through time I had to create a visual meme for my mind to use as a device to link to quantum space. At least that's what George said I had to do. I chose the Zellerbach Theater at Berkeley auditorium where I've always felt most comfortable lecturing. George suggested I imagine a door off stage that would extend my meme to include an illusion of making visual choices about where and when I wished to travel." She raised her hand and slowly shook her finger with each word. "It was a version of the King's Cross tube station in London. I guess that qualifies as my meme."

He raised his bushy eyebrows, and his eyes sparkled. "This is starting to sound like the memory procedure we used at university during the Middle Ages. You know, where you create a vision of a large mansion and place memories in different rooms, closets, and drawers to be retrieved by a simple walkthrough. Is that how you plan to expand your auditorium meme?"

She clasped her hands together in silent applause. "Great leap, Ollie. George said I would add more doors throughout the auditorium as I need for special connections."

"Ah, yes. Good. Your mind constructed a comfortable illusion for your means of travel. You made a visual meme. How does it work once you get to the King's Crossing part?"

"It looks like King's Cross station except it doesn't work by clicking my heels and saying where I want to do. It's all visual. I guess it is faster that way. Anyway, remember the columns of slats on the wall with destinations on them that would roll over until a specific trip was shown? The columns of destinations included special ones for selecting a specific time and a place. When I first looked at the information boards about destinations, the rows were blank. I quickly discovered that all I needed to do was to think of a where and when I wanted to go, and one of the empty slats would roll over until it spelled out my time and destination. Later, when I returned for my second trip, the slat for my first venture had its name permanently added on the big board." She coughed a laugh. "After selecting my destination, a ticket machine appeared next to me, which ejected a proper paper ticket . . . Printed with the current departure platform, the time, and the date of my train. After I ran through the passageways to the correct platform, I only had to wait a moment for my train to pull in. That resulted in a wild ride to my whenever and wherever."

Oliver, looking somewhat bewildered, put his empty glass on the table." And the young woman gave you the exact time, location, and date for your meeting, which was printed out on the ticket?" His empty was replaced by a full glass. "Thanks, Liz, you didn't tell me about these details before."

Seth extended his palm, fingers pointed down, pushing them in a go-ahead manner toward Elizabeth. "It seems to me you have begun a perfect meme, one well suited to your situation and experience. In your case, the ticket provides a focus, and the train reminds you of the journey within a vehicle you obviously enjoy and feel safe in. It allows you to actually be there at the correct time. Do you have any immediate concerns for this trip's timeline?"

She lifted her brows. What an understatement. It was intimidating . . . Or more like downright scary. "I assume the person I'm to meet will share all the necessary information."

Seth gave Oliver a nod. "You understand she will be traveling under the protection of an observer, so her trip will not adversely affect the timeline."

He sighed. "Lord, yes, please. I hope that means you will be there to watch over her and keep her safe."

Seth stretched his long arms overhead. "I will. My mind will be with her every second of her journey."

Elizabeth liked the sound of it, too. Although on the surface, it made no more sense than the concept of time travel in general, it cleared away the last vestiges of her concern. Tongue in cheek, she said, "Ollie, will you hold down the fort while I pop off to a meeting one hundred years in the past and some six thousand miles away?" She laughed out loud. "That's funny."

She raised her half-full glass in a toast as the men raised theirs. Returning it to the table, she vanished.

A VISION FROM THE ACROPOLIS

Acropolis 1888

Exiting the subway car and following a short loose gravel path, Elizabeth stepped through the hip-high gate into a small five-foot square open elevator. Electric elevator in 1888? With her entry, the gate closed automatically and starting its rickety ascent. She grabbed the railing that ran around the interior and wondered if elevators were part of the meme. She checked her ticket stub with her free hand. Yes. It said round-trip and her arrival time showed the correct date. She returned the stub to her pocket as she scanned as much of Athens as the view from the elevator permitted.

When the elevator stopped, she faced in the direction of the Caryatids temple on the far side of the rocky plateau and remembered from her own previous visits the uneven circuitous path from the main temple to the smaller Erechtheion temple with its six female Caryatid statues.

Sundown lurked and fell, but with an extraordinarily full moon, she navigated her way through large pieces of cut stonework and new renovations on the broken path. Funny seeing New improvements in 1888. Picking her way carefully over the rubble, she marveled at their ancient craftsmanship. All while she kept an eye out for the lone olive tree by the Erechtheion temple. The date, July 23rd, 1888 . . . Perhaps it was chosen with the brightness of the moon in mind. She found the olive tree nestled against the small temple. During the day it would get full sun, at night, however, it hid in the moon's shadow of the nearby temple walls.

At first, she saw no one. Then, the form of an old woman appeared hidden under the olive tree. Elizabeth strained her eyes to identify her, but the light from the moon faded. She glanced upwards, assuming clouds had accumulated and noticed a small bite had been taken out of the edge of the moon.

<Good evening, Daughter.>

<MeMa? I expected a young college girl from Berkeley. Did you get her to send me here?>

She ignored her question and gazed at the moon. <I see you noticed the eclipse has begun. Tonight it is one of the longest in recorded history. As your eyes adjust to the coming darkness, your mind may

become aware of other people gathered here. Many time-travel tourists come to witness this beautiful event, which is why I chose this date. Only we will be aware of them. They are not visible to the locals. Anyone attempting to locate us by tracking our minds will find the mental chatter of those gathered here too overwhelming to single us out. We can talk without detection. Take my hand, and I will complete the message you received from yourself a while ago on L2. I'll review it with you so that when you return to your regular time and place, you can share it with Oliver and Seth on your porch. It is time you were aware. >

<Why now and why here? Why not just give me the message?>

<No one is intentionally monitoring you here, and I need to be with you when you see it for the first time, so I can give assistance if you need it.>

<Assistance? For what?> She eyed the old woman in exasperation. She was never direct. She never gave a straight answer. Hell, you were lucky if she even gave an answer.

<The message will be alarming. Focus on the eclipse while you view the message. Are you ready?>

Elizabeth nodded, although the escapade was beginning to reek of cloak and dagger stuff she had hoped she was done with. An explosion flashed through her brain, and she had a terrible premonition.

To others, the two women appeared to be usual tourists standing at the corner of the small temple, with their heads angled toward the eclipse. All seemed normal until one of them slipped to the ground.

Elizabeth staggered and collapsed. Her heart raced like a terrified rabbit trying to escape the confines of its cage. The air surrounding her grew thin. She couldn't get enough. <What did you just show me? It can't be real. Is this some elaborate hoax? George?. Did he send you?> George . . . Something important he'd told her. What was it?

MeMa showed no reaction except to say, <Drink slowly from my flask. It's not a sedative in the clinical sense, but it will help you relax.>

Elizabeth pushed it away. <If there is any reality in this, I need a clear head.>

<It is all too real, Daughter, and now you must solve this problem.>

She held her temples in both hands. <My god, are you telling me I am supposed to do something to prevent this from happening?> She made a sound steeped in anguish before saying, <How can I possibly?>

<Do what you always do. Think about this problem and then fix it as I have seen you do many times before.>

<Fix it? Fix it?> She began to sound hysterical and knew it. Her brain wouldn't get off the track. <Are you kidding? How can I? Fix it?> She cried, <You just showed me the end of the world.> She took a deep breath, then another. Her brow lowered, as did her heart rate. Suddenly, anger replaced all other emotions. The old woman had a plan. <You've known of this for some time> A statement, not question.

<Yes, for a very long time.>

Although vague, it was an actual answer, and she hadn't even asked. <Is this is why you chose me . . . Chose my friends?> You knew about this when you selected us as undergraduates at Rice all those years ago. This is the reason we became . . . Us. You created us, made us Evolutis. It was part of your plan to fix this disaster?>

SHE ARRIVED BACK on her porch at the instant in time she'd left. It was as though she had never been away. The men, whose glasses had been raised in a toast, completed what they had initiated at her departure.

Wiping her eyes with her fingers, she took a shaky breath. Oliver gave her a questioning glance, but before he could phrase a question, she sagged into a rocking chair. “It’s done. I met with her, I met with MeMa as planned. Remember the uninhabited sphere at L2?”

The mystery had its beginnings months ago when they provided Cato and his Followers two of Tobin’s space-spheres to search for the parents, who they call The Children of the Light. Mysteriously, one of those ships had returned, abandoned, to its point of departure behind L2.

“When I examined it some time ago, I had an encounter with someone on that sphere who gave me a message.” She snorted a laugh. “I recently discovered I was that person, the visitor from our future.”

“What message, Elizabeth? You said there was no one there. That nothing happened. What are you saying?”

What was she saying, indeed? She didn’t want to repeat the message. In doing so, it would make it real, and she didn’t want that. The reality was too horrific to grasp. She put her empty glass on the table. “All memory of that meeting was removed from my mind at that time.”

“What? Speak louder, my love.”

She’d mumbled. She knew that. She didn’t want to articulate the facts. She glanced at Seth. He knew. She could tell by the grim set of his mouth. How long had he known? “Why had the facts been kept secret until now? If something were to be done about the situation, they needed to get started on it.

“The meeting I just had changed the apparent need for secrecy. I’ve been instructed to share the forgotten message, as well as my encounter with the messenger.”

She breathed deeply, reluctant to begin. The horror washed through her again, and her insides went liquid . . . boneless . . . Terrified. She gripped the armrest of her rocker for support. “I saw the record of a real event, one that hasn’t happened yet, but it will . . . And it’s . . . horrendous.” She swallowed and sat taller, much like a prisoner defying an interrogator. “Know that I am determined we will deal with this event. We have to.”

Oliver reached for her hand. “For god sake, Elizabeth. Tell us . . . Show us . . . what the hell it is.”

Seth reached for her other hand. <You've actually seen what you are about to share?>

The stark look on her face was the answer.

THROUGH ELIZABETH'S MIND, they watched the message she had carried all this time. Until MeMa released it, she hadn't realized she carried it in her mind. She sat with her hands clasped and her arms leaning on a lab table in Cato's abandoned sphere. A spectacular close up view of the moon and bright multicolored stars filled the background.

Within seconds, another Elizabeth, a slightly older, more mature, more confident version of herself, walked into view and sat opposite the first Elizabeth.

The new Elizabeth placed her palms down on the table and spoke first. <Before we begin, know there is nothing I can tell you other than I will give you a message you cannot share with anyone until someone gives you the keyword that will unlock it.>

Seconds of silence passed before she reached for the hands of the somewhat younger version of herself. <I will show you the message now. I warn you, it will be a horrible burden. You must not tell

anyone what you see here. If you do, you will corrupt the timeline, and there will be consequences. You will not be able to share the recorded message until someone of higher authority than I, determines it is the right moment. Do you understand?>

Elizabeth looked at the hands of her older version and after tightening her grip nodded. <I'm ready.> She closed her eyes and rested her chin on her chest. The point of view in the room rotated, and she saw herself sitting alone at the small conference table. The sphere's horizontal rotation slowly changed to vertical, and the moon sank from view revealing the deep blue and white orb of Earth beyond, a magnificent view of an Earthrise. Mesmerized, she watched hundreds of points of light from every direction converge on her home planet.

Her eyes shifted rapidly from Earth to the thread-like comet tails emerging behind each glowing point. She tried to steady her voice, but without success. "What had begun as hundreds of asteroids of points of light became thousands of meteorites raining their destruction down on the world insure planetary extinction."

They watched as the first arrivals struck San Francisco exploding into expanding rings of fire.

Successive hits interlocked a blazing blanket of death. The distinctive outline of the Americas disappeared, blending into blazing chaos. Eruptions exploded skyward from Earth's core to careen into the next round of inbound meteorites. Their collisions magnified the destruction turning the upper atmosphere into a blazing corona of red and white obliteration. Earth became a short-lived star.

Waves of nova-like explosions blasted through her brain, filling her soul with layers of death.

The sphere tilted and the moon rose, hiding the blazing mass of what had once been Earth.

A familiar voice jarred her. "You can help us prevent this attack, Sister."

Elizabeth dragged her gaze to her older self. She felt heavy. Her mouth barely opened. What was the point? "What could I possibly do?"

"We need your mind to formulate a plan to remove this terrible event from our timeline. Will you help?"

When the moon finally shielded them from hell's bright light, leaving only a faint corona of death and destruction surrounding Earth, the ambient light in the lab illuminated not the face of her other being, but the face of the young woman she'd met her on her porch.

No doubt in shock, Oliver said nothing, and although Elizabeth and Seth had seen the vision before, they were no less dumbstruck. Incomprehensible in its implications and horrendous in its reality, the message had left them speechless. Minutes ticked by. The sun dipped below the horizon. A damp breeze off the bay brought goosebumps to their bare arms. Lights came on in the distance.

Finally, Oliver rose. “I’ll be back with drinks.

Elizabeth pulled his forearm. “Are you okay?”

“What the hell, Liz? Earth just blew up.” Oliver gently removed her hand and wiped his own across his forehead. “That girl on our porch, how does she figure into all this?”

Elizabeth blinked in erratic syncopation with the banging in her chest. “I don’t know.” She turned to Seth. “You knew, didn’t you? In our near future, Earth will be destroyed.” It was a statement.

Seth appeared calm, yet when Elizabeth looked deeper into his eyes, she saw the same fear she saw in Oliver’s and shivered in dread.

As though he felt the message in her shivering, he reached for her hand. “Timelines can be changed. How much time do we have?”

“One solar year. That’s what MeMa told me. That’s the period of time we have until Earth is attacked. The message said it would be enough time to stop the attack. I am to put together a small team of our best Seekers and take them to work in a place of privacy and safety. A place where they can create the perfect solution to this threat."

Oliver repositioned from the kitchen and passed around the gin and tonics. "Is this a natural phenomenon or is someone behind it? This feels like some freaking bizarre space opera."

Elizabeth thought of Vlad's treacherous tactics at the crater on the island Jan Mayen when he ignored their rules of combat and murdered as many of Cato's Followers as he could before vanishing. "It is all too real. MeMa said Vald is attempting another pre-emptive strike. I don't know how he will manage it, but nothing is beyond his duplicity."

"Sarding bastard," Seth swore in an old language. "The damn man is a deathtrap and needs to be eliminated."

Elizabeth couldn't agree more. Earth's timeline would have been different if he had not been rescued when she ejected him into space. Guilt wormed its way into her soul. She should have been more thorough like Shannon said. She could barely wrap her brain around what she heard. The perfidy of Vald went much deeper than she could have imagined.

Oliver touched her arm bringing her back to the urgent problem. “Where can the Seekers meet in privacy and safety? Certainly not like this on our back porch.”

“We must assume Vald and his people, the Silva, carefully monitor our timeline,” Seth said.

“I would think if they detected any indication that we have knowledge of this cataclysmic event, they would launch their attack immediately. I think we should assemble our team at L3, on the other side of the sun, where there is virtually no chance of discovery.”

“Why are they waiting?” Oliver rubbed his hands together then rubbed his thighs and snorted. “Not that I don’t appreciate the opportunity it has given us, but what are they waiting for?”

Seth tapped the table with his finger. “We can only assume they need the time to complete their plan. We must act now.” He interlocked his fingers and reversed his hands in front of him, cracking his knuckles.

Elizabeth jumped, and Seth apologized. “I’m sorry. That’s rude of me. Can you believe my mother tried to get me to stop doing that over two thousand years ago.” He momentarily hung his head. “I was pleased you invited me to be here tonight, but I also wondered what motivated you.

While we have worked together at times, we have never socialized before. Now I believe I know the reason." He pointed a finger at her. "I'll wager the invitation you are about to extend for me to be on the team is no accident. It was part of the original message she gave you, yes?"

Before she could respond, he snapped his fingers. "And I just figured out why you need me." He laughed and abruptly stopped. <We need to speak privately from this point forward. I don't think we're intended to work on L3. I think we only need to assemble there. After the initial meeting of the team, the team must go to a time and place far from Vald's oversight, correct?>

Elizabeth had no idea how to make it work, but it made sense. She gazed so hard into his, she'd about fall in. She jerked upright. <What place and time do you have in mind?>

<The Time Overlords have monitored the timeline from such a place for centuries. We know it is safe from discovery and intrusion. After we get to L3, I can place the memory in your mind so you can share it with our team and they can reposition there directly.>

Oliver asked. <Who is the we you mention and are Vald's powers so strong we can't just block him? Better yet, why not kill him outright?>

She frowned. <That sounds good, but we don't know who Vald replacement is or if his weapon of earth's destruction is in place. We have a year to figure this out, so let's take the time to get the right answers. The day may come when we know it will be time for him to die.>

Seth stroked his short white beard before answering. <Good thinking, Elizabeth. As you know, I am a time overlord. Because you, and all those who will work with us, have or soon will experience their second awakening, we have the ability to travel through time. That capacity, we will have all the time we need to find an answer to preventing Earth's destruction.>

Elizabeth fumbled for Oliver's hand, needing an anchor for the mayhem swirling chaotically in her head.

<Did MeMa give you recommendations for a list of the seven-member team?" Seth asked. "If not, let's set them up.>

<For starters, I need the two of you.> She glanced at Oliver and sent up a little prayer in gratitude he had recently experienced his second awakening. It would kill him to be left behind, and she really didn't want to do this without him. <I have others in mind, and I'll share that with you on L3. Seth, will you travel with us or join us later?>

<Later, I need to collect some personal items first.>

Elizabeth turned to Oliver and wondered if they would ever enjoy a peaceful existence. “Well, here we go again. Grab our away gear while I setup up a meeting with George. Then you and I are off to L3. ”

Oliver reached for her hand. “What’s your plan after we confer at L3? ” He turned to their visitor. “It’s a good thing you have a safe place in mind. Can you tell us where it is?>

With a perfectly calm, straight face, Seth said, “We will travel several hundred years ago to the other side of the galaxy to a planet much like Earth called Torg.>

TOBIN AND TINA BUILD ONE

SPA's running tunnels

Tobin saw the one-mile marker on the wall letting him know he was near the end of his morning run through the service tunnels deep under the SPA. Taking a deep breath, he began his final sprint when someone rudely bumped his shoulder while passing. "Okay, big brother, how do you fold space to make something as intricate as the Disneyland sphere, Spaceship Earth?"

Tina's entrances stood on little formality.

He backed away from his sprint and matched her stride. "It's easy. The Spaceship Earth sphere is nothing more than a vast collection of equilateral triangles. They're two-dimensional and not difficult to make. I make one then I duplicate it many times into a row of them in a long flat ribbon of equilateral triangles with one side connected to the next triangle in the row. You know, sort of zig-zagging, to make a squiggly line. I fold them where they're joined until I can make a spherical shape. If I use pentagons instead of triangles, I get a large spherical dodecahedron shape, but since I want more flat sides, I'll use equilateral triangles. That makes the ball of flat sides look more like the Space Ship Earth model at Disney World.

Tina just stared at him. He knew she understood the principal. They'd struggled hours together to work the kinks out of the spheres. "It's a heck of a lot easier to make than describe."

Tina tapped her temple with her finger. "Come on Tobin, get on with it. A few big words don't hurt. So, then you blow it up like a balloon until it's corners fuse to the inside of the sphere."

"I did that once, and while the sides of the triangles reminded me of a lace framework inside the sphere, I was uncomfortable with the idea that the space between the flat triangles and the sphere was lost. I couldn't shake the feeling the lost space could be used for something special."

"How much lost space are we talking about?"

"Well, if I had put a sphere around Epcot's Spaceship Earth, the room between each folded triangle section and the sphere would be wide enough to hold a softball, perhaps a basketball, but I didn't do the calculations to find out."

She raised an eyebrow. "Lost space, huh."

"Think of it what it could mean when you scale up. Cato's two-mile radius sphere is tremendously larger than Spaceship Earth. It dawned on me that if I had constructed something like Spaceship Earth inside the sphere we built for Cato's people, they would be traveling inside a very special instrument."

"What the hell, Tobin? Get it out of your wetware and tell me what you mean by a very special instrument?"

"The sketches you saw in my viz of the notes I left with Sally were about creating freaking portals linking space and time. They show I built a prototype and hid it in a place in our solar system where no one from earth can see it."

"Did you use the space perpetually hidden behind the moon? L2?"

"No, too easy to find. I used the location of Earth's L3 point which is perpetually hidden behind the sun."

Without breaking stride, she slapped his thigh. "Well, what are you waiting for?"

Tobin grabbed Tina's hand. "Hang on."

WITH BOTH OF them standing inside the bottom of an empty giant sphere and after a quick scan of nearby space, Tobin repositioned them to L3 and sad, "TaDa! We're here."

Tina looked at the dark sky with its nearby bight sun and put her hands out in question. “What am I missing? Exactly where are we?”

He pointed at the sun and handed her a pair of dark goggles. “Wear these. While the sphere filters out many of the harmful rays of the sun, I don’t recommend looking directly at it.” He put his goggles on and continued, “Can you see Earth anywhere?”

In a sing-song school-girl tone, she recited the facts. “I don’t see the earth because we’re at L3 and Earth is hidden behind the sun.” She looked around. “You said we’d be on your sphere with the tiny time-space portals. Why can’t I see the special inner network of equilateral triangles?”

“When you look only with your eyes, the original sphere and my enhancements are almost transparent.”

“When I first fold the strip of equilateral triangles into a Portal ball it’s about four feet in diameter.” He held his hands that far apart. “Then, after I put it inside a plain sphere, I expand the Portal ball of triangles until the vertices, or points of the triangles touch and then meld with the inner wall of the outer sphere. Even though I didn’t wallpaper them together, the connections of the two spheres will make the final product stronger and provide the special space we need." He paused and tilted his head, barely containing a smile. "Can you guess why?"

"Ah ha. You need the special space that is left over between the nested spheres." Her face lit up. "The special space between them is the Portal." She gave him a high-five with her free hand. "That's great, but what do I have to do so I can use the Portals? I can't see them. Let's go. Let's use one."

"First you need an app."

She laughed. "Now you sound like Aunt Elizabeth. Okay, give it up."

"Here it comes. Only takes a few seconds."

She faced away from the sun and gazed into the stars. Then she lowered her chin and closed her eyes.

"That's it, Tina. With your eyes closed, tell me what you see?"

She bounced on her feet. "This is brilliant. I see five active portals with a view of a destination positioned on the inside wall within each portal. They look like travel posters. Holy shit. I can see details of the destination if I lean closer." She opened her eyes, and her face fell. "Oh, they're gone. It's like the lights went out." She eyed her brother's smug smile. "There more, what is it? Tell me."

"If you are in your apartment back at the SPA and wanted to travel somewhere you never been before, you would first remotely viz the inside of this sphere. You'd see the lights of the active portals looking like, as you said, large posters of places the Space Portal has been set up for you to visit. Say you want to go someplace new."

"Right, since I've never vized that place, I can't reposition there . . . ahhhh . . . without help." Her eyes shot open. "No way. Are you telling me we can share the places you've been via the portal? People like me who have not been to a given place can now go . . . Riding on the coattails of your experience? All I have to do is find a portal, one of the special triangles with a view of my desired destination?"

"Right, consider the inside of a Portal Sphere like a giant brochure." When the traveler sets up a portal to remember their trip, the knowledge to get there is available the next time. What's really great is the local timeline of the destination is also set and doesn't change with each trip."

She beamed. "Awesome. Sign me up. Where can I go?" She stopped to think. "Hey, why not show tallies of 'Likes' to help people discover the best places?"

DEADLY CONFLICT

Afghanistan near crater

Tobin's voice interrupted. <Aunt Elizabeth, you have to see this. Come quick.>

<I was about to call you. I'm here with Ollie and Seth. You sound upset.>

<I am. There's room, bring them with you. You know where I am, right?>

Without replying she literally grabbed Oliver and Seth. "Come with me. Tobin's has a problem."

THE THREE ARRIVED inside one of Tobin's twenty-foot spheres he liked to use for travel instead of repositioning.

Without a greeting, he launched into an explanation. "I wanted to figure some measurements of the sphere Vald used to escape from Afghanistan and possibly to pick up some soil and rock samples." They took off at high speed. "I was hovering high above the circular exit hole made by his departing sphere, and I noticed it hadn't yet filled with water, so I dropped lower." He pointed ahead. "We're almost there. While hovering, I saw something that didn't seem right. Take a look."

The sphere hovered about four thousand feet above the brown and tan badlands. Thin lines of low green shrubs gave emphasis to an otherwise bleak terrain.

"I see the crater," Oliver said.

"That was the first thing that caught my eye, as well. Broaden your scope and look closer."

Elizabeth pointed at the ground, drawing a large circle on the floor with her finger. "Do you mean all these big circling birds?"

Seth cleared his throat. "These birds are scavengers. You know it is easy to lose men in battle. That is how we locate freshly killed warriors."

Elizabeth felt her stomach drop. "Take us closer, Tobin. I fear I know what we'll see."

"I do, too but I don't have a satisfactory explanation." Tobin's rush to ground level gave the illusion the sphere fell away from under their feet. Knowing their internal inertia remained constant inside the sphere, its transparent floor did little to alleviate the feeling of free fall. Tobin stopped their decent about one hundred feet above the edge of the newly forming lake.

Elizabeth gasped. “I see hundreds of dead animals, ”

Oliver pointed behind them. “Oh my god. There are several dead people next to this dirt trail.”

“And more to our left,” said Seth. “What in hell’s going on?”

Tobin looked at him. “I can’t figure it out.”

Seth’s frown deepened. “Take us closer to the surface of the lake. Maybe there’s a clue there.”

“Is that an oil slick?” Oliver pointed with his chin to one side of the lake. “Tobin, did you measure how far from the crater the dead animals and people extend?”

“About five miles in each direction.”

“Not good,” Elizabeth said. “I don’t believe the crater’s the source of the poison. Someone must have dosed the area with it. Let’s pan out.”

Tobin cruised low and slow, and everyone got on their hands and knees and looked all directions, calling out what they saw.

“All dead.”

“Larger animal tracks look like escape efforts.” Oliver all but groaned.

“Nothing alive for at least twenty miles out.” Seth’s voice was deadpan.

Finally, Elizabeth stood. "Tobin, get some lab people out here and have them gear up to take samples. I'm pretty sure we're witnessing Vald's petty anger here. We made him cut his visit short, and the bastard retaliated. He has to be stopped. I'll be contacting you and Seth soon with our own problem, so get the SPA Cohorts on this fast. Oliver and I are to meet with George. It is good you found this, Tobin."

ELIZABETH AND OLIVER repositioned to the door of George's penthouse apartment in Chicago. After a brief welcome but seeming distracted welcome, they assembled on his small balcony with coffee and bagels.

Elizabeth spoke first. "Sorry, we're late. Tobin found something. Watch this." She shared with him a record of Tobin's discovery of the poisoned ground in Afghanistan.

The expression on his face told her he had taken it in. "My god, what won't that damn fiend do?"

"Unfortunately, not much." It was so obviously true she wondered why she wasted her breath. Exasperated, she addressed George. "You know why we're here. When I contacted MeMa about my plans to meet with you and her for ideas we can present to the rest of the team, she told me she had just left you moments before."

He seemed to diminish in size before her eyes.

"Yes. MeMa gave me the visual of the future. It was . . . too much to take in." He sat with elbows on his knees and stared at his clasped hands shaking his head. "I don't know what to tell you. It's too soon. My mind hasn't had a chance to assimilate the facts."

When he unclasped his hands, they trembled, and he put them back together.

Oliver touched his shoulder. "I'll remember that vision forever. How did MeMa react?"

Anger flashed momentarily across his face before he lowered his head and folded his arms over his chest, tucking his hands under his armpits. "She's known of it for hundreds of years. Did you realize we were always part of her solution?"

"I suspected as much, and she finally admitted she engineered our awakening. Yes. We were part of her long-term solution. She targeted us at Rice more than fifty years ago for this moment."

Oliver spat out in anger. "Why in the hell did she wait until there was only a year left?"

"Me and James." George cleared his throat. "We have been slow to awaken."

They looked at him in surprise.

"And possibly you as well Ollie. Have you had your second awakening? She had to wait until we, the seven of us from Rice, had fully developed. The three of us lagged behind Elizabeth and Shannon. Until we could all time travel, her plan wouldn't work."

Elizabeth tried to minimize everyone's feelings of guilt. "What you say about the timing of awakenings is true, but in fact, we have all the time in the world. For Pete's sake, we're freaking time travelers."

George sat upright and shook his head. "Its been longer, Liz, she's been observing us much longer than fifty years." He took a shaky deep breath. "Remember one of the first meetings you and I had inside our memes? We spoke of time-travel possibilities. Well, after you told me about your experience, I did what you did, I gleaned parts of my childhood."

She tried to be upbeat. "And did you have an enjoyable experience?"

He furrowed his brow. "While it was fascinating, it was also a bit disturbing. Why did you ask? What about you?"

"I thought it was a warm fuzzy. You know, nostalgic. I was surprised with some aspects of my circumstances, but I wouldn't say disturbing."

He raised his shaggy brows. "Are you sure? Nothing just a tab bit weird?"

"Oh." She put a hand to her mouth. "I didn't get your meaning, George. You recognized MeMa. She visited you, too, when you were a child."

Oliver slopped coffee over the rim of his cup. "She involved herself in your childhood? What the hell was that about?"

George wiggled his finger under his chin. "I know you often make fun of a physicist's way of observing data, but this was no outlier. I recognized her as a visitor at my house on several occasions." He rubbed his hands together fast enough to make fire. "I'd like to know what she was doing there. I wish my parents were alive today. I'd ask them."

She could see he was angry. "Go back and glean some more. It's possible, you know."

He gave a slight jerk of his head to acknowledge her suggestion. "Of course. Goddammit. She probably studied our parents as well as us. Lacking any real science or the technology to study our internal DNA development, she only had observations of family behaviors in her research toolkit. She couldn't tell us anything, though. Even to lie to us would screw up the timeline."

Her eyes widened. "George. It's beginning to sound like you think the end of the world is MeMa's fault?

"If it's any help," Oliver said, "I'll try my hand at, what did you call it, gleaning? And check out my family's entanglement with her."

Elizabeth patted his knee. "Interesting. I'd like to hear about that at some future time. Meanwhile, I think we shouldn't get sidetracked from what's most important . . . Finding a solution to preventing Earth's obliteration. Let's go straight to the source. MeMa."

MEMA SHARES SECRETS

MeMa's mansion High Wickham

Elizabeth, Ollie, and George lost no time contacting MeMa at her Victorian mansion near High Wickham, Hastings, southeast of London near the coast. Considering how often MeMa was unavailable, Elizabeth considered herself lucky. After exchanging the niceties, MeMa invited them into her sitting room and indicated Elizabeth and Oliver sit in opposite ends of the short sofa comforter. Then MeMa repositioned the short table with two overstuffed rockers allowing George to sit facing Elizabeth and Oliver next to her.

Elizabeth jumped right into the purpose of her request for a meeting and opened the discussion. "This tradition of kidnapping that Seekers employed basically recruits people into their ranks, Right?" She waited, allowing MeMa's silence to fill the room. Elizabeth locked eyes on the matriarch "You've been working your own angle on it for a long time, haven't you?"

MeMa's old eyes studied her. In truth, they drilled into her. She felt them impale her innards and her resolve slipped, just a little. She bit her lip and stared back. She needed these facts. They all did, and this time she would get an answer from the woman.

"I am not quite sure I understand where you are going with this."

Elizabeth continued. "I think you do, I'm talking initially about George, Shannon, and me. You added Shannon's adoptive twins, Tina and Tobin, along with Sarah and lately Benjamin. That initial seven you started does not include some in our social circle that may soon join us, like Aaron, Oliver, Doris, and others. My personal view is that the latter group was not recruited by you but by association with the former group. We want to know what you hoped to do with the original Cohort and how you recruited us. While we're at it, we want to know more about the second group and where all of us are headed in the near future." She paused again.

George said, "You remember, the initial seven of us."

Oliver added, "The Rice University Cohort."

Stoic as always, MeMa frowned and said nothing. She raised a finger and touched her temple. "Yes, Rice. That was more than fifty years ago."

Elizabeth raised an eyebrow. "Yes, a long time to see a plan come to fruition, wouldn't you say?" Would she finally get the answers they needed to quell their suspicions about MeMa?

The ancient woman said nothing for a heartbeat. "You keep asking the same questions, Daughter."

"Do I? Why did you choose us, as opposed to others? What methods did you employ to reset our genomes? What is your plan for us?"

Seemingly startled by the frankness and direction of Elizabeth's questioning, the matriarch folded her arms and pushed back against her chair.

Elizabeth's heart floundered. A response did not look forthcoming so she continued "I can appreciate the need for patience, MeMa, but you had to know the subject would be breached at some point. What occurred during our undergrad years at Rice University? We need to know what you did. How did you it and why did you it?"

MeMa's head fell momentarily to her chest, and Elizabeth assessed from MeMa's body language her question would be ignored, again. It was a favored tactic of the matriarch. She didn't dole out information on a good day and gave out none if she didn't want to divulge information.

She looked through each of them as she spoke. "To be accurate, Rice was not the beginning, but the end. Of course, as you may speculate, the how and the why are closely related to all of your concerns."

Elizabeth watched the old woman carefully, suspecting a straight answer was not forthcoming, yet MeMa surprised her closing her eyes while a small secret smile lifted the corners of her lips.

"The current crisis with Vald began for me in 1206. That was the year I met and fell in love with a young man." Her eyes opened sharing a dreamy, distant look that made Elizabeth glance away to give her privacy. She looked at Oliver and discovered he continued to stare at MeMa.

"We had many high adventures, some of which should have killed us." MeMa's smile spread. "But they didn't. It took a series of events to bring us to see the problem you will soon face. I am speaking about the timeline and its relevance to our problem with Vald. My journey toward you and the forming of the Rice cohort actually began during the time we called the Great Mortality." She waved her hand, "Somewhere around 1347. It was something we could not fight and were forced to flee."

"You mean the plague."

"Yes, it was a terrible time. Whole villages were wiped out. When we heard it was not so bad in Norway, we began a journey there to escape the pestilence. We left Europe by ship. I say ship when in truth it was a tiny wooden vessel, an easy mark for the unexpected storm that struck us. We immediately capsized in the North Sea. I was near hysterical with fright, but I managed to pull myself atop a piece of the hull."

Taking a deep breath, she swallowed. "Our now is many hundreds of years later, and the memory of that ship's destruction still chills me to the bone. As that young girl, I was terrified of drowning in that cold water." She wrapped her arms around her chest as if to warm herself. "When the storm passed, my hands were frozen to the wooden hull, my voice a mere rasp from calling out. No one answered." She hung her head. "The sea was too cold for survival. Those in the water died. "MeMa looked down at her lap and pulled at a thread on the small handkerchief she gripped with white knuckles. "All I heard was the moaning of the wind and the lapping of cold water. I was all alone lying on the frozen hull. I fought to stay conscious, afraid I would lose my grip and slip into the sea. In spite of my intentions, I dozed and dreamed I saw another figure sprawled across a large nearby piece of floating wood. The swells of the ocean brought him closer, and I reached for him. When I woke, he was unconscious and so very cold, but he was alive."

MeMa smiled at the memory. "Ever so slowly, I was able to work his body toward the top of the piece of the ship I clung to. I parted our clothes and pressed our bodies together. Throughout the long night, I hugged him close, sharing what body heat I had. The next day, the man only occasionally mumbled, and I was so afraid he would die and leave me alone again."

As if reliving the horror, MeMa stilled, and Elizabeth thought she was finished, but the ancient one continued, talking through the hand she held close to at her mouth. "That day was very long, and I saw no other survivors. I watched over the man and prayed he would gain consciousness."

"Just before sundown, a Norwegian fishing boat rescued us. The crew warmed us with blankets and fed us warm broth. The ship was headed for Bergen, and during the duration of the voyage, we slept together. The man survived."

George slapped his hands in his thighs. "MeMa, we all realize the cold water should have killed both of you within minutes. Is the story a fable or can you tell us why were you spared?"

She flashed three fingers. "Three days. We were afloat for three days. At the time, I gave credit to our survival to heavy long fur-lined coats and Devine Intervention. The crew of the boat that rescued us thought it was a miracle, but I know better now." She stood with outstretched arms. "Come close and hold me tight."

Glancing aside, the three guests encircled MeMa and held her close.

Within a moment her body temperature rose sufficiently to cause each of them to step back.

Before any would comment, MeMa staggered into her chair and briefly laughed. "Making the warmth makes me dizzy, and I must sit."

Elizabeth said, "Did you know you could do that, MeMa?"

She shook her head, "No, and I'll wager none of you realize you can do that either."

Oliver spoke softly. "You and this man stayed alive for three days in freezing temperatures cuddling within your fur coats."

"Yes, and we slept a great deal." She laughed and returned to her chair.

Elizabeth reached out and patted her forearm. "Ahhh, thank you, Mother. I will forever have a warm, loving feeling about proximity."

MeMa nodded and brushed her skirt as if to press out wrinkles. "You will get no more information on that subject from me."

The silence in the room was palpable, and for long moments, no one spoke. Finally, Elizabeth roused herself and spoke to the group. "No more personal questions. However, you did say this was the start of the Rice . . . What? Should I call it an experiment?"

MeMa shook her finger. "Always the scientist. I will tell you. After I lived with the people you mentioned and know as Followers for quite some time, I wanted to live in the world again, so I became a Seeker."

Elizabeth gasped, although she had assumed it for some time. "You kidnapped children?"

"Yes, although I am not proud of it. You know I have not condoned kidnapping for decades, but that is what we did in those early days." She sighed. "That is a story for another day, but I will say, my job as a Seeker involved something I thought most peculiar. We were required to live closely with the ones we kidnapped . . . for periods upwards to a year. Longer, if the child we took had not yet awakened, living in Proximity became the rule."

The ancient woman paused to pull her shawl closer around her shoulders and resettle herself in the chair. Elizabeth could see she hated making the confession and wondered at its importance in the story required it. The woman Elizabeth knew would not be sharing this information. She was sure it of its significance. MeMa indeed wasn't proud of what she and the Followers had done. Elizabeth decided it was a thing of necessity in MeMa's past and deserved her respect.

After a long period of silence, MeMa sighed, "What I have learned from my personal proximity experience has proved most interesting."

Elizabeth's impatience for her to continue showed in the crossing of her legs. She tightened the grip on her knee to rein her impulse to interrogate and allowed MeMa continue at her pace.

That tactic seemed to work as the old woman said, shaking her finger at each word. "Once I put the information together, I deduced it is possible that over time, the proximity of an awakened person such as myself, to another, specifically the kidnapped child, could, in itself, awaken the child."

Elizabeth spoke in her normal clinical voice and asked the question she knew others only thought about. "How old were the children you shared you micro biome with?"

The matriarch's eyes narrowed, but she continued. "I only held the newborn to close to me.

Once they became toddlers, I fed them a specially prepared soup of herbs and potions. The intimacy and the potions brought about the growth in the child's brain of what you now call Snyder's area."

No one spoke.

MeMa continued, "Forgive my apparent diversion, but one of Shannon's adoptive children, Chloe, knows how important microbiology is to our work. Yes, yes, that is the word she used. I think the process of awakening is related to our microbiology. Note that when I use words such as 'our or 'us' please remember I am talking about this new species we have become. "

THE EVENING BREEZE from the nearby coast turned the room cooler, but Elizabeth remained rooted to her chair. "An excellent perception, Mother. Microbiology may very possibly be at work here. Take us back to when you found us in college. Why did you choose us? Your technique seems to imply you could have awakened anyone."

MeMa pursed her lips and then smiled. "I knew you would return to the question. You never gave up on anything. So I will share part of the story with you. I wanted to test my theory about this proximity, so I searched with the Time Overlords long and hard for seven people who already had the intelligence, potential for leadership in their field, and would remain physically close to one another for a sufficiently long time. The most qualified group I found attended Rice University. Unfortunately, there were only six of you."

"Ah, yes, you needed the power of seven. That is very important."

She tucked her old-fashion skirts in tight around her legs while she ordered the facts in her mind. "I was on the verge of leaving the campus to continue my search elsewhere when I learned that after winning a prestigious national science competition, a gifted high school senior would be admitted to Rice as a second semester freshman."

"That had to be Shannon," Elizabeth said. "However, the question remains. How did you accomplish awakening with us?"

MeMa covered her mouth with a hand and debated whether to go on. She wasn't proud of what she'd done and didn't want to share it. Not now, not ever. "I've debated sharing this dark aspect of my Seeker life with you." She dabbled the corner of one eye with hankie she kept under her wristband. "You may not like this part, but I found a better method later, but this one didn't involve proximity and also worked." She squared her shoulders. "It is best to get on with it, and I have decided to do so." She softly cleared her dry throat. "I was getting good at the practice of herbs, and all of that but I found it too slow. Eventually, my lack of patience took over my judgment and caused much unhappiness."

Elizabeth knew the softly spoken question from Oliver was all they wanted to know. "What did you do, MeMa?"

"As I have mentioned, some Seekers used natural herbs to speed up growth in the time it usually took to awaken a kidnapped person. And with the help of my Seeker friends, I discovered a combination of such plants that practically did away with the need for proximity. One was a particularly potent, albeit a slow acting drug that caused not only a traditional awakening but eventually, one that led directly to a second awakening making the person a powerful Seeker."

"That's just good research, MeMa." Elizabeth placed her hand on the old woman's knee and could sense the old woman took some comfort in it. "Why does it bother you so, Mother?"

"Because I became a foolish old woman. I liked the success I was having and the elevated status it gave her in the Follower community." She shrugged. "Did that make me like Vald? Working selfishly toward my own ends? Surely not. I didn't stop my research there. I learned from a child development class at Rice, about the time I first thought of your group here, my initial research showed younger children, even toddlers made better candidates than teenagers. Something is forgiving about a toddlers body's ability to adapt to change. While a teenager's brain is the model of chaos. Therefore I sought out younger and younger candidates."

George said, "Where did you get the idea of it? Given the science of the time, the jump from natural herbs and diet to anything seems like a great leap of faith."

"Did you chose ever younger children? Just how young are you talking about, Mother?"

MeMa dropped her eyes. Elizabeth and her damn questions. Her answer was barely audible. "In utero."

"Ah," Elizabeth's face lit up in a reaction that totally surprised MeMa. "That makes perfect sense. That's before so many of the developmental genes are switched off, particularly the genes supporting the ability of regeneration and longevity."

The old woman nodded. She didn't exactly understand the details of the science, but she realized what worked would be used. "In one of my earlier experiments, the children awakened in utero and began to communicate with each other. Unable to understand what they said, I use my monitoring time to track their physical development. Then one day I heard mind speak from their mother's womb what sounded like a blending of English and Swedish. They were talking, trying to get their mother's attention from the womb." She stopped to drink her glass of water.

She stopped hoping that was the end of it, but of course, knew her audience would continue questioning.

Oliver said, "Did the mother know what was happening?"

The ancient woman sagged in her chair and shook her head in defeat. "If only she had. If only I had stayed with the mother and helped her through that difficult time." She snorted. "A difficult time? A bloody euphemism."

"Eleanor did not understand, and the pregnancy and her unborn drove her stark raving mad. In the end, afraid, horribly confused and unbalanced, she tried to terminate her pregnancy with a knife . . . She slit her throat. Her husband arrived to find his wife on the floor surrounded by a slowly growing pool of blood. He and the midwife thought Eleanor had bled out, and the experienced midwife boasted she knew how to save the twins. MeMa gulped back a sob and took a deep breath. She had cried over this too often to do it again. Besides, she was damned if she would show weakness. “The midwife saved the babies with the same knife their mother had used to try and kill them.”

Elizabeth was too shocked to speak.

George broke his silence and spoke softly. “MeMa, who was the mother of the twins?”

MeMa held Elizabeth’s forearm tight and shook it.“They can never know. The children, I mean. Don’t tell them,” the distraught woman pleaded. “They would assume the burden of guilt that is mine alone.” Tears pooled in MeMa’s eyes but she forbad them to fall. She stood with outstretched arms. “Please. Don’t tell anyone.” She stopped and looked at them and waited for comments.

Elizabeth placed her hand over MeMa’s tight grip.

“We will never tell them, I promise.” After a too long pause, Elizabeth asked, “MeMa, who was Eleanor?”

“Eleanor was my daughter.” With those words, the old woman vanished.

The remaining three stared at the space MeMa once occupied. Then Elizabeth spoke in a stage whisper. “It had to be them.” Elizabeth covered her mouth and shook her head. She snapped toward

Oliver, “The twins Ollie, MeMa is talking about are Tina and Tobin.”

ANOTHER REASON

Berkeley to L3

Oliver frowned, "I never knew MeMa had a daughter. Her name's Eleanor, you say?"

George stood. "This is all wrong. What MeMa said is tragic beyond any definition, but it couldn't happen."

Elizabeth managed to say, "Oliver—"

Oliver didn't wait for Elizabeth to finish. "That's a chilling, cruel assessment, George. How do you support it?"

George laced his fingers over his barrel chest. "I shall explain. Think timeline. MeMa couldn't possibly be talking about events that occurred some 60 years earlier. The twins are currently too young. If we assume, the events of that tragedy occurred in our time, and when we were Freshman at Rice, Tina and Tobin would be in their seventies today."

Elizabeth nodded, and Oliver said, "Right you are, George. What happened? Did MeMa make up a story?"

George tapped is tented fingers and grinned. “In the words of the 14th-century logician and Franciscan friar Occum, the simplest solution is almost always the right one.”

Elizabeth snapped, “So you’re playing the Occum Razor card? You have a simple solution for MeMa’s story?”

“Of course I do. I’m surprised you never asked the question. MeMa must be able to time travel to our future.”

She stood and countered, “George, I’m mad enough to spit. Future Time travel? Is Time Travel going to be our ‘go-to’ solution to every problem?”

George feigned hurt feelings. “You deny the possibility?”

She shouted, “Deny it? No, we’ve experienced too many time-travel events since my personal twining experience on L2.

Oliver put a hand on Elizabeth’s knee. “Don’t let the possibility interfere with your thinking. There must be another reasons we get no visits from anyone in our future. It’s not like you to give in to despair.”

George put his cup down and looked into the eyes of both of his friends. “You are correct. We must put the horror of that image of Earth exploding in deep storage for now except as it relates to finding a solution to that problem. If time travel is part of that answer, we need further investigation."

Elizabeth clapped her hands once. "You're right, George, we know how this works, one of us will figure it out, or stumble on to, a solution. At least we have a head start on it." She couldn't keep the sarcasm from her voice. "In a few hours, we'll be on L3 with family and close friends telling them the worst possible news of their future."

"They'll be angry and irrational," George said.

"And in need of support," Oliver said, "but their cooperation is the first step in the solution we seek."

"Well put. Oliver and I have a few things to gather before we go, George. You got my message about the timing of the team's rendezvous on L3?"

ELIZABETH PACED on the patio of her Berkeley home waiting impatiently for Ollie to return from gathering their gear for the trip to L3 and beyond to Torg. While he collected their personal items, she remembered George's suggestion, but she needed to hold those awful images close to badger her in every way possible. The horrendous images reminded her of what she had become. Everyone she knew and cared about had become people with unlimited power. We were now a people with the ability to travel through space-time. We must also become a people who could prevent the total annihilation of Earth. She reviewed her understanding of Evolutis' Second Awakening with seemingly unfettered power. Did development of these abilities portend abuse on the scale that obliterated planets? Would their critical thinking skills and reverence for life also improve?

The concept of time travel was something the scientist in her refused to accept on faith alone. To find a way to use time travel to save the world would test her intelligence, courage, and emotional fortitude.

Frustrated and depressed at her inability to even fathom what that solution might be, she continued her pacing. The fact that her Cohort could survive elsewhere by repositioning to another habitable planet did not appease her. Nine billion Homo sapiens and only god knew how many other forms of life would die within minutes of the attack. All efforts to even imagine a solution failed her. If her group couldn't even dream of a successful strategy, the chances, the greater science community actually finding one, seemed unlikely.

Furthermore, this was home. There had to be a solution for this place. Anger took over, and she threw the apple she'd been munching against the tree, which sent a cat yowling as it leaped to escape.

Immediately, she regretted her outburst. It was a final straw, and she lost the control she had so dearly held on to. She buried her face in her hands and groaned in frustration until the cat, unaware she'd hurled the apple, rubbed consoling figure eights around her legs. "Boots." She picked the cat up and rubbed her chin on its head. "Silkypuss, I'm sorry I threw the apple your way."

She stroked the cat's back and spoke nonsense through the loud purr. A small smile erupted on her face. "Oh, you dear inspirational sweet thing." She scratched the feline under the chin then settled it on a nearby chair. "I have to go now. You, however, have been most helpful. Thank you."

OLIVER APPEARED, and without a greeting, Elizabeth launched into her new idea. "I need your help. Boots just gave me a wonderful idea. We haven't told all the members of the team about what we know of Vald's plans for revenge. The first time I saw the explosion of earth, it removed all rational thought from my mind. I can't imagine asking our people to view the nightmares and then asking them to forget what they just witnessed and ask them to creatively brainstorm a solution. I need to have a solution ready to propose as a point of departure. One that is pure tactics that we all can create and support." She looked at him for understanding. "Does that sound right to you?"

"James would say it's a good business practice to lay out the first few steps and give the dog a bone to chew on. What do you have in mind?"

"Tobin shared one of his wild and crazy thoughts with me a short time ago. As you well know, like Einstein's mistaken theories, they often lead to good science."

Oliver smiled. "You have told me often that a new discovery often runs away on a different set of legs." He tapped her forehead, "And you, my love, just as often find new uses for the wildest and craziest of ideas of others. What does this one look like?"

"That's part of my problem. I need to present Tobin with a hypothetical. I want to hear his thoughts before he's shaken by the image of his world's demise. Am I wrong doing that?"

He pulled her close, and she leaned into him, taking refuge in his strong arms. "Oh, Ollie, how will this all end?"

She kissed him and then spoke to Tobin's mind.

<Meet me at L3 now in full mind-blocking mode for privacy. MeMa is suspicious of Vald intentions and warned me to protect our communication within the solar system. Ollie and I will meet you there.>

ALTHOUGH THEY ARRIVED ALMOST SIMULTANEOUSLY, Elizabeth spoke first. <I want to do this with you before the others arrive. Listen to what I have to say and raise your hand if you have a question or if I say something that doesn't sound right.>

Tobin raised his hand, and she frowned. It was a standing joke that he always had questions, but she didn't have time for shenanigans now. <No fooling around, Tobin. Let me rephrase that. Only raise your arm if I say anything about my assumption is not accurate. >

He lifted both hands. <Gotcha.>

<Again, for security reasons, we'll use mind-to-mind communication only. Okay. Here we go. Ollie, you weigh in, too. First, there is practically no limit to the size of a folded-space-sphere.> She paused for his nod. <And you can make a twenty-

sided pentagonal dodecahedron of any size as well.>

Although her statements were not questions, he nodded nonetheless.

She rubbed her hands together and took a deep breath to steady her voice. Even so, it wobbled. <Tina told me if you wanted to, you could make one, a sphere, just like Disney's Spaceship Earth made from 11,324 equilateral triangles or more. Correct?>

She leaned closer to watch for clues in his expression and spoke faster. <Tina said you could put this inside a sphere and together, they would be indestructible. She also said there would be sufficient room to carry something in the space between the flat surface of the triangles and the outside curve of the sphere because only the corners of the triangles or pentagons, or whatever you use to make the inside structure just touches the outer sphere at the corners of the flat geometric shape. Is that right?>

Tobin said, <Yes, Tina and I experimented with that.>

Elizabeth could see the wheels turning in his mind as he tried to figure out where she was going. <And I assume you could make the spheres large enough so the space between each triangle and the

outer wall of the circumscribed spheres could hold an asteroid one-kilometer wide. If we use a shape with fewer sides, so there was more space between each triangle and the outer wall.>

Tobin's expressions change immediately. He became suspicious. <Hold an asteroid? Whoa, Aunt Elizabeth, I never saw that coming. What the hell do you have in mind?>

<I'm coming to that, Stick with me a bit longer. You already came up with a brilliant idea to use these small areas within the Portal Sphere to launch people traveling to specific places and times. Correct?>

He nodded while he watched her carefully.

<Is it possible for them to function both ways? First as storage space and then, on command, as automatic portals?>

While she waited for Tobin to do the calculations in his head, she came up with another thought. <And how fast can we make the asteroid's arrival velocity?>

Tobin's eyes narrowed.<Oka-a-ay, Aunt Elizabeth, now you have to give me more information here. What are we talking about? I think it would improve my answers if I knew how you plan to use it.> Tobin glanced at Oliver for clues but got nothing.

Damn. Elizabeth didn't want to tell him just yet. She skirted the answer. <Let's just say, and I mean hypothetically, that I needed to blow up a planet. You know, destroy it.>

He grinned. <Oh, well then, that all makes perfect sense.> he lifted an eyebrow at her. <But can't you do better than that?>

Elizabeth put a hand on both Tobin's shoulders and looked deep into his eyes. There was no innocence there. She knew he had been through a lot, often with her, but he had not yet seen the worst of things. She squeezed his shoulders. <I need you to stick with me on this. I will explain all too soon.>

Tobin blinked in acquiesce and stepped back. <Well,> he said, running his fingers through fine blond hair, which immediately fell back over his face. <Default values for arrival speeds are attuned to the speed and velocity of the destination by the person using that portal for travel.> He shook his head. <This is crazy. Are you saying you want to store asteroids in the portals and then deliver them someplace at a given time in history? What would be their destination and how fast do you need them to go?>

She groaned inwardly. Her cheerful, brilliant, almost-nephew was not going to be the same young man when he found out the need for her answers.

She hated what he would learn. How one moment be so right, and the next, it could be so terribly wrong. She wished she didn't have to tell her nephew of her dark thoughts but managed to continue. <About 30,000 miles per hour, if I figured it right.>

His jaw dropped, and his eyes sprang wide. <Wha-a-at? A few mile-long asteroids striking a planet, for example, at 30,000 miles per hour would be an extinction event. Are you serious?>

She lowered her eyes and nodded once. <I am.>

He lifted both palms. <No, no, hang on. We need to change tack here. If you're looking for a sure kill one shot, we change direction and plan on only using one freaking colossal asteroid. He paced. Or rather he took two steps to the left then two to the right. <For the Portal Sphere, I suggest we go with creating an inscribed cube. It's a big box inside a twelve-mile radius sphere that can hold six of these planet-killing sized asteroids.> He raised a hand to his forehead. <God, aunt Elizabeth, I can't believe I'm saying this, or that you're asking me to do it.>

She ignored his last comment, and her voice became cold as ice. <You can do that?>

<Yes, and so can you, or you,> he said, turning toward Oliver, who had been silent throughout the

exchange. It's a simple matter of scale. Make a cubic sphere that fits in your pocket. You've done this before. Then double it, quadruple it, and so on to whatever size you want. A twelve-mile radius portal sphere with an inscribed cube creates six lens-shaped pods about 3.3 miles thick between the cube and the wall of the portal sphere at its widest place. Each lens-shaped pod has a circular base with a 6.6-mile diameter. The six pods are able to carry an asteroid of irregular shape as long as five or six miles and as thick as two to three miles. I suspect each one of those asteroids is a planet killer on its own, but we'll need to check out the numbers with Uncle George to make sure your calculations are correct.>

When Tobin vanished to retrieve Tina, Elizabeth reviewed what they discussed with Oliver. <You heard Tobin. We would only need to launch one colossal asteroid to destroy Vald's homeworld. So why the hell did Vald launch hundreds? Ahh!> She reached up with two hands to pull fists full of hair. <His overkill makes no sense. >

Oliver took her shoulders turning her to face him. <I'll go for the simple answer. Maybe Vald has no idea what it would take to destroy our planet. That would at least explain his overkill. Perhaps

he's not skillful at folding space like Tobin or even knows enough astronomical science to know how to locate and harvest the asteroids he needs. We can blame his actions on pure, stupid hubris.>

Elizabeth chewed on what Oliver had said. Maybe he was right, and she was giving him too much credit. <You know, I've always thought of him as the leader of a few hundred. Perhaps on his homeworld, he has thousands of Seeker-types. The destruction of the earth we witnessed could represent the work of five thousand Seekers, each in their own small sphere, with a single modest house-sized asteroid. Much like China putting thousands to work on a project we engineer and give to mere dozens. Oliver, you need to share your insight and genius more often. Your analysis of Vald's tactic may be spot on, and the overkill supports the idea he wants to kill everyone as fast as possible, so no one escapes his revenge. Let's strap him to a chair and ask him.> She spoke with tongue in cheek, but she'd love to make it real. <I never thought I could tolerate torture, but it doesn't sound so bad when you know someone is about to toss thousands of asteroids at you and kill everyone you love.>

DISCLOSURE

Conference on L3

After what seemed like hours, Elizabeth and Oliver had downed three cups of coffee and had dismissed countless possibilities. Still, they were not satisfied. So much hinged on their success.

"Torg is at a time and in a place the Time Overlords believe is unknown to Vald. Chances are good he won't be able to observe our work or know our plan to stop him from attacking Earth a year from today." Elizabeth reached for a chocolate biscotti and changed her mind. All they did was sit and eat and come up with no solutions. The pressure was killing her. It didn't need to make her fat, too.

"Chances are good? What kind of statement is that?" Oliver ran his hand across his forehead. "Chances? For Pete's sake, that's not good enough."

"I got the information from MeMa and Seth. I don't know how they know, but I trust their judgment. I should have asked if the Time

Overlords included Torg's timeline when they traced Earth's up to and after the awful event."

He sandwiched her hand between his. "And you're saying we are going off on this wild adventure to an earlier time, to this alien Torg planet, located in another part of the galaxy to practice . . . war maneuvers, for lack of a better phrase."

His look bore into her, and she felt his frustration and yes, worry. They were all worried. The plan sounded as ludicrous as any other they had dismissed.

"And when we're finished with all that, we'll return home . . . To our porch . . . to our place and time on the Berkley campus, without losing a fraction of a second?"

She knew the sick look on her face said it all. "Yeah, It's crazy." She nodded and shared a vision of the tree on the Berkley campus bu their home where, from experience, she knew the cat frequently slept on the lowest branch. "See Boots over there? If that cat were watching us, she wouldn't be aware of our departure. From her point of view, we never left. In her mind, we'd returned instantaneously. She wouldn't even blink, and your coffee would still be hot."

Oliver kissed her hand. "So, it's to be time travel to exotic places? We really do have all the time in the world."

Her eyes held his. "Yes, as long as we stay on Torg during that other time until we have a complete solution." She tented her hands under her chin. At this rate they were going, they could be on the other side of the galaxy forever. They had to get Vald to change his plans. The question was how? "We must persuade Vald to enter into a conversation that leads him to change his plans for us and create a working and lasting stalemate."

She drew her eyes from his and gazed down the hill toward the bay and the Golden Gate Bridge beyond. "Are you aware that we now have at least eleven members of our close Cohort who have had their second awakening?"

"Maybe we, as a new species, weren't meant to live close to each other."

"Where did that come from?"

"Remember MeMa mentioned that several of her friends vanished after their second awakening? Possibly they were concerned with the havoc they could wreck working in groups of seven or more and on the timeline with time travel. Or even concern for other biological consequences. You know, like a contagion."

"I see the timeline might be a problem. Hell. Maybe that's what we have. It is a problem. But biological consequences? What's that about?"

"Proximity. Like I said. Imagine if you and I were to take a year's sabbatical at The Chinese University in Hong Kong. How many awakenings could we spawn?"

"That doesn't have to be negative."

"Really? Remember that boy who disrupted our presentation and managed to get next to Shannon and me during a conference on the Rice campus last year? He was only twelve and before he set off a smoke bomb, he killed a security guard just to get into the lecture. Darkwood had abducted and conditioned him for years to be an assassin."

"Kyle, Yes."

"If it weren't for Shannon's adoptive daughter, Chloe, who reset his genome and gave him a new life, he'd be a powerful dark agent for Darkwood today. Both of them, Chloe and Kyle, are part of the group second awakenings I mentioned. Imagine a hundred assassins running amok, unleashing their powers for self-gain. We're an apocalyptic event just waiting to happen."

"Chloe did extensive work on our microbiome. She gave Evolutis the ability to be a self-immunizing species by customizing a CRISPR library of viruses for us to incorporate into our DNA. Why couldn't that be extended to develop a method to control the effects of our proximity?"

"Good thought. I'll bet Chloe could do it, too. Hmm." Elizabeth chewed her bottom lip. "Let's suggest it to Chloe, but not until after we take care of Vald and his plan to blow us all to hell. Her mind's like a rat terrier, and I don't want to go off on a bird walk on such an interesting research project that she forgets it's needed on the number one problem at hand."

"Speaking of bird walks," Oliver said, "we certainly got off track here. What about the solution?"

"What solution?"

"You've got one. I see it all over your face."

Elizabeth took an exaggerated breath and lifted her palms "It's not mine, and it's not a solution, at least not until we make it one. We need a quick consensus. As you know, by using two structures, Tobin put together a stronger framework for his giant sphere. He wanted to use some wasted space where the flat side of the inscribed dodecahedron met the round shape of the sphere. While he was at it, he came up with something I think we can use. I hadn't thought of a way to use it against Vald until I threw an apple at the cat. “You threw an apple at Boots?”

“Not on purpose.”

“Portals?”

Elizabeth laughed. Oliver always repeated stuff when he was confused, and no wonder. With all that was going on, she’d forgotten to tell him about them. “A few weeks back, Tobin invited me to L3 to see his new brainchild. He and Tina had been fighting about Tobin’s girlfriend. You know, Sally, the one he met in Egypt that lived in Australia.”

“Australia?”

She laughed again and took his hands. “Yes, Australia. Tina was wound up about Tobin’s blasé attitude toward proximity.” She lifted his hands up and down. “Ah. Here is an example of what we were just talking about. Evidently, Tobin’s proximity was in high gear when he visited Sally the last several times.”

“Back when Adrianne’s Seekers chased Tina and Tobin, you mean, and the twins got separated. That’s when Tobin first met Sally. Ah, I’d forgotten about his side trips.”

“Well, Tina didn’t, and proximity is more than a side trip. It’s serious. But get this, her main objection was that at some time in our near past, he visited Sally from his future and showed her what he was working on."

"This is getting interesting."

"The content of his notes was his spheres. He'd just learned a new way to fold space to make them better. His notes also included thoughts he had written that later led to his construction of what he calls the space portals."

"A good thing, yes?"

"You'd think. Except, Tobin may have screwed up the timeline. That was Tina's concern."

"Uh oh, why exactly did she think that?"

"When Tobin and Sally met the last time, she, Sally, that is, claims he was older than he is now."

Oliver said nothing.

"Right, the timeline. The issue keeps popping up, doesn't it? It was riddled with riddles, and the timeline seemed less and less stable."

"Well, Ollie, what potential problem in your view did Tobin unleash?"

"Tobin would have to be able to travel into Earth's future."

REVELATIONS

Tobin's massive sphere L3

Holding hands, Elizabeth and Oliver arrived in the center of Tobin's transparent sphere at L3 before the others arrived. Even at a full two miles in radius, the sphere's size was diminished by the vastness of space. It was lost like a speck of sand surrounded by billions of colorful stars shining as bright as the most magnificent and most expensive jewels in a museum exhibit.

<Remember we're going full security so speak mind-to-mind. Tobin ran off to confirm his ideas with George, and they may be delayed.> She began a slow walk across Tobin's floor extending her arm to point out each feature. We have some time to show you what Tobin's space portals may mean for us. This is his first model.> She laughed when she saw him staring. <After you examine the sphere's internal structure of more than eleven thousand equiangular triangles tiling its inside wall, that is. For an economist, you sure do like engineering type

things.> She knew until he inspected the configuration, she would not have his attention.

<It's magnificent, Liz. The reinforcement . . . It's brilliant, and you're quite the docent.>

<You think that's good? Wait 'til you see how we transformed this early concept into our of the portals into our weapon. You might as well get the full tour.>

Inside and off to one side, a small conference area without walls contained a circular table surrounded by everything a think tank would need. Empty chairs awaited occupants. Tobin had filled the sphere half full of dirt and rock, so the sphere had a flat bottom.

Pointing with both hands, she turned slowly. <The internal web of geometric shapes is not wallpapered to the sphere. They only touch it with their vertices, reenforcing the whole sphere and making it virtually indestructible. Tobin hated the idea of wasted space on a long journey and wanted to make use of the area between the flat of the triangles and the curve of the sphere. He discovered if the sphere were large enough, there would be sufficient room to reposition inside the space between the curve of the sphere and one of the triangles. At first, he thought the sector might serve as a small private room for long space voyages.

That's why this model is so damn big.> She laughed. <The first time he tried getting into the tiny space behind one of the triangles he felt so uncomfortable he immediately repositioned out of it and returned to his room at the SPA.>

<Claustrophobia?> Oliver asked.

She shook her head and finger, <Serendipity, Ollie. Serendipity. The next time he had business on the sphere at L3, his attempt to reposition close to the sphere automatically had him arrive in the same small space he'd vacated from the previous time. The exciting thing is this. After he repositioned from the cramped space to where we now stand, he looked back at the limited size of the triangle area he'd just left, he saw . . . Drum roll please . . . A tiny view of his room at the SPA.> She pointed to a lone, lit, triangle behind them. <See that one lit triangle standing all by itself? That's it! That's what he saw, His room at the SPA.>

She bounced on her toes in her excitement and Oliver placed his hands on her shoulders, grounding her and laughing with her. He squinted his eyes and thrust his head forward to see more, and she pulled his arm.

<No, my love, look with your mind.>

<So, here we are in Tobin's first Space Portal, and we've come to an end of the twenty-five cent

tour.> She stopped walking and tilted her head as though hearing something far away. <Hold on, if we're lucky, we should be here in time to see . . . Wait for it. Watch the empty portals close to Tobin's portal.>

On cue, six triangles lit with images followed by six people who repositioned to the conference table.

<This is mind-blowing.> He stumbled as he greeted the new arrivals. <Oops, I forgot about Tobin's flat floor.>

She extended her hand in a mock curtsy. <After Tobin suggested a flat surface to go with the artificial gravity created by the sphere I agreed with him that it's smart to have a well designed up and down in space for many medical and psychological reasons. I also suggested he install the arc of apartment cubes sitting on the flat surface at the end of the circular floor, each tucked against the curve of the interior sphere.>

Seeing the team walk toward them, She sighed,<Ah. But now the time had come, Ollie. I can't put off what we feared of doing any longer. We have to tell our brave band of warriors, her brilliant team of Seekers, what was going to happen to Earth in less than a year unless they were successful. That's gonna be rough.>

<Worse,> Ollie snorted. <It will be hell.>

ELIZABETH SAT at the round conference table in silence watching her family and friends experience the end of Earth video. She watched the horror grow on each face and despised the circumstances that made her part of the experience. Even more so, she hated being responsible for their future.

Tina and Tobin held hands, a testament to their extraordinary closeness. Shannon reached out to Sarah and Chloe, the most recent of the Cohort to have a second awakening and the last of her adoptive children. Although young, Chloe's powers were no less equal to the others. She would be a strong addition to the group. Benjamin and Seth had no change of expression. They stood stoically during playback. Elizabeth suspected they knew of the event before today's meeting. MeMa, who had arrived just before they began, sat opposite Elizabeth, who held Oliver's hand in a death grip while George watched open-mouthed to the same horror the entire group experienced.

MeMa lowered her chin and spoke softly. <Elizabeth, you and Tobin have prepared our facility well. When they have seen everything in the message, they will need time to assimilate the facts,

and they will struggle to confront their emotions.> MeMa tented her fingers and pointed to Chloe. <That one will have many questions.> She held her chin and tapped on her closed lips as she spoke in private to Elizabeth. <We will position coffee, tea, fruit, and loaves of bread on the table in case they are needed. I suspect we will be spending some time in painful discussion and questions.>

As she spoke, Elizabeth examined all the faces make the same transition from astonishment to disbelief, and then to horror and dread. Not surprising and as if on cue, everyone started to speak at once. What they saw was unfathomable.

Shannon slapped the table. <Quiet everyone. For the moment, Tobin, is the sphere blocking intrusion?>

He was quick in his response. <You're concern is well founded. While the answer is yes, the sphere should block intrusion, it would be wise for everyone to continue to use mind communication for the duration of this crisis until we get to our secure headquarters. Is that okay with you?>

The group sat in silence with lowered heads. Although they had witnessed Earth's destruction, questions were slow to override the stark horror of the event.

<When will this occur?> Sarah finally asked the questions that they all wanted . . . Needed. . . To know.

Elizabeth began the explanation. <365 days from this moment, Earth time.>

<Is Vald behind this?>

<Although we have no concrete evidence, we believe so. >

<How?>

<We do not know, but know this; we will create a solution that stops this event from happening. That's why you are all here. We will prevent it. >

Chloe sat with her neck resting on the back of her chair, gazing upward. <Other than being huge, this sphere is different. Any chance this is part of a solution you have in mind? You do have some ideas, right?>

Elizabeth glanced at MeMa in time to catch a fleeting smile. She was right about Chloe. <It is part of our first proposal for a solution, and of course Tobin and Tina get credit. They put it together.> She extended her hand in their direction.

<This is a prototype,> Tobin said, <proof of concept, for a portal system. Today we're going to use it to travel through space and time to a temporary headquarters where we can secretly work on a solution. Once there, we'll be off our solar

system's timeline, meaning we can work as long as we need to come up with a permanent solution to Vald's plans to eradicate us, along with our planet. We will be time travelers. Time will not be a factor because we can always return to this instant.>

Elizabeth could feel the energy in the air. Her band was eager to get started. It was time for the next thing. <Review the brief training overview Tobin provided the instant you entered the portal. Use the word Portal to trigger the review.>

After everyone reviewed Tobin's introduction, applause erupted.

Elizabeth stood and offered a hand to MeMa. <Grab your gear and form a queue behind MeMa. See the solitary top triangle? The blue one with the light yellow castle? When it's your turn to jump in, the castle will appear. Enter that pod, and you will come out at your destination on the other side.>

<The other side of what?> Oliver said from close behind her.

George stood next to Oliver and passed the question on to every mind. <Is that portal's pod set to get all of us to the same place? To the same when and where?>

Elizabeth squeezed Oliver's hand. <Yes.>

<Hold on," Shannon said. <When's when and where's where?"

<In Earth years, 1303. The where is a planet called Torg.>

George's eyes glowed with adventure lust. <That's clear enough for me. Let's go.> He waited for the light change, then stepped into the small space, to disappear.

Elizabeth spoke privately to Tobin. <You go last and take the Portal Sphere to the Maelstrom, the black hole at the galaxy's core, and put it in a degrading orbit. After you make a pocket-sized copy of it, abandon it for a personal sphere. Got it? From the safety of your personal sphere, give the Portal Sphere an extra shove that sends it into the black hole. Once you verify the Portal Sphere is beyond recovery, reposition to the castle's keep on Torg. Do you understand? Keep your copy of the Portal Sphere secure in your pocket until we next need it.>

Tobin nodded. <It's a good plan. Should anyone have the ability to track the Portal Sphere from L3 to the Maelstrom, they'll believe we lost control and died in the black hole.>

<Precisely. Moreover, it eliminates anyone else copying your latest technology> Elizabeth gave him an unexpected hug. <I'm so proud of you, Tobin. Make sure you remember to set the space portal to plunge into the black hole after you're safe inside a

personal sphere located a greater distance away. Promise me you will not take any risks?>

<Other than the ones you put on my to-do list?>

She hugged him once more. <That's for your mom. See you at the castle's square keep.>

FIRST CONFERENCE

Torg 1303 AD

Elizabeth shared a message with her team. <Everyone, our security on Torg is sufficient to speak aloud.>

Tina, Chloe, Tina, and Sarah stood atop the keep's square tower where they strained their eyes looking through the narrow arrow slits awaiting Tobin's arrival. Benjamin, Seth, and Shannon were having an in-depth discussion about some aspect of Tobin's spheres when she headed below to the large dining hall where she knew MeMa, Oliver, and George had already begun preparing for their meeting.

Pleased by the serious discussions, she kept an ear tuned above to Tina, Chloe, Tina and Sarah, youngest members of the team.

"I think he'll be delayed," she heard Chloe say. "I was at the end of the line waiting to enter the space portal, and I saw Elizabeth pull Tobin aside."

Tina added, “I think she was giving him instructions to do something or other.” It was a given that Tina wanted to keep tabs on her brother.

Sarah said, “Did you happen to hear what she told him?”

“It was a private conversation.”

Chloe’s natural suspicion kicked in, “Meaning you were blocked.”

“They weren’t talking to me, so I didn’t try to listen.” Chloe snorted. “I am betting I could have broken through their personal private screen if I wanted to.”

With second thoughts, Elizabeth returned to the top and filled them in. “It’s no big deal. So you will understand, Tobin is cleaning up behind us.”

The trio nodded.

“Don’t worry, you were good to be concerned and share that concern with others.” She smiled at her think-tank army. That’s what her band of warriors needed to be this round. They had to out-think Vald and come up with a strategy to prevent the destruction of Earth. She played with ideas of the possibility for stalemates, but it had not crystallized yet. She hoped her initial plan with Tobin would quick-start the discussion of some cold-war standoff strategy.

“Let’s get comfortable.” Elizabeth assembled the group in the shaded side of the high tower. “Although the temperature on Torg rarely rose above 88 degrees, the sun could feel brutal, especially when the humidity was up. While we’re waiting for Tobin to complete his short mission, Let’s join the others below, and I’ll give everyone a brief orientation.”

After everyone had taken their seats, Elizabeth gestured at the stone around them. “As you see, this keep is a fortified tower within the castle. It is the tallest of four. The other three are cylindrical, and all are connected by walkways. High walled ramparts protect them as well. Nestled within the protection of the four walls is a two-story-high meeting hall. Chose a top room in one of the corner keeps as your own for our stay here, leaving the bottom rooms for expansion should we need more people in residence. By the way, each room comes with a small suite.”

“Nice digs. How long will we be in residence?” Sarah asked.

“Good question,” Elizabeth said, glad of an opportunity to explain. “When we have a solution, we will return to Earth at the exact time we initially departed for L3. In that respect, we will not be here for any time at all.” Hold on, she raised a hand to ward off questions. "That said, if a perfect solution requires five years to accomplish on Torg, so be it. We will be here, in residence, for that length of time."

"So, you're saying as long as it takes," Tina said.

"What does a perfect solution look like?" Chloe emphasized her words.

"One that eliminates the conflict with Vald yet has no impact on the timeline of Earth." "Yes, it will be a challenge, but I have no doubt that our collection of minds is up to it. As a team, we are smarter than any one of us, and we will figure out what we need to with that brainpower."

Elizabeth paused while the group digested the information. They made comments and asked questions of each other. Such activity was constructive, and she was happy to let their minds work. Although she had spoken in terms of years, she fervently hoped it would be less.

"Take thirty minutes to move your gear into one of the rooms. Meet back here so we can continue."

After each team settled into their rooms, they assembled in the dining hall. Platters of simple food had been laid out consisting of flatbreads and fruit that looked familiar, yet different. "Everything is safe to eat," Elizabeth said, interpreting their expressions, "and delicious. Mostly, the baskets are filled with fruits, but some are vegetables. While the Torg people are not feudal in the classic Earth sense, the hominids living here are more like the Native American Plains people. They have made us welcome and have given us privacy. This castle has been here since before their collective memories and may well be the only stone building on the planet. They are happy to have us use it, and in return, we have bartered with them to keep us fed. They tend to be reclusive, and I doubt you will see much of them." She waved a hand. "We have a problem to solve, and the best way to attack it is to turn you loose for brainstorming I know it will be difficult to avoid getting bogged down with details but for now, look at the big picture and let's have some goals."

She turned to Oliver and MeMa. "While they are working on that, Tobin has made some suggestions he asked me to pass on to you for discussion. First, however, there is an aspect of this planet that has me in a quandary. I find the fact that Torg, this planet, is inhabited by a human-looking species is somehow suspicious. I'm not sure how different they may be from us. That will make for a fascinating field study after we achieve our immediate goal. Okay, Tobin."

He stood, and placed an oddly shaped sphere on the table and announced, “This sphere has been sized to allow you to view its properties. Know that my current calculations will require a similar sphere, one we plan to use on our mission, with have a six-mile-wide outer diameter. Pass it around while I introduce some aspects to you.”

Elizabeth liked his lecture technique and beamed imagining him speaking to graduate students about his new Quantum Spheres made from space folding. “Around the outside of the cube, 6 giant lens-shipped portals await their asteroids.”

Watching their enthusiastic examination of the miniature portal sphere, he almost wished he had made one for each member of the team.

CHLOE ASKED, “How do we get an asteroid of the size you mentioned inside one of the 6 lenses?”

Tobin dryly replied, “With practice. With a great deal of practice. We will operate in teams and use its combined strength to gently move and position each asteroid in its lens pod. The spheres are not balloons. Standing inside there is a way to gently poke three fingers through the wall of the sphere and make an ever-widening opening that becomes large enough for both hands to stretch apart until the hole is as large as you need.”

Sarah frowned, "That's it?"

Tobin replied, "Once the object is inside, you use your fingers to coax the edges of the opening closer. At a certain distance, the sphere completes the process by snapping the edges of the hole together sealing it."

Sarah's chin dropped.

Tobin said, "I'll be demonstrating this process several times. It is easier to learn this technique than it is to reposition ourselves through the sphere's wall."

Elizabeth said, "Tell them how we manage to reposition through a wall of folded space."

Everyone leaned a bit closer to get the science behind of one of the new skills they have often done but never understood.

Tobin shrugged, "I've given this some thought. The first dozen times I repositioned in or out of the sphere was scary as hell. I had no idea I'd live through the experience, and you guys have been brave to trust me on that." He glanced at George who nodded slowly.

Tobin continued. "I believe the mind gets us through the membrane of folded space exactly as we will get a three-by-five mile asteroid through folded space except our mind controlled repositioning is super fast. We cannot see it happening because," he glanced at George, "it takes place in a different dimension."

George laughed and clapped his hands twice.

Tobin smiled but refused to laugh. "Really, guys, when you see this done and after you have tried it yourself, you will agree that making a hole large enough for a three-by-five mile asteroid is easy."

Sarah didn't skip a beat and said,"I take it we will deploy the asteroids from the sphere's pods somewhere high over our target, but what makes the asteroid leave the pod and hit its target at the speed you mentioned?

He shrugged, "According to George, we owe that ability to load and link to the theory of Quantum Entanglement.

Hearing several audible groans, Elizabeth stood. "Are you forgetting how you learned to develop your new skills? You all have one thing in common. Each of you has had their second awakening and the new powers that go with that. Imagine the toddler who just witnessed its mother sprint by. What could you say to the toddler to make it understand your confidence that it will soon outrun the parent? Well, you have my confidence that you will learn how to do all the things we shall require of you. We are Evolutis. Enjoy the possibilities."

TORG ORIENTATION - PART 1

Safe Altered Timelines

The cool of the early evening had the assembled band adjourn to the large patch of shade in the square the rampart's corner. A breeze wafted up from the near-by sea, comfortably cooling them. Slabs of stone at the base of the wall made ample seating and MeMa used her power to reposition a stone that would hold three adults sitting together in front of the group. She smoothed her long black Victorian dress over her knees and the small Cohort settled in for the next session.

With her arms raised wide for emphasis, the ancient woman, with centuries of knowledge, began. "This place has long been the center of our galaxy for time travel research. Its name, Torg, is the acronym for the formal name of the team of Watchers assigned to monitor time travel. *Time Overlords Research Group*."

Seth winced. "The title *Overlords* is a bit much, but it is a very old title, as you will soon understand. If the record of our efforts to save Earth is ever written, Torg would make one hell of a backstory. So, bear with me, in what I am about to share might clear up what we mean by needing a *perfect solution.* For convenience we will use current Earth time for local Torg time. Since travel for us, even to this side of the galaxy, is essentially instantaneous, that convenience has real meaning. If we were to look at Earth from here on Torg through a telescope, we would be seeing Earth as it *was* about 60,000 years ago. That's how long it takes light to get here from Earth."

Elizabeth laughed at the expressions of her Cohorts Even though she knew they were savvy to intergalactic distances, they were caught by surprise. Their mouths open like trout.

"Give them more Torg backstory, MeMa."

"We chose to return to 1303 AD for this trip because by now, the planet Torg had already served as our time travel research facility for some fifteen centuries prior to this date."

"Are you saying the time research project began in 200 BC? Then, why choose that date?" Chloe asked.

"Indeed. 200 BC." MeMa scanned the group. "Any ideas why we chose that date?"

When no one ventured a guess, Seth lifted his palms. "I was among the early historians who were interested in early religious trends, especially the monotheistic movement, which I personally find fascinating, and since I already had a deep interest in time travel as well, it was a logical match. It did not take long, however, to realize the potential dangers and problems some individuals could create with the possibility of time travel."

A very somber MeMa picked up the thread. "Remember, time travel as an individual activity is only possible to individuals who have had their *second awakening*, or rising, as some call it. While the first awakening gives us repositioning and vizing skills, as well as intellectual skills like manipulating and folding space, you all know the *second awakening* gives us so much more, the merging of our mind to the greater mind, he folding of space, and the ability to travel in time. It has been a dream of many for centuries, yet people did not grasp the implications, the consequences, the ramifications, of single acts to future generations. It was not until several such disasters were *narrowly* averted, and I do mean narrowly, that seven of the most powerful Seekers formed a group of *Watchers* to monitor the negative side unbridled time travel.

"What happened?" Chloe leaned forward from her bench. "What prompted the watch?"

"Some fool thought he should do something about the Black Plague," Seth said. "He released a bacterium he thought would minimize the illness. In fact, it spread the disease, killing off countless generations who might have done miraculous things."

"Edward Jenner was almost killed in a street altercation with a traveler. Would we then have had a small pox vaccine? Perhaps. People wanted to go back and kill off Hitler, which sounds good on the surface, but the complications—" Seth stopped and slapped his hand on his forehead. "All well meaning? Of course, but the tragedies would be endless." He waved his hands "Enough. Look at *our* situation. We have the power to go back in time and kill Vald. It may be difficult to believe, but by killing him, we could unleash something worse. Our solution requires preventing the destruction of Earth and creating a lasting stalemate."

"These watchers," Sarah asked, "when did they get organized?"

Seth glanced at MeMa, who hesitated before answering in her own enigmatic way. "I can only say they exist, not when they were first functional. I am not at liberty to share more than that with you. Some periods in the timeline are better observed than others."

Sidebar conversions erupted and she waited. When it quieted, she continued. "Our community, long attuned to total freedom, began to sarcastically call the watchers, *Time Overlords*." As she spoke, she repositioned a small low table with a mug to her elbow. She took it and drank thirstily pointing to another larger wooden table lined with mugs and flatbread that followed it. "Once again, locals living nearby have left refreshments for us. The water is from an ice-cold well in the corner of the castle courtyard." After giving Elizabeth a sidelong glance, she raised her mug in toast. "Slainte. Let's take a short break. Help yourself at the other big table."

WHEN THE COHORTS REASSEMBLED, Seth continued his tale. "To prevent mishaps . . . perhaps disasters . . . the Overlords established rules for time travel." Seth had brought his mug with him and carefully set it on the floor next to where he sat. "Here is how it worked. If you limit yourself to gleaning, meaning residing in the mind of someone in your past, you were not monitored by the Overlords. Gleaning basically allows you to see and hear what is happening, or happened, but you have no control over your host and your host is unaware of your presence."

"So it impossible to alter the timeline when gleaning." Shannon reiterated. "Will we *ever* learn to glean the future?"

Seth stroked his chin and tapped his temple. "This is unclear. Who am I to say what we will eventually accomplish? At this point in time, however," he laughed at his choice of words, "the answer is no. What kind of risk does *gleaning* hold for our history?" Tina asked. "It seems to me there must be plenty of disturbances already. With so many Seekers monitoring the greater mind for troubles, they must be creating their own kind of fracas of their own. Is that a concern for the Time Overlords?"

"Yes, we take that into consideration."

"Let's look back at the past, where we *can* go for sure and pretend that there is more for us there beyond plain gleaning." Sarah held her hands out. "Let's *assume* there is interaction. Suppose someone makes a mistake . . . like rescuing their Great, Great Aunt Myrtle from a burning stake, put there by the hands of an angry mob of people who condemned her for witchcraft?"

Groans sounded around the room. Aunt Myrtle wasn't a favorite with the group and kind thoughts were suspiciously missing. Sarah frowned at her siblings. "It could happen."

"Your question's a good one and it moves us closer to understanding Torg. Something similar actually occurred. One of our gleaners happened across a distant relative being burned for witchcraft. She presented an appeal to the Time Lords."

Tina jumped in. "How could they even consider—"

MeMa held up both hands. "Please. We may have all the time in the world, but until we get a solution to Earth's problem, I am not interested in wasting our time on these speculations beyond the fact that this kind of situation plays into our job here at Torg. But to put and end to this speculation, I will say the Time Lords knew the Seeker making the appeal. He was a true historian who'd spent months pursuing the woman's single life thread for consequences. His records were meticulous, precise. He'd observed and re-observed the burning of his ancestor and found a solution, which he presented to the Overlords. According to him, there was a moment that existed during the death-by-fire-trial where the assembled witnesses could not clearly see the victim. He suggested they reposition the accused out of the fire while simultaneously replacing her with the body of a dead woman taken from a nearby community burial pit. All the records of the accused woman would attest to her death at the stake, although in reality, he would save her."

MeMa glanced about the group expecting questions. Not hearing any, she continued. "The Seeker's plan also included removing her from Earth's timeline and resettling her in a different planet in our galaxy, eliminating any chance of contamination of Earth's timeline. The Time Lords were new to their work and therefore inexperienced. They could not find fault with his argument."

"Wow. He was probably in love with her." Sarah studied Benjamin's face for clues. "The plan *sounds* foolproof. Why does it feel like something went wrong?"

MeMa gave her a knowing half smile. "Hindsight is easy. Even though he kept her safe on the other side of the galaxy, his logic was flawed."

Elizabeth listened as intently as the others. It was a story she had not heard. Did MeMa's face soften with tale or was it a trick of the rearrangement of her many wrinkles?

"While the man's immortality allowed him to think of it as a routine five-hundred year project, he didn't factor in the fact that the instant they allowed him to switch her from the fire, he had, in fact, significantly changed the timeline. Furthermore, his change made subtle changes in the timeline of any place he visited, including, Earth. We now know that by granting him permission to change his timeline, the future of Earth changed."

"Of course," Shannon said. "He was forever affected by her survival. It changed him. It changed his decisions about everything, no matter how small. No wonder we never get visitors from the future."

In a low voice, Tina said, "And if we did we wouldn't even know it. We wouldn't be aware of any changes to our timeline or our future because it would seem a natural sequence of events to our life, even though in fact, our lives may be a part of the consequences of *his* actions."

"The woman is buried beyond the courtyard. She died in the arms of the man who saved her after many happy years." MeMa paused for dramatic effect. "Here is my point. This single act of mercy, with no *apparent* ramifications, as long as the woman was hidden away on this planet so far away from Earth, in fact *has* changed your future. That single act cascaded through Earth's timeline and finally set into motion the up-coming destruction of Earth."

After positioning about the late round table next to the castle's kitchen Seth and Oliver passed out cold bottles of non-alcohol ginger beer. MeMa looked at the label and frowned. “This is purely medicinal, right guys?”

Oliver and Seth looked at one another and shook their heads. Ollie said, “I told you they would miss the point. You owe me ten dollars if you ever get to see money.”

Elizabeth checked out label on her bottle and laughed. “You guys are too subtle. You brought two cases of a brew from the 23rd century.” Her chin quivered and she took a swig.” Wiping a tear from her cheek, she said, this batch was capped after the pending end of Earth.”

Seth added, “Elizabeth has good eyes, but to set your hopes to possibilities, a pair of unnamed Time Overlords obtained this contraband to let you know that all of us are prepared to help you through this conflict so you can enjoy the fruits of Earth’s future.” He raised his bottle and shouted, “To possibilities and safe altered timelines!”

TORG ORIENTATION - PART 2

Work on a larger planet

Walking the long ramparts that connected the four keeps, Tina examined the two moons overhead. "Are they the same two moons from your second awakening?"

Chloe brushed off the question with a shake of her head. "Aren't you worried about Tobin? You haven't mentioned him since we got here. Where is he?" Although he was her brother as well, it was still a newly acquired relationship. She wasn't connected at the hip with him the way Tina was. A figure of speech, maybe, but Tina always knew where he was. Without admitting it, whenever she couldn't see him, she worried. Even if it sounded like she blew it off, Chloe knew better.

"Why worry this time? He's always doing some stupid risky experiment. I'd probably have ulcers if I always knew what he was doing."

Chloe had to agree with that was true and was glad he wasn't her responsibility. "He's probably taking a fly-by in his personal sphere around these two moons just to check them out."

Seth lifted his chin toward the opposite rampart. "He just popped in and is talking with Elizabeth again."

Chloe saw the relief in Tina's face and smiled. "What are they talking about?" She lifted a hand. "Oh no, I'm not going to listen in." Yet, even so, she paused and tilted his her head. "He's safe, and I have stuff to do, that's all that's important." She vanished.

WHEN TINA STARTED for her room, Elizabeth looked up from her conversation with Tobin called her to join them. Good, she wanted to know what was being discussed.

"One of the possible solutions we're considering is to create a modification of the space portal to use it to deploy or shoot for lack of a better word, asteroids at a planet." Elizabeth laid a hand on Tina's shoulder. "George has some questions for you. Could you two put your heads together with Tobin and see what you can come up with while the rest of us brainstorm other aspects of this problem.?"

Elizabeth was not only Tina's mentor but more than that, she was her beloved honorary Aunt. She would swim through the gates of hell for her if she asked. Hopefully, it wouldn't come to that. Without hesitation, she said, "Sure."

WEARING their serviceable tan hooded robes that had somewhere along the way become their uniforms, the trio looked like three monks. While it was a first visit to Torg for everyone, George assumed the role of a guide when they appeared at the castle's courtyard at the terminus of the ocean trail.

"Torg's just shy of being twenty percent larger than Earth." He pointed to the forest on their left and the rolling foothills behind the castle. "Notice the lower trees and low mountains due to the stronger gravitational pull?" He watched Tobin throw a stone down the path and eying the distance. "How did it feel?"

"The throw? Short." He picked up another stone. "And heavy. I'll bet the temperate zones are wider here as well, right?"

"Most definitely. Good critical thinking, Tobin. There are other differences too. Elizabeth suspects the local plants have some genetic variations, and the higher land masses aren't from tectonic plate shifts, but from extensive coral and volcanic build up, much like the Hawaiian Islands."

Tina waited for George to shake a small pebble from his shoe. "You mean this is a world of subtropical archipelagos?"

After replacing his shoe, he brushed the dirt from his hands. "You got it, but I want to know more about the native people, like what's with the Earth-like description Elizabeth gave the mentioned?"

Tobin, just as curious, searched all directions as they walked. "Do you think we'll encounter any Torg along the way?"

"No idea, except," George paused and waggled a finger, "the existence of Cato's Followers and Vald's Followers prove the species of hominid we call Evolutis is not unique to Earth. Although we know them from Earth, it now appears they are both from some other planet, Vald is from Spes and Cato's, well, we don't know. We just know he set off across the universe with his people to find his ancestors. We may only be the latest in a galaxy that has been home to a species that may have existed for millions of years. Are the Torg of our species or sub-species? I don't know yet, but I intend to find out."

He looked up into the sky then back to Tina and Tobin. “What does that larger moon tell you about this place?”

The three studied the two red-hued satellites of the planet. The second one had just risen and the first, although low in the horizon was halfway across the sky.

Tobin glanced at Tina and after a flash of a smile said, “Neither appears to have been hit by many asteroids. I also suspect the moons were recently acquired by passing too close to Torg.”

“Tina, Any observations from you?”

She sucked in her cheeks. “I’m guessing here, but Elizabeth has shown an interest in your portal sphere, Tobin, and I heard her mention asteroids several times. If that means we’re soon going asteroid hunting, I am guessing we’ll have to go farther from the Torg’s sun than we would in our system to find asteroids.”

George wiggled his eyebrows at her, and she laughed. “I take it that’s a yes, Uncle George.”

It never ceased to amaze him how quickly the twins took in information and rearranged it to see how it could best be used. From folding space to spheres, from dodecahedrons to space portals, their minds just kept churning out ideas. “Elizabeth has had several conversations about them with me, as well. Hmm. Asteroids hunting, huh?"

Tina's face grew dark. "It's payback time, and it's the best weapon we can put together given our existing toolset."

George put his hand on Tina and Tobin's shoulders. "Okay, guys, everyone here is expecting us to return within two hours for our meeting. I propose we skip the walk to the beach and since we agree that portals and asteroids are in our future, let's get some piloting time in and see just how far we have to go for some kick-ass rocks. After all," he struggled not to laugh, "if it takes us a week, we can always jump in time to return to our next group meeting."

CREATIVE REACTION

Torg Castle's Garden

Elizabeth and MeMa strolled the courtyard garden next to the large meeting hall while the others finished unpacking their personal gear in their suites.

"Daughter, you were wise not to assign rooms. They have begun to self-select their teams." MeMa walked with her hands behind her back and occasionally bent to smell a flower. "I do not find much fragrance in these things." She jerked her chin toward a patch of pink blooms. "It seems to me our teams need small distractions from the work and responsibility we've given them. What will be your distraction?"

"I plan to run in the woods, MeMa. And you? I've never seen you at play."

"Interesting choice of words, Daughter. I like to shoot my arrows when I run through the woods."

That was a surprise. Elizabeth never heard MeMa even mention archery. "I have a Japanese friend who combines meditation with the bow and arrow."

MeMa laughed, a surprise in itself. "I run against tree trunks and shoot the eyes out of rodents."

Elizabeth's eyes grew large, and she shook her finger in the air. Was that a joke from the ancient woman?

MeMa bent to a purple blossom with a long yellow tubular center and frowned. "Humph, there's no fragrance here either. In your opinion, what's our next step?"

"Not to go running when you're playing in the woods."

MeMa harrumphed.

"We still need to put them in teams. There are eleven of us, and three teams of three should work. I think you and I should remain apart from the groups to serve as monitors and backup for any unforeseen eventualities." She lowered her chin and spoke privately to MeMa's mind. <By unforeseen eventualities, I mean we should monitor local space for intruders and be prepared to reset the timeline in case it's required.> She paused and made direct eye contact with her matriarch. <And then there's the matter of you.>

<Me? What about me.>

<I believe the team needs to know more about you. It will give you an opportunity to fine-tune the concerns you have for our success.>

GEORGE CHORTLED and rubbed his hands together in anticipation. "I know this may be short notice, but what kind of sphere can you make for us that would be suitable for a quick fly-by of this solar system?"

Returning the grin, Tobin dug in a deep pocket. "I keep a few small copies of spheres handy for quick resizing. We'll use this one."

George leaned forward. <Good choice, the one that looks like a Ping-Pong ball.> He didn't know one from the other, but if Tobin chose it, it would be just dandy. "Go ahead and blow it up. Oops, sorry. Bad choice of words."

WITHIN MINUTES, the three explorers were traveling through space. "This is really Spectacular," George said, gazing in all directions at the heavens, "but I never get over the feeling I'm going to drop out the bottom. I don't suppose you could do something about that."

“You sound like Tina now. I’ll put in a flat floor with some carpet next time,” Tobin teased. “Will, that work?”

George nodded. “Perfect. Now, let’s hear your plan.”

“Right. I thought we could chart our initial course of exploration on a line away from the gigantic black hole at the center of the galaxy, through Torg, and on toward the galaxy’s outer rim. That path will also give us a good fly-by of this system’s Goldilocks region.”

George chuckled. “A zone around the sun too far out would be ice and any closer it would be steam. Therefore, it’s just the right zone where a planet could have water. Goldilocks, very funny.”

“Right,” Tobin said. It’s going to be Sub-light speed cruising and searching for asteroids in the Goldilocks region . . . until we find it boring.”

Tina socked his arm. “No hot dog driving. Swear you won’t run us into something just for fun.”

“If I do, you know the sphere will protect us. With your eyes closed, you wouldn’t know if we collided. We’ll simply bounce away.”

Tina ignored his reminder. “These asteroids we’re looking for are small, right? I mean less than ten miles or so.”

Tobin waved his hand in dismissal. "This expedition shouldn't be too difficult. We'll simply locate an asteroid belt close to a gas giant planet. The giant will be farther from the sun than the asteroid belt and the region between the rocky belt, and the sun isn't all that huge. Then that's where we'll find the rocky planets. Meanwhile, we'll slow down and pick up a few asteroids."

George asked, "You think that will actually work?"

It seemed far-fetched, but Tobin was known for not speaking until he had thought his plans through. "Why wouldn't it?"

"Because although finding the gas giant won't be a problem, I can't imagine you'll be able to see anything as small as a what?" Tina asked, "A ten-mile asteroid? Without special instruments?"

Tobin grinned and got in her face. "True. Asteroids are small concerning the vastness of the universe. So?"

Not intimidated, Tina stood on her toes, bringing her nose almost to his chin. "Listen, I've learned from Chloe how to micro viz a single protein within a cell." She pulled her chin back. "And that's about the same scale as this freaking solar system to your freaking asteroid."

George chuckled. "And now you know why Elizabeth, herself a microbiologist, asked Chloe to join us on this venture. Such skills could prove invaluable." There were many reasons why Elizabeth was in charge, and they ranged beyond the fact that she could assemble the best team. His favorite was her mind. It was brilliant, and she could make leaps in her thinking to propel them forward.

Tina stepped back and gave Tobin a roundhouse to the arm.

"Ouch."

"Ouch, yourself. Don't patronize me."

George patted each on their shoulder. Although he liked their competitive play, it was time to get serious. The period for their foray into space was running out. "Now, now, play nice. Although Elizabeth mentioned we might think we had all the time in the world, the team's mental and emotional stability will diminish unless we come up with something useful. Meaning we can't vanish from the team for hours at a time and return empty-handed. We need to catch some asteroids to show them it can be done."

He looked both in the eye. "This isn't a game. We will soon tire of looking death in the face."

Tobin sighed. "I hear you. Am I right to assume you have a plan? What do you propose after we find the gas giant?"

"Let's back up a bit," Tina said. "I think we agree that Elizabeth will soon want everyone looking for asteroids, but meanwhile, we're here, in space, right? Tobin, we always look for more than one application in our research or experiments." She extended a palm. "We have the means, motive, and the opportunity to look for habitable worlds while we collect our rock garden, yes?"

Tobin face lit up. "Yeah, you're right. That'd be a good use of our time."

"Won't that slow down our search for suitable asteroids?" George objected.

"Hell no. The Hubble and Kepler telescopes energized our astronomers to search for habitable planets. They've already found more than 100,000 possible candidates for habitable worlds. The only thing that will take time is making a list." Tobin grinned. "I thought I was the only one who saw Evolutis as a species of the galaxy. How about you George?"

"All right, then. I say we mimic what had worked for the astronomers when they searched for super habitable worlds. First, we'll keep an eye out for K dwarf class stars. They're slightly dimmer and smaller than our sun. When we find one, we first see if they have any gas giants, like Jupiter. We know gas giants come in two major types. Some are close to the sun protecting the inner, rocky water planets and some are much farther away and play a different role for gas and ice planets."

"I'm not sure if the word protect is an accurate description, Uncle George, but for our purposes, it should be okay to think of them that way." Tobin rubbed his chin. "It sounds to me like we should be looking K dwarf class stars with the first kind of gas giants, the ones near the inner rocky planets. The thing is, while it is all good theory, there are two problems. One, we don't have the technology needed to identify K dwarfs from a distance. Two, if we found a K dwarf star and got close enough to its system to see a gas giant near it, there's no way we could see or find the inner planets without the technology."

Tina tugged at his sleeve. "I figured we'd be doing something like this, so I have a mental image to share with you."

"You figured? How the heck did you do that?"

"Does it matter? Shut your eyes." She gave them a moment. "Got it?"

Tobin paced in front of them before responding. "I got a beautiful viz that looks like a video loop of a star." His eyes grew large. "Is that a real-time view of the closest K dwarf in this part of the galaxy?" He went nose to nose with his sister and his voice lifted in utter disbelief. "Where in the devil did you get this?"

Tina could not contain her giddy laughter. "I didn't get it from a YouTube or a National Geographic TV show, I can tell you. I located it from Hubble records and used the 8-inch reflecting telescope I built on my own for Girl Scouts several years ago. You now have a real-time record of the full-color image in your mind. With this K dwarf star on file in your mind, you can compare its light spectrum with other stars to see if you found another just like it."

"Are you saying your mind is comparing the K dwarf star's light spectrum with the star's light spectrum we encounter like a facial recognition app?"

"Exactly, Sir Physicist."

Tobin furrowed his brows. "You knew we would decide to go on this off-the-cuff trek today, Tina. And you knew the direction we would choose would put us near this particular star system? So come clean. Just how far into the future can you see?"

“Just far enough to know when to duck. Tina put her hand on Tobin’s shoulder. “Actually, it was just good, old-fashioned, de-duck-shun.”

Tobin groaned. “That is the worst pun I ever heard, but I forgive you. Okay, George, hang on. It’s fishing season.”

A SUPER HABITABLE WORLD

Deep Space

After an hour of charting their initial course of exploration away from the Maelstrom, the gigantic black hole at the center of our galaxy, the three were content to play the traveler and spent their time stargazing.

George rubbed his chin and spoke privately to Tina. <Why did Tobin say it would be boring?>

<Aside from the fabulous view of *distant* stars, we won't see much anywhere close to the sphere and that's where we'll be searching. The parallel important thought is that it's what Chloe experienced looking for specific types of proteins in her body. Just as she learned to find molecules, whose distance from other objects in the cell were proportionally about what we'll find looking for asteroids.>

<Ah, of course, The relative distances. I should have realized. This knowledge, and skill you presented in the viz for identifying K dwarf stars with potentially habitable systems, will facilitate

our search. Excellent, it will help the others too. That will take some pressure of the mission and the analytical geometry thinking required should keep our minds sharp.>

Tobin sat on the flat floor he had contrived at George and Tina's request. "Space is space. Nothingness. So, tell me Tina, let's hear more about the technique we'll use in viewing this emptiness?"

"Just *in case* we decided to begin prospecting early, this is what Chloe and I came up with."

Tobin grinned. "We *do* need to discuss your prediction skill."

Ignoring the crack, she said, "Okay, lay on the floor like you were making angels in the snow. Make sure you stretch out as far as you can."

"Like we used to in real snow when we lived in Stockholm? On clear nights the galaxy was superb, but to clarify what we're doing, this will help us find planets in all this these millions of miles of empty space?"

Tina slid away from him to make room for George and they all spread their arms and legs wide. "Tobin, rotate the sphere so the target star is directly overhead and we're perpendicular to the system's orbital plane of planets. Imagine a laser coming out of your navel. That's your pointer for hitting the K dwarf's planets."

He rotated the sphere slowly and when he made boy noises like a laser gun, he said, “We’re aligned.”

Tina gave her best classroom lecture voice. “Lacking the technology of powerful telescopes, we have to engage our minds. Open your mind and attune your microbiome to the star’s solar system. It may take a while, but once attuned, the brain is able to learn from the mind how to see what’s there regardless of the scale. Once you have done it a few times, it won’t take as long. Don’t try to force your concentration, simply focus on seeing the solar system as your mind, the collective mind, sees it.”

After a few seconds she added, “Now, close your eyes.” She waited. “Keep them closed and imagine the K dwarf star I shared with you. Make it larger in your thoughts then you rationally know it appears from this distance. Remember the image of it we shared moments ago and make the star a memory from that image. Keep your eyes closed and keep the image of it in your head. All you should see is the star. Let me know when other objects appear.”

George spoke first. “I’m not sure . . . I think I see a fuzzy point of light on the lower right side.”

Tobin replied. “Me too but if I open my eyes to look at it, it goes away.”

She jumped to her feet. “Sorry, I forgot. This will improve your reception.”

They gawked at Tina as she removed her robe.

“Try this. Nudity is best because it exposes more of your skin’s microbiome, but you can keep on your tighty whities. I defer to any degree of modesty you possess. After you learn to macro view, your clothes won’t be as troublesome.”

George and Tobin looked at each other before they loosened their belts and removed their robes. “That’s it for me,” George said.

Tina looked up from the floor and saw their hesitation. “Come on guys, we’re all family. I’m wearing as much as Brandy Chastain after she kicked the winning World Cup penalty point and the whole world has seen the David Beckham’s underwear ads.”

“Not so much,” George and Tobin said in unison.

With aid of the Tina’s viz, the honed in on a likely K dwarf. Their minds built had built three small gray dots from the faint signals of distant planets.

“We’re getting closer to the star’s elliptic plane. Adjust the sphere to keep us perpendicular to it,” Tina instructed. “Spatial relationships will be better.”

After adjusting their approach with a measured repositioning, Tobin returned to sub-light speed finally stopping when they felt could clearly identify the system's rocky asteroid belt.

George folded his arms behind his head, and stretched while admiring an emerging band of tiny points of light etched across the black sky in a brilliant swath. Space travel was great to his way of thinking. It was too bad they had to get back to the others and face the reality of why they were here in the first place. That sobered him fast. "Any guesses about how far it is to the system's sun from here? What do you think, are we about as far out as far out as Torg is from its sun?"

"I'd say we're within three hundred eighty million miles," Tobin said. "Give or take a few."

"Show off," Tina said. "But really Uncle George, the calculations are pretty simple. K dwarfs are about 50% to 80% the mass of our sun so, assuming an average diameter for that category of star, we calculate 65% of 432,450 miles or approximately 280,000 miles. Then imagine how many suns, placed side by side would be needed to line up between the sun and the ring of asteroids, and there you have it."

"Close, enough," George said. "What's next?"

Tobin pointed toward the arc of points of reflected light on his right. “Let’s check out the asteroid belt.” Then, as though tethered to the star, Tobin took the sphere through a gigantic arc, keeping the floor of the sphere perpendicular to the imaginary tether. Willing to be guided by Tina, he continued to move the sphere through that arc until they were again perpendicular to the star’s elliptic-orbital plane.

George’s face took on a suspicious frown. “I think I know where you’re going with this. By moving in an arc keeping our face perpendicular to the system’s ecliptic, the signal from the system to our microbiome raises or falls based on how perpendicular we get.”

Tobin smiled. “Right, if you were viewing the system from its edge, the signal from individual planets would be the weakest.”

Tina snapped her fingers. “Exactly. We it would be more difficult to make out individual stars.

She turned to George. “Each time we feel we have the strongest signal from the system, Tobin repositions us closer to the plane of the elliptic and it becomes easier to see. That should lead us closer to the rocky asteroid ring, *if* one exists.”

George's bushy eyebrows fell. "The best I can see right now are tiny points of light, so how will this work?"

"There's a bit of a learning curve. It took Chloe several days and several tries before she worked it out, but I think if the three of us can do this working as a group, and then we can transfer our cumulative skill and knowledge to the other teams."

George put his hands on their shoulders. "Well done. You guys just outlined an exciting day." He laughed.

"What's so funny?" Tina asked.

"I never imagined I would ever say something like *we'll need to time travel if we expect to get back by dinner*. An observer in this time line might wonder if we got lost on a bird-walk. It must look like we're wasting precious time." He swooshed his hands in the air. "But that's old-time thinking. We really do have all the time in the world."

Tina's stomach growled and she turned red. "Only *if* we had packed lunches."

"Well, I love the idea of finding habitable planets and considering where asteroids tend to hang out, we should be able to kill two birds at one time. Hang in there, Tina. We'll be home for supper." Tobin tapped his palm on a fist. "I agree. This is gonna be fun."

COVERT ACTION

Torg Castle's Meeting Room

Elizabeth sat with Oliver at the large round table, waiting for everyone to assemble for a working dinner. She planned to take notes on how each small group entered the huge dirt-floored meeting hall and look for logical groupings of the teams she would name shortly. Her band of space travelers had spent the past three hours engaging in a peer-based, social Q&A session. Oliver preferred the expression 'late-night dormitory bullshit sessions.' In the meeting coming up, she would help them focus their discussions.

By the time everyone gathered and selected a seat, Elizabeth had worked out the last couple of unresolved group assignments. That was the easy part. She stood, and the Cohort fell silent.

<I trust you had some productive conversations after you settled in.> With their nods, she added a housekeeping detail. <In spite of the earlier assurances we were safe from intrusion from Vald and his kind, MeMa and I think all conversations

and discussions must be mind-to-mind from this moment forth for security purposes. Although we believe this is a secure place, we can't be certain. Vald may somehow be observing and or listening. It is also feasible, although not likely that there are spies among the Torg people. Except for our group, make sure you set your mind to block all others from your thoughts.>

MeMa lifted a single finger, indicating her desire to speak. <We split you into three . . . uh, tactical groups.> She glared at Elizabeth and raised one eyebrow. <Meaning . . . > She waited.

Elizabeth gave her a funny look. <Meaning you guys who are the ones who are going to get this job done.>

<Thank you. We could have said that in the first place.> The shake of her head spoke volumes of her opinion of military jargon. <We had many reasons for composing the teams the way we did. Initially, we took your general knowledge, your temperament, and your abilities, into consideration, but to be sure the groups functioned at optimum effectiveness, we looked for more.>

Elizabeth liked the manner in which MeMa's gaze drilled into each of the Cohort band at the table. She had their attention and their anticipation. She picked up MeMa's thread. <That you are all

friends is a given. That each of you could work with anyone here is also a given. The work requires an optimum collaboration-productivity grouping.> When they all looked at each other, she contained a chuckle. She could just imagine the assortment of thoughts running through their heads ranging from who's in my group to when is a microbiologist preferred to a physicist? They all excelled in the brain department. Harvard and the NSA would kill for any one of them, but they were her team. They were in the palm of her hand, thank god, and she would use them.

<We left your gear in the center of the courtyard and had you select your own rooms for a reason. What we observed confirmed our expectations. You self-sorted yourselves into threes, and each group elected the top rooms in one of three available keeps.>

Elizabeth loved this cluster of people. They were her family, and there was nothing she wouldn't do for any one of them. At this moment, however, they were more than family. They were Earth's best chance for survival. She believed in them, and they all knew they had her confidence. This was for a good reason. <Our group, is unique in that all of us have had our Second Awakening. It means the magnitude of our thought process is leaps

and bounds higher than we could ever have imagined. We are the most significant brain trust that has ever been in one room, and we will use that brain power to save Earth.>

MeMa remained sitting but broke in. <Seth, do you want to speak to this?>

He laced his fingers over his flat stomach and looked directly at each individual present, MeMa and Elizabeth included. <You are all Seekers, which means you are the highest hierarchy of Cohort, but with your second awakening, your mind is connected to all minds, and to the collective mind. This gives you added almost unthought-of powers. When the Time Overlords met to solve a problem, they remained physically separate for security reasons, yet their communication was as precise as if the sat together in this very room. That skill, communication from any distance, is one you also possess. On this journey to stop Vald and save the Earth, you will use it to your advantage.>

Elizabeth grinned. <Thank you for being here with us in person.> She glanced around the table. <I can only imagine the questions racing through your fertile minds, but save them for later. Here are your teams.> She gazed around the table to check that all eyes were on her. <Team Beta is Oliver, Shannon, and George.> She knew as old college chums, their group would be a well-oiled machine and Oliver, and George would keep Shannon from haring off in her own direction. Team Gamma is Sarah, Benjamin, and Seth.>

She heard Shannon say, <If you don't like him that much, Sarah, why'd you sit next to him?>

<Mo-o-o-m.> Her face flushed and Elizabeth choked on a laugh. The two were getting along just fine these days, and since Seth and Benjamin had been friends for centuries, she had no concerns about the compatibility of the unit.

<Team Delta is Chloe, Tina, and Tobin.> The twins had worked together since the womb, and that was not hyperbole. Sometimes, it seemed that Chloe had been born their triplet. Yes, she was well satisfied with her units. <If you will notice, your group also reflects the seating company you chose when you sat for this meeting. I'm not sure if that is indicative of an emerging pre-cognition ability or merely good taste in friends.>

Murmurs erupted, and Elizabeth knocked on the table for silence. <Mind-to-mind. No exceptions. MeMa and I are Team Alpha. We are your back-up in all things. Now, on to the business at hand.> She paused and took in a deep breath. <Saving Earth. To save Earth from total destruction requires two separate strategic actions. The first requires we

create a plan that forces Vald to cancel his plans to destroy Earth. The second force him to meet us in a discussion that results in a permanent military stalemate. I believe we have designed the first part of a perfect plan to deter Vald's impulse to attacking us. Recalling the Cold War between the United States and Soviet Russia in the last century, we will present him with the same model. We will show him how we will blow his home world to smithereens if should Earth be attacked.>

<Meaning what, Aunt Liz?>

Tobin always asked questions, and she realized this was a good one. She often forgot how long ago the standoff with Russia was. <Having developed and used the nuclear bomb on Japan during World War II, with god-awful results I might add, we vowed not to use it again. When the Soviet Union developed nuclear power, we were not sure they supported our same attitude about using that power. US relations with them had grown hot, and their leadership was unpredictable.>

Oliver ran his hand across the back of his neck and brought it around to his chin. <People were on the verge of panic. Some actually built bomb shelters.> He shook his head. <Not that they would have done any good.>

<The fear that we would retaliate, should they use their bomb on us, was the only thing that kept Khrushchev's finger off the red launch button,> Shannon added. <The Kingston Trio sang it loud and clear:

> And we know for certain that
> some lovely day, someone will set the spark off
> and we will all be blown away.>

Elizabeth waited while everyone assimilated the information. Faced with a similar annihilation, Vald will be forced to meet with us to manage a lasting truce. To ensure his presence, today we begin the construction of that deterrence.>

She waited for a reaction but got nothing more than quiet resolution. She gazed around at the ardent faces. Clearly, her team was onboard.

MeMa reminded them of the time frame. <Earth has one year. Because we have jumped back in Torg's timeline we have centuries, should we need them, to create the construction of that deterrence. She smiled broadly. <I do not believe we will need that much time.>

In appreciation, everyone pounded the table with their hands and coffee mugs.

<With input from MeMa and George,> Elizabeth continued, <and with creative design from Tina and Tobin, each team will be assigned a sector of space where they . . . You. . . will search out and harvest asteroids of a specific size. You and your team will travel in portal spheres like the ones you used to get here. Tobin has modified one for each team.

<This is important. Once we give you your sectors, you are not to share that location with any other team.> Not an eye left her face. <Secrecy with a friend is a tall order.> She glanced at MeMa and gave her a tight smile. <Yes, military again. This is for a good reason. If you are captured, or if someone forces his presence into your mind, you'll only be able to give up the information you know, information on your team, but not that of any other. The entire mission, however, will not be compromised. It is not yours to give away.> She shivered. Heaven forbid, that scenario should unfold. <Tobin will share an overview of the mission with you and MeMa, and I will follow with a Q&A after.>

Tobin stood and held out one palm as though lifting a baby bird back into its nest. <I will

demonstrate your sectors.> A black cloud swirled above his hand for a few seconds and then a bright blue sphere the size of a volleyball appeared and floated to the center of the table.

The volleyball split into eight equal sections that slowly pulled away from the sphere's core like a slow-motion explosion. Tobin stopped their migration and let the image linger over the table. <Think of a three-dimensional cake sliced and generating eight equal pieces. Notice the three perpendicular red lines crossing at the center of the sphere? The planet Torg is at that intersection point. The red lines form the edges of the eight equal pieces of the sphere and also represent the flight paths of the three harvesting teams, Beta, Gamma, and Delta. Elizabeth will assign two random sets of numbers defining each team's flight path and slices of the sphere.>

Elizabeth pointed to Tobin's model, and as she did, each referenced item glowed for clarity. <If Team Beta has this axis,> she indicated, <leaving Torg in this direction is designated Beta-plus. The opposite direction is designated Beta-minus. Simple? Three teams, three lines, one center point. Knowing the coordinates of one line, will not enable the enemy to compute the coordinates of the other two lines or of the slices of territory.>

Not wanting questions, she waved her hands sideways. <You will see and understand the geometry of this better in your dream training. Each team will harvest a total of twelve asteroids. Since each sphere is designed to contain six asteroids, your team will create and use two separate portal spheres. You asteroids should be six to ten miles in diameter.>

<Not bigger?> Chloe asked.

<There's no need for it to be any bigger. One portal sphere of that size will be able to house six asteroids of sufficient mass to destroy any planet.> She knocked the table with he knuckles. <I repeat, do not share anything about the two insertion points of the space portals you will learn in your dream training with any other team. You will have to lock that information in your mind from intrusion. Nor are you to share anything about your navigational details to the other team.> She hated this secrecy required of them and knew she was not alone in her feelings. <One more thing. Don't share anything you might encounter during the gathering of the asteroids. This security is the top priority and essential to our mission. None of us can know all the details, that include MeMa and me. To put it in perspective, the mission is designed to achieve our goal even with a sixty-six percent failure rate.>

A collective gasp erupted.

Oliver spoke for everyone. <To see if I have this right if two teams fail, our mission is still safe. Humph. But not necessarily our lives. Did I get that right?>

Elizabeth relented to the roiling questions. <Yes, but it shouldn't come to that. As the dream training will show you, MeMa and I will continually monitor you for danger. Your team will leave Torg in one sphere and fill it with six asteroids. The training will also show you to reposition the filled and fully loaded sphere to some random point in the galaxy. You will program each portal to deliver six asteroids to Vald's homeworld. When a portal is triggered, its asteroid will travel at 30,000 miles per hour toward Spes, ensuring the total destruction of Vald's planet world. The trigger to launch uses a quantum entanglement with Earth in such a way that should Earth be destroyed, all your asteroids will be launched.>

<Okay,> Oliver said. <Then we get in our second portal sphere and go in another direction and repeat the process and get six more asteroids?>

She smiled and to him alone said, <Thanks, Ollie, you were right, everyone needed that clarification.>

Elizabeth leaned forward with her palms flat on the table. <Vald's homeworld, Spes, and his people, the Silva, have long been the center of conflict on this side of the galaxy.

Elizabeth slowly shook her finger at them to emphasize her point. <We must focus on today's mission of harvesting asteroids and position them, so our threat is real. It will Force Vald and his council to negotiate.> She made a fist. <We seek a permanent truce with Vald and his people by threatening the hellfire out of them. Trust as well as belief will be the issues.>

Shannon stood, and MeMa flashed Elizabeth a private message. <Careful. I sense pushback.>

Elizabeth loved and respected her life-long friend and research partner, but knew exactly what the old woman meant.

Flinty eyes locked on Elizabeth, and although Shannon who kept her arms at her side and spoke calmly there was anger to come. <Threaten him, Elizabeth? You really think that can work on a monster that respects no rules and honors no one except himself. Are you delusional? I know the pain he can inflict on families. Vald must be stopped so he cannot wreak havoc on the lives of others and you are saying you want to threaten him? Really?>

Elizabeth lifted her hands to calm her friend, but knew from experience, reason would not stop Shannon until she finished her rant. Although she wanted to move on with her plans, she also knew it was only fair to hear objections and Shannon's thoughts. Given her family's history with Vald, she was entitled to that. She took a deep breath and willed herself to patience.

SHANNON'S RANT

Torg Castle's Meeting Room

Shannon placed her palm on her heart. <While I was on the Sphere with Vald, I got to know several of the men and women of Spes. They are more like us than I thought possible, yet we threaten them as well as Vald with your plan. Why do we consider war with the people?> Her open palm transformed into a white-knuckled fist. <I'd gladly kill Vald right now with my bare hands if he were in front of me.> She paused and looked at her four children, who watched her intently. She turned back to Elizabeth. <More than gladly. It is, in fact, my first choice. The entire people of Spes, are not our enemies.> She sat, folding her arms.

Murmurs flew around the circular table like angry hummingbirds. Elizabeth was not surprised by Shannon's reaction, in fact, she had a certain empathy for it, even though the children were, not hers. She noticed Seth drumming his fingers on the table and privately addressed MeMa. <Do you know his thoughts on this?>

<It's time for Seth to speak.> She lifted her chin toward him. <Tell them. They need to know. It is crucial to the ultimate solution.>

Seth momentarily closed his eyes and then unfolded his long body to stand. <There is a history of Spes I thought would be better addressed during our second action. That is after we had the space portals in place. MeMa and I debated the wisdom of sharing this with you now, thinking its discussion fit in better with the agenda of our peace talks with the Silva once we get them to the table.> He nodded toward Shannon. <I am pleased that your need for blood has not overtaken our natural aversion to taking lives. There is more to the Silva of the Spes planet than the darkness of Vald. He began as a tool of a long-lived elite ruling class that constitutes the council, the governing body that makes the rules. Vald has ingratiated himself to them to the point that he has risen in power. He is no longer a tool. He has become a policymaker. The common people of Spes are far removed from the elite council. As a people, they are like the Evolutis of Earth. As a race, there seems to be one difference. Neither they nor the ruling class seems to have the capacity for a Second Awakening.>

Murmurs and raised hands erupted around the table. Seth held his palms out to hold their questions. <Indulge me in a few minutes of galactic history. MeMa and I once worked with Vald on this side of the galaxy. It was during a conflict between Spes and a planet that fought to secede from their empire. With good reason. The Spes upper crust bullied them, terrorizing them in many ways, from kidnapping to random killings. This was the empire, This was like a hundred thousand years ago. The people were more like early Homo Sapiens than Evolutis. Hmm. That wouldn't be right. Probably more advanced than that. The thing that confounds me is that for all their lack of development, they had space travel. Is it possible they got it from another sentient species, farther advanced?>

Chloe interrupted. <Do you mean to say they looked like early man? Or did they look like us.>

Seth rubbed his chin. <Mostly human. However, the characteristic I had in mind is a difference that forms the foundation of our conflict with the Silva.>

<So our efforts here go beyond our concern for Vald?> Oliver said.

<Until then, we had not realized the Silva, and other planet populations in the Spes empire were different from us,> MeMa said. <Only some of the people in Spes Empire had the ability to awaken. But only the First Awakening, mind you. No one had the Second Awakening. They were limited to

mind-to-mind communication and remote viewing, but couldn't fold space.

<For all that there were not many, during our interaction, Vald discovered we were different. We had powers he and his people did not. You can imagine how he felt about that. He was a general at the time and realized this difference could make his people subordinate to us. This difference presented him with a career opportunity.>

<Another critical element in this drama is that the upper class on Spes had a nasty, centuries-old practice, of taking children from other planets in their empire to serve as slaves on Spes. The Spes upper class controlled the captive by destroying the small portion of their brains that would emerge as what we now call the Snyder's Region. The slaves, therefore, never had a First Awakening. Except for a very few slave favorites who were permitted to mature into Evolutis, the captives remained inferior to the Spes Silva elite.>

<Did the regular Spes people have a First Awakening?> Tina and Tobin had voiced the question in unison.

<I think it safe to say so. Just as on Earth, a few exceptions existed that didn't have to live the theoretical 145 years to attain awakening. But it's important to note that none of the people on Spes or

of the children they apprehended had a Second Awakening. To our knowledge, this phenomenon occurs only in the Evolutis of Earth.> He paused and frowned.

<And although my parents were not born of Earth, I grew up there and developed as you all have. You know why.> He shrugged and continued with the history thread. <Eventually a one-sided intergalactic war developed and MeMa, and I did what we could to save the underdogs, the planets oppressed by Spes.> He hung his head. <it was almost too little so little.>

Questions erupted from about everyone, but Seth waved them off. <Not now, it is another story for another day. Suffice it to say we learned a great deal of unpleasant things about the Silva, things we will study in depth as soon as we establish the first part of our mission. I will tell you we finally escaped, saving close to three-hundred people Vald had condemned to die in a Black Hole.>

Elizabeth, along with the others, was glued to the story. With the unfolding of each new fact, she wondered how she might use the information in her plan. Of one thing she was certain, Seth had the same bitter hatred for Vald they all had.

MeMa rapped the table with her knuckles and took up the tale. <It was not until much later we

realized Vald had allowed us to escape. It is yet one more example of his diabolical mind. He planted one of his trusted security guards among our numbers with the mission to foster a relationship with a Seeker, once we arrived on Earth, the spy eventually convinced the Seeker to return him to Spes to rescue his family.>

Tina interrupted Seth's lecture. <But how did MeMa get there as a fighter?>

MeMa waved a limp hand at Seth to continue as if the telling of a more comprehensive story was exhausting beyond measure and Elizabeth wondered what else the old, old, woman had experienced in her lifetime.

<As I said, Vald's plan worked. The security man was able to befriend a Seeker, and eventually he pleaded with him to take him back to Spes. He said he feared his ability to reposition there alone and needed help to rescue his family. The Seeker, knowing the location of Spes through the viz of his new friend gladly helped. Once they reached Spes, Vald had the Seeker placed in their deepest dungeon with instructions to keep him well fed and drugged, but not to permit visitors or communication. All food, water, and any other needs were passed through a slot in the cell door.>

<The security man shared the return trip with Vald through a viz. That was the bastard's goal. Vald could now travel to Earth. He knew the way from learning what the security man knew.>

Elizabeth groaned inwardly. <So, that was where it had all begun. Seeing opportunities beyond the imagination of most, Vald had tricked his way to earth with careful long-range planning. How was the guard rewarded?>

Seth curled his lip in a giant sneer. <As you would expect. In his typical dastardly fashion of appreciation, Vald had him killed. With the Seeker out of commission and the security man dead, only he knew the way back to his new planet, Earth.> Seth dropped into his chair.

<Hey.> Sarah abruptly stood, shoving her chair backward. <Then what happened? There's more to the story, right?>

MeMa lifted a placating hand. <Yes, Daughter, there is more.> She looked at Seth with fondness. <Too much talk of Vald is not good for the soul, but I will take up the story. When Vald became a concern to the Time Overlords, they went back in time to find out what happened. They found that Vald initiated visits to the Seeker's prison cell daily and played a game much like checkers, which in

itself was a farce with a Seeker in a drugged stupor. She glanced at Elizabeth and then Shannon.

<Vald is far smarter than we want to give him credit for. He suspected close proximity to a Seeker, over time, would make him like the Seeker. It would eventually give him the skills of a Seeker. Proximity would make him develop the physical attributes necessary to experience a Second Awakening.>

It was a truth she and Shannon had gone round and round with. Elizabeth wondered how he had figured it out so fast. She rubbed her chin in memory of the pros and cons they had thrown back and forth. What could have set the man's mind on the right track? Seth. He knew Seth was not of Earth, yet he had achieved the awakening. What she and her Cohort had only theorized for far too long, he had figured out centuries ago.

MeMa continued. <One day, as the time traveler observed Vald, he vanished in the middle the game with his prisoner Seeker, only to return seconds later to slip the Seeker's throat.>

<Hold on. Why? What changed?> Chloe blurted out.

<Good question, Daughter. Indeed, what had changed?> She looked around the table expectantly, and Shannon gave her the answer.

<The bastard successfully repositioned to Earth. He could now visit there whenever he wanted and return when he pleased. As Seth said, 'He knew the way.'>

Vald returned again to Earth that very day and spent the next several centuries on Earth working to position himself as leader of the Followers.

Benjamin slammed his fist on the tabletop startling everyone. <Until the very end, that damn son-of-a-bitch had me, and the rest of the Followers conned. There is only minimal satisfaction in the fact that we were never so foolish as to make him the man in charge. He had to take the lead. He thumped the table again. I stand with Shannon. I say we kill the bastard.>

Seth, sitting close to Benjamin, reached out and patted his shoulder. <Vald had many of us deceived.>

<For clarity,> Sarah reached for Seth's arm. <So through his proximity to the Seeker, Vald's body had a kick start for a Second Awakening and with it came his ability to fold space and reposition across the galaxy?>

<For my money,> Shannon said, <Vald left Spes for Earth because he didn't want any of his rivals to achieve a Second Awakening due to his proximity to them.> She shook her head. <That

lowlife scumbag, what a greedy narcissist. Can you even believe it?>

<What about his slaves?> Sarah asked.

Elizabeth heard the more profound turmoil in Sarah's words and watched her flinch when Benjamin reached for her hand. He had kidnapped her, and she was slow to forgive him. The fact that his motives were genuinely protective and he was genuinely contrite did little to hurry the process. For a long while she didn't speak to him, and in fact, she had decked him more than once. She still gave him a hard time but showed grudging signs of wanting to be with him. Not that she had put them together for that reason, but working so closely together in one of Tobin's spheres could help them work out the kinks in their relationship. Perhaps proximity has other applications.

Elizabeth pulled the meeting back to the present time. <We have heard rumors Vald's current practice is culling the populations from the other fifteen planets throughout the Spes Empire for pre-pubescent children. I cannot emphasize this point enough. They are all and only what he takes. Almost all of those left behind, including adults, have had their Snyder's Regions removed with radiation. Those with brains allowed to mature become part of the bureaucracy for Spes' Empire.>

Oliver slapped his palms on the table. <Why weren't we told of this sooner?>

Seth started to stand, but MeMa grabbed his sleeve. <Seth and I have known of these abominations for years and could do nothing about them. The pain and frustration of that knowledge brought us to the decision to tell you about them at a time in history when something could be done. Today is that day.>

Elizabeth added, <When Tobin took George and me on a test run using the space portal for gathering asteroids at Alpha 11, on its fourth planet from the sun, closest to its asteroid belt, we observed a chain of coastal cities under an asteroid attack launched from space. We don't know how the Spes accomplished that without the use of spheres, but the missiles were of a size calculated to destroy the city. We learned from a family we rescued that the destruction was in retribution for the city's refusal to comply with requirements demanded of them by Spes. Included in those demands was the family obligation to give up one or more of their children to work on Spes as slave laborers. Further, they were required to annually provide the Silva homeworld a percentage of goods and services. Maybe they should have given Vald whatever it was he wanted.>

<You are exaggerating, right Aunt Elizabeth?> Appalled, Sarah stared at her.

She shook her head slowly, <It is difficult to imagine the suffering these families endured when they did not comply>

<And suffered worse when they did,> Shannon reminded her. <Losing a child is . . is . . . > She slouched back against her chair without finishing.

Oliver rose and before speaking looked at each person. <The behavior fits what we know of the Bustard. He must be stopped. The question we are faced with is how?. I remember the Cold War with the Soviet Union. School children were trained to duck under their desks for protection should there be an atomic attack.> He rubbed his forehead and shook his head. <Lord, what a ludicrous an exercise. Back then we had little appreciation of the concept and power of mutual destruction. Multimedia didn't pound it into our very souls back then. Wars weren't telecasted for all to view. Yet the wisdom of the idea of 'if you use a nuclear bomb on us we'll fire back', held credibility and promoted fear. If everyone was blown to bits, there would be no winners. I think the concept could work . . . will work. Our arsenal of space-portals, hidden in unknown parts of the galaxy, armed with asteroids aimed for Spes would be something Vald

understood. It would serve as a deterrent to Vald's planned destruction of Earth.>

That was all Elizabeth needed to hear. Oliver's mind was sharp. She knew he had considered all the angles and looked for flaws. He confirmed his confidence in her. <Let's harvest those asteroids today and begin the tough part tomorrow, that's getting that little weasel to bring his council to the table. Chloe has an app she and Tina put together to assist you in locating stars, planets or yes, asteroids, otherwise lost in the vastness of space.>

Shannon persisted. She tightened her folded arms and spoke to the group without speaking to anyone in particular. <I suppose losing two-thirds of this team, including our children, is a price we are willing to pay.>

Elizabeth pounded the table with her fist. <We may accept the risk, but we will not tolerate the loss.>

Seth stood and held out a hand to silence her. <Say no more, or you put us at risk.>

Shannon snapped, <At the risk of what?>

Before Seth could respond MeMa stood. <I promise you—>

Seth yelled at her, "Finna, be careful!"

At hearing his voice, everyone sat back and stared at MeMa.

She remained standing. <We owe them this much. I have been a warrior in active combat enough to know that once I bought into the cause, whatever war it was, I was prepared to die for it. That knowledge did not diminish my ability to my duty. I must trust our team and show them the respect we have for them.> She took a few seconds to make eye contact with each and held them on Seth before she continued. <I promise that anyone who dies in this effort will be redeemed without altering Earth's Timeline.

B - INTO DEEP SPACE

Teams depart

Later that evening, Elizabeth met with Oliver and Shannon. They assembled in a corner of the keep and stood in the breeze admiring Torg's twin moons.

He raised his mug in salute. <To beautiful women adorned by stellar moons.>

Shannon pointed to the moons. <Which one do you see as me?>

Knowing this first meeting with Shannon after she'd heard the payback plans for Vald was important, Elizabeth tried to keep it light. <That's easy, the faster, red one. You know you always want to be first.>

<Umm.>

Facing her friend, she leaned on the rampart with her forearm. <We'll shut Vald down. I guarantee it.>

Shannon gave a long sigh. <There is no guarantee, and you know it, but I appreciate the sentiment. MeMa's promise of Redemption opens

some hope, but I’m not sure the Overlords will support Redemption.>

Elizabeth shared a thoughtful <Hmmmm. I’ve been thinking about that. Here’s my take on MeMa’s promise. If it’s true Redemption is strictly forbidden, for any reason, we never would have heard MeMa’s statement to the contrary. Did you catch why that is so?>

Shannon's draw dropped. <Are you saying—>

<Yes, The overlords would have supported their position of no Redemption by making MeMa retract her promise by having her make a redo of her statement.> She shrugged. <It simply would vanish from our, and we would have no memory of it.>

Shannon’s eyes sparkled. <Oh, that’s comforting, Liz. Thanks. I’m really happy for what you have already done for my family and me.>

<No need, let’s look ahead,>

Shannon agreed and said, <I have to agree, Tobin’s preset portal spheres programmed to automatically deliver asteroid destruction is really kind of brilliant. They give me hope. I must admit I’m more than a little relieved to understand that I will not be one of the delegates on Spes when you and MeMa confront that monster Vald. I never want to see him again.>

<As crazy as we all thought you were, it once again demonstrates the courage it took for you to confront him in Afghanistan.> Oliver stepped close and gave her a hug. <I feel the same as you, but keep in mind, even if you keep some distance, you will continue to be a valuable part of this plan and our solution.> He gave her another squeeze. <Hang in there with us. Seth and Elizabeth are cooking up something so we can get a better handle on the bastard, like the number people working behind Vald who never show themselves. They lurk and remain hidden. We will keep everyone informed with what we learn in our initial meeting. There will be opportunities for all of us to play a more significant role in our future.>

Elizabeth touched her best friend's arm in the similar show of solidarity given by Oliver. <What Ollie said is true, Shannon.> They had been friends for decades and leaned on each other often. <I need your expert help with preparation for our first diplomatic meeting. We know too little about Vald's people. We always assumed that once Vald acquired his Second Following, he repositioned to Svalbard and lived there with the Followers, passing himself off to them as a Silva refugee.>

<We heard the bastard came to the Followers on Svalbard as a nobody,> Shannon said, gazing out

over the rampart. We know he weaseled his way up in their ranks. We also know in an immoral lowlife act so like him, he wrested partial control from the Followers and assassinated close to half of those who did not join him.> Elizabeth turned to stare out on the foreign world as well. She could just see the ocean over the top of the scrub-like trees. In contrast to the turmoil, she and her friends were experiencing it was calm and flat.

There was no disputing the truth in what Shannon said. They all knew the essence of that man. What they needed to find out concerned the others in charge.

Seth said, <Vald was far from being a nobody on Silva when he left. Although the watchers have observed him for centuries, what they don't know was how his brief visits to Spes kept him in a position of power. Furthermore, we are unsure of the structure of Spes' government. Are there others who wield the same power as Vald or is he their almighty? We can only guess that knowledge of Earth gave him leverage to gain higher positions within his government. He may have hinted at skills he obtained, yet he has not shared them. We just don't know. Our immediate problem is to convince Spes it is in their best interest to back off and leave us alone on our side of the galaxy or there will be

hell to pay. We need the stalemate to give us time to learn more about the Silva before we can be sure it will continue to work. We need to evaluate the Species>

Shannon turned to face Elizabeth. <Why did you say, 'Species?' You make them sound different from Evolutis. Are you saying you think they are?>

From what MeMa and Seth told us it seems that the people of Spes may very well be a subspecies of Evolutis.>

<Ah, Elizabeth,> Oliver groaned, <Explain it better for this dumb economist.>

<Dumb economist, my ass. Ollie. What is that? Levity? Lord knows we need it.>

Shannan said, <Let me give it a whirl, Liz, then we'll all be on the same page.> Shannon stepped away to face both of them. <A subspecies is the only taxonomic rank under that of a given species that can receive a scientific name. Homo Evolutis is the name of our species. So then, the Silva would qualify as a subspecies of Evolutis only if they existed geographically separated and isolated. For example, I know you like tigers, so you may also know the tiger's species is Panthera Tigris. A tiger named Panthera Tigris Sumatrae living on the isolated island of Sumatra in a different climate and terrain qualifies as a subspecies. A Bengal tiger

residing in India is a Panthera Tigris Tigris. These have the highest population. A South China Tiger is a Panthera Tigris Amoyensis and the Bali tiger, now extinct, is Panthera Tigris Balica. There are nine subspecies of tiger in all, three of which are extinct with all the numbers falling at an alarming rate.>

Oliver said, <Hmm, interesting. Well done, Shannon, I thought I had the simple answer, but you have provided a more in-depth understanding. Liz? What have you got? As far as the Silvia is concerned, these people are definitely isolated from Earth, all right.>

Elizabeth said, <Hence our need to investigate the Silva . . . And the Torg . . . More thoroughly. Meanwhile, we can call them Homo Evolutis Silvae Does that sound right? Even though their Snyder's areas were removed in all too many cases, they were there, to begin with.>."

Shannon laughed. <I don't speak for the International Code of Zoological Nomenclature, but when our friends in the scientific community recognize the need to establish an intergalactic code for all of Evolutis, I'll nominate you to work with them, Oliver.>

He bowed at the honor and left, remembering Elizabeth's original plan to meet with Shannon was for private time.

Shannon asked, <Did you just send him away? What are you about to ask of me?>

<You know me too well. A hypothetical, but I'll wager you can figure it out.>

<What are we talking about, Liz?>

<<I'm about to ask you to commit a crime. Hypothetically speaking, since we recently acquired automatic self-immunization, we will not require hazmat suits when we visit Spes.>

<No, why would you expect to? There is a history of contact, albeit limited, with the Overlords working on Torg and Earth. <I wondered how Vald and his council would react to a case of the chicken pox or maybe something lighter?>

Shannon's eyebrows rose. <Are you going where I think you are? Why not the bubonic plague if we're going to infect them?>

<Hmm, I like it, but for now, do you think you could give the council a light flu-like cold? That would be sufficient for our test. I want to know how it worked within twenty-four hours.> Elizabeth grinned as a thought came to her. <How would you deliver it, with roses? I'll have Seth contact you when he's ready. Have something for him he can put in the water with the roses.>

PART of the dream training instructed everyone to reposition to a round table in the center of Alpha team's space sphere. The teams were about to see what the finished product of their first task looked like. Elizabeth and MeMa had traveled back in time and tested their procedures for finding and storing six huge planet-killing asteroids. When they passed the directions on to their teams, Elizabeth wanted to be sure they were clear.

She smiled, watching MeMa turn in a child-like whirl of pleasure, the image of someone in wonder and surprise. A massive asteroid was enclosed in each of the portal's six pods. The enormity was unimaginable. The ancient woman stood in the center of the sphere and, spreading her legs wide, grinned at their achievement. <Look at this collection. Fantastic. They look like six floating gray to brown mountains.>

Elizabeth, she was reminded of entering NASA's Vehicle Assembly Building for the first time. It was the largest open room in the world at the time, and it housed the huge Saturn V rocket, which would deliver men to the moon. She had entered expecting a close-up look of the ship but was immediately swallowed by the vast emptiness above her. Visually stimulating and at the same time hugely intimidating, she had gripped Oliver's arm to steady herself. Her feeling of falling upwards in the VAB now translated to the sphere. Surrounded by six asteroids, she felt like an insect trapped inside a very large bag of potatoes worrying which way the spuds would fall.

MeMa stopped twirling. <I just grasped the full scale of this collection. It could not be anticipated. Repositioning into a transparent cube surrounded by six huge mountains floating within transparent sphere suspended in space with no apparent support— it would be a shock to anyone, Tobin included.

Elizabeth handed the old woman a mug of coffee while sipping from her own cup <I shared the test run you, and I did in everyone's dream training last night, including a detailed look at the manner in which we collected the six asteroids in the K dwarf star system. The crew should be awake and refreshed when they get here.> She paced as she spoke. This was it. Her band was going to execute the first part of the plan. They were on their way to a solution. She felt both giddy and afraid.

<I also included a survey of the planets George, Tina, and Tobin mapped out during their excursion yesterday. The scientific community calls them super habitable planets within K dwarf systems. I suggest we have all the teams record as much data

as possible. No actual landings, mind you, just what they can learn from their fly-bys. The record of such images of new worlds will be valuable to Earth scientists in the future.>

MeMa continued twisting her head in all directions. <I can't take my eyes off these giant asteroids.>

<They're hard to ignore. I'm glad we have them to show to the teams, but I can't get it out of my head that I am surrounded on six sides by potential planet-killers.> She refilled her coffee mug and yawned into the back of her hand. <They should make for good-table talk this morning.>

Elizabeth chewed her bottom lip while she ran her hand over and over her chin, then checked off an item on the list in her tab.

<You are having second thoughts about their mission.>

An inelegant snort escaped Elizabeth's lips. <Second, fourth, ninth . . . As many as you could stand to listen to. There are too many things that can go wrong. I'm deeply troubled by the possibility of a team getting lost, injured, or worse.>

<Ah, Vald. He could somehow find out we are here before we are ready to announce ourselves. He could do considerable damage. Is that why you keep

adding and subtracting things from your to-do list on that tab of yours?>

Elizabeth slid the tab away with her thumb. <I can’t turn my brain off. We need the teams working on this critical first step instead of spending valuable time envisioning future discussions with the Silva.> MeMa spoke in private. <Remember, Elizabeth, anytime we need to break away to discuss and fix a future concern, all we need to do is reset the timeline. If that concern takes a month to shake out, so be it. After we enjoy a relaxing beach party we return to the time we stopped the original project's timeline and continue on schedule.>

ELIZABETH CROSSED her arms and sat back with a groan.

<Sorry, I wasn't thinking in four dimensions.>

<Okay, Liz, who do you think will arrive first?> MeMa’s question was obviously one to distract her.

<That’s easy. Team Beta, with Oliver, Shannon, and George.>

<Why them and not Team Delta? After all, Tina and Tobin designed the spheres. I would think they’d be most anxious to get going. In fact, he’s been up for hours. He copied six complete copies of the space portal he had designed to house the

asteroids and placed them out of sight high above Torg's equator in high synchronous orbit.> Elizabeth shook her head. <It'll be George. This is just like Christmas morning for him.>

With soft pops and loud mind chatter, George arrived with an arm over Oliver's shoulder shaking a finger under his nose and pointing at the asteroids.

Team Delta arrived next, and within seconds, Team Gamma followed. Sarah hurried over to give Shannon a good morning hug while Benjamin and Seth argued about the decline of the crusader ideal.

All talk stopped at the impressive sight of the floating asteroids then resumed in a rush with questions about their size and appearance. Tobin continually gazed around the sphere as if checking all was right and every few minutes Tina patted his arm in reassurance. Elizabeth wondered what private conversations they were having. Whatever it was, it was one of support. She often teased them they had an exclusive mutual admiration society, and they made her wish she had a twin. Seth went to MeMa and hugged her warmly before sitting beside her. They turned their chairs away from the group and bent their head in close conversation. Elizabeth thought again of the portrait of the man in MeMa's living room. She left them to their privacy and went to sit with Oliver. She'd missed him, and they had their own catching up to do. He was as good as any twin.

It was not long, however, before more questions came her way. Sarah pointed directly overhead.

<Is this the same sphere like the one in our dream training? How long did it take to fill?>

<It took MeMa and me about two weeks. However, since we time traveled we were gone from here for only five minutes.>

Sarah's mouth dropped as fast as her shoulders rose. <When?>

<About one hundred years ago.>

Sarah grinned. <You got me. I forgot about the benefits of time travel.>

Elizabeth looked at MeMa, who had allowed Seth to solicitously turn her chair back to the group. <Do you want to jump on Sarah's segue?>

MeMa stood, mug in hand. <Did any of you observe Elizabeth and Tobin's discussion when we were all on the rampart yesterday? During one of the slices of time in that conversation, both of them vanished and did a week's worth of work constructing this.> She raised her outstretched arms and then leaned toward Tobin. <You tell them.>

Elizabeth smiled. She knew Tobin loved to be front and center and always gave his audience an informative show. <Once I had a prototype of the

space portal we'll be using, all I had to do was duplicate it until I had two for each team. Then I built this one for MeMa and Elizabeth's trial run.> He lifted his gaze then dropped it. <The only difference is you'll have to get your own asteroids.>

When the laughter settled, MeMa leaned closer again. <Are you ready to give your demonstration?>

<Can't wait.> He picked up a mug and held it to the table in his left hand and then looked down. After a brief pause, he raised his eyes and took a drink from the cup that was mysteriously in his right hand.

George slapped the table. <Dammit boy, you're quite the showman.> He laughed loudly.

Tobin raised his cup. <To those of you who may wonder about George's definition of entertainment, what I did wasn't a trick, but to demonstrate how time travel can influence productivity. After I grabbed the mug in my left hand, I went back in time. And checked in on your spheres. He has already built and positioned them. They have been placed in a high equatorial Torg orbit.> He grinned at the assembled group. <Before I returned, I refilled my cup with wine and switched hands.>

MeMa clapped her hands. <Thanks, Tobin. That's an excellent demonstration of the power of

time travel. You can see from that, and the dream training of how Elizabeth and I acquired these asteroids, the prospects such time travel presents. And that about covers your next task. I am sure you will enjoy your new spaceships.> She sat and rested her folded hands on the table.<Elizabeth, you're up.>

Elizabeth spoke from her chair. <MeMa and I will monitor each team in your journey to find and collect asteroids. As you saw in training, if something does go wrong happen, you can make your own small escape sphere and reposition here. But first,> she held up a finger and paused for effect, <send your harvesting sphere into Spes's sun. Is that clear? We want no evidence of your presence left behind.>

She waited for questions and then added, <By the way If you can't reposition, don't panic. We will come to you. Do not initiate any mind-to-mind communication with us. We can and will find you wherever you are. Questions?> When none came, not even from Tobin, she turned to MeMa. <What do you want to add?>

<On the off chance, and I do mean off chance, that you should be captured, tell them everything you know. Everything. You saw an example in your training of how to behave. Know that drugs, mental

controls, and even torture should be expected. As immortals, we will take the time to find and deal with those who harm us. But since you know nothing of our big plan or what your teammates are doing, you can do little harm.>

Elizabeth stood next to MeMa. <Your space-spheres have been stocked with food, water, and medical supplies. Remember to keep all talk mind-to-mind and no calls home. Stow your gear and be on your way. Good luck.>

When the team members gathered in small clusters, Shannon broke from her group. <Liz, remember what you said about the twins and Chloe. While I'm confident Seth and Benjamin will keep Sarah, I need your assurance that Chloe and the twins will be closely monitored.>

<Be assured we will.> They hugged one another. <I've discussed it with MeMa, and she's agreed. I'll be on their unit all the time while she splits her attention with the other two teams. You have Ollie's back. Take good care of him.>

Oh, god, what are we about to set in motion?

UNEXPECTED DEVELOPMENT

Solar System Alpha 11

Elizabeth knew MeMa's logic, ethical and moral codes dictated she monitor all the teams, which included keeping an eye on her as well. The difference in time and distance didn't affect the automatic monitoring process. Although she was sorry to pass off her responsibilities to the ancient woman, who had become her dear friend, it was essential to find the answers to questions brought up by what she witnessed on Alpha 11. Who was behind the mass extinction? What motivation drove the senseless killing?

Elizabeth's initial effort to glean with a member of the family and see the event first hand was inconclusive. She observed their flight through their eyes, but panic and chaos shut out logical thought. It only raised her level of sympathy and a desire to preserve them.

She had to record their last seconds on the boat. Did she need to witness their deaths firsthand? Fear washed through her like bad food. How could she make their extraction less horrific than it already was? She vized planet Alpha 11's countless archipelagos and felt its stronger gravity. Alpha 11 could have been a twin planet of Torg. Coincidence? Interesting. Maybe they needed to alter their perception that Earth was normal.

She had to meet them in private and at a safe place. Scanning the southern hemisphere, she found what she needed, a small collection of tiny coral islands too small for vacation or commerce.

She returned her attention to what she damn-well-hoped would be the last horrific replay of the family's demise. Were they a substitute in her mind for the people on Earth she wasn't sure she could save?

Holding her breath, she waited for the flash that preceded the annihilation blast by seconds. Before she could reposition the family, the EMP of the initial explosion disabled the electronic motor of the powerboat. Fortunately, it was not at the frequency to cause death. In an instant, before the powerboat was blown to smithereens, she realized the family was alive, and she repositioned them safely with the craft to the tiny coral island she'd found. The family, taking shelter below the water line in the bottom of their boat, was oblivious to the repositioning and the island she selected looked very much like the one they were near. Shoving thoughts of interference with the local timeline to a dark corner of her mind, she sat under a palm tree look-alike and waited for the family to come topside.

The powerboat drifts lazily in the calm water about one hundred yards away from the small spit of land.

When silence replaced the cries of fear, and before the people came topside, Elizabeth pulled her hood over her head and brushed sand from her robe. The next few moments would be tricky.

The tallest of the family appeared at the small opening of the foredeck holding a black rod. He shaded his eyes with his free hand and scanned the horizon before his eyes locked on her. Another head appeared from the lower deck. The person with the black rod motioned for the person to back down. <Stop. We are not alone.>

English? That couldn't be. She remembered George's theory of a universal translator in the minds of Evolutis. Was it possible? Could these people be like her? Like the people of Earth?

<Identify, or I will shoot.>

Oh boy. Elizabeth needed to earn his trust ASAP. She brought forward a gallon jug of water from behind her back she'd repositioned from her sphere to her hand.

The man, or at least she thought it was a man, raised his rod and repeated his demand. "Identify."

Hoping the universal translator worked both ways she raised her arm and spoke to his mind. <I am a friend. I bring you water.>

He lowered his rod. <What city are you from?>

She placed the water jug at the water's edge and stepped back next to the tree. <San Francisco.> She wondered how that would fly.

He handed the rod to the person emerging from below, who aimed the thing in her direction. He pointed to Elizabeth and then dove into the water. She kept an eye on both the swimmer and the rod.

He cleaved the water as though it was his natural element. When he stood knee-deep in the water's edge, she saw the fine-tuned muscles of a swimmer, the broad shoulders, the sleek, slim torso and waist, powerful legs. Everything about him radiated fitness. His only apparent alien aspects were very wide-set eyes and elongated fingers. When he finger-combed his shoulder-length black hair off his face, she thought she saw vestigial webbing between his fingers. His tall naked torso left no question, he was a mammal.

Lowering her hood and adjusting her belt so he could see her knife hanging from her left hip, she presented both hands and hoped the universal sign of friendship also applied to the people of Alpha 11. When he hesitated, she reached down to pick up the water jug and extended it.

He cautiously accepted the water and backed away.

<Wait.> She needs to keep him there longer. She repositioned food to behind the palm tree so its arrival would not be seen. Reaching a hand around the trunk to retrieve it, she handed him a net bag of coconuts, bananas, and flatbread. <I hope these are foods you know. The only other food I have is beer.>

He scanned the contents of the net bag and nodded. When he extended his hand to accept the offering, however, Elizabeth retracted the sack and patted her chest. <I will carry them to your family.>

Turning sideways to keep her in his sight, he spoke to the person on the vessel. <She brings food. Do not kill her.>

That was at least a good command. Glancing at the small craft for the first time since he'd finger-combed his hair, Elizabeth saw three people now standing on the bow. The man had turned and, undulating like a dolphin, closed the distance to his destination by half. The easiest thing for Elizabeth would have been to reposition to the boat. Resigned to the fact that was a bad idea, she stepped into the water, glad that it was warm, put the bag in her teeth, and set off with a backstroke. Normally, she thought of herself as a competent swimmer, however, having observed the speed of the Alpha 11 man, she swallowed her pride and focused on maintaining a straight line, hoping the Torg had wrapped the flatbread in plastic.

SEVERAL HANDS PULLED HER ABOARD, and she heard what the man said to the others. <She understands our mind talk. It is possible she is one of the Wooded Ones.>

<Were they the ones who attacked you?

She got no response, and the small group that had all the appearances of family stopped closer together. The presumed mother, although as tall as the man, had mammary glands and her face did not have the hard angles of the other adult. When she glanced at the smaller ones, she guessed with they were boy and girl, but only because of subtle differences. Not quite enough data to pass a peer review in a scientific article, but it was a good beginning.

Hoping it was not a cultural faux pas, she spoke to the group rather than to the man. <I am Elizabeth. I am not one of those you call the Wooded Ones.> Wooded Ones. Something clicked in her brain. Silva. Latin. Forrest. Woods. The Wooded ones? Was it possible? Her heart banged on her chest wall. <I come to learn how to protect my people from them. They plan to destroy my word. I need your help.>

She didn't have time to measure their reaction. She sensed another strike hit the mainland closer to this island and rather than wait to see how long the death cloud would from the asteroid blast take to arrive, repositioned the boat back seven days into the Alpha 11's past at the same location. Only extraordinarily high-speed cameras could have caught the change in scene. She glanced at the lone palm tree. Except for one additional coconut, a few birds, and clouds, everything was the same. She relaxed.

<Is this food to your liking?>

One of the smaller ones, the one she assumed was a young girl, had already taken a banana. <This tastes the same as our bananas only it is larger.>

Damn translator works like it's using freaking autocorrects.

<Were you able to save your entire family?>

The woman looked toward the distant horizon. <Our first is away for more learning. We pray for his sake the Wooded Ones spared that city.>

Elizabeth placed her hands over her heart in a prayerful position. <I pray for him as well, Sister. How can you remain so calm?>

The question went unanswered. <The ash is coming. We need to fix the boat and get far away.> The man turned to prepare.

She stepped into the family circle. <Have your people experienced this before?>

There was silence at first, and then the female spoke. <Yes, for years our people have provided young ones for service to the Wooded people. When we hide them or fall short of their quota, they destroy part of a city. This time is different. Some of us rebelled and killed five citizens of the Wooded people. What you see today is their retribution. They told us five cities would vanish. One for each citizen.>

Elizabeth had a bad feeling about the translator's use of the word serve. <How do your young ones serve them?>

His expression could have been made of stone. <We do not know. We never see them again.> The females face crumpled, and she turned away.

<Are there other members of your family?>

<None. The children's grandparents are dead. We have no other relatives.>

<What is your profession?> Time was a factor, and she realized she tone was urgent and harsh. She softened her mental tone.

<I am part of my city's government. What is it you do? What is an Elizabeth?>

<I am a physician. Elizabeth is my name, not a title. It is a custom of my people.>

<What do you want, Elizabeth?>

She took another intuitive plunge. <I can take you to a place where you and your family will be safe. It is a place where we can learn about each other. A place that will prepare you to help us deal with these Wooded people you have told me about.>

"When can you do this thing?"

The operative word is when. <I live on a world that is safe. It is in many ways like this world. What do you call this world?>

"Earth."

Stupid translator.

ELIZABETH DECIDED on Torg minus 10 years, a full ten years before the team arrived to solve

Earth's problem, as an excellent time to shelter the family. The castle would be vacant for at least another five years and the Time Overlords would see to their needs and possibly learn more about their culture and the Wooded Ones in spite of a somewhat sophomoric universal translator. The fact that the castle was empty didn't mean there were no Torg. The castle, as a gated community would endure the family would not interact with the Torg until the Time Overlords felt it was safe to do so. They would not be alone.

She wondered what MeMa's reaction would be to that. Truth be told, she held the ancient woman with more awe than she was comfortable with. Not fear exactly. More like the mystery of not quite knowing her. There were, after all, centuries to understanding her. Having broken the timeline of this planet, Elizabeth wondered if the woman would ever forgive her. Considering their goal for saving the earth, it was a paradox in logical thinking, and indeed she would come around to seeing that.

Although also concerned with Time Overlords reaction to breaking the Torg's natural occurrence of events, because she knew they had not embroiled themselves in other galaxies so much, she hoped she could slip this by them. Whatever she could expect, it did not deter her determination. She gathered the family together and prepared them for the journey they would take. <The world I will take you to is very much like this one with only one exception that I am aware of.> She bent closer to the two children. <It has two moons. One for each of you.>

They giggled, and Elizabeth smiled. It was the first emotion she had seen from any of them. Confident they would like Torg she broadened her smile to include the parents.

<The boat comes with us. I think we can fix its motor. There is a river and an ocean close by, and you will be glad to have it. I have a large stone building there you can call home. Close your eyes. When I tell you to open them, you will be at the top of my house where you can see a river, the hills, and the ocean. Your powerboat will be tethered on the shore. Is everyone ready?>

ELIZABETH HAD COMPLETED their tour of the castle when footsteps on the keep's internal staircase alerted her to someone's approach.

MeMa stepped onto the square flat rocks of the roof rampart. <Greetings, everyone. I am this

family's number one daughter. I am glad my Sister, number two daughter, could bring you here safely.>

Relief swept through Elizabeth.

MeMa spoke privately to Elizabeth. <Not that I am happy, but what's done is done. They had my attention when they mentioned slavery. I know what that's like. I will stay here as their mentor and go-between with the Torg.>

<Team Delta is having problems. Read my mind for their location and see if you can get them back on schedule without rescuing more species. Go!>

DELTA IN THE WEEDS

Somewhere in Deep Space

Elizabeth remained unaware of the sector *Team Delta* drew in the random selection of assignments. She also knew any information about their location in space and time would be removed from her mind by the app MeMa gave her to be with them.

She arrived not knowing where she would be, but surprised by Tina's greeting.

<Aunt Elizabeth, thank god you're here,> Tina said, looking ashamed. <It's my fault and we lost Tobin and I didn't know what to do.>

Chloe crossed her arms and also looked at a loss. <Tobin had an idea then poof, he was gone.>

This could be more complicated than she had thought. Hiding her alarm, Elizabeth took Tina by the shoulders. <Tell me what happened. Give me the bullet points from the beginning. If we need to go back for more details, we will.> She bent to look at Tina eye to eye. <We'll find him. Look at us, we're three bright women. How can we fail?> She pulled her close.

Tina blew her nose. <Look at the mess I made.> She pointed to one of the six pods that were waiting for asteroid storage.

<I don't see—>

<That's the point,> Chloe said. <It's full of water.>

<It's my fault, > Tina repeated and hiccuped. <On my first catch I had this huge asteroid, but I didn't check if it was solid rock. It wasn't. Just the outside was. When I repositioned it inside and it hit the local gravity it . . . it . . .>

Chloe said, <The shell of frozen rock collapsed and the warmth of the sphere melted the internal ice. Now we have a perfectly good fish tank but no fish.>

Elizabeth listened carefully trying to pick out salient points of what happened. The girls didn't make it easy.

Tina continued. <After I made this mess he didn't stay around to help me get rid of the water. I don't know how to reposition water, do you?>

<I see, am I correct to assume Tobin made a small sphere and went off on his own?> When a small nod affirmed her question, she reached into her robe then held out a closed fist. <Take it Tina, it's part one of our solution.>

Tina took the miniature six-portal sphere and held it in her hands to her lips, kissing it. <Yes. We didn't have a copy and Tobin told us to fix this one. He didn't have time and—>

Let me guess. Tobin had *an idea*.> Elizabeth gave Tina another hug. <You know what to do to make a copy for your pocket and then make another full sized six-portal sphere?>

<Yes, I can do that. It's easy, but Tobin asked that we not do that.>

Elizabeth took Tina's chin and gently shook it. <Leave that to me. He will see the wisdom of it.> She looked into her eyes for agreement and Tina grinned.

<Chloe, we need a second sphere. How about creating a fifty-foot one for us to use to search for Tobin?>

She made a thumbs-up gesture and moved off for more space.

Elizabeth turned back to Tina. <Are you okay repositioning the five asteroids into the new sphere? Chloe and I will find Tobin. Are you good with that?>

Tina mouthed the words *thank you*.

Elizabeth repositioned into the sphere Chloe had ready. <Let's see if we can sort out where your impulsive brother went. What were you guys

talking about just before Tobin discovered there was water in the last asteroid?> She hoped like hell there were going to be clues. It was a big freaking galaxy and Shannon would kill her if she failed in this. Not that *that* was the important thing. They had to find Tobin.

Chloe frowned in concentration. <He seemed generally pretty bored with the search for the right sized asteroids.>

<Nothing special or different grabbed his attention?>

<We passed the remains of a small moon closer to the sun.>

<What did he say about that?>

<Hmm. Let he think. He said we had all the time we needed to finish the job and that he wanted to spend some time with. . . no, to check *out* the remains of the moon.>

<Can you take us close to it?>

<Sure. It was one of the moons of the fourth planet inside this system's asteroid belt, but I don't like getting too close to the debris, it's . . . chaotic. We'll go in slow.>

Elizabeth admired Chloe's control. She piloted the small sphere as though she was just leveling up in a tough arcade game. <This isn't just the remains of one moon. It looks like the debris of as many as

three. Set a mind trigger to see flashes of reflected sunlight from the sphere. Do you know if he was looking for anything in particular?>

<Who knows what is on his mind?>

<Do what you described to me when you told me how you managed to see a given protein inside a cell. I've always liked your analogy of looking at a spinning barrel of spaghetti for a tiny diamond. Go ahead, I'll drive.>

Closing her eyes, Chloe sat and let her chin drop to her chest. She often mentioned how many variations of the Lotus position she could comfortably use and this had to be one of the strangest. It did not take her long to begin her mindful meditation. She opened her eyes and sat still. Chloe attributed much to her breathing, and pointed to their shared mind about Tobin's interest in a unique pattern of very large pieces of the remains of three moons slowly circling the fourth planet in the system.

A very small point of light flickered through her viz.

<There. He's there. He's preparing to reposition directly into the center of several oddly shaped rocks.>

He rebounded off one moon fragment into another, then another. He bounced and rebounded two-thirds of the way around the moon's ring of wreckage before shooting away from the remains.

<Look, he's back to start again. That rat,> Chloe said, <Look at him. While we were worrying about him . . . and us . . . he's playing celestial pinball. Wait 'til I get my hands on him. Wait 'til Tina see this. We'll kill him together.>

<How many rebounds did you count, Chloe?>

<Fifteen. Look, he's back and moving another large rock into position.>

Although not surprised, Elizabeth was peeved. He'd left the young women and his sphere to play. <Well, he's had enough fun. I'll get his sphere in here and we'll return to Tina. Then he's all yours.>

<Oh, my god. He's racing back to the beginning and positioning his sphere again. Count 'em with me, Aunt Elizabeth. He's off again.>

They watched his zig-zag perfect rebounding in three dimensions. <I count sixteen this time. Hell, he's just playing, Chloe.>

<Are you going to tell Mom?>

<Damn right. I'm telling everyone. This is pure genius. Wasn't it Robert Heinlein who said, 'specialization is for insects?' > This was more emotion she had seen from any of them. Confident they would like Torg she broadened her smile to include the parents.

<The boat comes with us. I think we can fix its motor. There is a river and an ocean close by, and you will be glad to have it. I have a large stone building there you can call home. Close your eyes. When I tell you to open them, you will be at the top of my house where you can see a river, the hills, and the ocean. Your powerboat will be tethered on the shore. Is everyone ready?>

ELIZABETH HAD COMPLETED their tour of the castle when footsteps on the keep's internal staircase alerted her to someone's approach.

MeMa stepped onto the square flat rocks of the roof rampart. <Greetings, everyone. I am this family's number one daughter. I am glad my Sister, number two daughter, could bring you here safely.>

Relief swept through Elizabeth.

MeMa spoke privately to Elizabeth. <Not that I am happy, but what's done is done. They had my attention when they mentioned slavery. I know what that's like. I will stay here as their mentor and go-between with the Torg.>

<Team Delta is having problems. Read my mind for their location and see if you can get them

back on schedule without rescuing more species. Go.>

INSERTION

Near Spes

Bowls of fruit and spicy chili awaited the bone-tired and emotionally drained teams in the castle at Torg-minus-zero. The band of asteroid hunters dug in while they awaited Elizabeth and MeMa' return. Oliver, restless and every bit as tired as the others, tamped down his anxiety as his mind relentlessly ticked off all things that might have gone wrong, reasons that might have held them up. The new fact that Tina had temporarily lost contact with Tobin proved things happened.

All the teams had returned with pods full of the requisite asteroids. Table chatter moved on to focus on Tobin's pinball games in the debris of the three moons of some unnamed planet. The most viewed viz was from his point of view inside his sphere as he went for his own record to complete a full circuit of the planet rebounding off one lunar rock after another, maintaining his direction and avoiding undesired collisions. The group groaned as one when he was slammed in the wrong directions and out of the debris field by a smaller stone that appeared from nowhere behind a gigantic one. An outlier asteroid that careened off the outside edge of his sphere and sent it back into play saved his game.

Olivier said, <I call it 'Space Ball Wizard' and I think it could catch on. Seriously. It's a great training exercise.> It was apparent Tobin had never felt lost and totally missed the suggestion he might have done anything wrong.

Tina and Chloe, who had been entirely furious at him, had relented and although not admitting it to him, made a pact they would give the game a try someday.

Shannon seemed content to merely give him a cool fisheye. While she acknowledged his brilliant computational abilities to adjust to the ever-moving changing path of each individual asteroid, she disapproved of his needless risk and told him in a not-so-subtle way. <Einstein once said, 'The difference between genius and stupidity is that genius recognizes its limits.'>

While Tobin's face turned red, Oliver saw George's eyes light up, and he knew his friend tucked the pearl away to misquote it, as he always did, sometime in the future. His amusement, however, was short-lived. Where the hell was Elizabeth? She was long overdue.

ELIZABETH AND MEMA FINALLY ARRIVED, breathless, some yards from the table. They had agreed to withhold Elizabeth's discovery of the attack and the subsequent rescue of a native family on Alpha 11. The attack on the planet used large asteroids to wreak havoc instead of chemical or nuclear weapons made it relevant to their mission. She believed Vald had a hand in this and knew they needed to dissect the attack from every angle to help them solve their own problems.

For now, the Alpha 11 family resided in this very castle on Torg minus 10 years. Knowing they were safe and content, Elizabeth focused on the next thing, and it was a bitch. She rushed over to Oliver, as much glad to see him as she was in need of moral support.

A big step had been accomplished, and MeMa began preparation for the next phase of the operation. <We have eight, twelve-mile radius portal spheres, containing a total of forty-eight planet-killer asteroids. They are in a parking orbit around Torg minus fifty years. We must move them to remote hiding places throughout the galaxy and set the trigger on each asteroid before they are

detected. Set the time for their relocation to now, Torg minus zero.

Elizabeth, who had sat next to a very relieved Oliver, stood. <This next phase is tricky and dangerous. As you learned from your dream training, the plan requires strict adherence to specific steps. The order of each step is designed to minimize your exposure, discovery, or god forbid capture. Do not deviate from the procedural order I gave you.> She sent a stern look to Tobin who raised his palms in capitulation. <MeMa and I will continue to monitor your progress and safety. Your first step will take place in this meeting room. You will be departing within the hour.>

Elizabeth followed behind Team Delta as they walked from the table to a place where there would be sufficient room to huddle up. They formed a circle for repositioning to the first of their two portal spheres already located at a random, pre-determined location somewhere in the galaxy.

Once each portal received the signal to deliver its asteroid to a designated, entangled point in space high above Spes' atmosphere, they would arrive with an initial velocity of 30,000 miles per hour to ensure maximum damage on impact. The entanglement process, the most dangerous part of their mission, could go astray.

Elizabeth assessed the composition of her teams for the billionth time. They would perform identical chores in different sectors of the galaxy and the individuals needed to work together as a cohesive unit. A well-oiled machine, Team Beta with Oliver, Shannon, and George, had known each other for over fifty years. Team Gamma, with Sarah, Benjamin, and Seth were an interesting mix. The two men had lived for centuries and had a great deal of shared history to discuss and squabble over. Sarah had confided she sometimes felt left out.

On the other hand, she admitted listening to what they said was fascinating. Furthermore, Elizabeth knew Sarah and Benjamin grew closer by the day. They weren't the only ones feeling a higher affinity. By the time this was over, this group would be the tightest group of friends she knew. In such a critical situation where teamwork was essential, they couldn't help but be.

She placed a small shopping bag on the table. <I want to show you something that may help you understand how this will work.> After reaching into the bag, she held up her hands and grinned. <Behold, in my left hand is a Torg potato-looking-thing. Think of it as one of your asteroids. In my right hand is a Torg cantaloupe-looking-thing. Think of it as Spes.> She placed them on the table about five feet apart with a finger on each. <I, the middle object in this demonstration, am your mind. Your mind knows the location of both objects. We know that is a basic requirement for repositioning from one place to another.

Oliver raised an eyebrow. <I take it this next part is more difficult.>

She raised her chin and then dropped it. <Right you are. George will elucidate.>

George stood and rubbed his hands together, then placed a small white sphere the size of a Ping-Pong ball next to the potato. <I admit these props look ridiculous, but they'll do. They represent our participation in a most serious event. One that requires we place billions of lives at risk in an attempt to establish a mutual non-destruction pact. He tapped the Ping-Pong ball as if telling it to stay. <Tobin and I will construct about fifty pairs of these entangled little devils and place each numbered pair in a numbered pouch for you>

He heard a private message from Tobin. <I think maybe we should tell them how we'll actually create the pairs of entangled spheres,>

George pulled on his chin and looked into near space. <Hmm. I was saving it for later, but maybe you're right.> He brought his gaze back to the group. <For your work with asteroids, perhaps a

simple explanation of entanglement is in order. We will employ the properties of quantum entanglement to link two places in the galaxy. In this demonstration, I refer to Elizabeth's potato as the space portal, the cantaloupe as Spes and the Ping-Pong balls as our entanglement vehicles.>

<The quantum requires an unusual and unique study. Some wag quipped that if you feel you understand the quantum, you don't. Einstein famously rejected quantum theory for its use of entanglement as 'spooky action at a distance.' Physicists have long since argued this point. Action at a distance basically means that doing something to an object in front of you cannot affect an object far away that is not physically connected to it. Note I am not talking the transfer of energy such as something like sound waves in the air, water, or some other substance.> He dropped his gaze on each individual. <Are you following?>

<Ye-e-s, Uncle George.> Tina spoke for everyone. <Please continue.>

Elizabeth barely swallowed a snort. It was her experience that her band gobbled up facts like toddlers ate Cheerios. As soon as they got one, they wanted the next.

<Hmm. Right, Tina. Okay, physicists discovered in their laboratories that the simple act

of observation by a person of an experiment conducted on the quantum level, would, in itself change the outcome of the experiment>

<And using other words that means what?> Oliver asked.

<Experiments and observation conducted by technology alone, without person a living mind present, will conform to outcomes predicted by theory. It is only when we introduce a person observing or making any measurement of the experiment, that the result of the experiment differs from theoretical expectation.>

<For example... ?> Oliver let the sentence fragment hang, and George held up his hands.

<For example, using a magnetic property of electrons called 'spin,' Dutch researchers designed an experiment that used pulses of microwave and laser energy to create the same spin in two electrons. Then they trapped each electron within its own diamond. They used their instruments to automatically measure the "spin" of the trapped electrons before placing the two diamonds on opposite sides of the Dutch Delft University campus, which put them 1.3 kilometers apart. One set of scientists set their instruments to record electron A during the appointed time, and another set of scientists initiated a change of spin in electron

B. At the scheduled instant of change in electron B, was instruments recorded the same change in electron A. Remember these two objects are only .3 kilometers away.>

<And this is quantum entanglement?> Oliver asked.

<Yes.>

Oliver nodded. <Gottcha.>

<Hang on,> Chloe jumped in. <Does entanglement apply to particles a million light years apart?>

George responded with a series of short head bobs as he spoke. <No matter how far apart the two points seem to us, the properties of quantum physics treat them as being adjacent. Once your portal asteroids are in place, each of you will begin the entanglement process using pairs of small Ping-Pong sized white spheres we'll deliver to you in sets of four leather pouches like these.> He held his four by their drawstrings. My pouches are numbered as five, six, seven, and eight. Inside each pouch is a unique pair of entangled spheres labeled with the same number as their pouch. Do not mix the numbers. Asteroid number five gets one of the number five spheres while its insertion point receives the other number five sphere. MeMa or Elizabeth will deliver the pouches to you in your space portal spheres and review the entire process with you before you begin your mission to hide each portal sphere.> He paused to wet his lips and then raised his voice. <Remember, each team has two space portal spheres each holding six asteroids to be positioned for insertion over Spes. Teams, Beta, Gamma, and Delta, yields a total of thirty-six asteroids.>

<Ah, nice,> Shannon said. <with this many asteroids, there's no way Vald or his minions could find them all.>

<And all it takes is one to terminate all sentient life on Spes.> Elizabeth added. <If Vald discovers one or more of the small white insertion spheres in stationary orbit he has no way of knowing how many are up there. He will never feel safe.> She shook her head, thinking of the innocent people on the planet. <What a tangle.>

George snorted at the unintentional pun.

<Planetary extinction of Spes is not our goal. We are removing the chance they will take to destroy Earth.>

George raised an eyebrow at Oliver, who had waved a hand.

<You've given us an excellent description of our task, and I for one intend to attend your lectures on Quantum Theory once this business is settled,

but in your description of transforming one white sphere into two, you used the word divide and not copy. You're a man of precision. Why use that word?>

George clasped his hands and gave a slight rocking bow. <Yes, two different words. The subatomic particles are paired and while what we did appear to be making a copy of them, we actually divided them in a subatomic mitosis fashion.> He shook his finger and laughed. <But, by all means, plan to attend my lecture for the explanation of the process after this crisis is over.>

With George finished, Elizabeth repeated her warning. <Hiding the space portal sphere is rather straightforward. Remember that the insertion of your personal sphere above Spes is the most dangerous part of the mission. You cannot be detected. With its blue oceans and white clouds, Spes is a beautiful reminder of Earth. Do not be lulled, sucked in, or distracted for more than three seconds by its beauty. Stay longer, and you will be observed.

At this stage, if even one of you is caught, it may well put an end to our efforts to save Earth. Rather than let the entangled sphere fall into Vald's hands, reposition to another time and send the entangled sphere into the nearest sun. Do not let Vald get his hands on you.>

Elizabeth made eye contact with each member of her team. <It's time. You have the information you need for success. You're ready, and MeMa and I have complete confidence in you. Let's do this.> She turned to Oliver and squeezed his hand. <Stay safe, my love. I know you have this under control. I'm going with Tobin and crew. Not that I think they need my guidance but they are the youngest. It's a precaution. Anyway, his mind works in fascinating ways. Maybe I'll learn something new.>

ALTHOUGH ELIZABETH'S rational mind knew that when she entered the portal of one sphere, she would be instantly repositioned across the galaxy another, suddenly finding herself surrounded by a half dozen six-mile long suspended monoliths, she needed a moment to synch her mind with the scope of her new reality.

Once placed in their hidden position, the portal spheres, each holding six potentially deadly asteroids, would never need to be moved again, unless they were needed. A dreadful quote from the Bhagavad Gita uttered by physicist J. Robert

Oppenheimer upon witnessing the first atomic explosion, repeatedly washed through her brain. "I am become death, the destroyer of worlds."

The thought of that made her stomach cramp. And they still had to come to an honorable agreement with Vald, the slippery, lying, cheating, kidnapping, stealing, son of a bitch who never honored anything. It was a nightmare that she couldn't imagine would ever end.

TEAM DELTA DECIDED Tobin should go first since he was the one who constructed the portals and Elizabeth waited the few seconds he needed to make one more sphere, his private 10-foot diameter sphere from which he would position the two entangled small white spheres. When he was ready, she placed four small leather pouches in his hand and repeated the insertion process procedure. <Tie these to your belt. There are two small spheres in each bag. The numbers on each ball are the same on the pouch. Do not mix up the numbers. After you reposition yourself and your personal sphere inside the lens-shaped portal containing your first asteroid, untie one pouch from your belt and remove one entangled sphere and wrap the pouch's strings

around one hand. Reposition the entangled sphere you're holding in your hand deep inside the asteroid. Then reposition your private sphere to the designated location high above Spes' atmosphere. Got that?>

He nodded. <Yes, Aunt Liz.>

She knew his mind was sailing steps ahead and she slowed him down. <Good. This is a review for Tina and Chloe as well.> She made eye contact with them and continued. Remove the remaining sphere from the pouch wrapped around your hand. Check that the number of the tiny white sphere matches the number on the pouch. And then recheck it before dropping replacing the sphere inside its pouch and dropping it to the floor. Having done all that, leave your personal sphere with the empty pouch and personally reposition,> her voice rose slightly, <leaving your personal sphere at the insertion point, back to your team's space portal and repeat the process with your second asteroid until you finish all insertions. Clear?>

<Crystal clear. I leave my sphere with the empty pouch in it. It cannot be detected from Spes. Correct? And it is the point in space that the asteroid will suddenly appear with a speed of 30,000 miles per hour?>

<Correct.>

<I like that part. May I begin?>

She gave him a quick hug. <Be safe, Tobin. Thank you.>

He vanished, and she turned to Tina and Chloe. <Who's next?>

Before either responded, Elizabeth got a message from MeMa.

<Sarah and Benjamin are missing. Seth was the last to go for Team Beta and when he returned from positioning the last paired entanglement, they where nowhere to be found.>

She didn't hesitate and repositioned to Tobin on Team Delta's space portal.

<MeMa, keep Tobin from leaving. The two of you need to meet with Team Beta. Stay together there until I report what I find.>

<Find where?>

<MeMa, I'm jumping back in time to attempt an observation of Sarah's disappearance.>

MESSAGE IN A BOTTLE

Elizabeth's sphere near Spes

Elizabeth knew the coordinates of Sarah's four insertion points above Spes and repositioned to the closest one in her small personal sphere. It only took her a fraction of a second to detect the tiny white ball of entangled particles floating within a copy of Sarah's personal sphere in the high geosynchronous orbit matching Spes' sidereal location.

She then located and verified Sarah's second and third successful insertions. Arriving at the coordinates of Sarah's forth insertion point she found nothing but empty space. Placing the sun at her back, she moved away to get a broader view. Opening her mind and her body wide, she brought her microbiome into play to sense Sarah's location.

Five long minutes later, her patience waning, she discovered Sarah's personal sphere halfway toward Spes' sun and repositioned her area next to it.

Empty. Her stomach fell to her feet. It had seemed so hopeful. With a devastating sense of loss, she enlarged her personal sphere and brought Sarah's craft inside to examine it closer.

Elizabeth couldn't concentrate. Still searching for Sarah, she had to drag her wandering gaze from looking beyond her empty sphere. She imagined Sarah floating free in space with no sphere for life support and forced the idea away.

The evidence she found on the floor of Sarah's sphere supported what she already knew. Three empty pouches, 30, 32, and 33, represented proof the white entangled spheres she found above Spes had been positioned correctly. Pouch 31 was missing. The fourth insertion was empty. Unexpected hope soared within her.

If Sarah still had the white sphere in pouch 31 tied to her robe, she could use it to find her. Maybe Benjamin thought the same thing and had already found her. Perhaps he got to her in time. Her feelings of elation plummeted. She was reaching for straws and knew it. Still, not willing to give up, she wondered where they might possibly be. Another thought struck her and her heart-strings, which were attached to a yo-yo, slipped again. Maybe someone took her . . . And Benjamin as well. But Seth told her about there was still a belief the Silva could not bend space to form spheres. That there was a good chance, their technology to detect them didn't exist. But what if Vald somehow managed to find them? What if he took them? A damn pair of big freaking ifs. She didn't put it past him. Lost in thought, she didn't react immediately when her sphere suddenly changed direction, and she sped toward the planet below, spinning wildly out of control. She fought to right it and repositioned far from Spes. If the same disruption happened to Sarah before she could insert the entangled sphere, she might have panicked and followed the escape protocol and send the white sphere into Spes' sun, and then reposition far away. If so, and is probably safely hidden somewhere and shit, at some time from here. But where? And in what time?

Hopeful that Benjamin had, in fact, found her, she reached out to him as well as Sarah with her mind. Rewarded with nothing but silence, she returned to considering what she knew. Her personal sphere had drastically and unexpectedly veered off direction wildly out of control. What caused that? Vald's technology hasn't reached the level to detect and shoot something that small and as far away as their insertion points. No, this was a local event, perhaps clusters of small rocks orbiting Spes.

She examined Sarah's empty personal sphere again. This time, sitting cross-legged, with her eyes shut, she looked with her mind and not her eyes and detected an almost transparent glob of thread on the floor of Sarah's craft. Cradling it in her open palms, she gently pulled the loose end and was surprised at not only at its length, but its vague familiarity. She had seen it before.

Carefully patting the string into a small ball, she placed it in the pocket of her robe and then lifted her hand to examine the cuff of her robe. Son of a bitch. The thread was part of the protective EMP lining George had insisted the tailors weave through the fabric of their robes. After taking Benjamin's thread from her pocket, she closed her eyes and vized the thread in the way Chloe had taught her, searching for DNA. She found some. Benjamin. Here was proof he had been here. He'd pulled a loose thread from his robe, but why? She quickly reexamined it with her eyes. Benjamin's thread contained dozens of Knots. Did he have to tie small pieces together? No, it was one long thread with knots, lots of patterns of knots.

"Oh my god, could this be . . ." Elizabeth whooped with joy. "Yes."

ELIZABETH REPOSITIONED TO TORG HEADQUARTERS, still in local time. “I got it. I have something.”

She rushed into the huddle where MeMa was filling everyone in. Oliver had an arm around Shannon, who was white around the mouth and lacked her usual vitality. Tobin and Tina stood pressed together at their shoulders whenever trouble appeared as they had since they were toddlers. Chloe clutched Tina’s arm, and George stood close behind them. All had long faces.

Remembering their communication mandate, she reverted to mind speak. <Who knows Morse Code?>

Tobin lifted his head. <I do. I learned it when I was five. Why?>

Elizabeth hustled to the large circular table and spread out the string for Tobin to examine. <I don’t know which end is the beginning, but I found this in Sarah’s personal sphere. I think the patterns of knots is Morse Code.>

<Sarah doesn’t know Morse code,> Shannon said.

Elizabeth put her hand on her shoulder. <I know, but Benjamin does. Do you see? He found her abandoned sphere before I did and left this coded message.> She raised her head to everyone gathered behind Tobin's side. <Viz my mind to catch up on everything I did leading up to the discovery of this thread while I help Tobin read it.>

Within seconds, they had digested her record of events and refocused on Tobin. Shannon, impatient, prodded him. <Can you read it? What does it say?>

Oliver stepped closer to Elizabeth. Slipping an arm around her shoulder, he kissed her temple. <How the heck did you figure out it was Morse code? It's brilliant. Benjamin did all right, too.>

Tobin held one end of the string, and slowly pulled it between the thumb and index of his other hand. <Bear with me everyone. I'm reading it as fast as I can so you may get words, not complete sentences. Listen.

Sarah safe.
    She had entangled ball #31
    returned to the portal
    removed, #30 from the asteroid
    and used #30 to look for a safe planet.>

ELIZABETH SHOT A GLANCE AT GEORGE. <She still has sphere #31. What do you think?>

<Useless. Once entangled particles meet up, all entanglement properties disappear. Tobin and I will I think of something.>

George vanished.

Three seconds later, Tobin vanished.

SARAH AND BENJAMIN

Elizabeth's sphere near Spes

While Elizabeth had scheduled their group meeting with the intention of catching up with the success of each team and lauding their achievements, the only relevant topic of discussion focused on Sarah and Benjamin's disappearance.

Except for the strumming of Seth's fingers on the Torg-minus-0 roundtable, silence followed Tobin's translation. His focus lay on a spot on the floor fifteen feet away from the table. <I hope they get it right this time.>

<What?> Shannon asked. <What did you say?>

<I said they are smart, resourceful, and have each other. They will be okay.>

Shannon, still pale, stood apart from the others. <I can only hope you're right.>

Elizabeth shot George a glance. <She has sphere 31. What do you think?>

George shook his head. <Useless. Once entangled particles are engaged, all entanglement

properties disappear.> He worried his chin with his hand. <Tobin and I will I think of something.>

He vanished.

Three seconds later Tobin vanished.

Elizabeth covered for their disappearance saying she'd asked them to put together some research for the meeting. Meanwhile, the remaining members of her team milled about the roundtable brainstorming ideas to locate and rescue Sarah and Benjamin. No one wanted to move forward to discuss Vald. She wondered how she could get them seated without offending their concern for Sarah and Benjamin. She reminded herself they had the time for them to heal, if necessary, and the reality of Earth's imminent destruction could wait.

Shannon's voice, raised in panic, disrupted her thought. "No, that's wrong, Chloe, We must not run off without more information. What good would we be without you? Then you'd be lost too. Just wait—"

<No need to wait,> MeMa said. I sense—"

<Yes,> Shannon cried, <They're coming.>

Tina and Chloe added their shouts. <They're here.>

With two soft pops so close together they might have been one, four figures appeared next to the table. The presentation of twin toddlers, an adult with a full beard and another adult fully pregnant was almost too much for the nearly exhausted team.

Seth watched Shannon race toward the couple and hug them before anyone else could react. Anyone except himself, that was. He remained sitting but spoke privately to Sarah and Benjamin's minds. <Remember our discussion. What you say is critical to the timeline. If you give the team too much information, you may adversely impact the timeline, and we may have to do this again.> He rubbed his hand across his close beard. He really did hope they got it right this time. They had arrived back five times now, or was it six? Each time, a slip of the tongue forced him to send them back in time so as not to change the timeline.

Their nods were lost in the face of family greetings.

Shannon ran her hand over Sarah's belly. <Thank god you're alive and well. You are, aren't you? Well?>

Tina, laughing, wiped her eyes with the back of her hand. "Sarah, what the hell happened to you guys?"

Chloe gripped Benjamin's full beard with both hands. <What's this all about?>

Tobin and George returned amid shouts of a million questions.

<Tell us,> Chloe said, <and I mean tell us everything.>

Seth stood behind Shannon's family, with his arms folded and a big smile he felt pull on his ears and spoke to Sarah and Benjamin. <Not quite everything. Once we accomplish the goal of saving Earth, the Time Overlords assure me your story will be safe to share without disruption of the timeline.> He crossed his fingers. <You can do this.>

Before moving onto the final stage of her plans for Vald, Elizabeth waited until the story of Benjamin's ingenious rescue of Sarah unfolded.

Benjamin spoke to the team and related their story. <We cannot share all the details with you for many good reasons. We ask you to respect our privacy in that regard. This is as much as I can share with you know. Sarah will begin our story.>

<Benjamin followed the entanglement of sphere 30 embedded in my asteroid to the current location of the 31st small white sphere where it resided in the pouch tied to my belt. I was unconscious but alive in my personal sphere in a synchronous orbit above an Earth-like planet not far from Spes.>

Benjamin added, <Realizing she had almost depleted the oxygen in her sphere, I re-repositioned her into mine and quickly re-calculated the sphere's oxygen level. Knowing we had less than two hours

to live and not knowing if anyone from Spes was in pursuit, I decided to land on the planet by doing a fly-by in my sphere instead of blindly repositioning to a place below.>

Sarah continued. <He quickly settled on a river fed valley near a large lake midway between the planet's equator and ice-capped poles. While we were elated to find we and the twins were alive and safely hidden, we had no idea we had landed in a field of sapping stones and were loosing powers until he tried to construct a sphere large enough to hold sufficient oxygen to get us far from Spes before repositioning to Torg.>

Benjamin spoke, <By that time, we had lost their abilities. Mind speak beyond a short distance was unavailable, and repositioning was impossible. We were being held captive by a planet that once promised a solution to their plight. What we hoped was nothing more than a field of sapping stones turned out to be the spread over the surface of the entire planet. For almost two years we searched for a location free from the mineral that sapped their powers. The numerous large freshwater lakes and even larger saltwater seas were teeming with killer octopus-like creatures making travel by small boat impossible.>

Sarah broke in with her first smile, <Fortunately, there were enough land bridges between the small archipelago like islands that we could continue south toward the broad areas of ice we observed from space during entry. We hoped we could, like the Followers of Earth, discover our salvation on an ice pack near the planet's pole.>

Benjamin spoke quickly as they approached the end of their oral report. <Our powers returned slowly and the day their ability to reposition over vast distances and through time was restored, we immediately returned to Torg on Elizabeth's scheduled day to resume our part in discussions of how to deal with Vald and the Silva. Sarah and I will be taking turns with the twins while the other attends to team discussions. We will not be discussing additional of the ordeal until we have successfully dealt with Vald.>

Benjamin and Sarah held hands with their twin toddlers and vanished.

BACK TO BUSINESS

Torg Castle's Meeting Hall

After Benjamin returned to the group, Elizabeth called the meeting to order. She could see the effort it cost everyone to respect Sarah and Benjamin's privacy. Elizabeth smiled to herself. There was apparently more to the tale, but she, along with the others, would have to remain satisfied with their safe return until they were ready to share.

<Good. Now we can continue with the work at hand. We all know there's going to be a confrontation and reckoning with Vald and the Silva in the near future. I know many of us have played and replayed that scenario in our minds every day since we first saw the images of the destruction of our future Earth. She glanced at MeMa, sending a private message. <Last chance to change your mind.>

A stony expression and a small shake of the head said carry on.

Elizabeth did just that. Standing in front of the group she began in a non-lecture mode. <Here is

my proposal and my rationale for that meeting with Vald. It comes from many conversations MeMa, Seth, and I have had with each of you during the Harvest and Insertion phase of our plan. It is based on the proven concept from international chess tournaments. Championships are often decided by well-placed stalemates.> She let that sink in and then said, <Let this be our strategy: Our encounter with Vald is but one match in a thousand-year campaign.>

She paused for questions and then moved on. <There is a strong consensus among the team that before we craft our demands for a peaceful stalemate, we must have a better understanding of who governs Spes and in turn, the Silva. We need to know their advisory council on a more personal level, meaning knowing who are the weak, the strong, the corrupt, the inept, and the traitors. We need to know how we can turn them into assets. Otherwise, we'll be shooting in the dark. I agree with this understanding and suggest it will drive our tactical design for the first encounter.>

The expected murmurs of table talk among the team erupted, and she waited for them to assimilate her statements. Surprisingly, Chloe spoke first. <If you are proposing we set up a fake meeting so we can establish long-term surveillance to research and

examine Silva's political and military structure and agenda, I concur.>

Elizabeth shot a private message to MeMa. <Where has this girl been the past three years?>

MeMa was quick to point out, <Be mindful of potential hubris Elizabeth, she agrees with you.>

Elizabeth's not entirely private response to MeMa consisted of a flash of a smile and a quick wink of approval. Then she continued speaking to the team. <Yes, good observation, Chloe. By accomplishing this, we will avoid mistakes and misunderstandings of our enemies due to ignorance. Our diplomatic discussions on his turf will play into Vald's hubris, and his self-confidence will go through the roof because he'll think he has the upper hand.>

She allowed herself a lingering smile. <We'll first appear unannounced, inside Vald's council's inner chamber and present him with a staged series of questions that lead to a presentation of our ultimatum.>

Oliver raised his hand and as usual, began his inquiry at the same time. <An ultimatum within 30 minutes?>

<Of course, Oliver, our ultimatum is the result of a simple collection of logical statements. Vald is to withdraw his weapons from Earth and terminate

his intention to destroy Earth. He is to cease and desist forever all hostilities, including all covert and overt actions against our people, no matter where or when they are within our galaxy.>

<Simple?> Oliver said. <It doesn't sound simple to me. Why should he listen?>

Elizabeth began to pace with her words using her arms to conduct the music of the logic. <The plan hinges on vast quantities of evidence that cannot be ignored. He will have to believe us. We expect our demands will be met with denial and a grudging offer to return at some future date to begin formal peace discussions. We will appear to comply with his apparent upper hand, further inflating his ego. Then almost as an afterthought, we will announce a demonstration of our power by presenting his council a proof of concept that will act as a proof of our power and intent.>

Elizabeth observed Oliver's expression was filled with doubt, and as she looked around the room, she realized several of the others radiated similar uncertainty. She ran a hand over her chin. She remembered the initial plan and understood their reluctance. However, she and MeMa had been over it again and again. With Seth's endorsement of their intention to assign powerful Seekers to monitor the minds of the top Silva political and military figures, she felt the package they needed for success was complete. The three instantly realized it would work. When Elizabeth enhanced Seth's idea to include the Time Overlords as monitors, they knew they had a powerful solution.

Elizabeth wanted her team to be that confident as well. With a consensus, they could move forward together. Seeing their hesitant expressions, she continued with her persuasion. <To validate the threat, we'll need to secure a barren planet, which is void of life and satisfies a long list of other requirements. For example, it must have the molten core of Spes and Earth, and its destruction must not affect the orbit of other planets or affect the timeline of Spes. Seth has been through this part of the galaxy before and thinks he knows of one. He and Tobin are prepared to insert six more asteroids of planet-killer size in a hidden space portal entangled to six insertion points about the barren planet.

<Once the asteroids we've hidden in the space portals are entangled, we will present Vald with a triggering object at our meeting. He will be told in no uncertain terms that if or when anyone moves or destroys the object we give him, the planet in our demonstration will automatically be annihilated.

Shannon had been uncharacteristically quiet, and Elizabeth knew she was afraid the plan was insufficient to keep Vald under control. That somehow, he would get away. <How soon will you confront Vald?>

Elizabeth continued in her lecture friendly voice. <We will stage our diplomatic ambush of him at one of his council meetings as soon as we hear that Seth and Tobin have successfully traveled back in time in order to outfit a barren planet adequately prepared for destruction.

Shannon snapped, <How are you going to do that? Just pop into the meeting and take him?>

<You are not the only one who wishes to assassinate Vald, Shannon, but I don't believe that act would be a complete solution. We don't know the Silva as a people well enough to gauge Vald's influence. We can't be sure if he's the top person in their government or not. Whatever the true situation turns out to be, we want our intentions known to the entire council, and we want to establish a permanent diplomatic stalemate. Once that is assured, we can consider settling personal grievances with Vald.>

Oliver's frown persisted. <This must be a certainty . . . Nothing less. If we are to use a diplomatic stalemate, it must work.> He spoke in his calm, logical voice. <We all know what's at stake. The only possible way to gain success is to inform the entire ruling class of Spes as well as the

entire Silva population that the cost of doing business in the galaxy has just escalated beyond their initial business plans. Vald's deputies and the ruling one percent need to know their choices. Unless they are as insane as Vald, they will settle for a stalemate. I'm okay with negotiations for the next thousand years if it prevents the total destruction of two planets. Which leads me to ask, Liz, how in the hell are we to locate and communicate with that one-percent of Silva leadership?>

MeMa rose from her chair and gave him a small smile before holding out her hand like a magician to an empty spot on the table. A chalice with a golden stem and rock crystal base appeared.

<Beautiful, isn't it?> Picking it up by its neck, she waved it in a slow, low circle so they could all see. <Here's how our plan begins. We will give this lovely art object to Vald and tell him it is the trigger to destroy the barren planet we positioned for the demonstration, reminding of course that we have similar asteroids aimed for Spes. The concept shouldn't be difficult for him or his minions. Considering it is so similar to what they have planned for us.> She held the chalice away from her face to admire it. <It has a history that suits our purpose well. While it is a thing of beauty, it is also

a vessel we drank from.> She supported its weight with both hands and tipped it to her lips. <Expensive as mugs go, don't you think?>

She continued to stroke the vase as she spoke. <Strange, there is much death associated with this lovely piece.> She placed it on the table with a thump <The historical value of this vase is that it is the only existing symbol we have today of a peace gesture between the Crusaders and the Persians, yet it sits here remembered only as a gift from a narcissistic King Louis VII to a greedy abbot.>

All eyes were glued to on MeMa while she paused, then picked up her tale.

<Eleanor of Aquitaine gave this chalice to Louis in the Cathedral at Vézelay, France as a wedding gift. The year was 1145.> She picked up the cup and held the bottom close to her face. <According to this inscription, added later by the good Abbot Sugar to support his view for history, Eleanor's husband, who later became King Louis VII, gave it to the Abbot for his treasury at St-Denis.>

MeMa rubbed her hand lovingly over the rounded middle of the vessel.<Did you know that in those times, rock crystal, you know it as quartz, was considered a symbol for the Fountain of Life?> She laughed. <I once stole it from them both, the king and the abbot.>

General laughter released some of the building tension that had gotten so thick Elizabeth thought at one point, she could touch it.

<To be honest, I cannot part with it,> MeMa said. <This is an exact copy I made to serve as the trigger we give Vald to show him our claim is not empty. That we can destroy any planet at any time in the galaxy from anywhere we choose.>

<Excellent.> Elizabeth picked up the meeting. <George, please entangle MeMa's copy of the chalice with the space portals of asteroids Seth and Tobin set up. I think that keeps it consistent. The rest of us will script our first step at nailing this bastard emperor wannabe. Give us the location of the target planet so we can project a real-time viewing of its destruction for vald and his chamber to see.>

George added, <This will be tricky. The images coming from the planet we choose to use could take several years to arrive.>

Elizabeth replied <I know, do what you can to make it seem real time.>

As she sighed, she spoke to MeMa. <Sorry, I'm tired of doing the math. George will come up with something Vald will understand.>

STALEMATE AT SPES

Vald's headquarters on Spes

For two hours Elizabeth and Oliver held a tenuous grip on their patience while Vald's minions completed their security check and scan. She had no doubt it was a power play, the bastard's way of saying he was in control. As they waited, she reviewed the stakes of the meeting. She suspected his acceptance to meet with her, was only another of his numerous farces designed to hide his real intentions. Vald had no reason to suspect they knew of his plans for Earth less than a year from now, but when she surprised him with her diplomatic entourage, and he showed no astonishment that she was on his doorstep in his part of the galaxy, she wondered if the bastard had been watching them after all. One way or another, she relished the opportunity to start their end game and get through it without any redos.

On the other hand, if he really intended to annihilate Earth less than a year from now, would he bother with a pretense of diplomatic relations?

Was he that arrogant or did she misread his response and was someone else of a higher rank behind the plan for Earth's demise? Is this nothing more than a trip back to square one? They knew so little about the Silva people and nothing about Vald's inner chamber of advisors, but wasn't that the purpose of this effort?

Elizabeth clung to the only comforting thoughts surrounding this circus. MeMa and her six strongest and trusted Seekers had their backs. They would be vizing Vald and his personal guards. In addition, Seth, who would soon join them in the discussions, had initiated another avenue of subterfuge with assistance from the Time Overlords. They would be collecting data on Vald's immediate advisors and co-conspirators. Their success to predict the near future might provide Elizabeth and MeMa with insightful clues for immediate tactical responses.

The first meeting with Vald would be as intensive as any high stakes poker game at a whale's table in Vegas. She had to know him, how his mind worked, how he saw things, what his reactions were. If they are wrong and took out the wrong Silva enemy, they might never recover from the outcome. She and MeMa worked on the tactics of reading Vald's mind for tells.

Elizabeth couldn't help but think it would be so much easier to simply eliminate Spes. Her head ached, stomach cramped while irrational thoughts swam in her mind, a pre-emptive strike on Spes, being one of them. She rubbed her temples with both hands and hung her head in shame. That would make her as depraved as Vald. No way was that an option. Her ruminating stopped when seven of Vald's Seekers surrounded her and Oliver. She held Oliver's hand and spoke to him in private. <I expected an escort, but these guys have freaking creepy eyes are , always probing our minds and clothing. It's indecent. Too bad for them it's useless.>

Oliver rubbed his thumb on the back of her hand. <That's for sure. My mind is locked as tight as the Fort Knox Bank.>

<Good one, Ollie. These guys have neither the power nor training you, and I did on our first attempt to meet with the Followers. It's odd Vald insists on calling them, Seekers. I wonder why?>

<Aren't Vald's Spes Seekers as old as the ones we first met on earth? I believe your assessment that they have been granted Seeker status by merely achieving old age.>

<Hmm. Its also possible few of Vald’s people have attained a second awakening over time. If that’s true, I'll wager they’ve flown the coop.>

<It’s for sure they’re not in this room, or we wouldn’t be able to have this private chat. By the way, I’ve been meaning to ask if there any new understanding about physical changes in the brain as a result of a second awakening?>

<Where did that come from, Ollie? Not that I am up on Evolutis research as much as I would like to be. God, I miss the lab. The event is more about generating additional neural connections in the brain. They are needed to read and interpret an expanding mind connection . . . To all brains, I mean, not just their own. Why do you ask that now?>

<I figured there should be some sort of a test. So we know what we’re dealing with.>

Elizabeth snorted. <It’s a great thought. I think we have a real test coming up in a few minutes.>

The double doors on the other side of the room opened and seven more guards, all with pain sticks, entered. It appeared the waiting was over. While Vald may have given them the false title of Seekers, the guards were tall, mean looking and brawny.

<Actual power?>

<Beyond being able to reposition short distances and communicate mentally, they have only their stick.>

The original circle of seven lined up behind them and indicated they should follow the new arrivals down the long red-carpeted hallway.

They stopped in front another set of majestic double doors. Vizing through, Elizabeth squeezed Oliver's hand and pointed with her chin. <Vald's chamber. His counsel is there as well, all twenty-one of them.>

<Crowded. Do you sense any real powers associated with second awakened skills in there?>

<Other than Vald, who we know has powers beyond simple repositioning and mental communication, none that I can detect. Just do what you feel is right. This will be full disclosure.> She laughed. <Except for the secret parts.>

The circular room had seven rows of tiered seats behind an ornate low wall of intricately carved wooden panels. The long carpet culminated in a raised platform with two sets of three high-backed chairs.

Not quite concealing the sneer on his lips, Vald sat in a highly polished, elevated wooden chair inlaid with gold and precious gems, flanked by two deputies waiting for her and Oliver to sit.

As the leader, Elizabeth sat in the center chair with Oliver to her right. The empty chair to her left awaited Seth's arrival. Twenty-one Seekers filled the first two-tiered rows behind Vald's throne and sat as one after all had entered.

Oliver nudged Elizabeth with his elbow. <Catch Vald's footstool. No doubt part of his vision of being emperor of the galaxy.>

Elizabeth bit her lip and dipped her head to hide a grin. She would keep her face expressionless or die trying. <He can keep the damn stool. We're about to draw a line through the maelstrom and inform his majesty which side is his. Let's tell them we'll blow up their world right now unless they give him to us. I want to kill the bastard.>

<Hang in there, Liz. Let's stick to the plan.>

<I confess I'm shaking in my boots. This encounter leaves no room for any mistakes or errors in judgment. You always said I could do anything. Today's the day I get to show you how right you are.> Lord, let that be so.

Sweat trickled down her back, and she clenched her hands to stop the trembling. Talking big kept her confident . . . She hoped. So did having Oliver at her side. Thank god she'd talked Shannon out of coming. There was no telling what she would have said. Nothing diplomatic, that was for sure. Damn.

She needed Seth, too. Where was he? She didn't want to start without him.

Vald neither stood nor acknowledge their presence for several moments.

She folded her arms. <To be expected.>

Finally, he gave a dry, patronizing salutation. "Welcome to Spes, I am confused, Sister, what brings you to my world?"

"We are here, Brother, to begin a dialogue that will prevent the total destruction of our homeworlds.> She paused and watched him carefully. "Yours as well as ours."

His face froze, and she knew he communicated mentally with several of his advisors. Good. She wanted tons of chatter for her team of Seekers and a team of Seth's Time Overlords to monitor, garnering information about Spes' leadership and their empire.

Vald tented his fingers under his chin and crafted a poorly disguised concerned reply. "Sister, to what do you refer?"

To what indeed. Elizabeth said, "To save time, I will share the viz of an event that is scheduled to take place within one of your solar years." Obtaining permission was not part of her agenda. "I trust everyone in this room will find it as horrific as we do."

Vald's eyes darted about, and his hands squeezed the arms of his chair. Before he could speak, she spread her hands wide, as though delivering a rare piece of art. Instead, however, she unleashed the scene of the death and destruction of Earth. In making her point agonizing, she began with close-ups of families in a park and dogs romping around them, of magnificent gardens and stately buildings, of breath-taking landscapes and hospitalized children. She shut her eyes, unable to stomach the images. When the final explosions annihilated her beautiful blue and white globe, silence reigned.

Elizabeth opened her mind's eyes to catch the reaction of those present. All but a very few exhibited shock, then fear of a spectacle that portended a dark change to their own future. Only Vald, his two aids sitting with him, and a scattered few of the twenty-one seated in the tiered seats behind him, maintained a stone-faced visage.

She spoke to Seth, who had arrived in time for the demonstration and Shannon who headed up the Torg team. <We have identified Vald's inner circle with that demonstration. Do the Overlords concur?>

Seth responded, <They concur. It was apparent some knew about the assault on Earth, but most did not. I'll be there shortly.>

<Affirmative on that one, good buddy.> Satisfaction sang throughout Shannon's response. <We're swamped with useful information from the collective reactions. Wait 'til they see what's next on the agenda.>

Elizabeth <Good. See George on your way here and pick up a dozen red roses. Put them in MeMa's chalice, the one with her special rose water, and bring both with you.>

Seth said. <Will do. I am not sure of the ramifications of your instructions, but I like the sound of them.>

Vald pushed his long stringy hair behind his shoulders and found his voice. "Why do you assume this terrible vision involves both our home worlds?"

Elizabeth, who searched her mind for a stalling tactic, released a pent-up volume of air when Seth arrived.

He gave her a lift of his chin and deposited the replica of MeMa's golden chalice, filled with a dozen magnificent red roses, on one end of the table and then took the last empty seat.

"Vald," he said, without the use of the tag Brother for respect. "The answer to your question, in part, lies with this chalice. It is entangled with a device that is waiting for a signal to destroy a remote, barren planet. That signal is triggered by the breaking of this chalice."

Elizabeth spoke only to and Oliver and Seth. <I have confirmation from MeMa and George that they have successfully linked the minds of everyone in this chamber to that event. George said the delay between breaking the chalice and the explosion of the planet is about 90 seconds. That is as close to reality as he can calculate the event given the distance is measured in light-years.> He turned to Elizabeth. "We are set to proceed."

Before she spoke, Elizabeth glanced at all the male faces and didn't know if she was disgusted or pleased there were no women present. "We have given everyone in this room an automatic visual link to the annihilation of the remote planet we mentioned so when you choose to break this chalice, everyone will receive a view of the planet's destruction as it occurs."

Vald gave no outward reaction either in his posture or tone of voice. "Interesting information, but of what value is it to me?"

Elizabeth replied. "Simple knowledge. From this moment on, should Earth be attacked it will trigger such an event that will destroy you and the planet Spes. So you see Vald, sharing the knowledge of how we can destroy a remote planet is fair warning for the safety of your homeworld, Spes. It lets us know that you understand that should our world fall to the terrible event you will witness, Spes will instantly experience the same fate as the Earth. Your entire homeworld and its population will be eliminated. Do you see any value in that?"

She knew Vald would not take the information well. He leaned forward and spit his words through clenched teeth.

"You dare to threaten us?"

Elizabeth wanted to say, 'yes, I do, you little bastard.' Instead, she said, "No, we prefer to call that a proportional response; a response in kind. What you do to us, we respond in kind. You bomb us, we bomb you. You blow us up, we blow you up. Make no mistake we can do it. In this demonstration, we use many asteroids to wipe out a planet about the same size as Earth and Spes. Right now, many more world killing asteroids are now aimed at your planet. For all that she had meant to remain impassive, she glared at him. <Maybe you understand tit for tat better.> At any rate, I think you understand your position."

"We have no intention of bringing harm to your people," he said with a sneer. Then it seemed he couldn't resist and he added snide, "Sister."

"Excellent. Then you will help us prevent its occurrence." She added no title of respect. She confirmed once more the demonstration set and kept her eyes on Vald. Would he pick up the cup that sat like a benign centerpiece on the long polished table? With the set of ethics he had, she wouldn't be surprised if he picked up even if he knew the destruction would be to a planet full of people. The one niggling concern she had was that he couldn't grasp the level of their scientific ability. That he wouldn't quite credit what she said was possible. This would only work if they made him a believer and if that meant planetary explosions, so be it. She was surprised when Vald spoke again.

"What do you propose?"

"We propose the dismantling of your plan, your procedures, and all the relayed logistics, designed to destroy Earth. Furthermore, we want a full disclosure of the plan. We want continued diplomatic contact between our peoples with the intent to resolve our differences. In turn, we offer mutual support against common enemies."

Vald sneered, "What you propose is ludicrous."

Elizabeth words were as frozen as ice. "What we propose will happen."

Vald remained still for several moments. Elizabeth could almost see steam rising from his ears. She didn't expect this to be easy, but the man was so furious she wasn't sure he was capable of coherent thought.

She continued. "Those are our conditions. You have twenty-four hours to make your decision. Meanwhile, move that chalice, and you will see the extent of our commitment and the rage of our disgust of your narcissistic vision." Her voice rose. "I repeat. What we propose will happen."

Vald stilled, and Elizabeth listened to his mental communication flying back and forth with his council. The little piss ant didn't believe her. He thought it was an empty threat. She took the opportunity to talk with her team. Although she and her Cohorts could listen in on Vald, he and his people could not do the reverse.

Oliver nudged her shoulder. <Liz, my god, you think he needs the demonstration?>

<Pretty sure. What chatter do you hear?>

He cocked his head and glanced at Seth, who lowered his eyelids in agreement with Elizabeth.

She said, <He's having more sidebar conversations with his minions, Ollie. You know our Seekers and Seth's Time Lords with Shannon and the rest of our group are recording everything.>

<Damn, woman, you move fast. Do you think he'll buy it?>

<No, but I bet his council does.>

Vald stood. He was so angry his hands actually shook as he hissed through his teeth. "It will take more than idle threats to impress this council."

Elizabeth stood as well. She was considerably taller than he, and although he was on a dais of sorts, the differential was evident.

"Your magic has no place here."

"Magic? She snarled in disbelief. You would call the obliteration of a planet, magic? I'll show you magic. She grabbed a rose from the chalice and whacked the vase with it, sending it crashing to the floor, near his feet spilling water, roses, and fragments of the golden chalice in every direction.

There was complete silence in the room for a full seventy seconds.

Vald started to speak.

Elizabeth held up her hand and stopped him. "Wait for it."

The chamber suddenly grew blindingly bright as a large image of a planet erupting into a ball of glowing red lava filled the room. Fiery magma and ejecta shot toward its three moons. No one moved or spoke through the validation of their power.

She returned to her seat and waited, glaring at Vald.

<You realize you lost it, Liz, my love. What happened to calm and cool?>

She poked Oliver with her elbow. <Yeah, I did. Wow, I recommend that for stress relief.>

Vald's lips moved, but no sound ushered forth. His face, ordinarily pale, had grown alarmingly pale. Elizabeth needled him.

He tried again."We will consider, yes, we will consider your proposal."

"Excellent, I thought you might." Elizabeth clapped her hands, and six Seekers appeared next to Seth, who stood to join with them. Seth addressed the council at large. "Our peace team and I will remain to begin the discussion of our mutual support of a plan that ensures peaceful relations among all sentient beings within this galaxy. We trust you find this acceptable."

She could hear Vald grinding his teeth, and she barely contained her smile of satisfaction. Oh yes, she got the vindictive bastard this time.

When the apparent leader of the council stood saying they wish to meet with her peace team. She thought Vald would choke over his next words.

"The Seeker Seth and his . . . Committee," more teeth grinding, "will be . . . Our. . . welcomed guests."

<He won't go for it.> Oliver said. <How can you even begin to trust him?>

<I won't, and I don't.>

<Nor do the Time Overlords,> Seth spoke to them in private. <They have done some digging on their own. They say Vald's council doesn't trust him in this matter either and the majority of the council wants time to learn more about us. Sound familiar? Meanwhile, Vald and his minions will be monitored until the Spes council has had time to evaluate Vald's actions. There is a fundamental awareness that they are outgunned, to use an old earth expression, and the members of the council fear they will lose if they confront us too soon.>

The three stood and then Elizabeth spoke to the council. "Perhaps in the ensuing eons, our people will become closer," Elizabeth said to the council at large. "As the immortal guardians of this galaxy, we need to find out what we have in common to make that possible. We look forward to building a relationship that will make us both stronger."

Vald spoke to her in private. <You take care of your Cohort admirably. I look forward to a long adversarial relationship, Sister.>

The little piss ant never gave up. <As do I, Brother, as do I. Be careful what you wish for.>

Turning from the table, she stopped by the large double doors and spoke to Oliver and Seth. <Before we leave, may I confirm we have mind links to everyone in this room?>

Seth nodded.

<Good. With the unbreakable bond to you, me, Shannon's group and the Time Overlords, Vald's cohort can be monitored for as long as we wish.>

He smiled and nodded. <What is next on your list?>

<I need a private meeting with the person next in line behind Vald. Which of them is most likely to step into his shoes and can he work with us?>

<The one called Tannic. He sits on Vald's left side. A pair of Overlords had left this time period to do an in-depth study of his timeline to learn how he got his current position. The three of us will have access to their report within seconds. Tannic fits the bill of the one you seek. Let's take him to Torg and away from this time. When we return him, he'll be the only one who knows he was gone.>

Seth appeared at Tannic's left shoulder and Elizabeth at his right. He opened his mouth in question, but before the words escaped, the three vanished.

BEYOND

Torg's rampart

Elizabeth, with Seth and Oliver, repositioned to the top of the square rampart on Torg minus 25 with Tannic in tow. It was a time of history unknown to her, but time didn't matter. They were safely away from Vald and any of his listening minions.

"Where am I?"

"Sorry about the lack of warning, but we have a proposition that demands privacy. Be assured we'll have you back shortly, and reappear at the exact time you departed. No one will be the wiser. Do you understand?"

Anger radiated from the man in palpable waves. "Why have you removed me from the council? Are you so fearful you can't make a statement in front of the council?" He glared at her. "Take me back instantly."

Seth stepped nose to nose with the blustering man, his height obviously intimidating the shorter Silva man. "We have no fear, Tannic, only a proposition, a recommendation for the council, if you will, which might come better from someone the assembly trusts."

The man stepped back tilting his head upwards to see the powerful Seeker. "That's certainly not you. What sort of proposal might it be?" While he asked the question casually, his eyes squinted in interest, or perhaps calculation.

<Ah, we have him now.> Elizabeth was sure of it.

"Many of us have grave personal grievances with Vald," Seth said. "It is of importance you realize we are angry individuals who possess great power. We have the strength to remove him on their own just as we removed you."

Tannic looked to Elizabeth. "We observed you took the position of leader within your group and you led the discussion with Vald. What do you propose?"

"The relationship between Earth and Spes is not stable." She paused, considering her word choice. "I use the name of our home world and not its dominant species for a reason. We know our species already exist throughout the galaxy. Therefore, no matter what we do today, our species will continue. Our concern is for our planet and all of the life that currently resides on it."

She stepped closer and lowered her voice. She wanted Tannic to listen and listen good. "For centuries Vald has infiltrated worlds to satisfy his personal ambitions. Millions have been casually slaughtered to satiate his thirst for power. At this moment the existence of Earth and Spes is in his hands."

Pinching his chin, Tannic maintained a mulish glare "Your proposal?"

Seth observed, <Good, he's beginning to question.>

"I propose we convince several serious members of your council that to protect Vald from radical fringe elements on both planets, you need to put him in a safe place under trusted guard."

Tannic's face wrinkled up more so than usual. He shook his head. "Imprisonment? Why would he go for that? What you—"

She raised her palms. "What we propose is not exile or prison. We propose a safe haven where Vald can govern privately in a safe place."

"Can you see the advantages?" Oliver said. "Without his presence in your council room, there will not be the tension and potential disruption he brings. Your council and our delegation will have the time to find mutual understanding and a possible resolution of our differences. Tell him he'll only need the extra protection until your people learn more about us." His vanity will refuse to see this internment as only the desire of his people desire to keep him safe.

"I see," he mumbled.

Elizabeth wondered if he did, in fact, understand his position and mission. She watched the transition from belligerence to a resignation in the subtle droop of his posture. Traces of fear crept over his countenance.

<I think Tannic just realized how powerful we are,> she said to Oliver and Seth. I also think the penny finally dropped in his mind that Vald's behavior could be a danger to his own people, meaning his own life shares that danger.>

"To be clear about this, we need you to propose a plan to your council to protect Vald that hid him safely away, anywhere in the galaxy. In turn, we would promise no one of earth would harm him. Thanks to you, Vald would be safe."

"He hardly needs you . . . or me . . . for his safety." Tannic shook himself, as if settling ruffled feathers, yet his confidence went begging. "Go on. You might as well clarify what else you snatched me for."

Elizabeth could see that Oliver and Seth wanted to shake the politician, but doubted Tannic realized his immediate peril. “This action would guarantee you and the others on the council time to create a peaceful working relationship with Earth.” She paused and intentionally made her face go seriously dark. “Either way, I cannot promise revenge will be avoidable or preventable.”

“What’s to stop you from taking Vald?”

“Absolutely nothing. For anyone of us, it would be as easy as bringing you here, but that doesn’t guarantee a peaceful solution for our species or preservation of our homeworlds.”

“I understand.”

He extended his arm. “I give you my hand on it.”

Suspicious, Elizabeth took it. He should have taken more time to deliberate on his decision. How much honor came with the action? “Do not delay in giving your proposal to the inner council. Do you have any reservations?”

“Of course. I do not know you. Vald will learn of my involvement and destroy my family.”

She placed a hand on his shoulder. “We are well aware of Vald’s ability to do so. You will need to convince others to propose and support the plan. Play your role in the background as much as possible.” She glanced at Seth and Oliver before responding. Their slight nods told her she had their support to continue. “We understand the risk you are willing to endure for the sake of your people and planer. If you learn that you, your family, and those close to you are ever in mortal danger, say the words Volo sanctuarii and we will provide the sanctuary you request.”

He appeared to be surprised by her offer. “You speak the ancient words, why is that?”

She tilted her head. “I do not know, but that is a topic of interest we both need to discuss at another meeting.”

Oliver jumped in. <What the hell Seth? This isn’t the first time we’ve seen evidence of Latin in their history.>

She ignored Ollie’s excitement and continued with Tannic. “If you have no other concerns at this time, then we will return you now.”

After repositioning him back to the meeting at precisely the time he left, Elizabeth remained on the rampart and gazed at the distant Torg Ocean. “I’d say part one of the plan has been accomplished. Tannic may need ongoing support and guidance, so have the Time Overlords assign him to Ollie and me as Tannic’s liaison, with you watching Vald. Until this potential disaster has been resolved, they will not be able to shake us loose. Plan to be in their heads day and night. If we detect any actions or new plans for earth, we can intervene in an instant. Now we can build the agenda for our first real conference, the one where Vald is not sitting in the first chair."

Seth wiggled his finger at her. "You are the sly one. You never intended that meeting to lay the groundwork for a peaceful relationship with the Silva. You wanted this meeting because you knew that Vald could not resist showing off what he thought was his cunning power over us."

Oliver smiled. "Liz, your meeting was a cleverly conceived sham. You set Vald up so he would fill that assembly hall with the top power people on Silva, and—"

"Bam," Seth punched his open palm, "we got them. Bagged and snagged. Isn't that what your hunters say?"

Elizabeth huffed a small laugh. "Close enough." Seth tried to keep up with all the modern terms, but after so many centuries, he sometimes mixed them up.

Oliver lowered his voice to a conspiratorial tone. "You got Vald to fill that room with Silva leadership so we could learn their identities. Now we can observe their behaviors and get into their minds."

She shook her clasped her hands over her chest. “Exactly. With assistance from the Time Overlords were able to entangle their minds with the specific Silva leadership in a way that allows us to observe what they do. We’ll be present at every secret meeting, every whisper in the shadows and every tete-a-tete among the Silva elite, whether it is mind-to-mind or spoken.”

“Shrewd.” Oliver covered his chin with one hand while a widening grin erupted. “When did you decide on this multi-step process of guile?”

Elizabeth stretched with her hands high overhead hoping to release some of her tension. It had been several long days, and there were still problematic hurdles to leap. “Not that I didn’t already suspect it, but during my conversations with MeMa, I learned some things about Vald that explained his current behavior. Vald was a documented psychopath from the early twelve hundreds, at which time he was among the lowest of the upper Silva government officials. He took advantage of every opportunity, or more likely created opportunities, to haul himself higher.nHe fell into difficult times with the Silva leadership when he attempted to slaughter 900 of the people who wanted to and break away from the empire and follow their own path.”

Oliver nodded in agreement. “That sounds familiar.”

“Doesn’t it though. MeMa was present when Vald had captured and attempted to massacre many of Cato’s Followers. She played a large part in rescuing the survivors of the 900 by helping them escape and find new homeworlds. When several spoke of a planet on the antipole of the galaxy settled by their ancestors, MeMa helped them make the journey.”

“Hold on,” Olivier said. “Are you saying MeMa is not from Earth and the Silva empire had space travel?”

Seth “Good question. You know how MeMa siphons out information, with a total lack of clarity. I know her father was from Earth and her mother wasn’t, but I could never get her to tell me one way or another more about her parents or her birthplace.”

Oliver persisted. “You’re talking, what, some 60,000 light years to a planet that existed in their folklore? MeMa?”

Seth lifted his hands in front of him. “Cannot help with that one. I did not know of her existence until the 1200s.”

“Yes, Ollie.” Elizabeth tugged at his sleeve. “At that time, during our 1200’s, the Silva governed some fifteen planets in their empire using spaceship technology advanced only a generation or so beyond current Earth technology."

He held up his hands and stopped her. "But, but that still doesn't let them travel 60,000 light years. They would still be traveling, barely away from their home system."

She took his hand to get his attention. "Ollie, listen. MeMa repositioned their spaceships. They escaped Silva's fleet."

His eyes widened. "MeMa repositioned blindly?"

Seth interrupted. "It wasn't MeMa's first jump."

Elizabeth dropped Oliver's hand. "Oh my god, Seth, you never mentioned that before. And what happened to her mother's body?"

His face dropped. "Buried on Torg by the castle."

Elizabeth focused her shaking finger on Seth. "I cannot say this with any less emphasis. You and MeMa will have a sit-down, come to Jesus discussion with us about your combined knowledge concerning the Silva and our boy Vald immediately." She placed her hands on her knees and pushed back against her chair. "Start right now by telling us how Vald managed passage to Earth."

Seth pinched his chin with thumb and forefinger. "Good, we need to get back to Vald. The escape from Spes cost lives and injured many. They initially fled the planet on several old metal cargo spaceships used by the empire. MeMa's first repositioning took them to a planet on the fringe of the Spes empire where they were joined by other Followers with supplies, not for the journey which would lasts minutes, but for their subsequent housing on Earth at where their folklore told them their parents originally fled, to a frozen glacier in northern Norway."

Her fingers tapped on her knee impatiently. "And Vald?"

Seth inhaled deeply. "He had hidden his identity behind the confusion of escape in burn dressings and only revealed himself once they landed safely on Earth. The Followers by now were so grateful for their survival they were willing to take his contrition as a sign of transformation and let him live a plain life among them."

She heard Oliver swear something in Swedish, but didn't comment on Seth's narration.

Seth continued. "A few years later, about the time some of the people fleeing Europe's Black Plague joined their small community as Followers, our boy had already cooked up a plan with to infiltrate the community's new home on Svalbard as a part of its leadership. By now the majority of the Followers were from Europe and allowed him to play a low management role in the community which, after several hundred years led to his position as their supreme commander, for lack of anything else to call it."

Oliver slapped his knee. "That bastard. There is no doubt in my mind he lied, cheated, and bullied his way in and up."

Seth folded his arms. "I do not know many of the details, but MeMa made it her lifelong goal to prepare the Followers for his evil ways."

WHEN HER EFFORTS with the Followers seemed she had failed, she left Svalbard to become a Worlder and put distance between herself and the Svalbard community."

"That's probably what led her to cultivate her own set of Seekers," Elizabeth said, "Meaning us, of course. At first, I didn't follow your logic, but now I see how that explains her desired readiness to deal with the bastard. She knew his plan included bringing the Followers of Earth under Silva control to his control." She tapped her chin. "I wonder, does that mean he intended to make them return to Spes?"

Seth leaned forward, elbows on knees. "No, his desire to become the emperor of the galaxy included making Earth his center of power on this side of the Maelstrom."

She sat back as if to focus her eyes on him better. "You mentioned MeMa sought out her own Seekers." She shrugged, "How could she do that? Did she need to find them or create them herself?"

He smiled. "That's one of the details she shared with me. I was found."

"When?"

"In the mid-twelve hundreds."

"Where, Seth?"

He shook his finger. "That is not important. MeMa found me by accident after she, made . . . assisted two others with their second awakening."

"I don't follow." She frowned. "Why leave the Followers? Why not find and assist a few there and then dump Vald?"

"I am sorry, I did not explain that well. The Followers of Svalbard remained like the Silva. They didn't have the capability for a second awakening. A very few did, but they refused to stay and ran off to other places and times.

"So MeMa already had her rising, or second, and took off to find or make more." She looked away and thought of her next question. "She's not a scientist, what made her think she could successfully do those things?"

He raised his chin. "MeMa is smart and has genius-level intuition. She saw something, and it gave her the idea that Earth was different. The Followers who took Earth partners and raised families had grandchildren who had their first awakening in the womb and could rise to a second awakening before they reached 145. Today we have a positive label and attitude toward hybrids." He snorted a laugh. "Vald spoke openly against inter-Species marriage and labeled their children unkindly. No wonder they fled."

Elizabeth's eyes flew wide. "You mean specifically grandchildren of Seekers who have attained their second awakening? Does he feel cheated about how he got his second awakening from a prisoner he was forced to play checkers with? And why he's so angry with me?"

"I do not believe his thinking is that convoluted. I believe his anger comes from his perception you took Earth from him."

“By god, Oliver said, gripping his hands in fists. The maniac believes himself to be emperor of the galaxy.”

RETURNING TO THE HOMEWORLD

Earth

Elizabeth had gone to the top of the square keep on the Torg castle to be alone and reflect.. An ancient Chinese saying kept running through her mind. 'May you live in interesting times.' Some may view that as a blessing; however, to her way of thinking, it was a curse. Things were too freaking interesting for her. She longed for a dose of boring.

Tobin's space-ball diversion made more sense to her now. What great release . . . And the viz had served them all vicariously.

Her self-awareness included shameful pride in knowing others whispered at her luck in having a record of serendipitous science hacks. Her idea of heroic behavior in the lab goes to an American colleague working with a crack European team of researchers developing a molecular toolbox. Their CRISPR/Cas9 system used a special bacteria protein to splice the DNA of foreign genetic material and insert strands of modified it creates into the bacteria's genes as part of a process to create automatic immunity to the foreign material. After conferring with Chloe, one of Shannon's adopted children, she realized that a slight modification of the bacteria's process, now referred to as Targeted Genome Editing could result in Evolutis becoming a truly self-immunizing being. Her giant leap involved the host's microbiome made the perfect hack. Working together, she and Chloe developed the first CRISPR-Library of viruses that granted the user immune from 99.99% of Earth-based diseases.

During her brief lecture to her teams of asteroid harvesters about their assigned sectors of space, she added, as an afterthought, they search for and record all K dwarf stars with super inhabitable planets. That led to the discovery of sentient life on Alpha 11 with substantial evidence of a Silva slave trade. From that brief contact, she developed a theory that the Silva are Evolutis that do not possess a second awakening. This, if true, currently makes the Silva a sub-species of Evolutis.

These revelations, now constantly on her mind, portended a dark future of new conflict for her Evolutis. Vald, not play, remained the object of her thinking now. His last words, 'A long adversarial relationship,' troubled her. It had been long enough as far as she was concerned, but she knew he would never ever accept defeat. It was not in his nature to believe or admit her proposal gave him no choices. His response was as close as he could come to stating a possible truce.

Elizabeth chose the abandoned and vacant space sphere that had unexpectedly appeared a short while ago at Earth's L2 to meet with her team. She knew the brilliant minds of all her Cohort were working overtime assessing the massive amount of information the Time Overlords amassed monitoring Vald's council. Their efforts to learn more about the Silva were coming to fruition.

She prefers to work alone. Using her mind's entanglement to monitored Tannic regularly. She approved his headway in fulfilling his promise to convince the members of Spes' inner circle that Vald needed to be protected from those on earth who would harm him.

Tannic was able to tell them of Cohort powers. He relayed his own experience with emphasis on his removal from a secure chamber, undetected, right from under their noses to a place and time far removed from Spes.

Shannon, her longtime buddy and research lab partner, joined her on the rampart. <How is it working so far?> She wanted no part of this ‘handling with kid gloves,’ as she called it. Elizabeth knew her friend wanted to go straight for the juggler with no survivors.

<Tannic is rapidly building consensus with the Silva leadership to ensure they have the time needed to understand our powerful skills. Vald’s sheer unmitigated gall to set a date for earth’s destruction only 274 days away, may not give the Silva enough time to avoid the same fate. Earth’s destruction had been made the trigger for Spes’ destruction to guarantee Vald wouldn’t attack us sooner.

While the Silva will need more than a year to attain mental power parity with the Cohort, a year should be long enough for Tannic to establish a rational government that does not require Vald’s methods to achieve dominance over us.

Should the day arrive that Vald actually attempts the destruction of the earth will be the day she kills him. For now, she would settle for a good night’s sleep.

www.ingramcontent.com/pod-product-compliance
Lightning Source LLC
Chambersburg PA
CBHW051933020726
47501CB00001B/108

* 9 7 8 1 3 1 0 6 4 5 0 6 8 *